THE OTHER TIMES OF CAROLINE TANGENT

IVAN D WAINEWRIGHT

GRIMSDYKEPRESS

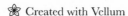 Created with Vellum

Have you ever wished you had more time to listen to music?

PARIS, OCTOBER 1935

We're in Le Gerny's in the Pigalle district of Paris, sitting at a table so close to the stage that I could almost reach out and touch it. Jon picks up a bottle of 1930 Château Haut-Brion and empties it into our glasses. I've never tasted such delicate wine. The musicians are warming up, playing scales on their trumpets, tapping cymbals, balancing a double-bass. Around us, everyone is smoking; I try not to cough but the low ceilings in the club create a permanent haze above my head.

I lean over to my husband. 'You know, I forget sometimes how smoky bars can be.'

The bandleader on stage sits with a cigarette nonchalantly dangling between his lips, tuning his guitar. In his suit and tie, he is the epitome of cool.

'Do you know who that is?' Jon whispers to me. I shake my head. 'Django Reinhardt. By this time, he and Stéphane Grappelli are already famous. He'll go on to tour with Duke Ellington in the States in a few years.'

I catch my breath. 'And I think I saw Maurice Chevalier earlier. What an era to be living in.'

Jon catches the waiter's eye and he hurries over, weaving elegantly between the tables. My husband taps our wine bottle. *'Encore, s'il vous plaît.'*

'Oui, monsieur.' The garçon dashes off.

A couple at a nearby table glower jealously.

'Isn't the wine expensive?' I say in a low voice.

'The dearest on the menu. It'd be out of our reach if we didn't benefit from such an amazing exchange rate.'

We both burst out laughing.

Jon scratches his leg. 'These trousers are so uncomfortable, Caz. How did people put up with this material?'

'It was normal for them. And you look very handsome. The double-breasted style suits you.' I smooth my hands down the front of my silk Madeleine Vionnet dress. 'Personally, I love the clothes. But I'm not sure if I want to keep this perm.'

The hubbub of voices around us changes from loud murmurs to excited chatter, and a few people clap. I turn back to face the stage. A petite woman dressed in a black dress is walking on. She approaches the microphone and nervously nods at the audience.

I grab Jon's arm. 'Jon! It's Edith Piaf. In the flesh!'

Jon's grin is as broad as the Seine. 'Can you believe it?'

'No, I still can't.'

'Me neither. But it really is. And we're really here.'

'I wish we could tell our friends how incredible it is,' I say wistfully.

But we can't. We never will be able to.

The audience hush, Reinhardt taps his feet and the band strikes up. A few feet in front of us, twenty-one-year-old Edith Piaf begins to sing and I sink back into my chair, my eyes glued on the diminutive artiste.

Perhaps of all our trips, this one is the most unimaginable.

But we don't have to imagine it. We're here. In 1935 Paris.

In a few years, Adolf Hitler will invade the French capital; in May 1968 there will be protests and wildcat strikes in the city; and less than twenty years after that, the Musée d'Orsay will open its doors. Fast-forward to 2021 and Pigalle will be famous for its neon-lit red light district rather than smoky jazz bars and artist studios.

But not yet.

Tonight, Edith Piaf sings and we can watch undisturbed.

1

London, 2021

I scan the room: places set, wine glasses ready, fresh-cut tulips and ranunculi in vases. I nudge a pepper grinder a few millimetres to the left, then pull it back to its original place. Nina Simone's *'Nuff Said!* is already on Jon's turntable. I stand beside it, turning the album cover between my fingers. I can't tell if vinyl has more soul, as my husband claims, but I know how much I love her music. She's still on our bucket list.

Bolan, our British long-haired cat, twines himself around my legs. I dim the lighting slightly and look up to the walls where two of my paintings hang. One is a self-portrait of the two of us with a young Bob Dylan, circa 1963. I tell everyone I painted it from my imagination, of course.

It's the first Saturday of the month, our regular dinner party date, and this evening it's our turn to host. As I peruse our dining room, our grandfather clock in the hallway chimes the hour and I close my eyes, wait and... yes, within seconds, our doorbell rings. Bound to be Andrew and Bee.

Andrew swears they don't linger outside in their Range Rover until exactly seven, that he simply times their arrival to perfection. I'm not so sure. Not that it matters.

I open the front door. 'Hello, you two. On time as usual.'

Andrew swings his arm from around his back, presents me with a bottle of expensive red wine. 'Of course, Caroline. We like to be punctual.'

'It would worry me if you weren't.'

It's a ritual we've developed over the years. He steps forward, hands me the wine and his goatee grazes my cheek. His wife kisses me more comfortably and gives my forearm a squeeze.

'Jon around?' Andrew asks.

I stop myself from smirking at the cravat he's recently started wearing. 'In the kitchen. Finishing up his pièce de résistance for dessert. Go through.'

Andrew strides down the hallway and Bee and I link arms as we go into the lounge. She admires my dress, which, even with its narrow shoulder straps, is demure compared to Bee's attire, and I tell my best friend how lovely her hair looks when she wears it up.

'The magic of root spray,' she says, patting her head. 'Next thing you know, I'll have to start dying it.'

'You're only forty-two, Bee. It'll be years before you need to do that.'

I hope I'm right; we're the same age, both of us have long hair, and I share her apprehension. We hear the men's laughter from inside the house.

'Jon sounds in a good mood,' Bee says quietly.

'He is. He's doing well at the moment.'

'Has he found a rare album or something?'

'God knows. I mean, yes, all the time. You know how he is. At least in the old days he had to browse in second-hand record shops. Now I think he props up eBay all on his own.'

Our doorbell rings again. 'That'll be Teri and Zaina. Pour yourself some wine while I fetch them.'

I return with the two women, who sit closely side by side on our sofa. They complement each other more every year. We fall easily into time-honoured conversation.

'That's such a beautiful sari, Zaina,' Bee says.

'Thank you. I so rarely get the chance to wear my Indian clothes. Teri would prefer me to wear my trouser suit every time.'

Her wife opens her arms in mock horror. 'What can I say? I'm an old-fashioned girl.'

We all laugh. Nothing could be further from the truth. Teri was ahead of her time when we met at Bristol University back in 1996, and since then she's done nothing except grow more contemporary and more radical. The only thing that hasn't changed is her short, spiky hairstyle.

We eat, avocado salad followed by my lamb stew, alongside a vegetarian version for Zaina, and consume three bottles of wine before we finish the main course. Jon interrupts his consumption twice, first to flip over his initial record (the Stones' *Sticky Fingers*) and twenty-four minutes later to replace it with a new choice (Miles Davis' *Kind of Blue*).

Andrew wipes the edge of his plate with his finger. 'You do know this is all available on Spotify, Jon? Why do you insist on playing those old records?'

'Because they sound so much better.'

'With the pops and clicks?'

'That's real music. Unsanitised.'

I don't know why Andrew bothers. He tries every few months to persuade Jon to migrate to a digital platform but he'll never succeed.

We clear the dishes and Jon brings in his retro baked Alaska for dessert. It's delicious, one of my favourites;

doesn't matter to me whether it's on-trend or not. We're scraping our bowls with our fingertips when Bee taps a wine glass with her spoon.

'I have an announcement,' she says and reaches for Andrew's hand. He beams and grips her fingers. 'Mel is pregnant. We're going to be grandparents!'

'Oh, that's marvellous news!' I'm the first to jump up and hug my friend. Melanie is Andrew and Bee's daughter and although she's only just turned twenty-one, I'm sure she'll be a terrific mother.

Teri and Zaina hug the happy couple and Jon stretches across the table to shake Andrew's hand, then sits back in his chair. He blinks a couple of times and his knuckles shine white as he grips his glass. He maintains a happy expression but I know he's hurting inside. Bolan chooses this moment to jump onto Jon's lap. My husband's face instantly relaxes and he strokes our cat lovingly, disregarding all the cat hair shedding over his expensive shirt.

We have a group rule that no one washes up during a dinner party. We only see each other once a month, so why waste the time we have together. But I let Bee help me carry the crockery into the kitchen while the others retire to the lounge.

'You must be so thrilled,' I say to Bee as we find space on the countertop for the dirty bowls. 'It only seems like yesterday when I was babysitting Melanie. Playing with her on the swings.'

'And when she ran away to your house as a grumpy teenager because her parents hated her!'

We both laugh. 'Did you know they were trying?' I ask.

'I don't think they were. Mel says it just happened.'

'The fertility of the young,' I say.

'Oh.' Bee bites her bottom lip and half raises her hand. 'Oh, I didn't think. That was wrong of me. I shouldn't have… I mean, I could have been more heedful.' She steps towards me and lightly touches my hip. 'Do you think Jon's okay? He didn't say anything.'

I place my hand on hers. 'I think so. Hope so.'

'Really?'

I sigh. 'No, it still tortures him, even now.'

'But it's, what, eleven years since you lost it?'

'That doesn't mean he can't hold a grudge. He's good at that.'

'He blames you still?'

I rub my arm. 'You can understand why.'

'No,' Bee says firmly. 'You mustn't think that.'

I force a smile, manage a half-laugh. 'Oh, that's unfair. He's fine most of the time. But every now and then, when things like this happen…'

I'm staring down at the floor. When I look up, Bee wraps her arms around me.

'I'm sorry. Should I say something to him?'

'God, no. Let sleeping dogs lie. Or hope they're snoozing anyway.' I roll my shoulders. 'Come on, remember the rules. Let's get back to the party.'

Bee grips my elbow and we make our way down the hallway to the lounge, where the others are slumped in the sofas and chairs, whisky and wine glasses already filled. My favourite Van Morrison album, *Veedon Fleece*, is playing on the turntable – yes, Jon has two sound systems, one for the dining room and one for the lounge.

As Bee and I sit down, Bolan jumps onto Andrew's legs. Andrew roughly pushes our cat off.

'Hey!' Jon shouts at Andrew. 'What are you doing? I've told you before about not hurting Bolan.'

Andrew shows mock fear, holding up his hands, pretending to shiver.

The room goes quiet. Jon sweeps up Bolan from the

floor and the cat nestles in his lap, my husband gently stroking his ears.

Bee breaks the ice. 'Oh, Caroline, I meant to say earlier: Michael adores that portrait you painted for his twenty-first.'

'It wasn't too erotic?'

'That's why he loves it.'

'I hope it didn't offend anyone. Has he got a girlfriend?'

'That depends on your definition of girlfriend. He seems to be talking about a different woman every time he comes home.'

We all laugh and the room relaxes again. Bee updates us with more news on her son's university life. Teri extricates her Rizlas and passes around a joint.

'The students have to work so hard these days,' Zaina says.

'Lucky it wasn't like that when we were at Bristol,' Andrew says. 'You'd never have hacked it, Jon.'

'What are you talking about? I worked hard. I got a first.'

'In mechanical engineering. They gave out mech eng degrees like confetti.'

'And I got my masters in mathematics.'

'That's exactly what I'm saying. We were lucky, we could do postgrad courses knowing we'd get a job somewhere. Our kids don't have that luxury.'

Jon bristles. 'I became a lecturer because I'm a good teacher. If you want to start comparing degrees—'

Andrew grins. He deliberately winds Jon up all too often, much to my frustration. I tap Andrew gently on the knee.

'How's Chen, Zaina?' I ask. 'Is he thinking of going to university?'

Chen is Teri and Zaina's sixteen-year-old adopted son. A lovely boy, definitely got his head screwed on.

'I think so.'

'Which one?'

'He doesn't know yet. He's more interested in music and hanging out with his mates.'

'Good man,' Jon says.

'He's obsessed with Janis Joplin right now. Even plays Andrew's old CDs.'

'Good taste,' my husband adds and winks at me. 'I'd love to have seen her live, wouldn't you, Caz?'

Andrew raises his eyebrows. 'I didn't know you liked Janis, Caroline. I thought that was more Jon and me.'

I swirl my wine around my glass casually. 'We've been married for nearly twenty years, Andrew. You think some of Jon's musical tastes can't rub off on me?'

Teri stubs out her joint. 'He certainly rubbed off other things on you, Caroline, didn't he?'

We all erupt. I chastise Teri, affectionately, Jon grins stupidly behind his glass of whisky and Teri feigns innocence with raised hands. Zaina howls with laughter. I risk a quick glance at Andrew but, thankfully, he's happy to join in with the sexual innuendo rather than interrogate us further about our wishes to check out a rock singer who died fifty years ago. My heart rate returns to normal.

Later in bed, I gently berate Jon. 'You almost slipped up tonight when we were discussing Janis Joplin.'

'It wasn't my fault,' he snaps. 'I was still caught up with Bee's news. I didn't think.'

I stroke my husband's arm but he pulls away, avoids my gaze. I press my fingertips together, wait a few moments. 'We need to be careful, darling. Especially when Andrew's around.'

'It was the whisky. It relaxes me, and it all came out before I could stop myself.'

'It's okay, he was just trying to provoke me. You didn't

say anything that would make him suspicious. But you know Andrew's like a dog with a bone when he does think he's onto something interesting.'

'You're right, Caz. I'll watch my mouth.'

I harrumph.

He chuckles. 'But it was only a few weeks ago. I can still remember so vividly how amazing she was.'

I purse my lips, but I can't stay annoyed; my mouth breaks into a furtive grin. 'It was a special concert.'

Jon turns to me and props himself up on his elbow, his long legs touching the footboard. 'I've been thinking about our next trip. What do you reckon to Simon and Garfunkel?'

'Really? When?'

'There's only one choice. 1981, concert in Central Park.'

'That would be incredible. Can we get tickets?'

'No need, it was free. One of the easy ones.'

I smile. 'I love it. When shall we go?'

'How about tomorrow? No time like the present.'

We laugh and fall into each other's arms.

2

Our first trip was a day I'll never forget. It was a late midweek afternoon, three years ago, and I had just finished painting for the day. I was sitting in the kitchen stroking Bolan, waiting for the kettle to boil when Jon came in. He was wearing a Led Zeppelin T-shirt, an old pair of Levi's and his walking boots. It was a look that suited his physique, which was still slim, despite the fact he'd celebrated his fortieth birthday only a few weeks prior.

I held up a mug. 'Want a cuppa?'

Jon shook his head. 'I've got something far more exciting to show you.'

'Have you?' I grinned slyly. 'Well, go on.'

'It's in the basement.'

'Oh, well about time. You haven't let me down there for months.'

'I know. I'm sorry I've been so secretive. But it's ready now, what I've been working on. You'll see why I couldn't tell you, I promise.'

He reached out. I left the kettle to turn itself off and

took my husband's hand, and he led me downstairs to our basement.

When we moved across North London into our Crouch End house in 2012 – partly for a 'new start' after our dysphoria following my miscarriage – the cellar was a dingy, forgotten place, but that didn't stop Jon from immediately commandeering it for his laboratory. We cleaned it out, wired up power sockets, installed heating and bright lighting, made it into a usable space. That was fine by me; I had my artist's studio at the bottom of the garden where I could work, so Jon could have his inventor's den. It was important for him. He was content enough with his lecturing post at the university, but whereas that was all he had needed in his twenties, it was creating inventions that excited him by the time we moved here. It made me happy seeing him so busy, so driven and reminded me of the man I fell in love with.

The cellar was and still is very utilitarian: stone floor, bare-brick walls, tall aluminium shelving, old wooden workbenches for his experiments. His servers – Jon didn't just have a single computer, his experiments required far more power, he claimed – were stacked in a metal rack in one corner. On the wall was a framed A3 poster advertising The Woodstock Music and Arts Fair in August 1969, signed by Roger Daltrey and Pete Townshend.

As I followed Jon down the stairs, I saw three large computer monitors on one of the benches, flashing symbols and graphs and line upon line of programming code. Had he bought even more tech since I'd last been down there? That was what, nine months previously? Jon had banished me from the basement since. And was that a 3D printer on a table?

But it was the centre of the room that made me do a double take. Bolted to the floor was a square sheet of metal, maybe three feet across, and hanging vertically from the

14

ceiling directly above it was… well, something akin to a two-foot steel lightning rod. Its tip was pointing directly at the metal sheet on the floor. Cable conduit ran from the top of the device across the ceiling and down towards the bank of servers.

'What on earth is that?' I asked.

Jon grinned. 'We're going on a trip, Caz.'

'What do you mean?'

'You'll see.'

'And what's this thing? Something we need to take with us?'

My husband laughed. 'Sort of.' He loped over to his computer screens and tapped on the keyboard.

I folded my arms. 'A trip.'

'Yep.'

'Do I need to change?' I asked heavily.

'What you're wearing is perfect.'

I looked down at my faded Grateful Dead sweatshirt and jeans. I've managed to keep myself as slender as I can, but my painting attire isn't the most flattering look.

'This?'

Jon turned. 'Really, Caz, it's just right. And we'll only be gone for a couple of hours.'

I fiddled with my stud earrings. They're an heirloom from my mother, common opal, but incomparably precious to me. I never remove them unless it's imperative.

'How about these?' I asked.

'You look beautiful in them. But you will need this.'

He bent down and fumbled under his workbench, then straightened up and held out a pair of blue wellington boots.

'Is this some kind of joke?'

'Please put them on, Caz, then I'll reveal everything. I promise.'

I sighed, slipped off my sandals and pulled on the boots. With my long hair, I looked like a poorly dressed hippie impersonation of Paddington Bear. When I stood up, I noticed Jon had donned his forties style fedora hat, with the dark blue ribbon band that he has rather romantically kept from our wedding day. He usually wore that when we went to gigs.

He rapped a final few times on his PC's keyboard before picking up what looked like a thick pen. He slipped it into his pocket, crossed the room and stood on the centre of the metal sheet. He held out his hand.

'Quickly, Caz, we've only got sixty seconds.' I plodded over to where he was standing, giving him a dirty look. He grinned again. 'Whatever you do, don't let go of my hand.'

I shrugged and gazed at his workbench. On one of his computer screens displayed flashing numbers, counting down: 20, 19, 18…

Jon gripped my hand tightly. 'Here we go.'

The numbers reached single figures. As the counter turned to zero, a flash of light shot down from the lightning rod above us, seeming to pierce my body from head to toe. I couldn't feel anything, but I instinctively flinched and shut my eyes.

A moment later, I felt unsteady on my feet, swaying backwards and forwards as if I was a little tipsy. But I didn't fall down, and in fact, my boots immediately felt as if they were squelching in something. I would have sworn it was mud if I hadn't known better.

A breeze blew across my cheeks.

I opened my eyes. What the hell? It *was* mud. I gasped.

I was no longer in our basement.

It was dark, night-time, but there were no stars. Light was glowing from somewhere not far away and I could hear music in the distance, and was that cheering? I shivered. It wasn't so warm.

I looked around. Not only was I standing in mud, but I appeared to be in a field, surrounded by small tents pitched close together and, more disconcertingly, one or two people sleeping on the ground nearby. Or maybe they were passed out.

I couldn't fathom what had happened. Had Jon created some sort of virtual reality game in our basement? A 3D video adventure, complete with sound effects and fake wind turbines?

Someone touched my elbow and I spun around. It was Jon, grinning insanely. He held out his arms. 'Surprise!'

I stared at him. Turned around again. Saw a couple emerge from a tent but they ignored us. I heard another cheer in the distance and turned back to my husband.

'What the hell is happening? Is this a new computer program you've invented? Some sort of VR?'

Jon took my fingers in both his hands. 'Caz, this is Glastonbury.'

'As a VR simulation? It's very lifelike, I'll give you that.'

'No. The real Glastonbury. In the real world.'

'The music festival?'

'Yep.'

'But it's the wrong time of year,' I said feebly.

'It's exactly the right time of year. But it's not now. We've gone back in time. It's 2015.' Jon shook my wrists up and down. 'Caz, it worked! I've done it. I've invented a time machine.'

Jon started talking quickly and excitedly, throwing his hands in the air, laughing. He even did a little jig on the spot at one point. In the mud. It was the mud that made me believe it might be the real Glastonbury Festival. Even a VR simulation couldn't create that. But no, how would that be possible? I couldn't believe it. Although clearly, it was, had to be, because I was there. Whenever there was – 2015, if my husband was to be trusted.

After a few minutes of Jon's chattering, I held up my hand. 'Wait a minute. You say you've invented a time machine?'

'Yes! Exactly!'

'How?'

'Haven't you been listening?'

'I've hardly heard a word you've said.'

'Caz.'

'I've just been trying to accept I'm not in our basement anymore. And I don't understand anything you've been saying.'

A huge cheer went up from... the pyramid stage, I presumed. Jon glanced at his watch. 'Look, I'll explain everything again when we get home.'

'We can get home, then?'

'Of course! What, you thought I'd brought you on a one-way trip to a muddy field in Somerset and we were going to stay here?'

'I hope not.'

'Listen, Kanye West is on in ten minutes. We need to get going.'

'Kanye West? The American rapper?'

'Yes, him.' He grabbed my hand but I pulled back. 'I'm not going anywhere. Not until you tell me what's really going on.'

My husband rubbed his chin. 'There's only one way for me to persuade you that this isn't fake, and you're not dreaming or part of a simulation. And that's to show you why I've brought you here. Trust me, Caz, please.'

I hesitated but, well, what the heck. I had nothing to lose. If this was a simulation, then it was ridiculously huge and real and damp. But if it really was Glastonbury in 2015, if Jon really had invented a time machine…

I forced my mind to allow that possibility. My husband held out his hand again and I gingerly gripped his fingers. We started walking steadily towards the noise of the crowd. We passed a few people coming in the opposite direction but as we walked further, more men and women ambled alongside. They were mostly young twenty-somethings, but there were couples of all ages so we didn't stand out. They were dressed in everything from T-shirts and short dresses to rainbow-coloured jackets and bin liners. Plenty of other wellington boots. There was even the ubiquitous, nearly naked man caked in mud. My wellies already felt heavy as the mud glued itself to them, but I was glad Jon had given them to me. I caught my breath as I considered that. I was starting to think as if it was real.

I grabbed Jon by the elbow; if that was the case then I didn't want to lose him.

As we walked, as the crowds got denser, as the noise increased, and as the first light from the main Glastonbury stage filtered into my eyesight, I started to forget about what Jon had done, and how and why, and instead, the excitement and adrenaline which I knew so well from so many other gigs and festivals we'd been to over the years kicked in. This was real, it had to be. I could tell now. It would have been impossible for Jon to replicate this.

But it was also impossible to travel back in time. Wasn't it?

A young man standing beside me in a George Ezra T-shirt looked me up and down. He was young enough to be my son if I had one. At first, I thought he was staring at me because of my age or my mixed heritage; my mother was Caucasian but my father was from Jamaica and I've inherited most of his genes. Then the kid smiled and winked.

Forty-two (well, thirty-nine at the time), but I've still got it! I grinned back and squeezed Jon's arm.

Jon led me as close to the stage as he could before it became impossible to push forward any farther and we staked our place among tens of thousands of excited revellers. I rested my head on his shoulder. He looked down at me. 'Alright?'

'I think so.'

'Can you see okay? Need me to ask anyone to move?'

He always asks me this at gigs. At nearly six foot, he inevitably has a good view; but I'm only a few inches shorter than him, so the crowds don't usually bother me.

'I'll find my spot when it starts.'

'Do you believe me yet?'

I nodded, smiling. 'I think I have to. Because the alternative, that this is a simulation you've created, is even more ludicrous than you inventing a time machine.'

Jon laughed. 'I think that was a compliment.'

'One thing, though. I never knew you liked Kanye West. Is that a guilty secret you've been hiding from me?'

'I don't.'

'What?'

'I'm not a Kanye West fan.'

'Then… why have you brought us here? I assume you could have chosen any year, so why now? Why 2015?'

'Because this set evolves into one of the most controversial performances ever seen at Glastonbury in recent years. There was even a petition before the festival to replace West with a "proper rock act". But to see this, well, this is special. It's so much more than just another gig. Do you understand?'

'I guess. But I wouldn't have minded seeing The Stones.'

'Trust me, Caz, this will be incredible. And anyway, we can always go and see The Rolling Stones another time.'

I was just about to ask how that would be possible when there was an enormous wall of sound and the strobe lights on the pyramid stage started flashing and all around us people held their arms in the air and cheered and screamed. And as the electric beat of 'Stronger' pulsed through the enormous speakers, Kanye West walked onto the stage and raised a fist.

I was at the Glastonbury Festival in 2015. I really was.

Jon was right. It was a phenomenal experience. I'm not a Kanye West fan either, but the atmosphere, the crowd, the artist himself, the feeling that we were witnessing an exceptional moment in music history was extraordinary. The fact he forgot his words at one point and re-started a song just added to the reality of the occasion.

When the rapper left the stage, I felt elated. During the set, I even forgot that I wasn't in my, what should I call it, normal timeline? The crowd began to disperse, returning to their tents or heading off to late-night silent discos and comedy shows, and Jon and I walked slowly back to the spot where we had 'arrived' two hours earlier. There were still a handful of concert-goers lying on the ground, but that part of Worthy Farm was mostly quiet. It was a clever 'landing place' Jon had selected.

'How did you know to bring us to this location?' I asked.

'I looked at the campground online. There are plenty of maps of the site. And I chose a point as far from the stages as I could but inside the perimeter fence, of course.'

'But how do we get back, oh smart scientist? I can't see a time machine here.' Jon reached into his pocket and extracted the pen-like object I saw him take before we left our house. He held it up. 'That? That's a time machine?'

'In effect. It's linked to the machine back in our house, at the other end of the wormhole.'

'The what?'

'Weren't you listening to any of my explanation earlier, Caz?'

'No. At that time I was trying to work out why you were fabricating such an elaborate lie.'

'Fair enough. Look, I'll explain everything again when we're home. But yes, this is the device that's going to return us to our time.' He gave the top of the pen a twist and reached out for my hand. 'Remember, don't let go!'

I glanced around. No one was looking in our direction. He depressed the top of the pen, there was a puff of smoke that seemed to emit from his fingertips and I felt the same slightly dizzying sensation for an instant as I had when we had left our home. Moments later, I found myself back in our Crouch End house, standing a little wobbly on my feet on the square metal plate on the stone basement floor.

Jon raised his arms high into the air. 'Welcome home, Caz!'

I touched my forehead, focused on Jon's Woodstock poster, and as my mind cleared, my jaw dropped and I flung my arms around Jon's neck. We stood in a tight embrace. Jon stroked my hair before he eased me away from him and held me at arm's length.

'You okay? You don't feel nauseous or anything?'

'I feel fine. Better than fine. Oh my God, Jon, I can't believe that just happened. I can't believe you did that.'

My husband held out his arms. 'I told you I had a surprise.'

'It was real, wasn't it?'

Jon threw his hat into the air. 'One hundred per cent. You just travelled back in time to Glastonbury 2015.'

We linked arms and swung each other around on the

metal plate. Then I noticed Jon's empty hands. 'Oh, but your… pen thing. The device that got us home. Where is it? Did you leave it at the festival?'

'No, don't worry. It's a one-time-only controller. Programmed to return us to where we started. But unfortunately, the power it needs means it burns up and evaporates when it's used.'

'You mean that was a one-time trip? You can't use the time machine again?' I was dismayed at the thought.

'No, it's fine. I can make another one.'

'Oh. Thank God.'

'I take it you enjoyed that, then?'

'I loved it! It was amazing. Unbelievable. Impossible!' I kicked off my wellington boots.

Jon laughed. 'Let's go upstairs and make that cup of tea you promised me a few hours ago. And I can tell you again how I did it.'

We climbed the basement stairs and as I pushed open the door at the top, I was bewildered to see that it was still light outside. Surely after all our time away, it should have been early evening dusk. I walked into the kitchen and as I picked up the kettle to refill it with fresh water, I found it was still hot to the touch. I turned towards my husband.

'How is this possible? Hasn't any time elapsed since our trip?'

'It's a time machine, Caz. I returned us to the same minute as when we left. The two of us, at least our bodies, are two hours older, but we've come back to exactly the same moment.'

I shook my head in amazement and poured two cups of tea. We headed into the lounge. Jon put Pink Floyd's *Wish You Were Here* on the turntable and sat down beside me on the sofa. Bolan sprang onto his lap and curled up.

'Okay, Einstein. Start at the beginning and don't spare the horses.'

Jon sat forward. 'Actually, Einstein is a perfect place to start. It's because of him that I was able to create the time machine.'

'You mean you've met Albert Einstein?'

'No. I mean that Einstein was the original proponent of time travel through wormholes, back in 1935. Him and his colleague, Nathan Rosen. They conceptualised the theory into what we now call Schwarzschild wormholes, or Einstein–Rosen bridges. I took his work, reimagined it somewhat and adapted it using twenty-first-century technology that the great man would never have had. And added contemporary mathematics to fill in his gaps.'

'So you invented a wormhole.'

'I don't know if I invented wormholes, but I adopted the concept.'

'So how does it work?'

Jon put down his cup and held up his hands as if he was playing cat's cradle. 'Think of a wormhole as a tunnel. This end is now, here, and the other end is a specific time and location somewhere and sometime in history. That was Einstein's theory as well. But what he could never do was create enough power and accuracy to be able to create a wormhole large enough to send two humans along it. And bring them back. What my equations and computer servers have done is create that wormhole in a controllable way and so accurately that I can land us in pretty much any location within a few feet of my target, and almost to the second of when I want to be there.'

'That's incredible.'

'Thank you. I think so. I obviously have to be careful to research when and where we're going, otherwise one could end up in the middle of someone's house or in a lake or something!'

'So that device downstairs is what, your launch pad?'

'That's exactly what I call it!'

'And the pen you had to bring us back?'

Jon stroked our cat. 'That was one of my biggest challenges. Once I had figured out how to open a wormhole and send something or someone through it, I had to work out how I could bring them back. The time machine clearly isn't portable, it requires too much computer power.'

'So what did you do?'

'Well, think of the wormhole as a long piece of elastic. A huge rubber band stretched between two points in time.' He held his hands apart again. 'When I land us at the other end, in history, we are in effect tied to that elastic band, but somehow I have to, ah, ping us back to where we started.' He clapped his palms together.

'Ping us.' I laughed. 'Is that your scientific phrase?'

'Why not? That's what it does. That's why I invented the pen as you call it. Actually, that can be any handheld device: a pen, a water bottle, a TV remote. You name it. But something purporting to be a pen is useful in case someone in the era we're visiting catches sight of it. Ballpoint pens have been around for most of the twentieth century, so it wouldn't make anyone suspicious even if someone in, I don't know, 1930 was to see it.'

I thought about this as the saxophone solo from Pink Floyd's opening track faded away. 'That's so clever,' I started.

The clatter of our letterbox in the hallway interrupted me. I turned my head, suddenly worried that we might have been overheard, but the thud on the doormat announcing the arrival of a small parcel or a free newspaper relaxed me again.

I patted my chest. 'You were saying.'

Jon grinned. 'The clever bit is how it works. We need a serious amount of power to return us to our time, and because we are still tied to that wormhole elastic band, the pen creates the power we need to send us back when I press that button. But as you saw, it does mean it disintegrates when it's used. So I need to program a new one for each trip. It takes a few days as I have to create all the pieces on my 3D printer.'

'It's ingenious, Jon. You're a genius.'

He shrugged. 'It's mathematics, computer programming and one heck of a lot of power. I'm afraid our electricity bill is starting to mount up.'

'Stuff that! You've invented a time machine! I'm so proud of you.'

'Thanks, Caz.'

'And I love the fact that you used it to take us to Glastonbury. It's brilliant.'

Jon's eyes lit up. 'That's just the start. Think of all the other gigs we can go to. All the amazing concerts and bands that we never got to see. Zep, Elvis, Woodstock! We can go to watch whoever we want.'

'Bee's mad about Elvis. Could we take her, too?'

Jon dropped his eyes. 'No, we can't. Sorry.'

'Why not? She'd love it.'

He took both my hands. 'This is really important, Caz, so listen. We can't take Bee or Andrew, or anyone else. We can't even tell them about the time machine. Ever.'

'Why not?'

'Because they'd tell someone else.'

'If it's that important to you, we can insist they don't.'

'It's not that simple, Caz. Are you sure they could keep such a secret? Look how hard you're finding it.' He gently squeezed my fingers. 'Listen. If anyone else did discover what I'd invented, do you think they'd be content to simply go back in time to see gigs?'

'Well, no, I guess Andrew might want to visit the nineteenth century, you know how he loves steam trains. Or Teri might want to meet Harvey Milk.'

'And that would be quite innocent. But other people would want more. They'd want to use it to change history. And that's so dangerous. Imagine if a far-right group got hold of it. For us, it's an incredible invention. In the wrong hands, it could be the most horrific weapon ever invented. A doomsday machine.'

That was a terrible thought and I understood his concerns. But did it have to mean we couldn't share the time machine with our closest friends? Would that be so bad?

I rubbed my cheek. 'Are you sure we can never tell anyone else?'

'Let's put it this way. I haven't printed a single page from my research notes. They're all in encrypted files on a USB stick. I don't even know how long we can risk using the machine. Maybe only a few years. Have some fun, see some great concerts. But the longer we have it, the more we risk it being discovered. I'm even wondering if I'll need to destroy it eventually to ensure that no one else can get their hands on it.'

'That's so sad.'

Jon sighed. 'It's ironic. I've finally created the most significant invention in history, exactly what I wanted to do, and I can't tell anyone except you.'

'Maybe you can use the core concepts in your next invention.'

'Maybe.' Jon smiled again. 'But none of that stops us from enjoying the time machine now.'

This was Jon all over. While other people would be thinking about visiting a famous person in history, or finding out what happened to the *Mary Celeste*, or even selling their invention to the highest bidder, my music-obsessed husband was purely interested in going on a world tour across time to see all his favourite bands and artists.

I nestled into Jon's chest as he reeled off more acts, more ideas he'd had about which gigs we should go to. I gently stroked his forearm. But for the second time in three hours, I was only half listening. I was thinking how there were other as yet unasked questions about how we might want to use the time machine. Well, one specific question. Jon must have thought about it, too. But I wasn't going to bring that up there and then – at that moment, he was so happy, and I had no desire to change that.

But I knew then and I still know now it is going to happen, we can't avoid it.

3

I love Zaina's cooking. She seamlessly and with consummate ease fuses Indian cuisine with any other culture she chooses; Western, Japanese, she's even concocted a Kosher Indian meal for her Jewish friends. So I'm delighted that this evening, it is her and Teri's turn to host our monthly dinner party.

Our friends' house is in a leafy street near Kew station, a lovely part of London, and it means Jon and I can drink all we want and fall asleep on the last train home. I'm wearing my favourite red dress and Jon is looking smart in his button-down shirt and black jeans. As we walk from the station, I remind my husband to keep his cool if Andrew starts arguing tonight. Jon scowls but nods.

Teri and Zaina's son, Chen, is sitting at the kitchen table when we arrive. He's fiddling self-consciously with his earring, which he's only recently been allowed to acquire. Andrew and Bee aren't here yet so Jon and I join the family in the kitchen, sipping cocktails while Zaina prepares her dishes. Jon looks nervously at Teri and Zaina's Staffordshire bull terrier, a Battersea rescue dog. My husband is far more a cat man than a dog person. We acquired Bolan as a kitten two years after my miscarriage and it was one of the things that helped Jon slowly get out of his funk. Now he dotes on him.

'How's school?' I ask Chen.

He shrugs. 'Okay.'

Teri smooths his hair and he flinches. 'Actually, Caroline, Chen has some coursework where he would like your help.'

'Oh? Is it art related?'

'No. It's about Britain in the sixties, and what it was like for the immigrants of the time.'

'Ah, I see. And you'd like to know how my father found it living here?'

Chen nods awkwardly. 'Yes, please. I don't know anyone who grew up in London at that time.'

My father emigrated from Jamaica to the English capital with his family when he was a teenager close to Chen's age now. They weren't trailblazers but Ealing wasn't used to West Indian families in 1967. I tell Chen some of the stories I remember my father telling me when I was a child, of the racism he experienced, the problems he had at school, and ultimately when he fell in love with a white woman, my mother-to-be, the resentment they received from some of the community. It was far simpler for Jon and me when we married in 2001: his parents flew down from Scotland, we tied the knot in a registry office, had a meal at a pub, and they rushed straight home the same evening while we partied with our friends. We barely see his parents now.

My father was constantly angered at how the British accepted then prime minister, Margaret Thatcher. He felt that her policies and attitude were responsible for much of the discrimination he suffered.

'He hated Margaret Thatcher for what she did to the working class,' I finish telling Chen. 'But at least he got to see her deposed by John Major just before he died.' I sigh. 'He was far too young.'

'How old was he?' Chen asks.

'Forty. I was twelve. My mother brought us up by herself after that. That was a challenge in its own right, a single white woman raising two mixed-race daughters in the late eighties.'

The doorbell rings. Teri says, 'That'll be Andrew and Bee. Must be seven o'clock.' We all laugh. I tell Chen to phone me if he wants to ask any further questions. He scurries away to his bedroom, sensibly avoiding further adult interaction.

Andrew walks in ahead of Bee, wearing a casual jacket. He's exchanged his contact lenses for clear-framed glasses; they rather suit him. His wife follows, radiating beauty in a stunning blue maxi dress with orange tulips.

I kiss my friend. 'That's a gorgeous dress, Bee.'

Bee extends her arms sideways. 'Thank you.'

'It looks familiar. Wait a minute… Is it the same one you wore when you opened your fashion shop?'

'It is. I wouldn't normally keep a dress that long but this one holds a special place for me. I like to wear it every now and then to remind me.'

'But that was five years ago!' Teri says. 'It still fits you perfectly.'

Bee smiles. 'I know. I think it must have been a bit too large for me when I bought it.'

She moves off to talk to Zaina.

Teri folds her arms. 'It certainly wasn't too large before. How does she keep her figure?'

'You know she's always been like that,' I say. 'Ever since we met her.'

Teri grunts but it's true. Tall, blond, she had half the

31

boys at university running after her in our freshers' year. I spent half my time carried along in her wake.

We decamp to the dining room as Zaina brings through the food: samosas for starters, but unlike any I've ever tasted, and the most delicious vegetarian curry. I don't know how she makes her rice so perfect.

We're starting dessert when Chen sidles in to tell his parents he's going out to see a friend. Teri strokes the back of his neck and he pulls away.

'Back by eleven!' she calls after him as he leaves. She smiles lovingly. 'He's planning a holiday to Spain with his mates, which he's very excited about but Zaina constantly worries over.'

'He'll be fine,' says Andrew. 'What's the worst that can happen?'

'He could get led astray, get into drugs,' Zaina says.

'He won't do that,' Andrew replies.

'How do you know?' Zaina asks.

Jon puts down his spoon. 'He's more likely to snog a young Spanish girl.'

'Or boy,' Teri adds.

'Or boy,' Jon confirms.

'Or get cajoled into getting a tattoo,' Bee says.

'Hey, that was your idea!' I say quickly.

'Maybe…'

'Let's get matching tattoos, you said. It'll be cool, you said.'

Zaina looks horrified. Bee leans on her elbows. 'We were five years older than Chen when we went on holiday together, and he's far more sensible than we were.'

Teri, who has a beautiful sleeve of tattoos, says, 'Do you regret doing that?'

'Of course not,' Bee answers. 'I love my dove tattoo. It's very discreet.'

32

'Even I haven't seen it,' Andrew interjects.

We all laugh.

I lean back in my chair. 'I do, however, regret allowing Bee to talk me into doing shots on our last night on that holiday. My God, I could barely get out of bed the next day. And when we took off on the plane...' I make a retching sound; my husband shakes his head in disgust.

'What about you, Jon?' Teri asks. 'You ever done anything on holiday you regretted?'

'Not really. There are worse things in life than getting pissed in a foreign bar.'

'Of course there are. But, come on, you've never been embarrassed by something you did on holiday?'

Jon scratches his chin but before he can answer, Andrew pouts and flicks the stem of his wine glass. 'I tell you what's embarrassing. Losing a pair of tickets to see an Oasis gig after promising you'd look after them, when your friend takes you on a weekend away especially for that concert.'

Jon tilts back his head. 'Oh, God, that was twenty-five years ago, Andrew. I said I was sorry.'

'Hmph.' Andrew continues to tap his glass.

Jon folds his arms. 'Jesus, I can't believe you still go on about this. I thought I'd made it up to you a year later when I bought you that rare Hendrix CD.'

'It wasn't that rare.'

My husband rolls his eyes. 'Look, if it makes you feel better, I'll put it at number one on my list of what I would do to change history if I could do. Just before preventing *Apollo Thirteen* from exploding. Is that acceptable for you?'

'Well...' Andrew starts.

'Wait a minute,' Teri interrupts. 'Jon, are you telling me that stopping that spacecraft from blowing up would be the most important thing to you if you could change history?'

'Number two if it makes Andrew happy,' Jon snarls.

'Oh good God.'

'I'm sure Jon would want to do both things,' I say quickly.

'I think that's very honourable,' Zaina adds.

'Even though there'd be so many better things to change that would make the world a better place,' Teri mutters.

Bee turns to our host. 'Well, what would you do, Teri? If you could change history? What would be your number one concern?'

'If I could change anything?' Teri says.

'Sure.'

Teri thinks for a moment. 'Hmm. I'd stop that mother-fucker David Copeland from bombing the Admiral Duncan pub in Soho. Back in 1999.'

'Interesting,' Andrew interjects. 'How?'

'I'd fucking kill him so he'd never get near it in the first place.'

Bee sits upright. 'Oh, I wasn't expecting something so… serious.'

'You did ask,' Teri says.

Zaina takes Teri's hand. 'It's a great idea. I'd support you.' She gives her wife a kiss.

Andrew stares nonchalantly into his wine. 'Except…'

Teri spins her head towards him. 'What?'

Andrew looks up. 'Except, the problem with that would be, just because you stopped Copeland from doing it, would that mean the bombing never happened?'

'Yes, obviously!'

'Ah, but we've all seen the sci-fi films, read the novels about alternate histories. How if you go back and kill Hitler then Germany would win the war because his number two, Göring, was more ruthless and a sharper tactician than the Führer.'

'So I shouldn't try to stop Copeland from killing and wounding over seventy people?'

'I'm not saying that. I'm just pointing out that different events might unfold if you did.'

'Christ, I don't think David Copeland had an accomplice like Hermann Göring.'

'Well, I'd stop Nine-eleven from happening,' Bee says firmly.

Andrew sniffs. 'Same problem, sweetheart. So instead of the twin towers being destroyed, the following year, Bin Laden blows up the White House.'

Bee and Teri complain loudly. Andrew holds his hands up. 'I'm just saying that's possible.'

I dig my fingernails into my palm. Partly to stop myself admonishing Andrew for his annoying habit of arguing for the sake of it, but also to calm me down. I don't like the direction this conversation is going, and as the others are arguing I sneak a glance at my husband. He's sitting at the end of the table looking perfectly relaxed, sipping his wine, turning his head towards whoever is speaking. I can't tell if his heart is beating as fast as mine.

'Okay, clever clogs,' Teri says to Andrew. 'What would you do?'

'Me? I'd go back and buy stocks in Apple when they were a fledgling company. Think what they'd be worth now.'

'Boring!' Teri complains and looks down the table at my husband. 'Come on, Jon, I bet you've got a better idea.'

'Yes, come on, Jon,' Andrew echoes. 'You're being very quiet. What world event would you influence if you invented a time machine?'

I try to smile encouragingly at my husband, but inside I am willing him not to rise to the bait.

Jon sips his wine. 'The problem with all your suggestions, as Andrew is insinuating, is the butterfly effect.'

'The what?' Zaina asks.

'Classic chaos theory. The belief that every action causes another reaction, no matter how small or seemingly insignificant. The classic example is how a tornado is influenced by something as simple as a distant butterfly flapping its wings hundreds of miles away several weeks earlier.'

'How would that happen?' Bee asks.

'The butterfly is purely metaphorical. Look, take this scenario instead: In 1850, a young woman attends a picnic and a spider runs up her leg. She screams and a young man gallantly plucks it off her. They fall in love, have a son and he invents the telephone.'

'Did that happen?'

'No, of course not. Just listen. Imagine instead that I invent a time machine, go back to that same day of the picnic and accidentally tread on that spider. Therefore, the young woman has no need for her beau to rescue her and they go their separate ways. Hence, no son and the telephone is never invented.'

'That wouldn't happen,' Andrew retorts. 'Someone else would invent the telephone even if your young Alexander Bell had never been born. Don't forget Elisha Gray was working on his own project independently.'

I can't believe Jon is discussing this. I jump in quickly. 'Well. I tell you what I would do—'

'You're right, Andrew,' Jon says over me. 'But even so, history has changed. The world is no longer the same. Your examples are more contemporary: Stop Nine-eleven, and instead, the following year the president is killed.'

'Exactly,' Andrew says.

'You have to be very careful if you invent a time

machine, you see,' Jon continues. 'You can do all sorts of untold damage if you aren't careful.'

'You're taking this far too seriously,' Teri says.

'I agree,' I say, giving my husband a meaningful look.

But Jon is into his flow. 'I mean, if you had a time machine, why would you want to use it to change history? Wouldn't you use it to travel somewhere, to a time or event you'd always wanted to go to? The best concert you never saw. And think of the souvenirs you could bring back.'

'Oh, here we go, typical Jon,' Teri says.

We all laugh, me included, my laughter being one of relief.

'Wait, what do you mean, souvenirs?' Andrew asks.

'Oh, just let him go to his historic concerts,' Zaina says. 'That's what he loves.'

'Yes, I think that shows far better imagination than killing Hitler or buying Apple stock,' Bee adds.

'No,' Andrew says sharply. 'I want to know what Jon means.'

Everyone in the room falls silent. Teri reaches for Zaina's hand and Bee's wine glass hovers in mid-air. She glances at me. The two of us know exactly what Andrew is referring to.

It had only been a brief phase of our husbands' lives, but I wasn't proud of it. Jon and Andrew had got into the racket together when Jon had first started using Photoshop to aid his designs and inventions. It must have been around 2005. Just for fun initially and to test his software skills, he had mocked up a fake photo of Keith Moon of The Who, pretending he was at an early Rolling Stones gig. But when he'd shown it to Andrew, his friend had told him he knew someone at his office who was a massive Stones fan and would undoubtedly believe it was genuine. Especially if he printed it in black-and-white and crinkled up the photograph. Andrew sold it to his workmate for fifty quid. That set them off down a two-year path of creating more fake items, old gig tickets, autographed photos, rare retro concert posters. Jon designed and printed them at home, Andrew sold them at record fairs and car boot sales, one or two things on eBay. Neither of them told their wives what they were doing, and it was only when Bee and I found out that we made them promise to stop doing it. Andrew was sour about it for months.

My husband looks at his friend and blinks. 'I don't mean anything by it, Andrew. It was just a throwaway statement.'

'But—' Andrew starts.

'And anyway,' I cut in quickly, 'Jon hasn't really answered your original question, Andrew.'

'What?'

'You know, what great historic event he would choose to change if he could do.' I turn to my husband. 'Darling, why don't you tell him. You've often said that there's one particular thing you wish had never happened.'

'Okay, but wait—' Andrew says.

'No, Caz is right,' Jon interrupts. 'I do know what I would do. I would go back to December 1980 to stop Mark Chapman from shooting John Lennon. How about that?'

'Oh, it's always about the music, isn't it!' Teri says.

'But that is a fair answer,' Bee says. 'It's changing a significant event in history, after all.'

The debate continues. But on the opposite side of the table, I see Andrew peer quizzically at Jon, who simply acknowledges his friend and turns to speak to Zaina. Andrew looks across at me instead. I narrow my eyes and set my jaw, shake my head slowly, hoping he understands that I would be angry if either of them intended to start producing fake rock memorabilia again. He nods, sighs and briefly raises his fingers, which I hope means he recognises my point. He looks away, reaches across the table for a wine bottle and asks Bee if she'd like anything more to drink.

I bury my face in my wine glass. I don't care if Andrew is suspicious that my husband might be restarting his dodgy business. I wouldn't let him do that anyway, but I do worry when Jon begins to talk about time machines, insinuating they're real.

I exhale a long, silent breath.

4

I was still experiencing the high of our Glastonbury adventure for weeks after our trip to the festival. I would be working on one of my paintings and suddenly the realisation that my husband had invented a time machine and we could go anywhere to any time in history would overpower my mind and I'd stand stock still with my brush raised, staring out at our garden while I contemplated the astonishing feat and incredible possibilities.

Jon, however, was busy planning our second trip. He wanted to go back to August 1966 to New York, but, he told me, we had some preliminary challenges to overcome.

'Like what?' I asked. I was perched on a stool in the cellar, wiping my hands with white spirit after a painting session while Jon created a new 3D pen. I reached out to examine a printed piece but he snatched it away from me. I dropped my hands into my lap. 'Don't worry, darling, I won't spill anything on your workbench, I promise. Now tell me about your challenges.'

Jon grimaced. 'Logistics, Caz. We'll have to buy tickets

for the gig, although I think we can do that at the door, but we'll need appropriate clothes.'

'For the swinging sixties? There's plenty of stores here in London selling stuff that'll look fine. Or I bet we can get originals on eBay.'

'I hadn't considered that. But there is a larger issue: money.'

'I'd have thought that was the least of our worries. The inflation since then must mean our present-day pounds would buy an abundance of sixties dollars.'

Jon rotated an image of a 3D circuit board on his computer screen and started to print another component.

'That's not what I mean,' he said. 'I mean we need US currency from the sixties. Hard cash. How do we get that?'

'Hmm. Maybe eBay again? Do people sell old banknotes?'

We checked and found that they did, but they were few and far between, and most were for the wrong era. Hence, they were now treated as collector's items and the price was extortionate.

'So what do we do?' I asked.

'I have got one idea, but strictly speaking, it's not legal.'

'How strictly?'

'Well. Back in the sixties, traveller's cheques were used far more widely.'

'Um, what?'

Jon opened a browser on his computer and tapped a few keys. I stood up and looked over his shoulder. He pointed at the screen. 'Traveller's cheques. They were hugely popular before credit cards. I remember my parents taking me on holiday to France and using them. Think of them as a pre-loaded credit card like we have now, but paper-based. You bought them before you left home and when you got to your destination you could "cash them in" at a bureau de change or a bank. Some shops and places would even accept them directly in lieu of cash. American Express was the largest vendor, they sold millions every year.'

'So, we would buy some in our present and cash them in sixties America?'

'No, that wouldn't work, they look very different now. We'd have to, ah, print our own here at home to replicate how they used to look in 1966.'

I crossed my arms. 'Oh, I see. Yes, that would be illegal.'

'Only if we get caught.'

'Hmm, that's not quite true. Plus, wouldn't you need ID or something to cash a cheque back then?'

Jon paused while he read something on the screen. 'Some exchange bureaus insisted on ID to cash them but I'm sure there would be others who wouldn't. We'd just have to find one.'

'We'd still be committing fraud.'

'One-time only. If we cashed a large cheque for, say, a hundred dollars, that would keep us going for several trips to sixties America.'

Several trips! Of course, we could go back again anytime we wanted! I peered more closely at the article Jon had been reading. 'So how would we make it look real?'

'Easy. Find an image on the web for an old sixties version, save it on our PC, touch it up in Photoshop and voila. I've got a colour printer we can use to print it.' He smiled slyly. 'You know I can do it, I have history.'

'Hmm.'

'Come on, it'll be fun – a little drop of danger would add some spice!'

I thought we had enough danger in not being spotted as twenty-first-century time-travellers, but Jon had the bit between his teeth. He spent the next three evenings finding the best image, adjusting it to the finest detail in Photoshop and experimenting with different types of paper until we felt it was as good as we could achieve. I spent the same time having much more fun, buying us appropriate garments: a cotton tunic shirt for Jon and a beautiful blue and white kaftan dress for me. I loved it. I also bought a small, vintage shoulder bag which I fancied could pass for a sixties or seventies-era handbag.

'You still haven't told me who we're going to see,' I complained as we were dressing up for the evening.

'Wait and see.' Jon grinned. 'And don't bring anything with you from our present time. No cash, credit cards, obviously not your mobile phone, and I have no idea what the tampons of 1966 were like compared to today. And definitely no identification like your driving licence.'

'Why not?'

'For a start, imagine if we lost any of that stuff and someone found it! I hope they would think it was a joke, but it's not worth the risk.'

I looped a bead necklace around my neck, purchased the previous week at Camden market. 'Because of the potential butterfly effect?'

'Exactly. But also, if we did get stopped and searched by the police or the authorities in the past, how would we ever explain that? Better to have no ID at all and use my handheld device to ping us back out of there as soon as we can.'

I ran my fingers nervously over my beads. 'Are you expecting the police to catch us again?'

'Of course not. I'm just being careful.'

I recoiled at the memory. It was a long time ago, in 2003. Jon and I had joined one of the Stop the War protest rallies in London. We had been unfortunate: caught campaigning with a group of hardcore anarchists who were set on attacking the police, even though we weren't part of their faction. We were arrested, fingerprinted and slung in

43

the police cells for several hours before they released Jon and me with no charges. It wasn't an experience I wanted to repeat.

'Wait. Couldn't we use your time machine to stop that from ever happening?' I asked.

'Absolutely not,' Jon replied firmly. 'Not only would that set off God knows what in terms of the butterfly effect, but we can never meet our younger selves. I don't know what that would do to us now or then.'

We descended into the basement, where I discovered Bolan sleeping behind the servers; I shooed him upstairs, out of the way. When I returned to where Jon was working on the computer, I noticed the pen device lying on the workbench – the 'time-pen', as we'd dubbed it. I nudged it towards my husband.

'Don't forget this, whatever you do, or we'll never get back!'

Jon glanced down. 'I thought about that when I was designing it. I've built in a fail-safe – when we're standing on the launch pad, the computer always checks our bodies for the time signature the pen emits, and if it can't find it then it automatically aborts the launch.'

'Good thinking!'

'Hey, as much as I'm dying to see all these great gigs, I want to make sure we can always return!'

I waited for Jon on the metal plate while he programmed the final coordinates into his PC, pocketed the time-pen and put on his fedora hat. As he joined me, I held his arm tightly, closed my eyes and seconds later felt the same temporary, wobbly sensation as my legs adjusted to another era. I opened my eyes. I was standing under the broad canopy of a tree with a large expanse of grass in front of me, but with the sound of car horns and loud voices only yards away. It was a bright, hot day.

'Where are we?'

'Washington Square Park in Greenwich Village. Should be around one o'clock in the afternoon.'

'Aren't we early?'

'It's an afternoon gig, and we've got to cash our traveller's cheque, remember? That might take a little while. Besides, let's soak up the park. Come on.'

'Soak up the park? What are you – oh!'

I had barely stepped out, over a flower bed, when a Frisbee flew within inches of my nose. Jon grinned, threw it back to the owner and swivelled around to open his arms to me. 'Welcome to 1966 New York!'

I was already gaping. The park was teeming with sixties American life: buskers, protesters, hippies, dancers, jugglers, roller skaters and the aforementioned Frisbee players. There were ice cream vendors, weed salesmen, the odd prophet and, of course, throngs of tourists. In the middle of the park was a fountain spouting water twenty, thirty feet into the air, while nearly naked people danced in the concrete pond surrounding it. The other immediate clues to the era of our arrival were the clothes everyone wore and the lack of mobile phones. On the one hand, I was thankful we had appeared under a tree where no one would have noticed us, but even if they had, they would probably have simply applauded, suspecting we were illusionists or something.

'If we were here another day, we might even have seen Allen Ginsberg reading poetry,' Jon said.

He flicked the large lapels of his sports jacket and we walked as casually as possible onto MacDougal Street. I'd visited Manhattan several times as an adult and I was fascinated to see that some aspects of sixties America were no different: yellow cabs rushed everywhere, steam rose up through the streets, hot-dog vendors loudly advertised their wares. And it was just as humid as a summer visit I'd once experienced with Jon in my thirties.

Jon saw me fanning myself. 'Sorry, I should have warned you. This is the hottest summer in New York since 1869.'

As we skirted around the park, I saw a street sign for Washington Square North. I grabbed Jon's arm.

'I've just realised where we are!'

'About time, Caz.'

'No, I mean specifically where we are. Washington Square North. This is where Edward Hopper lived for fifty years.'

'Edward Hopper the artist?'

'Who else?' I tugged his jacket sleeve. 'Oh, you know that, darling. I've told you so many times how much I admire Hopper. He was one of my greatest influences when I was studying art.'

'I've never understood that. Your paintings are nothing like his.'

'Well, the band you were in at college was nothing like Edith Piaf or Amy Winehouse, but you still love listening to them.' Jon shrugged and craned his neck to peer at the buildings across the road. I squeezed his forearm tighter. 'I've had an amazing idea. Could we come back here another time in, say, the thirties or forties? I could visit Hopper in his studio. Oh my god, that would be incredible!'

'We'd have to be very careful. Interacting with someone famous could have unforeseen circumstances.'

I gripped the strap of my shoulder bag. 'I know that. But to have the opportunity to actually meet Edward Hopper, that would be life-changing. You can understand that, can't you?'

'Of course. Look, maybe we can do that next time. We'd need to work out how we can do it safely, okay? Right now, we have to concentrate on cashing our traveller's cheque. If we can't do that, we won't be going anywhere.'

He strode off down the street. I paused for a moment to ponder further what it would be like to talk to one of my favourite artists, then hurried after him, my mind whirring with possibilities.

The first bureau de change we found insisted that we present our passports to cash a traveller's cheque. Jon looked suitably abashed, claimed he'd left his in our hotel and announced he'd return later. The second had a cop queueing up behind us so we felt we couldn't risk it, but then Jon spotted a classy-looking department store on 5th Avenue.

'I read that some stores would let you pay by traveller's cheque and then give you change in cash. Shall I buy a new tie?'

Somewhat aghast at Jon's bravado, I followed him into the store and Jon picked out a garish purple and orange number. He strode up to the counter.

'Hi there,' he said in an extreme English accent. 'I was hoping to pay for this using an American Express traveller's cheque, but I've left my passport at the hotel. Is that a problem?'

The assistant didn't even blink. 'Of course not, sir. Happy to help.'

Jon gave her a wide beam and signed his fake hundred dollar cheque in front of her. We had a few moments of panic when she called her manager over but it was only because the cheque was for such a large amount; coming from 2018, we'd underestimated the impact that would have. Fortunately, five minutes later, we were walking back onto the street with a horrible tie and over ninety-seven dollars in greenbacks. Jon passed half the cash to me, 'so you can buy drinks as well if you need to,' and I pushed it deep into my handbag. We bade a hasty retreat into the heart of the village and found a bar where we could hide for a couple of hours. I listened to conversations about the Vietnam War, gay rights and the race riots that had happened the previous month in Chicago. It was a peculiar sensation.

Did I feel guilty about defrauding that store out of almost a hundred bucks, closer to eight hundred dollars at today's exchange rate? I might have done, except really they should have checked our ID, plus I barely worry about it now because of what happened afterwards.

Mid-afternoon, we headed back to MacDougal Street and Jon led us into a club called Cafe Wha?, a classic, dark downtown New York joint with a small stage, tables packed in, a jukebox and waitress service. On the way in, I glanced at the crudely printed, black-and-white poster tacked to the brick wall that listed the acts billed to play; I didn't recognise any of them.

'Are you sure we're at the right place? Or even the right time?'

'Trust me, Caz. Wednesday, August third, 1966 is a seminal day in rock and blues history. You'll see why.'

We took a table towards the back of the club, ordered beers and sat through a decent but in no way exceptional band before a bearded man with long hair came on stage.

'That's Manny Roth,' Jon whispered. 'The owner of this place. He unwittingly gave Bob Dylan his break here a few years prior to this.'

Roth stood with his cigarette rubbing the mic. 'Time now for one of our hootenanny sessions. Please welcome a young man just arrived in New York, Jimmy James.'

And on walked a black man with wild afro hair wearing a deep red velvet jacket, a Fender Stratocaster slung over his shoulders. He plugged his guitar into an amp, nodded to the rhythm section of the house band and played his first chord.

'Holy shit!' I said too loudly. A nearby couple glanced towards me. I lowered my voice. 'That isn't Jimmy James, it's Jimi Hendrix.'

'Before he changed his name,' Jon said excitedly. 'And this is his walk-on gig, which persuades Manny Roth to give him a residency here, which in turn means The Animals' Chas Chandler will later meet him and invite him to London. Which is where he truly makes it. So this gig is the reason the world came to know one of the greatest guitarists who ever lived.'

I watched in awe as the young Hendrix began his set. Within minutes, the wailing guitar, the lightning speed of his fingers and what I instantly recognised as his distinctive voice were blowing away the audience. He played covers of 'In the Midnight Hour' and 'Knock On Wood', and Howlin' Wolf's 'Killing Floor', before launching into the bent notes and accompanying feedback of a tune that was clearly an early version of what would become one of Hendrix's greatest songs, 'Foxy Lady'. I sat through the entire set without touching my beer. At one point, a photographer took some photos of Hendrix playing, and a few snapshots of the audience watching with their mouths open, as if we all knew we were seeing something special.

When he left the stage after just half an hour, he brought the house down.

There was no point in staying for anything after that, so after using the restrooms, we sidled out and went for a coffee, sitting at a sidewalk table without speaking. There was simply no need. Until Jon said, 'Wow.'

I smiled. 'That was incredible.'

He blew out his cheeks. 'I never dreamt it would be that good. Andrew and I used to talk when we were younger

49

about these small club gigs he did in New York. Andrew became quite obsessed with them, started tracking down bootlegs, keeping a record of the set lists.'

'He'd have loved it.'

'I know.' He sighed. 'I do feel a tiny bit guilty that he couldn't have come with us. But we have to stick to our rules. We can never tell him or anyone else.'

I nodded solemnly.

Jon looked amused. 'You alright? You look quite consternated.'

I tapped my forehead. 'I'm just trying to hold the gig in my mind so I don't forget it.'

'I know what you mean. But I did, ah, actually get one souvenir.' He reached inside his jacket pocket and unfolded a piece of paper, about the size of an A4 sheet. It was one of the posters with the running order that I had seen pinned to the wall of the bar.

'Where did you get that?' I asked.

'Pulled it off the wall in the gents.' He smoothed it out. 'Remember when we nicked things from gigs when we were younger?'

I shifted in my chair. 'I didn't steal things, I always asked. The odd track list that the band used, a flyer for an upcoming event. You were far more brazen.'

'This isn't so bad. No one will miss it.'

I bent over to look at the poster. 'You know you can never show Andrew this.'

'Don't worry, I'll frame it and hang it in the basement. He never goes down there.'

'Hmm. I suppose that's safe enough.'

Jon folded up the poster again and slipped it into his pocket. We finished our coffees, walked back to Washington Square Park, found a quiet corner and returned ourselves to the twenty-first century.

5

I'm meeting Bee at The Crouch End Art Centre today. It's a compact, maze of a gallery tucked away in the outskirts of our North London community, cleverly designed with multiple spaces and glass walls, the rear of the building hidden from nearby residences by tall poplar trees. They have a new exhibition, and Rosie, who owns the gallery, has several of my pieces on display, which she thinks will sell 'quicker than the prime minister can drop his trousers'. That's Rosie for you. I haven't known her long but most of her explanations revolve around sex or slandering politicians. Or both.

I'm given a glass of prosecco as I walk in. As Bee isn't here yet I wander over to my artwork to see if any of them have a red dot attached to them. I'm amazed and delighted to see that two of them do: 'Paris Jazz 1935' and 'New York Guitarist (unknown)', but who might, if you look carefully, have a passing similarity to a young Jimi Hendrix. I wind my fingers happily around my pashmina.

Someone coughs behind me but before I can turn around, they start to read out my biography, which is written on a small, raised plaque beside my work: 'Caroline Tangent has always been influenced by music in her art. In her latest works, she explores the history of music and its connections with contemporary multi-ethnic culture.'

I turn to see Bee grinning and Rosie standing beside her, looking proud. I kiss them both. Bee is looking beautiful in a long V-neck Winslow dress; Rosie, our age too, is wearing a tighter, peacock feather-print African Dashiki dress which neither Bee nor I could get away with but suits her perfectly.

'Contemporary multi-ethnic culture, eh?' Bee repeats.

'Does that sound too pretentious?' I ask. 'It does, doesn't it?'

'Nonsense,' Rosie declares. 'It's eloquent and illuminating. I should know, I wrote it.'

We all laugh.

'And it's true,' Bee says. 'You can't deny it.'

'Well, yes. I know I told you about my love of music,' I say to Rosie, 'but when I was a teenager, I harboured ambitions to become a musician myself. But I was rubbish. Never got past grade four on the piano. Then I realised I could paint, and my musical tastes naturally made it onto my canvas.'

'Thank fuck,' Rosie says. 'I couldn't have sold a piano concerto.'

'This one reminds me of some of your work when we were at uni,' Bee says, indicating the not-Hendrix painting.

'Ah, my constructivism and experimental abstract days.'

'They were wonderful,' Bee says to the gallery owner. 'She painted these weird images of The Spice Girls as concrete buildings, and you did those bizarre masquerades of Jarvis Cocker and Liam Gallagher.'

'Hmm, yes, not my greatest work.'

'And who was that handsome guitarist you kept painting? Oh, yes.' Bee snaps her fingers. 'The man you ended up marrying.'

'Yes, well, that's true, too. I still wanted to be a musician, even though I knew I never would be. Which is why I fell for Jon – he was doing everything I wanted to do. Play in a band, gain people's admiration, have free drinks.'

Rosie's eyebrows are stretching beyond her forehead. 'You never told me this, darling.'

I shrug. 'It's ancient history. I painted so many abstracts of Jon. Then he got drunk one night and slashed half of them with a Stanley knife.'

'He didn't!' Rosie exclaims.

'That's when you split up for a while, right?' Bee says.

'And ironically when I realised I was in love with him. I knew I must be when I forgave him just a few days later. Anyway, he was right, they were all shit.'

'They weren't.'

'Hmm.'

'He was an angry man then, wasn't he. Remember how jealous he would get if he thought another guy was looking at you lustfully?'

'He never did anything, though. I think he might have warned off one or two, but that was it.' I lower my voice. 'I'm rather ashamed to admit that I found it quite alluring.'

Rosie winks. 'Your knight in shining armour?'

I grin. 'God, I was infatuated by him then!'

'You're not now?'

'After twenty years? It's different isn't it, after that time?'

'Oh, I don't know,' Rosie says haughtily, 'my husband and I still have great sex almost every night.'

We watch the gallery proprietor glide off to schmooze potential buyers.

'Talking of angry husbands,' Bee says. 'Andrew was in a filthy mood after last month's party at Teri and Zaina's. He's convinced Jon is planning to start selling his fake concert stuff again but without cutting him in. He was seething all the way home.'

'Trust me, Jon is not going to start doing that. With or without Andrew.'

'That's what I told him, but I'm not sure he believes it yet. I think he still feels as if he's in Jon's shadow sometimes, even after all these years.'

'That's ridiculous. Andrew owns his own tech company.'

Bee holds out her arms in exasperation. 'What can I do?' She studies my latest works again. 'I do like them,' she pronounces. 'But don't you ever think about painting more commercial pieces again? It would help your cash flow. For Veronica.'

I tense at hearing my sister's name. I try not to think too much about her in environments like this, it makes me too sad.

'These are commercial. Look, two of them have sold already.'

'You know what I mean,' Bee says.

I do. Bee is referring to my one truly commercial success, which I painted in my early thirties. An image of two French horns with a hint of female torsos locked in a passionate embrace. It was used initially in an advert for a sports car, which was so successful that the proceeds were enough for the deposit on our Crouch End residence complete with artist studio at the end of the garden. Something I had always dreamed of. I subsequently donated the painting to an HIV charity, who used it in their awareness campaigns for several years.

'It's not that easy,' I say. 'I didn't set out to paint something so commercial. It just happened that an advertising executive saw my work in a tiny gallery and immediately wanted to use it. That's just lucky.'

Bee squeezes my fingers. 'It's more than luck, Caroline. It's down to all your hard work and ability.'

I squeeze back. She's very kind, my best friend, and there's some truth in what she says. I have painted so many pieces over the years and I hope that my work has improved. I've gone from painting what were pretty much abstract caricatures of nineties rock and pop stars, to more sophisticated abstracts of musical concepts, sounds, the feelings you get from an intimate musical experience, through to my, well, yes, current more commercial paintings, which I hope the well-off of North London will want to hang on their Hampstead walls. Not forgetting my post-miscarriage period, when my work expressed my anger and frustration – not just at losing the baby, but at the doctors who explained that I could never thereafter bear a child and at my subsequent relationship problems with Jon. It was a bad time, and painting was one of the few things that got me through it.

But I've worked hard since then, the last eleven years, building my career. Although it's not been easy. I was happy in my twenties painting whatever took my fancy, and if I sold a few pieces every now and then I was delighted. I did have long-term aspirations of being a famous artist, but it didn't seem so important, so urgent. After my miscarriage, I changed my direction, became more focused. Now I'm heading where I want to be. I know my goal.

'Well, when I have my *own* gallery,' I say. We both laugh.

'I can't wait for that,' Bee says.

'It will happen, you'll see. I might have to move to the coast to open it, but I can see it in my future. I promise.'

'I'll hate you for moving, but I'll do everything I can to help.'

I smile, embrace her. 'Well, it's not as if you've got nothing to celebrate. What about your—'

'Shh!' Bee puts her finger to her lips.

'What?'

'I'm not talking publicly about that yet,' she says in a low voice.

'You mean your new shop?' I say in a theatrical whisper. She nods. 'Why not?'

'I don't want to jinx it.'

I put my hand on her forearm. 'Bee, it's going to be just as successful as your current store. I promise.'

'What if it's not? Andrew will think I've failed.'

'Of course he won't. He's just as invested in it as you are.'

'That's true.' Her shoulders relax. 'But I still need your input. You're coming round for dinner next week, yes? To discuss how you can help?'

'Absolutely.'

'I can show you some of the designs I'm thinking of buying.' She holds out her arms. 'What do you think of this dress, by the way? Do you like it?'

'I love it. You look gorgeous.'

'Thank God!'

A woman passing by tilts her head graciously. Bee and I bite our lips and stifle a laugh. Neither of us has stepped inside a church for any reason other than weddings since we've known each other. We move on from my artwork and follow the woman.

'I'm hoping to acquire an exclusive range from the woman who designed it,' Bee continues. 'Do you think that's a good idea?'

'Do you think it will sell?'

'I hope so. Yes, I'm sure it will.'

'Then yes, I think it's a wonderful plan.'

Bee grabs my elbow. We explore the rest of the gallery. There's some wonderfully talented young artists' work on display, and some stunning sculptures that we appreciate for some time before Bee goes in search of more prosecco. As I study the figurine in front of me, I notice out of the corner of my eye that someone is staring at me. I straighten up and my heart leaps unpleasantly in my chest: it's Pieter.

Pieter smirks as he sees I've noticed him and strides over. It's too late for me to avoid him so I adopt a fake smile and let him air kiss me. But when he places his hand on my back for a few too many seconds, I wriggle to loosen myself from his grasp. Pieter stands back.

'Caroline, you look beautiful.'

I grip my handbag and peer over his shoulder hoping that Bee is on her way back. No sign of her yet. I avoid the young man's gaze. 'Pieter, it's been a few years. What are you doing here?'

'Didn't Rosie say? My first painting is on sale here.' He points to a distant wall in the gallery.

I'm genuinely surprised. When he was one of my students, he never showed any true promise. He must have knuckled down.

'That's wonderful,' I say.

'Would you like to see it?' he asks and smirks again. 'You might recognise some aspects of it.'

Oh, Christ, I think. He hasn't. But there's not much I can do to avoid his offer and I let him guide me over to where his picture hangs.

'How is your husband now?' Pieter asks me bluntly as we cross the gallery. 'Is he still a bitter man?'

'No. He's perfectly fine. And that's not appropriate for you to ask.'

Pieter shrugs. We reach his painting. It's a large three-foot square canvas of a half-naked woman lounging in front of a TV with a selection of remote control handsets strategically positioned across her body. It's bloody awful. What is Rosie thinking of? Unless she's...

57

'What do you think?' Pieter asks with puppy enthusiasm.

I pretend to consider it. 'It's very... contemporary.'

'Do you like it?'

'I—'

'Do you recognise the model?'

My heart sinks. Fortunately, it is just her back you can see, but yes, I can guess who he has based it on. Not that he ever saw that much of my body – it is all in his imagination. Which, I have to admit, is vivid and remarkably accurate. Even the dove tattoo that I stupidly admitted to having one evening.

'There you are.'

My shoulders rise again. Bee is back. She hands me a glass of prosecco. I down half of it on the spot.

'Oh,' she says, looking at Pieter's painting. 'That's, um...'

'This is the artist,' I say quickly, pointing to Pieter. 'Pieter Novak.'

'Ah,' Bee says and hides her smile behind her glass.

Pieter smiles back.

Bee takes my hand. 'Caroline, I think someone was asking about one of your paintings. Maybe we'd better see if we can find her.'

I nod vigorously, say goodbye to my ex-student, and Bee takes my elbow and leads me away.

'Oh my God, Caroline. Isn't that that chap you used to teach? I remember you telling me his name.'

'When I was an art tutor, yes.'

'I thought so. Didn't you two...'

'No!' I say sharply. 'Never.'

'He's very handsome.'

'So?'

'And that tattoo is just like yours. Like ours.' She winks.

'So?'

'It's okay, you can tell me. You never did say at the time.'

'I told you everything, Bee. And nothing happened, nothing like that, anyway.'

Which is true. But Bee still gives me a wicked grin.

What I didn't tell her is that I had thought about it.

It wasn't long after Jon and I had lost the baby, during my angry period, and with no income, I had turned to tutoring. Jon was at his lowest, we hadn't had sex for months. And when Pieter turned up in one of my classes, I couldn't help but admire him – he was, as Bee says, extremely handsome. And when he, a twenty-one-year-old at the time, came on to me, in my early-thirties as I was, how could I not be flattered? Or tempted. But I didn't do anything. We went out for dinner after class once or twice, but that was it. He wanted to take things a step further, but I kept saying no until, in the end, I told him to cool it.

Unfortunately, he somehow found out where I lived and sent me a huge bouquet of flowers. And as much as I insisted time and again to Jon that they were simply from a grateful student, my husband didn't believe me. He more or less blatantly accused me of sleeping with Pieter, just assumed I had done so. It hurt more than anything. Add that to Jon's constant depression and rage, and I was as close to walking out on him then as I've ever been.

But I didn't. And I'm proud now that we came through that time, for the better. I know he can still be difficult sometimes but we're stronger now than we were. With a better relationship.

Before we leave, I find Rosie to thank her for her patronage. She has a gleam in her eye.

'Caroline, I have someone who wants to meet you. A very influential person,' she hisses. She takes my hand and drags me towards a blond woman wearing a black trouser suit. She smiles as we approach her and her teeth are so white they dazzle me.

'Priscilla, this is Caroline Tangent, the artist you wanted to meet.'

Priscilla offers her hand. 'You painted the New York Guitarist?'

'I did.' She has a lilt to her accent; I'm guessing Scandinavian or German.

'It is wonderful. Reminds me of Jimi Hendrix.'

'That's very perceptive.'

She smiles again. 'Rosie tells me you were also responsible for the Bugatti advert, with the French horns.'

'Yes. That's a while ago.'

'I still remember it. It was very sexy.'

I feel Bee prod me in the small of my back. I don't flinch.

Rosie is almost hopping from foot to foot. 'Priscilla has an offer for you, darling.'

'Oh?'

'Yes,' Priscilla says. 'I am representing an exclusive jewellery brand, Esposito. You have heard of them, I am sure.'

'Of course.'

'Their founder, Bruno Esposito, used to work for Verdura,' Rosie says.

'That is true,' Priscilla confirms. 'I am looking for a new piece of art to launch their new season. Would you be interested in designing our composition?'

Now I feel Bee place her palm on the small of my back and I'm so glad she does; I think I might have toppled over otherwise. I don't know what to say.

Rosie flings out her arms. 'Caroline? What do you think? Come on.'

I place my hand on my heart. 'I would love to. Thank you.'

'Good.' Priscilla shakes my hand again. 'I will be in touch next week with a contract. The package will include the initial artwork and further additions if it is used more widely. I don't think you'll be disappointed with the offer.'

I'm abso-bloody-lutely sure I won't be. I thank her again, Rosie takes her guest to meet other artists, and Bee and I leave the gallery.

Well, I drift out, floating on air.

6

Over the last two or three years, since Jon has been promoted to a more senior position at the university, he has started to receive more work-related phone calls at home, even at the weekends. I don't mind, I'm glad he's more engaged with his job. So this evening, when we are in the kitchen preparing dinner, it doesn't surprise me when his mobile phone buzzes and he raises his eyebrows at me; it must be someone from his office. I wave my wrist at him and he steps out of the kitchen door but I can still hear some of his conversation.

'I've told you, it's not that easy... I can't do that... You know I'd like to, but I can't... Well, if you put it like that. Okay, let me see what I can do.'

He comes back in.

'Who was that?' I ask.

He tugs at an ear. 'My head of department. It seems that my colleague's jury service has been extended and he was supposed to be presenting a paper at a conference next week. My head's asked if I can go instead.'

'That sounds a great opportunity.'

'It is, but it's up in Manchester, so I'd have to stay away for a couple of nights.'

'That's okay.'

'And, er, it's quite soon. When we were planning to go to that exhibition at the Tate. I'm sorry, do you mind?'

'Hmm. I guess we can go another time.'

'Thanks, Caz.' Jon kisses me hard on the lips.

'But you can make it up to me,' I add.

Jon squeezes me around the waist. 'Always happy to do that.'

I smile and place my palms on his chest. 'I mean,' I say purposefully, 'that if you're going away on a jolly, then I get to select who we go see on our next trip to the past.'

'Fair enough. What gig are we going to crash?'

I tap his nose gently. 'I think it's time we go for a biggie. I choose The Beatles.'

My husband holds me at arm's length and grins. 'I had a feeling you were going to bring them up again sometime. So I've been doing some research just in case.'

'You know me too well.' I turn back to my bolognese simmering on the stove.

There's no doubt that seeing a band before they hit the big time has an extra attraction. And what better example of that than The Beatles? I've been bugging Jon about seeing the Fab Four since we returned from Glastonbury. But I have some very specific criteria: it must be with Ringo, it must be when they play songs that I know (i.e. not too early) and it shouldn't be a stadium concert (i.e. not later in their career when they're so huge that you can't hear them sing for all the screaming girls in the audience). I'm so excited by the prospect.

Jon picks up his iPad from the kitchen counter and scrolls his finger down the screen. 'Bearing in mind your conditions, we have two options: the Cavern Club or Hamburg.'

'Oh, the Cavern. Liverpool in the sixties, how amazing would that be?'

'Okay. In that case, we can go in, say, August 1962, one of the first gigs after Pete Best leaves the band.'

'Have they had a hit by then?'

'No, it's just before they release their first single, "Love Me Do".'

I clap my hands. 'Cool. Can we wear the same clothes we bought for Hendrix? That's the same sort of era, isn't it?'

'Your kaftan dress might be a few years ahead of its time, but I don't think people will notice. They'll be far more interested in Lennon and McCartney's latest hairstyles.'

'Me too!' I whip a wooden spoon through the sauce.

Jon taps the iPad. 'But there is a significant challenge.'

'Tickets?'

'No. At least, not in the sense that all you have to do is queue up and hope you get in. But the Cavern was a members club and you needed to show your membership card at the door.'

'Hey, you mocked up a sixties AmEx traveller's cheque, I'm sure you can print a membership card.'

'I'm sure I can.' Jon grins. 'Actually, one of my students, Elise, has a real eye for creating smart designs. I could ask her to help.'

'I don't think we should get anyone else involved, that's far too risky. Anyway, when do you teach design work on your maths course?'

'Artists have used mathematics for hundreds of years. You should know that, Caz.' He smirks. 'Don't worry, I'll do it myself.'

'So, what's the problem? Money?'

'No. I've found out you can buy old English coins from that period on eBay and even five-pound notes. Not cheap but simpler than risking our traveller's cheque racket in England.'

'That's all fine, then.'

'Well, there is one more thing I have to address. The Cavern is right in the centre of Liverpool, on Mathew Street, which means we can't just materialise halfway down that road.' He clicks his tongue. 'I'll need to find a quieter location.'

I dip my little finger in the sauce and hold it up for Jon to taste. He sucks it gently and nods.

'Delicious.'

'Right answer.' I turn the heat down and reach for the spaghetti. 'Now what were you saying about finding somewhere to arrive?'

'I've already been looking—'

'Wonderful!'

'— but I can't see anywhere that isn't in one of the more dubious parts of Liverpool unless it's two or three miles away from the Cavern Club. Down by the docks, for example.'

'What do you suggest? Do we have to land further out and get a taxi in?'

He shakes his head. 'That would be highly problematic. No, I have an idea but I'm going to have to be extremely accurate when I program my landing coordinates.'

'Because…?'

'Well, my idea is to arrive just one block away from the club, on a road called Harrington Street. From the sixties' maps I've seen, I'm guessing that's a quieter road on an evening. But there could still be people passing down it, so I'm going to have to land us on a first-storey fire escape.'

My hand holding the packet of pasta freezes above a pan of boiling water. 'On the outside of a building?'

'Yep.'

'How big would that be?'

'A few feet wide.'

'And if we miss it?'

'Then we'd end up in thin air and drop twenty feet onto the pavement.'

I grimace. 'Do you think you can do it?'

Jon shrugs then smiles. 'I'll have a go. It'll be a good test of my programming skills, right?'

'Hmm, but what if someone see us appear? It'll still be light at that time of the year, won't it?'

'We'd have to be very unlucky if someone was looking up just at the moment we flash into view. Look, just in case, let's land as late as possible in the evening, just before the gig starts. It should still give us enough time to get to the Cavern.'

I agree. While I finish dinner, Jon goes down to the basement to start programming the time machine.

Two days later, we're all ready. We dress, go down to the basement and I wait on the launch pad while Jon double checks his coordinates. The small Café Wha? poster that Jon stole from our Hendrix gig now has pride of place next to his Woodstock poster. He has some brass, my husband.

Jon joins me and crosses his fingers. 'Here we go...'

I close my eyes, brace my knees, just in case – although I doubt that will help if I do fall twenty feet – and trust my husband. Three, two, one... I feel the usual dizziness and then I hear a clang as my feet touch the metal of a fire escape. The air is warm, a balmy August evening. I breath out and open my eyes and see Jon. We are indeed on the

66

first-floor fire escape on the outside of a building, looking down twenty feet to the pavement below. And Jon is standing with one foot on the fire escape, one in mid-air, his hand clutching the metal handrail while his body wavers in the air as if he's doing a Tommy Steele impression from *Singin' in the Rain*.

'Jon!' I gasp.

'Shush!' he loud-whispers. 'There are people directly below us. Give me your hand, quick.'

I reach out and grab his wrist. With a heave, Jon swings himself around and lurches beside me, clasping me in his arms. For a moment, we stare into each other's eyes. Then we burst out laughing. With relief.

'Come on,' Jon says, 'we're going to be late.'

He leads the way down the metal staircase and as we reach the bottom, I see a group of three middle-aged women dressed in buttoned-up coats and pillbox hats watching us descend with suspicion sewn into their brows.

'Evening, ladies,' Jon says nonchalantly, holding my hand, and we jog away up Harrington Street, still laughing.

Three minutes later, our merriment ceases when we reach Matthew Street and see hundreds of people packed in the narrow road outside the entrance to the club. My heart sinks.

'Oh, Jon, look. We'll never get in. I can't even see where the queue starts.'

We push our way through the throng to within a few yards of the doors but we're not going any further. There is a sign on the wall saying 'Club Full' and a doorman shouts to the crowd that they're not letting anyone else in.

'My God, imagine what it's going to be like in a few years,' I say.

'This night is worse than normal,' Jon says. 'I should have expected this.'

'Why?'

'Because many of the people who go tonight are fans of Pete Best, and they're pissed off that Ringo's taken his place. There's even a bit of chanting inside the club saying they want Best back.'

The crowd surges forward and back. A few scuffles break out and we get propelled back down the street.

'Let's go home and come back,' I say. 'That's one of the beauties of the time machine, right? We can just do the same thing but program it so we arrive a couple of hours earlier. Especially now we know you can get the location of the fire escape pretty much spot on.'

Jon doesn't answer, just nods. We walk back to our landing place. We wait until no one is around, then walk briskly up the staircase and Jon presses the button on the time-pen to take us home.

We land back in our cellar and I clap my hands together. 'So, get cracking, darling! Start work on another pen and we'll go back in a few days.'

Jon takes off his hat. He turns it around between his fingers. 'There's something I haven't told you about the time machine, Caz.'

'Oh?'

'The thing is, I don't know if we can have two versions of us in the same place at the same time. That might disturb the wormholes that carry us there.'

'In what way?'

'I don't know exactly, that's the problem. But I'm hypothesising, and it's possible that if two wormholes open too close together, they could get combined.'

'How close?'

He places his hat on the workbench. 'Well, let's put it this way: if we went back three or four days before or after another trip we'd done, then I'm pretty sure that shouldn't pose a problem. But if we tried to return in anything less than, say, one or two days either side, that could present all sorts of risks.'

'Like what?'

'Well, the wormholes could break up or even collapse. We could potentially end up stuck in the past.'

I steady myself against a wall. 'You didn't tell me that!'

Jon tugs one of his ears. 'I didn't have a need to. I never thought we would want to go back to the same time and place twice. To be honest, being stuck in the past could be the best-case scenario.'

'What's the worst case?'

'We could get... dematerialised.'

'In English?'

'We could die.'

'Oh.' My shoulders slump. 'Well, I guess even an early Beatles gig isn't worth dying for. Is it?'

Jon picks up my nuance and smiles. 'Not in that way. But don't worry, it doesn't mean we can't go see the band, we'll just have to go to another gig.'

So we do. A week later, and we're back in the basement, this time planning a trip for a few months downstream, to December fifth, 1962, a night when The Beatles are playing with Gerry and the Pacemakers. That's better than our original plan. 'Love Me Do' has been released by then and reached number seventeen in the charts.

We know it is going to be a chilly evening, so we've bought retro coats; they're one of the easier things to acquire in 2021 and I adore my emerald green classic swing number. I'm going to wear it this winter in our present-time, too.

This time, we're landing two hours earlier in the day to

give us plenty of time to get to the club ahead of everyone else, and Jon has adjusted his coordinates so that both of us hit the fire escape with two feet on the stanchion. The bitter December cold immediately smacks me in the face. I pull my belt tighter, clasp Jon's arm and we retrace our steps slowly towards the Cavern.

I can't believe it. There's already a queue, over an hour before the doors open. But it's more orderly this time, so we join the end of the line. The crowd is full of teenagers and young twenty-somethings, most of the men wearing suits, the women, cardigans on top of their dresses. There's barely another coat to be seen. And very few non-white faces. We stand out like a Dalek in a Victorian theatre.

It's not long before we're on the end of a few jibes. Some are fatuous, references to grandparents and Jon's hat, but I'm shocked when someone calls me a darkie. I tell the lad to keep his mouth shut but that just sparks further invective. I take a step towards my abuser, but Jon holds my elbow and says softly, 'Not the time, Caz'. I grit my teeth. He's right, sadly. No matter how much I want to castigate the lad, we mustn't draw further attention to ourselves. We aren't supposed to be here.

I clench my fists and turn away. Cue more hoots of derision.

I ignore another woman when she mentions my long straight hair, but it's clearly not in fashion and I should have done something about that – made it more Samantha Stephens from *Bewitched*.

I'm relieved when the doors open and the queue begins to move. But as it does, people also start to enter the club from the other direction.

'Jon,' I say urgently. 'I'm worried we won't get in again.'

My husband cranes his neck. 'I've got an idea. Wait here.'

Before I can say anything, Jon leaves the queue and marches up to the club doors. I pull my coat around me and ignore the stares and wisecracks about my husband leaving me. I lean out and see Jon is talking to the doormen. After a few minutes, he reaches inside his jacket pocket and appears to shake their hand. He turns around and beckons me to join him. The wisecracks turn to howls of disdain as I march past those still waiting.

Jon holds his arm out. 'Come on, we're in.'

He raises his hand once more at the doorman who gives a fleeting nod in return and opens the doors for us. We walk down slightly crumbling stairs, past bare brick walls, the hubbub of raised voices growing louder as we enter the club. My heart is beating a little faster than normal.

I look around. The ceilings are low brick domes, as if I'm standing under a railway arch, and I remember the Cavern's design was based on the Paris jazz clubs of the time. It is dark, hot, really quite dingy, and there's a nasty smell. The floor is sticky and the air is already a fug of cigarette smoke. At the front, the stage is constructed under a low whitewashed arch and I think taller band members could scrape their heads on the low points.

'How did you get us in?' I ask.

'A fiver for both the doormen.'

'Is that all?'

'In 1962 the average wage for a manual worker would have been around fifteen pounds a week. Five pounds for them was too good to turn down.'

I find a copy of *Mersey Beat* on the floor, hold our coats and read a sixty-year-old music paper while Jon pushes his way to the bar. He returns with two Cokes.

'No alcohol,' he explains. 'I think they get a licence a few years from now.'

'At least it's cheap.'

'Hmm. The coins I got on eBay cost me a pretty penny.' He looks towards the stage. 'But it'll be worth it.'

We clink glasses and squeeze ourselves against a wall at the back of the club. And wait to see a band – two of whom are dead in our time – that I have dreamed of seeing since I was a child, never for a moment ever contemplating the possibility that I would actually do so. Why would I? But here I am. I listen to Gerry and the Pacemakers' set and know I should be excited by seeing them, but I don't know their music except for 'Ferry Cross the Mersey', which they won't even record for another two years. I'm just waiting for the highlight of the evening. My legs are getting tired, my shoes look muddy – how is that possible? – and my dress is going to have to go straight to the dry cleaners on our return. God knows what the cigarette smoke is doing to my lungs.

But when John, Paul, George and Ringo do come on stage, it is worth every aching limb, every inhalation of cancer-inducing vapour, all the heat the club can throw at me. The boys look so happy – so young! They're dressed sharply in matching waistcoats and narrow ties, pointed, buckled shoes, neatly cut hair. It's something George Martin insisted on, apparently, and although they say a few quips between songs, they don't swear like I've read they did when they first played here. They sing 'Love Me Do', 'Please Please Me', 'PS I Love You', 'Twist and Shout' plus other songs I do know and some I recognise but wouldn't be able to name. The crowd scream and cry out between the songs, but it isn't the Shea Stadium mania that the band will experience later in their careers. Instead, the audience stands, bopping their heads, staring admiringly at the four men who in the years to come are going to change the world. There's even space nearer the front for couples to dance together. Jon and I remain at the back, grinning like maniacs, singing along and joining in with the ooohs when Lennon and McCartney chorus together at a single mic. By the end, the sweat is dripping down the singers' faces.

It is one of the best hours of my life.

When they finish, we exit back onto Matthew Street, but we're too high, too elated to go straight home, so we find a nearby pub and brave a smog of smoke to have a half-pint each. We're laughing and singing and I can hear other people in the pub also talking about the gig. Could anyone ever have predicted at this time that they were witnessing the beginning of the career of one of the most influential bands to ever grace this planet? Based on what we saw, maybe they could.

We leave the pub and stroll back to the fire escape we landed on, ready to return to 2021. Jon reaches into his jacket pocket. Shifts his hand around inside it. Frowns. Pulls his hand out, pats his sides and feels in his trouser pockets. He yanks out some coins and they spill onto the pavement and dance away down the street. He doesn't chase them.

I can see my breath in the night air. 'Come on, Jon, stop messing around. It's freezing. I want to go home.'

'Caz, did I give you the time-pen?'

'No. You must have it.'

'I… must do.' There's mild panic in his voice. He takes off his coat and shakes it upside down. Nothing falls out. He pulls off his jacket and holds it out to me. 'Here, search my pockets. Maybe I'm being stupid.'

I rummage in all of the cavities, several times, but apart from his wallet, they're all empty. We don't bring anything on these trips, after all, except money and the pen. I hand the jacket back to him.

'Have you… lost it?'

My husband pushes his fingers through his hair. 'I can't have.'

73

'That's our only ticket back home! Tell me this is a joke. Tell me you're messing around.'

'I—'

'I'll forgive you, I promise.'

Jon holds his arms out and then clasps his face. 'I wish I was. But I'm not. I've lost it, Caz, I've lost the time-pen.'

He slumps down onto the pavement. I stare down at him, willing him to look up at me, grin stupidly and whip out the pen from a hiding place in his sock. He doesn't. He must be telling the truth. I squat down beside him. A hundred thoughts are flying through my mind. I want to scream and shout and tell him what an idiot he is, jump up and down in anger, punch him. But I rein myself in. Place my hands on his shoulders. What would I say if he had lost his car keys?

'Darling, think. When did you last see it?'

Jon talks through his fingers. 'In the club. I think. I remember taking out my wallet when I bought the Cokes, moving some coins to my trouser pocket... and I think I remember feeling the pen in my other jacket pocket. I hadn't meant to put it there, so I moved it. To one of my inside pockets. To keep it safe, I thought...'

'And then?'

Jon shakes his head. 'I don't know. I wouldn't have needed to check for it until now. The bands came on, I got caught up in the moment, we went to the pub... That's all.'

I straighten up. 'So, there are only two places it can be. The Cavern Club or the pub we've just been in.'

'Unless it's fallen onto the street somewhere. Then we're fucked.'

Then we're fucked. But we can't think that. Not yet. I stretch my arm down to him. 'Come on. We're going back to look for it.' Jon doesn't move. I thrust my hand in his face. 'Come on, Jon. Both those places are going to close soon,

74

and I'm not spending the night freezing my arse off in 1962 Liverpool.'

Jon continues to look fixedly at the pavement. He raises his shoulders, takes a deep breath and reaches for my hand.

We try the pub first. It's in the throes of closing, so while I rush around the emptying tavern, scanning the floors and sticky tabletops, Jon asks the bar staff if anyone has handed in a pen. No one has, and I can't see it anywhere. Not where we were sitting, not on the floor, not shoved behind a curtain anywhere. Of course, someone might have found it and pocketed it already...

'If someone does find it,' I ask, 'can they make it work?'

'In theory. They'd have to swivel the top around a couple of times, and then hold down the button. There's no reason someone would do all that consciously but if you were just messing around with it...'

'Let's try the Cavern.'

Jon nods wearily and we make our way back to the club. The doormen we met are still standing outside and after a few minutes, Jon persuades them to let us back in. 'I told them you'd left your purse inside. Sorry, but at least they believed me.'

'Fine, blame me.' I snort.

We hurry down the stairs. Everyone has left except a few people who are clearing up and two men sitting at the bar, holding drinks that don't look soft to me. I catch my breath. They aren't just two men, they're John Lennon and Paul McCartney. And then I see what else Lennon is holding: our time-pen. He is twirling it between his fingers like a mini-baton, stopping occasionally to click the button up and down, and then rolling it along the bar counter to McCartney, who absent-mindedly rolls it back.

I grip Jon's arm. He has seen it too.

'Can they damage it?' I whisper.

He shrugs. 'But they might unintentionally activate it.' He takes a deep breath. 'Come on.'

We walk towards John Lennon and Paul McCartney. Two of the most famous songwriters who have ever lived. In another time, I would happily have agreed to be dropped in the middle of Dartmoor to have the chance to be doing this, but now, if we don't get the pen back, we could end up lost in the past. Or worse: if Lennon does accidentally swivel the top around and click the button, history could change forever. This is what Jon meant by the butterfly effect. Only this wouldn't be a butterfly, it would be a bloody great big pterodactyl.

We walk up to the two Beatles.

'Mr Lennon?' Jon says.

Lennon turns around. 'Who are you?'

'Ah, Jon Tangent. This is my wife, Caroline.'

Lennon looks me up and down. I brush back my hair over my ears, demurely; I can't help it.

'Interesting hairstyle,' Lennon says. I mumble something about coming out late. Lennon frowns. 'What are you doing here? Were you at the gig tonight?'

'We were,' I reply breathlessly. 'It was fantastic.'

'You're a bit older than most of our fans.'

'Yes, well, we've heard a lot about you, thought we'd come and see what all the fuss was about.'

'Huh. What are you? A and R?'

'Um...' What the hell does that mean?

Jon steps in. 'Yeah, that's right.'

'What label?'

'App— er... Grapefruit records.'

'Never heard of them.'

'We're quite new.'

'Right, well, we're already signed to Parlophone. You probably know that.'

Lennon turns away from us and knocks back the rest of his drink. He taps the pen on the bar counter. I nudge Jon.

'Mr Lennon, that pen you have. Where did you find it?'

Lennon flicks his head at the barman. 'Dave said he found it earlier. Tucked it back there among the cans 'cos it looked a bit unusual. I thought so, too.'

So Jon must have dropped it here on the bar like he said, when he paid for our drinks.

My husband taps his fingers together. 'Only, ah, the thing is, it's actually mine. I left it in the club when we were here earlier.'

'Oh?'

'And, ah, well, I was hoping I could have it back.'

'It's just a pen.'

'It is, but it's… quite special to me.'

'Special?' Lennon spins the pen around in his fingers and my whole body tenses. 'Why's that?'

'Well…'

'I gave it to him as a gift,' I say quickly. 'A wedding present. Years ago.'

'Did you?'

'I did.'

'And you still carry it around now?'

Jon nods. 'It means a lot to me. As you can imagine.'

Lennon tilts his head and flicks the button a few times. My heart skips a thousand beats.

'You want to arm-wrestle me for it?' he asks.

'What?' Jon says.

Lennon flexes his bicep. 'Come on. What are you, man or mouse?'

'Well…'

Is this happening? Is my husband going to have to arm-wrestle John Lennon to get back our portable time machine? Seriously?

I see McCartney trying to suppress a grin. Lennon stays stony-faced for a few more seconds before laughing. The songwriter picks up a napkin and smooths it out on the counter. 'Well, of course you should have it back. Why not?' He flicks the button again. 'You want an autograph, too?'

Jon and I stare open-mouthed. Lennon looks at us. Paul McCartney laughs. 'Sure they do, John, they're just too embarrassed to ask you.'

Lennon grins and presses our pen to the napkin. Of course, no ink comes out. He rattles the pen and tries again. 'Fuck me, it doesn't even work.' He shakes his head. 'You must really love her if you're carrying around a pen she gave you years ago that doesn't work.'

Jon half laughs. 'Well, er, they do say that all you need is love.'

John Lennon and Paul McCartney stare at my husband. He swallows and smiles back.

I tense. Oh God, has Jon messed up? What if… What if he has quoted some of the most famous lyrics ever written to the men who are going to write them but… they have already written that song and no one else knows? What will they think then? I bite my lip and think of timelines. I'm sure they can't have done so yet. This is 1962 and they don't release 'All You Need is Love' until 1967. Do they?

Lennon purses his lips. 'Yeah, I like that.' McCartney nods thoughtfully.

John Lennon passes the time-pen back to Jon, whose hand is shaking as he takes it. Lennon smiles. 'Dave,' he calls out to the barman. 'Give us a pen, will you? One that works. And find some paper of some sort. This napkin is going to disintegrate, it's so wet.'

Five minutes later, Jon and I are walking out of the Cavern Club in December 1962 with our time-pen tucked deep in Jon's pocket and a personalised autograph on

Cavern Club headed notepaper: 'To Jon and Caroline, Stay young and in love. John Lennon and Paul McCartney.'

We don't even speak. Just exchange a single, long look and walk as briskly as we can back to the Harrington Street fire escape. It's nearly midnight now and although a few people are wobbling drunkenly up the road, no one is paying attention to us. I hold my husband's arm tightly. He removes the pen from his pocket, carefully swivels the top clockwise and depresses the button. We hold our breath.

Christ, it had better still be working.

Moments later we are back in the warmth of our basement and I let go of Jon and sink to my knees. Jon stands still and gazes towards his computers. I compose myself, look up at him and ever so slowly, a smile creeps across my face.

Jon grins back and reaches down to me. 'Come on, I have to check something.'

He pulls me to my feet and drags me towards the basement stairs.

'Hey, slow down!' I laugh. 'What is it? What's so urgent?'

'It's just a thought, but what if... No, it can't, can it?'

'What? What!'

Jon tugs my wrist. 'Come on, let's go see.'

He leads me quickly up the stairs and into our lounge. God, it's good to be back indoors again, out of the cold. Jon wrenches his coat off and flings it across the floor. Bolan is sleeping on a chair and looks disgusted to have been woken. I drop onto the sofa and ease myself out of my outerwear while Jon heads for the cabinet holding our vinyl. Well, some of our vinyl. He has collected so many records over the years that much of it is stored in boxes in one of our spare bedrooms. He gets down on his hands and knees and starts flicking through the albums on the left-hand side of the cabinet. They're stored alphabetically by artist so I'm

79

guessing he's looking for a Beatles LP. He pulls one out, spins around on his haunches and holds it up for me to see. Yes, it's an orange cover with 'Beatles' spelt out in yellow stars and the album name bursting out of the foot of the cover in their famous rainbow letters.

I clap my hands together. 'The *Magical Mystery Tour*. That's one of my favourites. I love the songs on that.'

'Me, too.'

'You want to play it?'

'In a minute. There's something more important to do.'

'What?'

'This is the US version, the first release of the full album.'

Which, of course, Jon has a copy of.

'Right…'

'In the UK, they initially released it as an EP. But the US version contains several extra tracks, which the band decided they'd add to try something different. Including–' Jon stabs his finger at the back of the album cover '–the last track, "All You Need is Love".'

'Well, that's a relief. At least we didn't change things so they ended up writing it earlier!'

'True. But that's not what I wanted to check.'

'Oh?'

Jon holds the album in one hand and opens it out with the other – it's a gatefold sleeve, more popular for double albums, but The Beatles were important enough by 1967 that they could demand they had a special cover. Jon runs his finger down the inside of the gatefold and pauses at the base of the cardboard. He looks up at me and his face breaks into the widest smile I have ever seen on anyone! He can't stop beaming. He blinks a few times and I think he might even start crying. Instead, he pushes himself up and comes to sit beside me on the sofa. He points at the inside of the sleeve.

'Look, Caz. Look. The last sentence. Read it out.' His voice is cracking.

I cast my eyes over the words he's pointing at. 'Ah... copyright of this sound recording, dot dot dot, exclusively licensed to Apple Corp... Oh!'

My hand flies to my mouth. At the very end of that paragraph, after all the legal stuff, it says, 'With thanks to J and C. Stay young and in love.'

Jon is still grinning like the Cheshire Cat. I stare at the album cover and then place my hand on my husband's thigh. 'How is this possible?'

'Butterfly wings, Caz. Tiny ones.'

'Are you sure?'

'Of course.'

'I mean, are you sure that wasn't there all along? And it's some other J and C they're referring to?'

'With the same words as Lennon wrote on our notepaper? No, that dedication definitely didn't exist before.'

'In which case, that means...'

'Yes, we changed history. In the smallest possible way. And with no nasty knock-on implications. But it happened, it really did.'

I can't believe it. But I have to. Like I have to believe everything else we're experiencing because of Jon's revolutionary invention. But I'm still astonished. And delighted. And... scared. I can't help it. To have changed history, changed time, no matter how small. That is one hell of a weight to carry on your shoulders, even if the fluctuation is tiny.

Jon sits back, leaves the album open on his lap and looks so content I think he might unwittingly drift off into meditation and reach nirvana. I grin and stroke his thigh. But as I watch him, his face changes again. His smile lessens, his neck tips back and he cocks his head to one side. Then his eyes widen as if he's just learned the most important secret anyone has ever heard, which maybe he has. Almost imperceptibly, he shakes his head. The smile returns.

I should be happy for him. I know that. But I know my husband, know what goes on his head, at least some of the time. And I can see he's churning something over in his mind.

I hope it's a good thing. But I'm not convinced it is.

7

Creating art is my passion. Everything about it intoxicates and thrills me: the initial inspiration, the rough drafts, the time I spend in my studio as I watch my vision appear on the canvas. And, of course, seeing the delight on people's faces when I reveal a piece of work.

This evening, I am especially excited about a new project I'm starting.

I'm driving to Bee's home in Muswell Hill, just a few miles from our house. My route takes me past the ladies fashion shop which Bee opened a few years ago with Andrew's investment. It's been doing so well they've found a location for a second store in Highgate and I've promised to design some bespoke artwork for the opening.

I always enjoy visiting Bee's house. It's a classic Victorian semi-detached with a black-and-white tiled floor in the hall-way, a modern extension at the rear and high-ceilinged rooms throughout. We've shared laughter and tears in these rooms for nearly fifteen years.

Bee shows me into her lounge. It's bright, tastefully decorated and I love their gorgeous oak floor. There are model steam trains on the sideboard that Andrew built years ago and a piano that their children used to play until they got bored of it. And despite Andrew's continual protestations as to how Jon should listen to music on a streaming service, he still has hundreds of CDs lined up on their shelves.

'Andrew's at the gym, but Mel will look after you while I'm cooking,' Bee says and disappears into the kitchen.

Her daughter, Melanie, is sitting on a high-backed chair, flicking through a mother and baby magazine. I haven't seen her since I learned she was pregnant and I give her a warm hug. Her face is glowing with happiness.

'Uncle Jon isn't coming?' she asks.

'He's in Manchester for a couple of nights, speaking at a conference.'

'So you're footloose and fancy-free.'

'Not exactly!' I sit on the sofa, opposite the mother-to-be. 'How are you feeling? You look so well.'

'I'm a bit nervous, to be honest. I think the reality is starting to kick in. I even cried on the phone to Mum the other night.'

'I did that when I was pregnant!'

Melanie bites her lip. 'Oh, I'm sorry. I'd forgotten what happened for you. Here I am talking about my concerns and you went through far worse.'

'Your mother is a great listener. When I had my miscarriage, I phoned her at two in the morning and turned up on her doorstep some evenings in floods of tears. I couldn't have got through it without her.'

'Mum says Uncle Jon is still upset even now.'

I hide my face behind my wine glass. 'Some of the time.'

'It must have been tough. I didn't know too much when it was all happening. I vaguely remember people would go quiet when I came in the room and you were being talked about.'

'You were how old? Ten? I'm not surprised if you don't remember! Your mother was amazing. So supportive. She listened to me for hours, she was always there, gave advice when I asked. She'll help you, too, whenever you need it.'

'I know. Thank you, Auntie Caroline.'

I sit back against Bee's cushions and look at the piano. There are a series of photo frames standing on it displaying family photos from the last twenty years. They include one or two when Andrew and Bee were sent to live in Australia for a year by Andrew's then-employer, when Michael and Melanie were still babes in arms. He always says that year abroad inspired him to start his own company. I missed Bee so much when she was away for those twelve months. I think Jon also missed having Andrew around, but he'd never admit it.

Bee serves dinner and after Melanie leaves, the two of us sit down side by side on her sofa with another glass of wine.

'I can't believe I'm going to be a grandmother soon,' Bee says.

'You'll be just as good as you were a mother, except you'll spoil your grandchildren more.'

'Probably. I just hope Mel isn't too young.'

'You were near enough the same age when you had Michael.'

'I know. I just don't want her to regret it in the years to come.'

'Did you?'

Bee hesitates. 'Of course not.'

'Well, there you are.'

Bee smiles. 'How is your commission going for your jewellery company? Have you started yet?'

'Esposito? I'm just waiting for the contract to be signed.'

'Did you see that they were in the news recently?'

'No. What for?'

'I saw it on Sky. Their headquarters in Rome was invaded by human rights activists claiming their suppliers don't pass ethical checks.'

'I hope that doesn't include me. Priscilla never mentioned anything.'

Bee nudges me. 'What if she finds out about that ex-student of yours that we met at Rosie's gallery the other night?'

'Hmm.'

'Are you sure you never got up to anything with him?'

'No! Absolutely not.'

'I was just asking.'

'I tell you everything, Bee. I've no secrets from you!' (Well, apart from one rather large, temporal one). 'Anyway, you were the one who snogged that boy on holiday before you got married.'

Bee slaps my arm. 'You didn't try to stop me.'

'I wanted you to enjoy yourself!'

We look into each other's eyes and collapse into hysterical giggles, hugging each other.

'Now listen,' Bee says. 'Talking of commissions, I am going to pay you for whatever you paint for our second shop.'

'You are not.'

'You'll have no choice; I'll write you a cheque.'

'I won't cash it.'

We grin at each other. 'Okay,' Bee says. 'Well, first of all, let's agree what your artwork will be.'

'Actually, I've had an idea for that. I'd like to create a mural on one of your walls. Make it a feature of the store.'

'Oh, I love it!'

'I'm not sure if I can finish it in time for your opening,

86

but I thought we could maybe make it into an organic piece of art. I could come into your shop every now and then even after it's open and continue to paint. You could publicise it as a series of events and invite people to come and watch.'

'Would you do that? It's very brave of you to let people observe you while you work.'

'It'll be good publicity for me, too. Win-win!' We clink wine glasses. 'And I'll sketch it out first, make sure I know exactly what I'm doing. Then it should be fine. What do you say?'

'I say yes!'

We clink our glasses again.

Bee says, 'Dani and Glenda have also agreed to come to the opening, so we're going to be snowed under with local celebrities.'

'That's wonderful. But I'm not famous.'

'You will be. Anyway, I think I might have to go on a crash diet before the event if I'm going to be photographed with them.'

I tut. She's far too self-conscious about her body and already has a perfectly slim figure. 'You have no need to lose any weight.'

'Hmm. You do know exactly what to say, Caroline. But I'm still going to pay you for your work.'

'You're my best friend, Bee. Just tell me you'll stay that way forever. That's all I need from you.'

Bee's eyes glisten.

The following day, with Jon still in Manchester, I visit my sister, Veronica. She's two years my elder and, indirectly, she could be seen to be partially responsible for Jon inventing the time machine.

Twenty years ago, aged just twenty-five, Veronica was diagnosed with Huntington's disease. It's a horrible condition that stops parts of the brain working properly over time. It's usually hereditary, so when Veronica was diagnosed we couldn't understand it as neither of our parents had suffered from Huntington's. My mother was sure that none of her family had ever had the disease, but we managed to contact my only uncle on my father's side and he confirmed that his mother in Jamaica had suffered from similar symptoms. Only affected children can pass on the gene to their offspring, so we had to assume our father also carried the gene but was never diagnosed with it.

There's no cure.

The brain cells deteriorate over a long period of time, usually fifteen to twenty years, and during this time, the affected person loses their abilities slowly. Gradually, walking, talking and eating all become harder and then all but impossible. This did mean that for some years after her diagnosis, at least, Veronica managed to live a normal life, relatively speaking. But over time, she began to need a part-time and now a full-time carer. We are fortunate that her carer, Zoe, is a wonderful woman. But she's not cheap. The only reason we can afford her is because when our mother died, we were able to use our inheritance to pay for her services, and when Veronica reached a point where she needed a full-time carer, she sold her swanky London pad and relocated to a small cottage in Suffolk. This meant a cheaper cost of living and had the bonus of being near a part of the coast that she loved. I try to supplement all that with some of my income when I can afford to.

I drive through her small village, past the green (and only) pub and up to her cottage. Zoe opens the door and we exchange a brief hug.

'How is she today?'

'Not too bad. Anxious but her energy levels are better than normal. She's in the back garden.'

Depression and anxiety are classic problems caused by Huntington's. And low energy; so it's good to hear she is more spirited today. We exchange further information about Veronica while Zoe gets ready to go out. It's good for her to get some time off while I'm here.

When Zoe leaves, I enter the front room straight from the street, walk through the kitchen at the rear of the cottage and out to the small but pretty garden; there are roses and delphiniums everywhere. Veronica is sitting on a swing seat under her apple tree. She waves. It's ironic that despite their decline in thinking and reasoning proficiencies, people with Huntington's disease usually remain able to understand and recognise others. I walk over to my sister and hug her tightly.

I sit beside her, hold her hand and laugh as I see what she has placed on a small table in front of her.

'Jon's drinking machine,' I say. 'Do you still use it?'

Veronica nods, laughs.

'I guess it's more useful to you now than it was ten years ago!'

My sister gives me the thumbs up. I tell her about my latest art, including my commission from Esposito, which has now been confirmed. Priscilla was correct; I am blown away by their payment schedule. It will mean I can acquire Veronica more support in the months and hopefully years to come. And if Rosie is right about Priscilla's influence in the industry, there is every chance that other contracts could follow; this could kick-start a new stage in my career.

My sister squeezes my hand and places her head on my shoulder. Tears well up in my eyes. How many more times like this will we have?

I smile again at Jon's invention.

. . .

It was just after our wedding when we heard that my sister had been diagnosed with Huntington's. Jon was almost as devastated as me and he swore he would help in any way he could. We were living in a tiny flat in Islington at the time and for weeks, the kitchen table became his work-bench as he worked on something he was sure would help her.

'What's he actually doing?' Veronica asked when she came to see us soon after her diagnosis.

'Inventing,' I replied.

'Inventing what?'

'I don't know. He won't tell me. He's very secretive about his inventions.'

'This isn't his first?'

'Oh no. Look around. See all these things hanging off our ceiling? They're either prototypes or occasionally successful gadgets he's created in the past. But he hasn't designed anything for over a year now, so I'm very happy he's started again.'

'My God, what's that?' Veronica asked, pointing to something that looked like a medieval thumbscrew.

'Automatic bottle opener.'

'Doesn't he know they already exist?' She laughed, her bangles jangling as she lowered her arm.

'That's not the point, apparently.'

'And that?'

'Musical egg timer.'

'Oh, I like the idea of that!'

'His greatest inventions are music-related. That's what he knows best, that's how it all started.' We sat down for a cup of tea. 'The first thing he ever built was a guitar, back in college. When he was in his first band.'

Veronica slipped off her sandals and stretched out her legs. 'I never knew that.'

'"Well, if Brian May can do it, why can't I?" That's what he said. So that's what he did. He still has it somewhere, still plays it. After that, he created a drum machine.'

'What for? I assume there were plenty on the market when he did that.'

'Of course. But like I said, apparently that isn't the point.'

'But why invent one if he was in a band?'

'Hmm. That's Jon for you. Music lover, short fuse. He fell out badly with the other guys in the group, or rather, they kicked him out over some stupid squabble. But instead of joining another band, he told me he was going to "get even with those bastards and show them they need me more than I need them".'

Veronica tried not to laugh, failed, spat her tea out. 'He built a drum machine just to... get even?'

'My new husband.' We clinked mugs.

My sister looked up again at the contraptions hanging from our ceiling. 'I remember you told me you met him at a gig. But I didn't know he was in the band.'

'I must have said that. No? Are you sure I haven't told you?'

'Maybe…'

'Anyway, it didn't last. The band phase, I mean. When he finished his masters in mathematics, he carried on with his academic career, became a lecturer, of course. Stopped playing on stage. But I think he missed his creative side. He still played guitar occasionally, but by combining his maths knowledge with his mech eng degree, he found that inventing things spurred him on.' I looked around the kitchen at the mess of bottles, loose springs, pieces of wood and broken plastic. 'Not that it helps me.'

We started to laugh all over again. It wasn't long before we found out what Jon had invented for his sister-in-law: a device for holding multiple drink containers, sucked through a built-in straw, each of which played a random set of musical notes when it was empty – and which the owner could operate without needing to use her hands. It was completely unnecessary for Veronica at the time, but she was overcome by the thoughtful gesture. In recent years, when her involuntary movements meant that holding a glass could result in it being sent spiralling across the room moments later, Jon's invention came into its own.

As I sit now in Veronica's garden, I wonder whether I can share news of my husband's latest invention with my sister. We used to tell each other everything about our lives; now it's just me who can provide updates. Surely telling her wouldn't be dangerous? Even if she fully understood what I was saying, who would she tell? Yes, she might open up to Zoe with her limited communications, but her carer would simply think she had misunderstood something I had been saying. I assume.

So I do.

I tell my sister all about what Jon has done: the time machine, how it works, the gigs we have seen, the change on the sleeve credits on the *Magical Mystery Tour* album, our plans for further concerts. And my sister listens, waves her arms, cheers, sips from my husband's drinking machine, and we laugh as the music plays. I hope she remembers what I'm telling her. She probably doesn't believe me – why would she? It's such a tall story, why would anyone trust my account? But I hope it makes her happy for a while.

Sadly, Jon's greatest invention cannot provide a counter-measure for Veronica's condition. Her die was cast the second she left her mother's womb. Nothing a time machine can do to change that.

Once her diagnosis was confirmed, and we all began researching and learning more about it, we discovered that I, too, had a fifty per cent chance of being affected sometime in the future. I also found out that I could have a 'predictive test', which would tell me whether or not I would develop the condition. That caused some soul searching for me. Was it something I wanted to know? We also read that a parent with the Huntington's gene has a fifty per cent chance of passing it on to their children, and even though this was several years before Jon and I were considering a child of our own, I realised I had to know. I had the test, held my breath and when the results came back to confirm I wouldn't develop Huntington's, I felt a dreadful combination of relief and happiness, yet terrible guilt that I was lucky and my sister hadn't been. Veronica, of course, was delighted when I told her I was clear, told me to 'stop feeling so fucking remorseful' and 'get on with your life'.

A kitten suddenly bursts out of the flower bed and we both coo over it. Veronica's next-door neighbour's cat has recently had a litter and they are apparently forever finding a hole in their fence and scooting through to my sister's garden. The neighbour has said he'll fix the gap but he hasn't.

As much as I enjoy watching the kitten wave its paws at a passing butterfly, observing it here with my sister makes me reflect, not for the first time, how sad it is that our family's lineage will die out after Veronica and me. Veronica hasn't had a boyfriend for the last five years. She was always perfectly happy flitting between relationships in her early twenties. Since her diagnosis, she only met one man who she felt comfortable with and who accepted her and her Huntington's. Sadly, as the disease progressed into the later

93

stages, he couldn't cope and they broke up. At that point, she wasn't in a position to consider babies.

I remember a conversation we had in my back garden a few years after my miscarriage when she was still about able to converse. Veronica had been in a reflective mood.

'You've stopped talking about having children,' she said.

'I hadn't realised.'

She pouted. 'I can't believe that.'

'I don't know if I want to discuss children anymore.'

My sister squeezed my hand. 'But you were so keen. So was Jon.'

I swung my ankle against the leaves of a pink cordyline growing in our flower bed. 'I know. But we've gone over this, Vron. There's no point in wondering what if.'

'Doesn't it scare you?'

'Not having children? Why would that scare me? I'm far more worried about whether anyone will buy my artwork.'

Veronica slapped my forearm. 'You know what I mean, sis.'

'I'll be fine. I'll still have Jon.'

I took a step back towards the French doors of our house, but Veronica grabbed my elbow. 'I thought you were going to consider adoption.'

'Yes. I was,' I said heavily.

The problem was Jon wouldn't countenance it. Once I had understood and finally accepted that I would never bear a child, my mind turned to the possibility of adoption. I tested the waters with Jon, mentioning over dinner that an artist friend of mine had recently adopted and seemed so happy, but Jon didn't bite. I left it for a few weeks and tried a more direct route.

'Remember I told you about Rowena, how she had adopted a baby recently?'

'Mmm.'

94

'I was talking with her again yesterday and she reminded me that we could still adopt, we're a perfect age, she said.'

'So?'

'So… I wanted to do some research on that. Understand how we could maybe progress that. What do you think?'

Jon grimaced. 'I have no desire to adopt whatsoever. I don't want someone else's offspring, I want my own child. Unfortunately, I can't because of your body.'

I bit my tongue. 'Why won't you even consider it? The baby would still be ours. We'd be doing a wonderful thing, and I—'

'No!' Jon shouted. 'I don't want to. I'm not going to. I never want to talk about this again. Understand?'

My hackles rose and I yelled back how selfish he was. He returned with more admonishments about my inability to have a baby, I told him he was a terrible, callous man for saying such things and we carried on shouting and arguing for ten minutes until we ran out of words. An hour later, Jon was apologising, saying he hadn't meant what he had said about me, but he was still adamant that he didn't want to adopt – sorry.

The only thing that comforted me was that even if Jon had said yes and we had started the process of trying to adopt, I was very aware that our friends would be asked, in effect, to provide a character reference for us. When Teri and Zaina had adopted, Jon and I had been one of their references and I was surprised at how blunt some of the questions had been, including our view on their fortitude and any past examples of where we had witnessed any insta-bility. Of course, we were able to give our friends a glowing reference, but it had been worrying me what they would, in turn, say about Jon if they were asked the same question. Would any of them mention his mood swings, how he took a knife to my paintings, how he would react towards fellow students who he deemed to be looking at me inappropriately when we were at uni? It was all a long time ago but even so.

I never raised the subject again.

I leave when Zoe returns. Cry half the way home. Partly because of my memories of Jon's refusal to consider adoption but mostly because every time I leave Veronica's house, it breaks my heart not knowing if I'll ever see my sister again. And when that fatal day does arrive, and it will do soon enough, not only will I be devastated at losing my only sibling, but then I will have to face the fear that I denied having. Because then it will just be Jon and me.

That brings me back to my concern about Jon and his time machine: how one day he is surely going to confront me with our life-changing moment from our past. And when he does, despite my apprehension, I will have to be strong enough to stand up for what I know is the right thing to do. Not the expected thing.

I clench the steering wheel. I am ready.

8

Bee has never understood the attraction of music festivals. 'Why would you want to stand in a field in the pouring rain?' she'd ask, 'drinking warm wine out of plastic glasses, surrounded by thousands of sweaty bodies?'

Jon and I, however, love these outdoor events – although I have to admit, they are better when it is sunny. Which is why, when speculating about which historic concerts to go to, we often consider great festivals. And as the Knebworth Festivals of the seventies staged some of the most iconic music acts of that era, that is what we've got planned for today.

We've decided to attend the inaugural event in 1974, aka 'the Bucolic Frolic'. It featured The Allman Brothers, The Sensational Alex Harvey Band, The Doobie Brothers and one of my all-time favourites, Van Morrison. I can't wait to see him live, and in the year he releases *Veedon Fleece*. Beautiful.

And it didn't rain.

Jon works out that we can land inside the festival perimeter, on the edge of the grounds behind one of the toilet blocks where it's least likely we'll be spotted. It'll be daylight, but it's a low risk.

'Anyway, most of the people there will be stoned or pissed, so if anyone does see us materialise, they'll just put it down to a hallucination,' Jon points out with a sly grin.

It also means we won't need any money; we can take our own alcohol and gorge ourselves on a meal when we get home.

We have enormous fun selecting our clothes; I sometimes think this is one of my favourite aspects of our trips. I know we could wear them at a retro party in 2021, but it's not the same as donning outfits that everyone else is wearing and where no one is being ironic. I select a white cheesecloth top, red and white gipsy skirt and adorn myself in more bangles and necklaces than a Maori tribeswoman. They complement my earrings perfectly. My long hair is already ideal for the era. Jon wears a shirt, waistcoat and faded bell-bottom jeans he's picked up on eBay. I try to persuade him to grow a moustache the week before we go but he refuses; says he has no desire to look like Tom Selleck, even for a day.

We're laughing as we descend to the basement. I practice some hippy twirls, dancing on the spot while Jon is programming the computer. Jon initiates the launch and we stand hand in hand in the centre of the room – fifteen seconds to go. As I watch the countdown on the computer screen, I spot Bolan slinking out from behind the server stack. He stretches and yawns. Ten seconds. He scrutinises us and starts padding in our direction.

'Bolan, where are you going?' Jon says.

The cat pauses. Five seconds.

Then he leaps. Up. Straight at my chest. And I have no choice. Instinctively, I let go of Jon, open my arms and catch our cat.

'No!' Jon cries and grabs my elbow a split second before the expected flash and moment of instability.

As my pupils adjust, I see I am standing at the edge of an enormous tree-lined field. A nauseating smell confirms we are almost certainly behind the loos. Loud music is pounding in my ears. The guitar has a wah-wah vibration and I guess The Sensational Alex Harvey Band are performing. I crane my head and see thousands, tens of thousands of people sitting on the grass enjoying the warmth of the afternoon, looking towards a canopied stage large enough to park a bus on.

Bolan wriggles in my arms.

'Bolan!' Jon calls out.

Our cat squirms again, yowls and swipes at my fingers with his claws. I yelp and snatch my hand to my mouth. As I do, Bolan writhes one more time, loosens himself from my clasp and jumps. Onto the ground.

And he's off. Running, tearing away through bemused concert-goers.

Jon flies after him, screaming our cat's name, dodging one couple but slamming his shoulder into another man in his urgency. The other man whirls around angrily, his long hair flying across his face, but my husband is already sprinting away. I jog forward a few paces, but I lose sight of him within seconds. I stop, sink to the ground and hold my head in my hands.

Alex Harvey continues to sing.

Twenty minutes later, as the band leave the stage, I am still sitting here, with no sign of my husband. Or our cat. I stand up and peer over people's heads, looking for either of them. Everywhere I look I can see long hair, beards, happy faces, waistcoats, denim jackets, flares, bare skin and sunglasses in abundance. But no immigrants from 2021. My problem is that I can't leave this spot, can't go chasing around trying to find Jon because I may never do so. Or not for hours, anyway, maybe not until the concert finishes, when it will be after midnight and dark and what are the chances of us finding each other then? I'd have to wait until dawn.

So I wait. Biting my nails. One or two women ask me if I'm okay and I nod glumly. They don't persist. I wrap my arms around my body. He is coming back, I tell myself. Isn't he?

It's an hour since our arrival when I see Jon slowly trudging towards me. He is sweating, breathing heavily, and as he gets nearer, I see his cheeks are tear-stained. He isn't carrying a cat. He reaches me, head down, and I throw my arms around his neck and pull him into me. He doesn't react, just stands still with his arms hanging limply by his sides. Then he slides his hands up between our bodies and with a loud sob, he shoves me away. I stumble backwards, almost fall. I gawk at him in shock. He glares back, raises an arm and points a finger at me as if he is condemning a witch.

'This is your fault,' he hisses.

'What?'

He clenches a fist. 'Your fault. You brought him with us.'

'Wait, I—'

'You could have dropped him when he jumped into your arms.'

'I couldn't! I didn't have time!'

'You could have held onto him when you got here.' Spittle flies out of his mouth with his vitriol.

I open my palms. 'I tried! But he scratched me.'

'So?'

'So I had to let go.'

'Because a cat gave you a tiny scratch? Are you that pathetic?'

I stand with my mouth open. I've not heard my husband speak to me like this since... since we lost the baby. It's terrifying. All sorts of frightful thoughts fly through my mind. A few people are watching us but no one is intervening. I take a small step towards him.

'Did you find him?'

Jon flings his arms out wide. 'What the fuck does it look like? You think I've got him hidden in my pocket? With this?'

He yanks out the time-pen and waves it. My eyes widen and I take another step forwards.

'Jon. Be careful.'

My husband swishes his arm around as if he's holding a lightsabre. More people are staring at us, but still no one does anything. This is 1974, when men could speak to their wives like this without expecting anyone else to get involved. But I am seriously worried. What if he accidentally presses the button, disappears, goes back to 2021. Without me. I swallow, then remind myself that he can't do that accidentally, he has to swivel the top first. I take a deep breath.

'Jon, let's sit down for a minute. Come here, please.'

He gives me a venomous look but at least he brings his hand back to his side and shoves the time-pen back in his pocket. I take another breath and hold out my arms. After a moment, Jon slowly trudges towards me and lets me wrap myself around his body. I walk him to a boundary fence and we slide our backs down it until we are collapsed on the grass, me clasping Jon's head against my breast, caressing his hair. We sit like this for another half an hour, all through another band, which I think is the Mahavishnu Orchestra. Van Morrison is on next.

'Jon,' I whisper. 'Do you want to go and see Van Morrison?'

Jon raises his head. 'Do I what?'

'Want to… see the next act?'

Jon rolls his shoulders, pushes himself away from me. 'No.'

'Oh.'

'No, I fucking don't. I don't want to see some crap Irish singer, I don't want to see any more bands, and I don't want to be here. I want to go home. Now.'

'But… are you sure?'

Jon snarls. 'Yes, I'm sure, Caz. Now come on.'

He stands up, marches back towards the toilet block where we arrived less than two hours ago. I don't have a choice. I have to almost jog to keep up. He pauses, looks around and heads for a large oak tree a little further away. Now I do run to catch up with him and as we move around to the hidden side of the tree, Jon thrusts his hand into his pocket, pulls out the time-pen and spins the top of it. I only have seconds to reach his side and seize his other elbow before he jabs his thumb down on the button.

We're back in our basement. Before I can say anything, Jon springs away from me, stalks up the stairs and slams the door at the top. I clasp my face in my hands and stand where I am for I don't know how long.

The time machine has caused its first tragic butterfly effect.

Jon doesn't speak to me for two days. He goes to work, comes home, doesn't eat and either disappears down to the basement or goes to bed. I resign myself to spending solitary hours in my studio, working on Priscilla's commission.

On the evening of the third day, I finish painting, shower, change and make myself a cup of tea. Bolan's food bowl is on the floor of the kitchen and I cry a few tears. I can't remove it yet. I sniff, wipe the back of my hand across my eyes and walk into our lounge.

Jon is sitting there, a near-empty bottle of whisky on the coffee table, a large glass of Scotch clasped between both hands. He hasn't even put on any music. He looks up as I come in, blinks several times, his eyes puffy. I half smile, nervously. He shifts very slightly on the sofa, indicating I should sit down beside him. At least that's a start. He hasn't wanted to come near me since we got back from Knebworth.

Still cautious, I sit on the end of the sofa, not so close to him. He puts his glass down and lifts an arm sideways. I hesitate but slide across, rest my head on his shoulder and accept his embrace. We sit silently for ages. My tea goes cold.

'He was such a wonderful cat,' Jon suddenly says, his voice breaking.

'He was.'

'The house feels so empty without him.'

'I know.'

Jon kisses my hair. 'I'm so sorry I yelled at you.'

'That's… okay.'

'I know it wasn't your fault. I was just so… startled. Shocked. Sad.'

I sit upright. 'I know. I was, too. And you're right, I should have tried to cling onto him.'

'How could you? His claws are so sharp. I know, he's scratched me before.' He half laughs. 'It's my fault. As soon as we landed, I should have immediately used the time-pen. I could have guessed what was going to happen. If I'd only done that directly…'

I stroke his cheek. He doesn't flinch away. 'I don't know if you could have done that quickly enough, darling. And reached out to both of us.' Jon nods and squeezes his eyes shut. I touch his forearm. 'What happened when you ran after Bolan? Did you see him at all?'

'Only for the first few yards. I saw him dart between someone's legs and then I heard someone else call out "cat" and I ran towards their voice. Three or four people were laughing and trying to peer over the wooden perimeter fence. I snapped at them, asking whether they had seen a cat run past and they carried on laughing and pointed at the fence. That's when I realised Bolan had jumped over it or sneaked through it, it was full of holes, after all. I knew there was no way I could scramble over, so I tore along the boundary until I found an exit gate, ran out and retraced my steps back to where I thought he had escaped. I don't know how long I spent searching.' He sighs. 'Once I realised he had gone and I wasn't going to track him down, I came back to find you. Although I almost didn't get back in again.'

'Why?'

'Well, I didn't have a ticket, of course, so I tried to talk my way back in with the bouncers or whatever they were at the entrance, but they weren't having any of it.'

'Shit! What did you do?'

'I waited. Fortunately, a scuffle started – a man accused someone else of stealing their ticket and the staff had to go off and sort it out. And I snuck in. I just hoped that you had stayed where you were, otherwise I didn't know how I would find you.'

'Yeah, I thought that, too.' I hesitate. 'I did wonder for a bit whether you would definitely come back for me.'

'Caz.' Jon sounds aghast. 'I was angry with you, furious, I wanted to yell my head off at you. But I would never leave you.'

'I know, I'm sorry.'

Jon grunts.

'Can we not go back and look for him?'

He shakes his head. 'Like I told you after the first Beatles trip. I can't risk placing two wormholes so close to each other. Even to find Bolan.' He pauses. 'He's gone, Caz. Bolan's gone. I have to accept that.'

I nod, sadly.

'Don't worry,' Jon says, 'I'm sure that one day you'll be able to forgive yourself.'

He squeezes my shoulder. Tightly.

9

One of the incredible things about the time machine is, of course, that we can go somewhere at, say, four o'clock on a Saturday afternoon, spend hours or even days in the past, and be back at one minute past four, still with three hours to prepare for a dinner party that same evening. It's kind of freaky. This afternoon we are taking a trip to see David Bowie. And not just any Bowie concert; we're going to his infamous 1973 gig at the Hammersmith Odeon when he killed off Ziggy Stardust.

I've suggested David Bowie as I hope it might spark Jon out of his depression over Bolan, but although he's agreed to go, he's barely acknowledged the fact that we're going to see one of Britain's greatest ever pop stars.

We buy tickets from a tout at what would be a crazy cost if we were truly paying seventies' prices and mingle with the audience before the show. I watch the excited fans stream in, some dressed up with Aladdin Sane streaks painted on their faces or wearing Ziggy Stardust-inspired outfits. Many of them are discussing the hundreds of shows that Bowie has played on this tour, the songs he might sing, what he and his guitarist, Mick Ronson, will be wearing. Someone beside me lights up a spliff and I inhale the sweet aroma.

We walk upstairs to our seats in the circle, although no one sits down. I spin slowly around on the spot, admiring the arena. I'm a big fan of the 'Hammy Odeon', as many music lovers referred to it back in the seventies; it's such an iconic venue, with three and a half thousand fans all focused on that famous stage. I've seen numerous other concerts here, on our historic trips and in our real-time.

Bowie comes on stage to the backing track of Beethoven's Ninth Symphony, dressed in his outrageous costume and accompanied by his band, The Spiders from Mars. He kicks off with 'Hang On to Yourself' and works his way through an eighteen-song set, with most of the tunes, much to my delight, coming from his more recent *Hunky Dory*, *Aladdin Sane* and *Ziggy Stardust* albums rather than his late sixties work. Even though we're in the upstairs seats, it's still an incredible experience. Jon nods his head to the songs and applauds with everyone else, but I can tell his heart isn't in it. He loves it when other musicians do unexpected guest appearances at a gig, but he barely shows any emotion when Jeff Beck comes on stage to join the band for a medley of 'The Jean Genie' and a cover of The Beatles' 'Love Me Do'.

As for myself, I become quite emotional, even though I know what is going to happen at the end of the concert. The closer we get to that moment, the more on edge I become. When Bowie finally speaks those famous words, telling the astonished and subsequently heartbroken audience that this is the last show that he will ever do with the Spiders, I scream as much as everyone else. People, men and women, are crying as we leave the arena.

It takes me a good couple of hours to come down from the show when we get home, so I have less time than normal to get ready for our evening soiree. I leave Jon to himself while I dash around and make sure the dining room is prepared.

It's not just my husband's mood I'm concerned about; the other awkward issue we have to overcome this evening is the fact it was Andrew's birthday earlier this week and because of Jon's funk, it wasn't until yesterday that we remembered. I made Jon jump on Amazon and order a book as a present, which, thankfully, arrived this morning. We'll have to eat humble pie over forgetting to send a card.

The first thing we do when our friends arrive (after offering belated birthday wishes to Andrew) is to tell them sorrowfully that Bolan has run away. They're horrified. Bee hugs Jon as she sees he is, quite genuinely, moved to tears. I know he still misses his cat. And I think he still blames me for my part in it.

'He might come back,' Zaina says. 'I've heard that cats can go away for days before returning, even weeks.'

'He's never done so before,' I answer.

'You shouldn't give up hope. It might just be a matter of time.'

Well, she's right there.

Jon shakes himself down and puts on a Supertramp album, followed by Led Zeppelin's *Houses of the Holy*. He starts to talk to Andrew and Bee quite happily. I'm delighted he's picked himself up, but it concerns me how his mood swings are becoming increasingly more extreme. After eating, we move to the lounge and Jon asks Andrew if he will select the next record. Andrew sighs theatrically but gets down on his hands and knees and flicks through the albums.

'Have a look towards the right of them,' Jon says, 'you might find something new.'

Andrew shifts his stance and starts from the Z-end of the records. He's clearly not keen on taking orders from Jon but he complies. Then his face changes. He stops searching through the vinyl and slides out what he's found: a square, record-sized box wrapped in birthday paper.

Jon grins. 'Happy birthday, mate. You didn't think we'd forgotten, did you?'

Andrew smiles wryly and returns to his armchair. He unwraps the present and holds up what is inside. He turns it around in his hands. 'Oh, that's cool.'

We all crane to see what he's holding. Even I don't know, because Jon didn't bother telling me what he'd bought.

'Show us what it is,' Teri says.

Andrew holds up his present. It's a coffee-table book, a large, glossy hardback with a black-and-white photo of Pete Townshend of The Who on the front, looking very young. The title of the book is inscribed in white Times Roman font: *Before They Were Famous*.

Bee claps her hands. 'Oh, that looks perfect.'

Andrew grins. 'It is. Thank you.'

'What is it?' Zaina asks.

Andrew slides his hand across the cover. 'A book of photographs of famous guitarists, but all the photos were taken before they had their big breaks. Before they were famous.' He opens the inside cover. 'And it's only just been published. Fantastic.'

I squeeze my husband's thigh. It is perfect; what a great gift.

Everyone starts talking again. Andrew turns over the glossy pages. I can hear him and Jon cooing over a series of names: Pete Townshend, Eric Clapton, Johnny Marr. I chat happily to Bee. I'm just wondering if I should make the coffee when Andrew's tone changes.

'What the fuck is this?' The room goes silent. Andrew

stabs his finger at a page in the book. 'Is this some kind of joke?'

Jon frowns. 'What do you mean?'

'Are you taking the piss or something?'

'What are you talking about?'

Andrew opens the book violently and holds it up so we can see the photographs on a particular page.

'You know what I mean, Jon. This photo, here. Taken at a Hendrix gig in the sixties.'

Jon peers forward. 'That was taken when he was still calling himself Jimmy James and the Blue Flames. What about it?'

I catch my breath. That name. I remember it.

Andrew bangs the inside of the book aggressively. 'Are you winding me up? You've got one of your fake photos published in a book and not told me you were doing this again.'

'What are you on about?' Jon says. 'Of course I haven't.'

'No? Then how do you explain this?'

Andrew thrusts the book at my husband and Jon takes it gently and places it on his lap. Sitting beside him, I look down at the photo Andrew was pointing to and my heart almost stops. I remember there was a photographer at our Hendrix gig in New York, taking photos of the audience. At the time I didn't think anything of it, but now... Holy shit, this could be seriously bad news for us.

The photo Jon is pointing at is black and white, taken from a wide angle and pretty grainy, thank God, because when I look closely, I can see towards the left of the photo, at the back of the club, two people who I instantly recognise. I should do – it's us.

Jon, however, remains composed. I don't know how. 'It's a great photo,' he says. 'Bit blurry, but cool to see. I should show one of my students, Elise, she loves old black and white photos.'

'You don't see anything strange about it?' Andrew spits.

'No...'

'Take a closer look.'

Jon and I peer down at it. My heart rate must have hit a hundred and twenty but I manage to remain as composed as I can.

'Look at that couple on the left-hand side of the photo,' Andrew continues. 'The one where that man has his arm around his date. Don't they look familiar? Don't they look just like you two?'

'Really?' I say with mock surprise. 'Let me see.'

Jon shrugs and passes the book to me. I pretend to examine the photograph more closely. There's little doubt. It does look like us. Obviously.

I scratch my cheek. 'Hmm, I guess they could look, well, I suppose they look about the same age as we are now. But I can't see any other similarity. I wonder what they were doing there? Everyone else in the photo is much younger.'

'You don't say,' Andrew retorts.

Jon takes the book from me again, frowns and shakes his head. 'I don't know what you're talking about, Andrew. What are you saying? That a middle-aged couple looks like Caz and me? I can't see it myself, but I guess if you want to believe it.'

'I do,' Andrew says. 'And there's only one answer. You've started mocking up fake photos again and you've sold one to the publishers of this book, and now you're rubbing it in my face by giving it to me as a present.'

'I wouldn't do that. Why would I do that?'

'Oh, I don't know. To make some money on the side without having to share it with me. To have some fun at my expense. You tell me.'

'Let me see,' Teri calls from across the room. Jon hands her the coffee book. She skims her fingers over the page and hoots. 'Oh, they do look quite like you two. How funny. Do you know if you have any relatives who lived in New York in the sixties?'

'No, of course we didn't,' Jon says more sharply.

'And anyway,' Andrew cuts in, 'how could they be relatives of both of them, looking so similar?'

Teri passes the book to her wife, who cocks her head. 'I can't see it myself. I mean, she has your nose, Caroline, I'll give you that.'

'Thanks,' I say indignantly and everyone laughs.

Jon sits forward. 'Andrew, I promise that I didn't make that photo. I said I would never do that again and I haven't. You have to believe me.'

'You swear it?'

'On Bolan's life,' Jon says.

Andrew purses his lips. He knows how much Jon doted on his cat.

Jon stands up. 'Why don't Caz and I make the coffee? Feel free to select some music, Andrew. Really, please do.'

Andrew nods sullenly.

Jon and I beat a hasty retreat to the kitchen. Once there, Jon puts his fingers to his lips, checks that no one has followed us down the hallway and gently closes the kitchen door. I run my hand across my forehead but Jon just grins and says quietly, 'Nice one, Caz, you did really well there. I don't know how you kept so calm.'

'Me? I was freaking out. Here, feel my pulse. I thought you were the calm one.'

Jon bounces his palms up and down to show I should speak more quietly. He holds his finger up and we wait in silence until the first notes of a Van Morrison record emanate from the lounge. I feel sad as I think again of Bolan. Jon doesn't notice or chooses to ignore my reaction.

He leans back against the kitchen countertop. 'I can't believe that.'

'Me neither.'

'I mean, it's so cool.'

'Cool? What are you talking about?'

He waggles his fingers in front of his face. 'Tiny butterfly wings again, Caz. It shows that although time changes imperceptibly, what we're doing is safe as long as we're sensible. It opens up so many possibilities.'

'We've just seen a photo taken of us three years ago when we were visiting 1966 appear in a book published in 2021.' I rub my forehead. 'It's so confusing.'

Jon giggles. 'It's quite funny.'

'Funny? Are you kidding?'

'It is, Caz, come on.'

He reaches towards me, but I yank my hand away. 'It's not remotely funny,' I say. 'Our friend thinks that you've been fixing photos again and he's really angry.'

'It could have been worse. He could have accused us of actually being there in New York. How would we have explained that?'

'It doesn't matter. You shouldn't have given the book to him as a present.'

'I'd no idea that photo would be in there,' Jon hisses. 'Do you think I would have given it to him if I had known?'

'Well...'

We stop talking, listen to the sound of Van Morrison drifting down the hallway.

'He seems very convinced that photo is of us,' I mutter.

'Which is fair enough, I guess.' Jon laughs.

'I can't believe you're finding this so amusing.'

'Why not? He can't prove anything. Don't worry, he'll

have forgotten all about this by next month.' I bite my nails; that's not the Andrew I know. Jon places his hands on my shoulders. 'Seriously, you need to calm down. As long as we continue to act exactly as we did just now, there's nothing to worry about. Let me finish up here and make the coffee. You get back to the party.'

I nod, take a deep breath, slide my hands down my dress and open the kitchen door. Back in the lounge the women are all perched on the sofa and chairs, chatting, while Andrew is sitting on the floor looking through our albums.

'It is a great collection you have,' he says, 'regardless of the media. There are some real classics here.'

'Thanks. We like them.'

He stands up. 'Look, I'm sorry about my outburst just now. I love the book, honestly. Thank you.'

'Don't worry about it. Jon isn't doing anything untoward, I promise. I'd kill him if he was, you know that.'

Andrew gives me a crooked smile. 'Let me see if I can give your man a hand with the coffee.'

He leaves the lounge and I sink into a chair beside Bee. The three women stop talking and Bee turns around to face me.

'I'm sorry about Andrew's tantrum.' She places her fingertips on my forearm.

'You have nothing to apologise for, Bee. Don't be silly.'

'They're so competitive still, aren't they? It's ridiculous.'

'I guess they've always been this way,' Teri adds. She raps her fingernails angrily against her wine glass.

'That's true,' Bee says. 'Do you know, I remember after we left uni, Andrew used to come home in a sulk even if Jon beat him at squash.'

I cross my legs. 'Yeah, Jon wasn't much better when he lost.'

'At least your husband was the cool kid in the band. I think Andrew still wishes he could have been more like him.'

'But Jon used to say how impressed he was that Andrew had started his own tech company. He even thought about asking him for a job a few years ago.'

We shake our heads in exasperation.

Jon and Andrew don't appear with the coffee for half an hour and I wonder if Andrew is still giving my husband the third degree. When they do arrive with hot drinks, the women chide them that they must need their help even to make coffee.

An hour later, the party starts to break up. Teri and Zaina are the first to leave. Bee says she wants to use the bathroom before going. Jon takes the empty glasses and mugs back to the kitchen. Which leaves Andrew and me alone in the lounge.

'You know, Caroline, you really have the most extraordinary husband.'

'Ah, thank you?'

'I mean, I've known him as long as you, although in a different way, of course.' He laughs suggestively and I curl up my lip. 'I remember when he built his own guitar, but I never dreamed he would turn into, well, a mad inventor.'

'What do you mean mad? He's just created a few gadgets for us and Veronica.'

'Yes, I know about them. But tonight, when I went to help him with the coffee, he showed me his latest invention.'

'He did? Which one?'

'The one in the basement, of course. You mean there's more?'

My knees almost buckle beneath me. What on earth was Jon thinking? Has he decided to go back on his demands, on our agreement? What has he done?

'I, um…'

'It looks amazing, doesn't it. He even turned it on to show me it working.'

'No!'

'Yes.'

'I… can't believe he did that.'

'Well, he did.' Andrew guffaws. 'Of course, it didn't work. I mean, it's pretty unbelievable for someone like him to do, right?'

'Er, yes…'

'Really. Trying to create a Faraday cage in his cellar. I mean, why bother anyway? Doesn't he know it's already been done many times before?'

A Faraday cage? He expected Andrew to believe that? I glance around for a glass of water, wine, anything for my suddenly dry mouth. But all the glasses are empty; I lick my lips.

'I… don't think that matters to Jon,' I say. 'Look at when he invented a drum machine back in Bristol. Just because he could.'

'Ah, that's true! Still, good for him for trying. Keeps him busy, eh? He seems to genuinely believe he can do it.'

Andrew continues to chuckle to himself. Bee and Jon return and we all kiss each other goodnight. I shut the front door behind them and turn on my husband.

'What the fuck, Jon?'

Jon looks shocked. 'What? Did I do something wrong?'

'You know what you did,' I say, poking him in the chest. Jon takes a step back. 'You showed him the fucking time machine. What the hell do you think you're playing at? We agreed we'd never do that.'

'Oh, yes, that.' Jon runs his hands through his hair. 'God, that was awkward. I didn't want to, I promise. Why would I?'

I cross my arms. 'I don't know. Tell me.'

'It was so difficult. We were walking back to the lounge. I was carrying the coffee, Andrew was beside me, talking about Janis Joplin or something, and of course, we passed the door leading to the basement. Oh, Andrew says, it's years since I've been down there. Can I have a butcher's? At which point I just ignored him and carried on walking, but when I realised he wasn't beside me anymore, I turned around and I saw he'd opened the door and he was on his way down the stairs.'

'Shit!'

'Precisely.'

I tap my chin. 'I thought we kept that door locked.'

'I do. When we're not here.'

'Wouldn't it make sense to also lock it when other people are in the house? That's so irresponsible of you.'

'Christ, Caz, it never occurred to me that one of our friends would wander down there uninvited.'

Jon throws out an arm towards the basement door. I sway backwards, involuntarily. Pause for a moment.

'Hmm. Of course Andrew would,' I say. 'Especially if it seems you don't want to show him something.'

'Yeah, you're right.'

'What did you do?'

He glances down the hallway. I follow his gaze. 'I put the tray of coffee mugs down immediately on the floor where I stood and raced after him. By the time I caught up, he had turned the light on and was halfway down the stairs. You should have seen his face when he saw the time machine. It was as if he'd walked into the laboratory of some evil genius.'

'Crap.'

Jon snorts. 'You'd have been proud of me, though. I remembered how you reacted when you first saw it, and I was sure he couldn't guess what it was. But I knew I couldn't pretend it was some small gadget I was inventing, so I told him what he obviously wanted to hear.'

'That you were trying to invent a Faraday cage.' I stand with my mouth open while Jon nods eagerly and holds his arms out in a ta-dah gesture. I blow out my cheeks. 'Jeez, you're a quick thinker, I'll give you that. I would never have thought of saying that.'

'Hey, I've done enough research that I can bamboozle most people by talking about electromagnetic radiation.'

A thought occurs to me. 'Wait a minute. What about the Hendrix poster that you nicked from the gig in New York? Did he see that?'

'I hope not. No, I don't think so, he would have said something. He was too busy studying my invention.'

'What if he had seen it? After all the shenanigans from earlier.'

Jon shrugs. 'I'd have told him it was real and I'd bought it on eBay. Something like that.'

'I don't know if he would have believed you.'

'So what? Who cares?'

I'm shocked by my husband's defiance. 'All the same, it shows we have to be careful. Maybe you should take it down.'

'Don't worry, he didn't see it.'

'Well, do you want me to check the lock on the basement door in future?'

Jon's face darkens. 'You don't trust me, Caz?'

'What? No, of course I do. What do you mean?'

'Well, it sounds as if you think I'm not concerned about keeping the time machine secret.'

'No, I know you are.'

'Or maybe you're blaming me for leaving the door open so Bolan could find his way down there. And it's my fault I'll never see him again. Is that it?'

'No, Jon, no. That's not true.'

He shakes his head. 'I don't want to talk to you anymore about this.' He turns his back on me and storms off down the hallway.

I watch him walk away and wonder how my evening has changed from being at a nice dinner party to having an argument with my husband.

10

Jon's been suffering from a bout of man-flu in recent weeks, so we've not been on any trips. During this time, I moot again my desire to visit Edward Hopper in Manhattan in the thirties or forties, but as before, Jon refuses, cutting me off mid-sentence, saying he needs to plan carefully for such a trip. I even suggest I could go on my own if he doesn't want to come or he's too ill, but he won't even contemplate that. I retire to my studio, disappointed, and try to think of ways to persuade him to change his mind.

Now he's recovered, we've reconvened at our kitchen table – he's sipping tea, I'm preparing dinner - discussing which band we want to see next, and reminiscing about some of the concerts we've been to in the last twelve months.

Our gigs in the last year have been a who's who of classic rock, plus our incredible trip to see Edith Piaf in Paris, 1935. But we've also seen: Led Zeppelin's famous 1971 concert in Osaka (our only trip outside Europe and North

America); Pink Floyd playing their original tour of *The Wall* — we saw that in Dortmund in February 1981; in 1985, it was the incredible guitarist Robin Trower at the original Marquee club in Wardour Street — God, I love that venue — where Trower recorded the live tracks on his *Beyond the Mist* album; and we finally made it to the Woodstock festival in August 1969.

It's impossible now to imagine a festival the size of Woodstock being curated. Estimates are that between four and five hundred thousand people made it to Max Yasgur's six-hundred-acre dairy farm in Bethel, and thousands more were turned away by the police. Local roads were so jammed they became parking lots as festival-goers abandoned their cars and walked the final distance to the site.

We went for all four days, enjoying performances by Arlo Guthrie, Santana, the Grateful Dead, a six months' pregnant Joan Baez, The Who, Joe Cocker — the list went on and on. The bands were flown in by helicopter direct to the stage — that was the only possible way they could enter and leave. We sang along to the songs we knew and those we didn't and joined in with everyone else to accompany Country Joe and the Fish as he sang the 'Vietnam Song', dressed in his patterned bandana and US army shirt. We slept wherever we found a patch of grass or when someone offered us a tent for a few hours. We relied on the generosity of others for our bed, our sustenance, our drinks, and happily partook in whatever else we were given by fellow music lovers. We watched the audience almost as much as the bands; I've never seen so much bare skin, beards, hair bands, leather and flower necklaces, tie-dye, Lennon glasses, guitars and tom-toms. It was chaotic but also self-organised, with specific tents erected for food, alcohol and first aid, and even a tripping tent.

When we got home, one minute after we originally left,

adorned with more beads and bangles than we had been wearing when we set out, we crashed for forty-eight hours and missed a play we had booked with Andrew and Bee. The clothes we had been wearing I put through the washing machine twice to ensure the mud, dope and any other sixties aromas and remnants we had returned with were completely washed away.

Our most recent gig was Paul Weller in June 1992 at Subterania in London. I'm not going to forget that trip, partly of course because The Modfather was fantastic, early on in his solo career. But also because afterwards, as we often did, we went for a walk before coming home, and on this occasion, we strolled down towards Notting Hill. It was a Sunday night, very relaxed, a warm evening, and eclectic groups of people were hanging out at the trendy pavement cafes and bars. But one place, in particular, was so noisy with people singing and dancing outside, we had to investigate. As we got closer I could see Danish flags draped over chairs and women's shoulders, and plastic Viking horns shoved down on men's heads.

'What's going on?' Jon asked a huge, long-haired man who was swaying around with a beer glass.

'Danmaaark!' the man hollered. 'We win! We win!'

'Win what?'

'Win what?' The man turned to face my husband and clapped him boisterously on the shoulders. 'The Euros. The football. The European championships, you know. We are the champions!'

'Champions!' echoed another five or six people.

'You must drink with us, drink!' the man insisted loudly to Jon and thrust a beer in his hand.

We left two hours later, Viking football songs ringing in our ears, ridiculously drunk, not having spent a penny.

. . .

'That was some evening wasn't it,' Jon says as we recall it.

'What I can remember,' I answer. I slice a carrot in two.

We grin at each other.

I put down my kitchen knife. 'You know who I really want to see? The Stereophonics.'

'We saw them before, 'Jon replies. 'In real-time, remember? 1997 was it?'

'Ninety-eight. The Forum in Kentish Town. We hitched to London and I thought you were so cool the way you stuck out your thumb! It was such a great gig.'

'So we've seen them, no need to repeat that.' He sips his tea.

'No, that's my point. I enjoyed it so much, I'd love to go back and see it again. The same gig.'

'But, Caz, we can't. I've told you. We can't go back to where our timelines cross.'

'No, you've told me that we can't go back to the same time and place in history where one of your wormholes has already opened. This would be different. You haven't created a wormhole there yet.'

Jon taps his mug. 'That's true.'

'So?'

He frowns. 'I'm not sure. It sounds risky.'

'Why?'

'What if we see us?' He stops, rubs his face. 'God, it's confusing talking like this, isn't it? What I mean is, what if 1998 Jon and Caz see 2021 us? What on earth would that do to our timelines?'

'Why would our younger selves recognise us as we are now?'

'Andrew spotted us at the Hendrix gig in a grainy black-and-white photo. So surely, we... 1998 us would be suspicious if they saw someone who looked vaguely like them?'

'We're twenty years older now.' I pause, do a quick

calculation in my head. 'More, twenty-three. And anyway, we're not the suspicious type, unlike Andrew. From what I remember, we were more interested in sex and drink and rock 'n' roll.'

'Mmm...'

I pick up my knife again and swivel the carrot around on the chopping board. 'Okay, listen. What if we go in disguise and keep well away from where we stood originally? The Forum's a huge venue.'

'Maybe. It could be fun...'

We agree that is what we'll do.

I'm so excited.

Over the following week, Jon grows a beard and I dye my hair red (I think I look rather Bohemian!), and we both don spectacles with plain glass. Jon has one more precaution.

'As soon as we land in 1998, if you feel any different than normal, or if you look at me and, I don't know, see my body shimmering or I've only got one arm or something, then you shout immediately and I'll press the time-pen and get us back here pronto. I hope. And trust we haven't done too much damage to the timeline. I'll watch out for abnormalities in you, too.'

'Abnormalities. That's nice.'

For some reason, I'm not as worried as my husband. If everything he has told me is correct, then the wormhole has no reason to cave in or anything. At that point, we won't even have seen ourselves, but I don't point that out to him.

We stand on the launch pad to leave and Jon holds the time-pen in front of him as if he's about to stab someone with it. The countdown reaches zero, there's a flash of light, I feel my usual wobble for a moment and I find myself standing in Talacre Gardens in Chalk Farm. Being

November, it's bloody cold, and I'm regretting our decision not to bring any coats simply because they'd be a faff once we're inside the arena. I look down at my body: two arms, two legs and yes, Jon has the same. I raise my eyebrows and he breathes out and slips the time-pen into his pocket. He shrugs nonchalantly. I shiver, pull myself into him and we walk quickly towards Kentish Town past the Fuzzock & Firkin pub and a billboard promoting *Meet Joe Black* (with a handsome young Brad Pitt gazing down towards me).

Ten minutes later, we arrive at The Forum. Hundreds of people are milling around outside. There's a surfeit of stonewashed jeans, short dresses, unkempt hair and a few men are even wearing shades despite the fact it's dark. We are definitely outside the average age demographic. But no one cares, it's a relaxed atmosphere.

We buy two tickets from a couple who need to sell theirs, go in and stand self-consciously at the back of the hall on the ground floor, by the bar. The downstairs arena is a large, standing-only area, already filling up, ultimately holding a thousand plus people. I spot a couple who look like Mark Lamarr and Ulrika Jonsson, who I don't remember noticing twenty years ago. I'm excited; it's a fantastic place to see a concert.

Despite our excitement, we're equally terrified, because what would happen if 1998 us did see twenty-first-century us? At the same time, we have an uncontrollable urge, we cannot help it, we have to look for ourselves. We both crane our necks. I'm pretty sure we stood halfway from the stage on the left. I suddenly let out a cry.

'There! There, I can see us!'

'Where?' Jon is like a meerkat.

I point. 'Can't you see? There's you, looking thin and handsome in your deep blue shirt. I'm standing beside you in my, oh, that's my black dress with the flowers. I loved that dress. I bought it after I saw Shannen Doherty wearing something like it.'

'Oh my god, yes!'

'I thought I looked so cool.'

'You did look cool.'

'Aw, thanks, darling.'

We grin uncontrollably. Watch as 1998 us hold hands, hug, knock back our beer from plastic glasses; 1998 me does a dance on the spot.

'Christ, I had some energy,' I say. 'I wish I was that skinny now.'

'You were only twenty.'

'Don't I look it.'

'You still have a wonderful figure now.'

I kiss my husband. He rubs his hands together. 'Now I'm here, I so want to go over and say hello.'

'No! You can't. We promised.'

'Just a few words. It'd be so much fun.'

'Jon, no. Swear to me. If you recognise you, then we don't know what would happen. To us now, to us in 2021, both our timelines – the wormhole itself. That's what you said!'

Jon cocks his head. 'Okay, you're right.'

All the same, I grab my husband's arm, but as I do, the lights dim, an enormous wall of sounds hits us and the Stereophonics appear on the stage. It's loud, so loud. Kelly Jones has such a presence and a gravelly voice made for live rock. I quite fancied him at the time, with his sideburns and sultry looks. They play for well over an hour, including two of my favourite songs, 'Last of the Big Time Drinkers' and 'A Thousand Trees'. I almost forget there are two versions of us here. It's a brilliant gig and I'm very glad we came. Nevertheless, I recognise that the first time was the best; gigs of this type with such intense energy and electricity belong to the age of those who were here at the real time. It's sobering but I'm not disappointed. I remember how much I loved it and this has just confirmed that. It's a peculiar but comforting feeling.

When the lights come up, Jon taps his feet. 'I've got to find the loo.'

'No, we should leave. Immediately. You can go when we get home.'

'I've got to go now, Caz. We're in the middle of Kentish Town with thousands of people leaving gigs and bars. It might be a Tuesday night but it could still be ages before we find somewhere where we can safely ping home.'

He dashes off and I stand with my back to the bar and wait. I remember this happening at several gigs, being left on my own like this. I glance across to where 1998 me was and sure enough, I see me again, on my own. But I don't look worried, I'm doing a cool dance on the spot with my eyes closed, arms occasionally waving above my head. Oblivious to anyone else. I chuckle to myself. Go, me! Just because 1998 Jon has pissed off and left me...

Wait a minute. If 1998 me is on her own, then that means that 1998 Jon has slipped off somewhere. The most obvious place being... the toilets. Where twenty-first century Jon has gone... Oh, the devious little— He'd better not be speaking to himself. If he is, I'll kill him. As long as I get the chance. I cross my arms and wait.

Ten minutes later, Jon comes sidling up to me, looking sheepish. He sees my scowl and holds his hands up.

'Don't worry, I didn't say anything bad.'

'But you spoke to him?'

'Mmm, yes.'

'For Chrissakes, Jon, that was so irresponsible.'

'I only said a few words. Nothing dangerous.'

'How do you know?'

'We're still here, aren't we?' Jon looks around. 'Come on, let's go. I'll tell you what happened when we get home. We do need to get out of here in case 1998 us does notice 2021 us. The audience is thinning out and I still don't want them to see us.'

'Bit late for that now,' I mutter.

We hurry outside, my ears ringing. After the heat of the arena, the chilly night air smacks me in the face and I wrap my arms around my body. But I don't care – the high from the gig, from seeing our younger selves, means I soon forget the cold.

We know that we, 1998 we, went to a bar in Camden after the gig so we, twenty-first century us, walk in the opposite direction, up Fortress Road towards Tufnell Park. As we walk, we see street vendors on the pavement opposite us selling jewellery, felt hats, waistcoats, candles, all sorts of hippy stuff.

I grab my husband's arm. 'Oh, Jon, look. I used to love all those trinkets and stuff. Can we take a quick look?'

We cross over and I start to flick through some tie-dye dresses on one of the racks. I hold one or two up against my body but I can't see me wearing them now; they belong to 1998 me. I smile wryly. I look up to see that Jon is studying the jewellery on a stall further along the street. He picks up a silver necklace incorporating an intricate feather pendant, says something to the saleswoman and hands over some money. I'm just about to rush up to see what he's bought, but as soon as he pays for it, he slips it into his pocket and looks around furtively. I grin. How cute – he's going to surprise me later! This must be his way of apologising for breaking his word when he talked to his younger self. What a lovely gesture.

I play along, pretend not to notice and wait until he waves at me. 'Come on, Caz! We need to get home.'

I take his arm, squeeze my body into his and we walk further up Fortress Road. We turn into a quiet residential side street, duck into a doorway and Jon presses the button on our time-pen to take us home.

We climb the stairs out of the basement and Jon leads us into our lounge. I plump myself down with my arms folded. Jon perches on the edge of the sofa, facing me.

'That was the strangest experience of my entire life,' he says.

'Talking to yourself?'

'Seeing ourselves like that. Us, twenty years younger. Don't you think that was bizarre?'

'I do. And that should have been that. Why did you want to go and risk talking to your younger self? Did he recognise you?'

'Nah. He hardly any paid attention to me.'

'What did you say?'

'He was standing at the urinals when I went in. There was no one else there so I stood right at the other end.'

'And?'

'I just said something like, "Good gig, that, wasn't it, mate?".'

'And what did he – you say?'

'He just grunted and agreed with me. Didn't even glance in my direction. I think he was just trying to be cool.'

'God, you and your need to be aloof with people.'

'I wasn't like that.'

'You bloody were, Jon. You still are now sometimes.' My husband shrugs, barely looks chastened. I sigh. 'Why did you do it? You were the one who said it could be dangerous.'

'I know.' Jon reaches over and strokes the end of my fingers. 'But once we were there, I couldn't help it. I wanted to test something. See if it was possible. I mean, I never even knew that we could visit our own timeline in the past, let alone talk to ourselves and return without causing a butterfly effect. At least, I hope we haven't. I can't see what we would have done. And you were right, it had no impact on the wormhole at all.'

'Well, we're still alive and living in the same place.'

'There you go.' Jon taps his fingers together. 'Are you going to bed?'

'Well, I thought I'd have a cup of tea, and—'

'Okay, sure. Would you... would you mind if I did something back downstairs? Got a couple of things I want to test, I mean check. One or two ideas. Is that okay?'

Without waiting for an answer, he rushes down the basement stairs again. I watch him go. It may be completely innocent, what he has planned, but that wasn't the impression he left me with. I'm not sure what he's doing downstairs but I am sure I don't like whatever it is. And I guess I'm going to have to wait a while longer before I'm given my necklace.

11

It's been three days since we saw ourselves at the Stereophonics gig. Jon's been rather distant, but sadly that's something I've become accustomed to in the last few months, even with the time machine.

This evening, we're sitting side by side on the sofa in the lounge listening to Van Morrison's *Moondance*. We've drunk a whole bottle of wine between us. Jon turns to me.

'Remember I told you that we could never use the time machine to change our timeline. Or anyone else's.'

'Of course. And I agree, you know that.'

'Yes, well, I've been thinking. There is one thing we could do. I want to do.'

I examine his hyperactive face. I think I know what's coming; I've been expecting this. Ever since we returned from that first trip to Glastonbury, I knew that this would have to be discussed at some point. Seems like that time has arrived.

Jon starts to pull at his fingers. 'It's about… our baby.'

I was right. I've thought a lot about this, so I know what I'm going to say. I know Jon isn't going to be happy, but I have to see it through. But I have to manage this so carefully.

'You mean my miscarriage?'

'Yes.'

'Go on.'

'Well, I've been thinking. Why don't we go back and reverse it? Stop the accident from ever happening and change our lives. Have the baby!'

'Oh, Jon. Really?'

My husband's face lights up. And I panic. My reply was supposed to sound sad but he's misinterpreted my words.

'You think so too? I wasn't sure you would.'

'No, I—'

'I mean, it won't be easy, there could be all sorts of complications, but I'm sure we can do it.'

'Wait.'

He is so excited. 'Oh, Caz!' He moves to give me a hug but I back off and hold up my hands.

His face drops. He realises I don't agree. His arms slump to his lap and his head droops like a forlorn puppy. I move my fingers towards his arm but think better of it and sit back. I have to say my piece.

'Darling, you know that there was nothing I wanted more. At the time. But that was over ten years ago.'

'So?'

'We can't just change ten years of our life.'

'We can, Caz, we can.'

I rub my forehead. 'But my body couldn't cope. That's why we had the miscarriage.'

'I know, I know.' He turns to face me again. 'But only because of the accident.'

'Not only—'

'That was the root cause.'

'It might still not change what happened.'

'But it will. I know it will.'

I close my eyes and think back eleven years. There was a time when this was all I thought about, but not anymore. Not now.

I force myself to replay in my mind the night in question.

It was the evening before the opening of an exhibition at a small gallery who were including some of my work. I had stayed until the end of the set-up, determined to help clear up afterwards, even though I was coming towards the end of my second trimester. By the time I piled my unneeded frames onto the passenger seat of my car and began to drive home, it was getting late. I only closed my eyes for a second but the next thing I remember was the strip lights of a hospital ward and Jon sitting beside me, his face streaked with tears. He told me I had crashed my car into a tree and my airbag hadn't inflated properly. I'd hit the steering wheel, my seatbelt had snapped into my stomach and the corner of a picture frame had pierced my abdomen. I wasn't badly injured but the doctors couldn't save our baby and, worse, the operation meant I could never again conceive.

It was devastating.

But it happened. And we moved on.

Now Jon is making me revisit that terrible time. It's so painful.

I try a different tack. 'Okay, let's just say for one second that it is possible. Somehow, we could go back and prevent the miscarriage. I have the baby. What then?'

'Then we live happily ever after.'

'Seriously?'

'Yes.'

'How?'

Jon splays his hands out. 'Isn't it obvious? It's all that we wanted. We'd have the baby, we'd be happy.'

'And practically? Are you suggesting we live these last eleven years all over again?'

'No, that would be impossible. For a start, there would be two pairs of us in 2010. Our original selves from that time and then us from 2021. Getting older together, at different ages, from different timelines. That's a time paradox if ever I heard one. Apart from that, we, 2021 us, couldn't go near the baby.'

'So what are you saying?'

He leans towards me, one of his knees jiggling up and down. 'We go back and talk to 2010 you. Explain what's going to happen. Make sure you understand you mustn't fall asleep at the wheel.'

'That would be crazy.'

'No, it wouldn't.' His knee stops twitching. 'That's what I learned we could do from our trip to see the Stereophonics. It made me realise this is possible. I still can't create two wormholes in the same place at the same time, but there can be two versions of us at the same time in history if we, 2021 us, just visit that time zone and location once. I never knew all that before, but now I do, it's revolutionised my understanding.'

'But, Jon—'

'No, Caz, *listen*. This will work. But I need you to do this. It won't work without you.'

'Jon.'

'I've thought a lot about this. It has to be you. If I go back on my own to warn you, 2010 you won't believe me. I know that. I mean, why would you? But if you, 2021 you, goes back and tells your younger self not to take that trip, she'll listen to you. I know she will.' He drops his eyes. 'Trust me, if I could think of an alternative plan I would do it. I've even considered whether I could simply go back and hobble your car so you can't drive it home that night.'

'You don't need me for that,' I whisper.

'I know. But I don't think that will work. You'd just fix it or find another car and the crash would occur the following evening.' His shoulders heave. 'I can't do this without you. You're our baby's mother.'

Tears prick the corner of my eyes. I swallow. Stare at my husband. I'm slightly in awe of him. He's thought this through more than I believed he would. Both in terms of the plan and his emotional blackmail. Although with hindsight, I don't know why I didn't expect him to be so thorough. I suspect he doesn't even think he is intimidating me.

I drag the heel of my palm across an eyelid. 'O-kay. And then what? We arrive in our basement, walk up the stairs, and sitting in our spare bedroom is our ten-year-old child?'

'Yes!'

'Wow. But we wouldn't even know him or her. We'd have missed all their early years. We'd be starting from scratch. How on earth could we do that?'

'No, don't you see?' Jon sits forward. 'The timeline would fix itself. We'd come back with all those memories suddenly in our minds.'

'What? How?'

'The butterfly effect working positively. I never realised it was possible, but look at what happened after we met Lennon and McCartney in 1962 and I inadvertently said that all you need is love. When we got back and checked the record, we saw that reference in the sleeve notes saying thanks to J and C. The world can change for the better! Time can change as we want it to!'

Jon is now sitting inches away from me. My back is squeezed against the arm of the sofa and I'm shaking. Jon sees this and laughs. He probably thinks I'm excited. He couldn't be more wrong.

'But what about anything else that might change? A new

person appearing in the world who wasn't supposed to be here is more than a delicate pair of beating butterfly wings. Anything might happen. He or she might turn out to be a terrible person. We might be terrible parents. It might mean that someone else who was supposed to be born isn't. We don't know how that works. And what if that person is supposed to go on and, I don't know, cure cancer or something?'

'We'd cope. I know we would.'

'But what if—'

'What if, what if!' Jon stands up abruptly and throws his arms out. 'It doesn't matter. It won't matter. The world will sort itself out. Like it did with The Beatles. It will all be fine.'

'But we don't know that.'

'We don't have to.'

'And what on earth are our friends going to think?' I add quickly, playing another trump card I'd forgotten I had. 'What will Andrew and Bee, and Teri and Zaina all say when a new ten-year-old child suddenly appears in our life and we say we're parents? How will that work?'

'Aren't you listening to me? The timeline will resolve itself.' Jon starts pacing around the lounge and I watch in horror. He's just trumped me straight back. 'Look, I didn't create the time machine to do this. I never believed it would be feasible. I thought it would be too dangerous. But I was wrong. I thought that changing time was the worst possible thing that someone could do. And for what it's worth, I still do for most things. As we've always said, kill Hitler, Göring wins the war for Germany. Stop Nine-eleven, and the following year—'

'I know all that,' I snap.

'So what's your problem? Why won't you do this?'

'Because I don't want to have a baby anymore.'

The words burst out of my mouth before I have a chance to stop them. And oh, shit, that wasn't supposed to happen. Not like that. He caught me on the back foot. I meant to build up to that point, ensure Jon was prepared. But I haven't done that and he isn't.

If I thought he seemed disappointed a few minutes ago, now he looks as if someone has just told him his child has died. Maybe they have, in effect. He stares down at me with utter disbelief. I hold his gaze for a moment but I can't maintain it. I turn my head away, let my shoulders slump. Close my eyes. I hear Jon clump across the room. The needle jumps on the record deck and Van Morrison ceases with such a jolt, I fear for the vinyl's surface. Then there's silence.

When I open them again, my husband is sitting on the floor with his back against the wall, his forearms resting limply over his knees, staring glassy-eyed into the distance. I have no desire to say anything, but I have to. I owe him that. I take a deep breath.

'When we had the miscarriage, I thought the world would come to an end. We both did, I know. And it took me a long time to get over it. Years. It was even worse when the doctors told us that it meant I could never have a baby. Since then, I've thought a lot about that period. Even before you invented the time machine I asked myself, what would I do if I could change what happened? If I could have a baby after all. I even talked to Bee about it. At first, I thought I would of course change my life, have the baby if I could. But slowly, very slowly initially, I changed my mind. I realised that not having a baby was who I am, who we are.'

I pause. I wish the record were still playing; the silence is harrowing. I clasp my palms together and continue.

'I understand why you think I would want to change all that. Why wouldn't I want to prevent such anguish? All the

137

pain? And yes, there is a tiny part of me that finds it terribly tempting. But… it's not the right thing.'

'Yes, it is, Caz. You know it is.'

'No, Jon, it's not. It's what you want to do, what you think is the right thing. I know it isn't. Your suggestion is the wrong way to confront our past, our traumas, my fears. It's the wrong way to live your life. The right approach is what we are doing now. I know that's right for us and I know you'll understand that if you think about it. We shouldn't change our past, because the past is what happened.'

I lower my voice. 'This… this is our life now. I've reconciled that and I want to carry on being me. With you. As I am now. And I am this person partially because of all that happened. Can you understand that? Jon? Darling?'

Jon's head has sunk between his knees. He isn't moving. I think I can see tears running down his cheeks. I want to go to him but I daren't; it won't help yet. For minutes, we remain silent. An occasional car passes by outside. Then Jon gets up and walks to the door of the lounge. Where he pauses.

He doesn't look at me, just grips the doorframe and says, 'I'll never forgive you for this. Never.'

He walks out of the room.

I go to bed and lie in the dark, his accusations ringing in my ears. I think of what I should say to him and wait for him to come up. I hear him go back into the lounge and then go downstairs to his lab. I force myself to keep my eyes open, but it's not easy – a combination of too much wine and tiredness born of frustration, anger and sadness.

A while later, I don't know how long, he comes upstairs to our bedroom. He undresses and slips in beside me. He doesn't say anything. Lies down with his back to mine.

We lie in silence.

12
———

For the next few days, Jon and I avoid each other. He goes to work, I head for my studio. He comes home, I go out to see Zaina or an artist friend. I even go to the cinema on my own to avoid being in the house at the same time as him. After three days, I tell Jon I am going to stay with Bee and Andrew for the night.

'Do they need someone to look after Melanie?' he asks.

I growl 'something like that' and slam the door behind me. I spend the evening at my friends' house, bleed my heart out to them, confess all that Jon and I are going through. At one point, I nearly mention the time machine, but I catch myself just as I'm doing so and turn my stammer into a sob. They comfort me, say I can stay as long as I like. But I can't stay here, I have to go home and confront Jon. I discuss this with Bee when we're alone in her lounge.

'He's so selfish, Bee. He never thinks of how I feel.'

'He's still hurting.'

'You don't think I am?'

'You've reconciled how you feel about your miscarriage. Jon never has.'

'I know. But I still can't believe he said all those horrible things.'

Bee takes my hand. 'How does that make you feel about him?'

I think about this. I'm just about to say how much I hate him but I stop myself. I look up at the ceiling.

'You know what? Despite what he said, I do still love him.' I catch my breath as I say this.

'Are you sure? What he said was nasty, vindictive.'

'Yes... I am. How is that possible?'

Bee picks up her glass of wine, swirls it around in front of her. Stares into it before facing me again. 'When I had Michael and Mel, I was so young. But I was so happy. It never occurred to me I was missing out on anything. But I gradually began to realise I couldn't pursue my hope of working in the fashion industry, at least not for some years, and when I watched you and Teri and Zaina going out so much more than me, well, there were times when I wondered if I had done the right thing after all. And I needed someone to blame. So I blamed Andrew. I mean, he was still happily working his way up the corporate ladder, while I was staying at home. What was he missing out on? Oh, don't get me wrong, I loved – love – my children more than anything, but it felt unfair.'

'I remember. You told me some of this when we had that night out for Teri's thirtieth.'

Bee's hand flies to her mouth. 'Oh God, yes. How long ago was that?'

'Ten, twelve years.'

'I was so pissed! But that was because I hardly ever went out at that time!'

I nudge her knee with mine. 'You kept showing strangers in the pub photos of your children!'

'Because they were so beautiful. Mel was, what, nine

then? How could I not?' Bee laughs but then her face drops. 'It wasn't long after that when I found myself questioning if I still loved Andrew for who he was, or just because he was the father of my children.'

'Oh, Bee.'

'It was so personal, something I knew I had to work through.' She sighs deeply. 'And I did – we did. I realised I had to open up to Andrew about it, so I made myself do that. We talked, a lot. It helped so much. Maybe the same approach can help you.'

'Hmm.' I stare listlessly at the family photographs displayed on their piano.

Bee follows my gaze. 'Look, Andrew was – is – a wonderful husband. He loves me, always does his bit around the house—'

'So does Jon. Most of the time.'

'It's a different sort of thing that Jon has done to you. You have to decide if you can accept it, maybe even understand why he said it.' She takes my hand. 'We know what sort of temper he has, you know better than us how he can blow hot and cold. But if you love him still…'

The following day, I go home. I arrive early evening, hoping that Jon is already back from work. I don't want to be waiting for him. I turn the key in our lock, push the front door open and walk into the lounge. Jon is sitting there, unshaven, a Nina Simone album on low volume, a cup of tea in front of him where I might have expected a glass of whisky. He sees me, his face crumbles and he walks over to me. He offers me his arms and after a moment, I inch towards him. He embraces me so tightly I think he might be trying to crush the breath out of me. He rubs his cheek against mine and his is wet. I gingerly curl my arms around his back and place my fingertips lightly on his shoulder blades.

We don't discuss what happened. I just can't find the words, the right things to say, and Jon doesn't seem to want to. But his demand to reverse my miscarriage is never mentioned again in the subsequent weeks. I go back to my studio, Jon continues to work at the university and we come to a silent if mutual understanding. After close to four weeks, I am surprised but happy that Jon hasn't once flown into a mood. He is always asking if he can do anything for me. He gives me space when I want, and puts his arm around me when I need that. If this is his way of saying sorry, I can accept that.

I finish my commission for Esposito and deliver the artwork to Priscilla. She's thrilled by it and loses all her Germanic composure when she tells me it's better than they ever could have expected.

'We will celebrate!' she adds. 'I will take you all for dinner. My treat!'

I feel fantastic. We agree that before the jewellery company use it, we will also display the painting at a private view at Rosie's gallery in Crouch End. It will give the whole project additional publicity, and it will boost Rosie's exposure and mine.

There is one thing Jon and I don't do: We don't go on any trips to any gigs. We don't even mention the time machine. Not once. Do we both feel it is to blame for what happened? If so, that is, of course, ridiculous and unhelpful. Not only are we not confronting our feelings around it, we're also cutting off our nose to spite our face because we both love the trips so much.

I finally decide enough is enough and on the morning of my private view, while having breakfast in our kitchen, I moot the possibility of going on another trip.

Jon smiles. 'You don't know how long I've been waiting for you to say that.'

I return a rueful smile. If that's true, and I do think it is, then more kudos to my husband. He could easily have gone away somewhere himself (although I suppose I'd have no idea if he had, other than by the fact he would probably be so high for days after he got back that I would guess), or suggested a trip himself, but instead, he waited for me. I lean across and kiss his cheek.

He butters a piece of toast. 'I do have to admit that I have been doing some research.'

'Oh, have you?'

'On one particular singer. Someone we both wanted to see, but I always said it was too difficult unless we went to one of her bigger concerts.'

'And that is…?'

'Amy Winehouse.'

He crunches on his breakfast.

Some singers make the hair on the back of your neck stand up. Amy Winehouse's voice does that to me. I'd been pestering Jon about going to one of her gigs almost since he invented the time machine, and finally, it appears that he's zeroed in on one.

My eyes widen as he continues. 'As I was saying, it's tough trying to find one of her gigs unless we go to one after she broke through. But I'd rather go to an earlier one.'

'Me, too,' I say. 'Something more intimate.'

'Good. Well, I think I've found the answer. July 2003, a few months before *Frank* was released, she did a series of underground gigs at The Cobden Club in Ladbroke Grove.'

'Never heard of it.'

'I'm not surprised. I don't even know if it's there anymore. Trendy part of London. It's quite likely investors have come in and snapped it up. The building would be worth much more as residences.' His finger chases the last of the breadcrumbs around his plate. 'Anyway, Amy played there a few times as a way of building up the buzz about her. She had a smart manager.'

'Can we get tickets?'

'Pay on the door. It wasn't quite an open-mic night, but the organisers talked about it later as a showcase for up-and-coming acts. KT Tunstall and Tom Baxter both played similar gigs there. We'd go to the first of the three nights she played there, so it shouldn't be so popular.'

I blow on my coffee. 'That's what you said about some young band called The Beatles.'

'Hey, you got to see them eventually. And meet the song-writers!'

'I did.' I grin sheepishly. 'And we can even use our current money, right?'

'Afraid not. The banknotes were still paper back then, remember? The plastic notes we have now weren't intro-duced till years later.'

'Oh, yes.'

'Don't worry, there's plenty of people selling old notes on eBay. I can buy an old twenty-pound note for just a bit more than its real value and we can spend that to get legit change for the rest of the evening.'

'So let's do it!' We clink coffee mugs. 'When shall we go?'

'I need to print a few parts for another time-pen, and I do have classes today... We're having dinner with Priscilla and Rosie this evening, right?' I nod. 'Then how about tomorrow? We can go to see Amy during the day and then go to your private view in the evening.'

'Sounds fantastic!'

Jon scurries off to his lab to print the time-pen and buy our required cash before heading off to work at the univer-sity. We arrange that I will meet him in his room there in the afternoon and go on to the meal together.

For the rest of the day, I am so excited. Like a child on Christmas Eve. I've forgotten how this feels. The anticipation, the thrill, even a certain amount of trepidation in case something goes wrong – maybe we'll be found out or we'll dress incorrectly and everyone will stare. It's such a buzz.

Mid-afternoon, I get dressed for our meal. Priscilla has kindly offered to take Rosie, Jon and me to Hakkasan Mayfair for dinner. We would never normally eat at such an expensive restaurant so we are touched by her generosity. I wear my silk Madeleine Vionnet dress, which I bought for our Edith Piaf adventure, and hope that I don't look too out of place.

I am ready by four o'clock but I'm so high from the anticipation of our Amy Winehouse trip and going to such a swanky eatery that I can't sit still. It's earlier than I had told Jon I would meet him but I decide to leave anyway; I can wait in his room at the university if he's still teaching. I splash out on a taxi and it drops me off at the university campus. I receive a few sideways glances from the students as I stroll through the corridors of the central building, but I ignore them and walk confidently upstairs to the second floor, towards Jon's room. It's several years since I've been here but the college has barely changed and I know my way.

I pause outside Jon's room, smooth my hands down my dress and knock on his door.

'Come in.' Jon's voice is high-pitched, happy.

I push the door open. The room is as I remember it: small, cluttered, overflowing bookshelves on one side; diagrams, charts and a large whiteboard clinging to a wall opposite. The window is wide open but the space still somehow permeates a musty, professor's smell. Jon is perched on the edge of his desk, smiling, holding a sheaf of papers, shirt-sleeves rolled up, his tie dangling halfway down his chest. Sitting a few feet in front of him on plastic chairs are two young women and one man, students, I presume. They are relaxed, legs crossed, and look equally amused. Jon does a double take when he realises it's me, stands up abruptly, his eyes widening. He looks momentarily ruffled.

'Caz!'

I smile coyly, lower my eyes for some reason. Nod at the students.

'I didn't realise it was so late.' Jon cranes his neck to look at a clock behind his desk.

'I'm sorry. Actually, I'm early. I hope that's okay.'

'Ah, of course.' Jon swivels back to face his students. 'This is my wife, Caroline. Ravi, Kim, Elise.' He waves his arm at the three young people. 'We were just finishing our tutorial.'

I smile at the students. 'Sorry to barge in like this.'

They murmur suitable platitudes. The boy then scrutinises his phone but the two women cock their heads as if examining me. The redhead in the middle, Kim, I think, turns to talk to Ravi, but the woman with long blond hair, Elise, holds my gaze for a moment longer, reaching up to her neckline. For an instant, the sunlight streaming through the window illuminates the sparkle of silver dangling from her necklace, then she elegantly tucks the jewellery inside her shirt. I can't help but stare at her, she's so beautiful. She shifts in her chair and looks away.

Jon sweeps his hand through his hair. 'Let's call it a day. Ravi, don't forget to re-examine your equations. Elise, remember what we agreed for how you're going to proceed with your project.'

The blond nods quickly and shuffles out behind her fellow students, flashing me a cute smile as she leaves. Jon watches them go and comes over to kiss me.

'I'm sorry if I interrupted,' I say. 'I didn't know you'd be

146

teaching in your room. I thought I could wait here until you'd finished for the day.'

'Don't worry, we were nearly done.' Jon walks back behind his desk and taps at his computer. 'Give me ten minutes and we can be out of here. Sit down.'

I sit, but I feel awkward so I stand again, walk to the window. I look out. Below me is the main quad, a grassy area with dozens of students laughing and chatting. I search for Jon's three pupils, but I can't see them.

I sigh. 'Were we ever that young?'

Behind me, Jon laughs. 'You know we were. It wasn't that long ago that we saw ourselves at that age.'

'That's true. We were so carefree.'

'Hey, we have a pretty amazing life now, don't we? You never could have imagined at that age what you'd have achieved by now. And the sort of trips you're taking.'

I turn back to Jon. He winks at me. 'Ready to go?'

He moves into the middle of the room, eases his tie up so it fits perfectly into his collar and offers me the crook of his elbow. I grin and slip my fingers through it. 'Lead the way, Mr Tangent.'

Jon kisses me again, hard. 'I haven't even told you how stunning you look in that dress. Is that the one you wore when we went to... Paris?'

'It is.'

'What a trip that was. And what a foray we have planned for tomorrow, yes?'

'God, yes, I can't wait.'

'Let's not get ahead of ourselves. Tonight is all about you!'

We leave the university campus and stroll down the backstreets of Fitzrovia to Hakkasan Mayfair on Bruton Street in the early evening light. Priscilla and Rosie are already at the restaurant when we arrive, a bottle of wine ordered and chilling beside them. Hakkasan is fine dining, modern Chinese cuisine, lots of neon blue lights, dark walls, straight lines, glass ceiling and low-hanging lights. Very stylish. The two women are wearing smart evening dresses but both of them compliment me on my attire. I smile sheepishly. We order food and begin to discuss tomorrow's private view and who will be attending – a combination of senior business figures and significant players from the arts.

'I can't believe who you've managed to invite,' I say.

Priscilla twirls her wine around her glass. 'I just made a few phone calls, you know.'

'You did more than that. You've corralled half the London glitterati!'

We all laugh.

'And where is Caz's painting?' Jon asks. 'Is it already at the gallery?'

'In our back room,' Rosie answers. 'We're hanging it tomorrow. Just in time for the viewing.'

'I can't wait to see it,' Jon says.

'You mean you haven't already?' Priscilla asks.

'Oh, I saw it early on in its development, but I haven't… had a chance to see the completed work yet. It'll be a surprise for me as well as everyone else.' He squeezes my hand under the table. 'I know it's going to be amazing.'

'I'll drink to that.' Our host smiles.

We eat Hakkasan's signature Peking duck with Prunier Caviar, followed by green tea and yuzu, and I'm glad I'm not paying for it. Priscilla fills us in on the company's plans for how they're going to launch their new range with my artwork alongside it. She casually mentions that they're already planning next year's products and wonders if I might be interested in further work. Everyone laughs at my open mouth.

It's raining when we leave the restaurant so we catch a

black cab back home and flop onto our sofa. Jon brings me camomile tea and puts on Miles Davis' *'Round About Midnight*. I'm nodding off.

'I think it's time for bed,' I say sleepily.

Jon puts down his tea. 'Actually, I feel wide awake. I think I'm too wired thinking about tomorrow. In fact, if you don't mind, I've got some final checks to do before our trip, so maybe I'll finish them off now.'

I kiss him and go upstairs, get into bed. Although I'm exhausted, I, too, have a dozen things flying around my mind: the private view, what might come of Priscilla's future plans, our trip tomorrow to see Amy Winehouse. I can't believe I am finally going to see her.

I listen to the familiar, comforting noises of Jon moving about the house downstairs. Doors opening and closing, Jon stacking the dishwasher, the kettle clicking on and off again. *'Round About Midnight* is now playing at a low volume. The album comes to an end but a few moments later, I hear music again – Madeleine Peyroux's *Careless Love*. It's beautiful. I snuggle into the duvet. There is an occasional clunk as Jon moves something. I listen to the rain outside. Jon stops moving around – he must be working down in the basement now – and the music lulls me to sleep. Sometime later I feel my husband slip into bed beside me and peel off his damp T-shirt. He curls up around me. I press my body into his. He gives me a tender kiss and I fall asleep again in his arms.

13

The following day, as soon as we finish breakfast, we leave the house to go on our Amy Winehouse trip. We're both wearing jeans and long-sleeved, patterned shirts, and of course, Jon dons his fedora. It's a rare thing for us, going to an evening gig in history in 'our' morning time. But it's a rather wonderful feeling, leaving home mid-morning and arriving at our concert just as everyone is leaving work. We feel rather like naughty schoolchildren bunking off from class! And having a drink! On a practical level, it also means Jon can go into work this afternoon.

Jon lands us in 2003 a short walk away from the Cobden Club, inside one of those private gardens that belong to local residents. I usually hate their exclusivity but arriving there just as they're closing for the night with hardly anyone around is the perfect cover. Our landing point, Meanwhile Gardens, even has high trees around the border so no one can see in. We sneak out of a gate and walk briskly to the club. It's July when we are, so it's warm, with birds singing above us. A young woman passes us wearing an absurdly high cropped top, mirroring Fergie from the Black Eyes

Peas, the ring in her navel prominently displayed. Her boyfriend swaggers alongside her in low-slung jeans. It's a good thing Jon and I haven't tried to emulate the in-vogue fashion on this trip; we'd never carry it off.

The building that houses the Cobden looks more like a small industrial unit than a music venue. There's no queue so we waste a few minutes trying to work out where the entrance is. We pay with Jon's specially acquired twenty-pound note, which causes the doorman to be somewhat pissed off as he has to give us so much change, but we don't care. They won't see us again.

We find a position halfway towards the stage. We watch a few average singers, but we're happy to wait. By the time Amy Winehouse comes on, the club is busier; clearly, her manager has spread the word. Even so, there can't be more than a few hundred people. Amy walks on stage with an acoustic guitar and stands behind the mic, looking shy, skinny, smaller in stature than the exhibitionist she will become. She's wearing a plain blue dress and doesn't yet have the cat-like eye make-up she will apply in later years.

'She reminds me of Edith Piaf,' I murmur to Jon.

'Does she?'

'In her demeanour, I mean. She couldn't be further removed visually! I don't think Piaf ever had a beehive hairdo and tattoos.'

Jon puts his arm around my neck. The audience shuffle and cough, as if they are not sure what to expect. It's a strange sensation for me being one of the few people here who know how this incredible musician is going to sound. I turn to give Jon a covert wink and as I do so, I notice one of his fingers resting on my shoulder has dry blood on the knuckle. I'm just about to ask how that happened, if he's okay, when Amy strikes her first chord and she begins to sing. I forget all about bloodied fingers.

What a voice!

Within seconds, you can see people watching her in awe – me included. It's all very well hearing someone on a record and seeing YouTube videos, but hearing Amy Winehouse's vocals live, in a small room accompanied by just her guitar is breathtaking.

She plays 'Stronger Than Me', 'In My Bed', 'October Song' – the list goes on. She plays numbers I don't know. The audience is quiet while she sings and erupts with applause after each tune. It's a similar reaction to Jimi Hendrix's gig; talent like this shines through. Amy smiles at the ovation but barely says anything between songs. Her confidence will increase during her unfairly short career. When she leaves the stage, you know that each person here is going to tell another dozen people about this phenomenon.

We walk out, clear our heads with a short walk along the Regent's Canal, eulogising about the singer, before finding a quiet spot to send ourselves home. I remember when we did our first few trips, I would cling to Jon's arm as if my life depended on it, especially on return journeys. But I'm so used to the experience now, I hardly touch Jon when we take the trips in either direction.

We walk up our basement stairs (it's barely a minute after we left in our real-time, of course) and head to the lounge without a word. We both want to hear her voice again, so Jon plays *Back to Black*, the songs she couldn't have sung at our gig. We sit on the sofa in silence, sipping sparkling water. Jon says he has to get ready for work and goes upstairs to change. I nod, sink back into the sofa, think again of what we've just seen using my husband's remarkable invention.

My phone vibrates on the coffee table. I'm just about to

push it away, let it go to voicemail, when I see it's Priscilla calling. I'd better get this.

'Priscilla! Hello again.'

'Caroline?' She sounds tired.

'Yes. Thank you again for last night, it was wonderful. Jon was just saying how—'

'Caroline,' Priscilla interrupts. 'Where are you?'

'At home, of course. Why?'

'Caroline, I...'

'Is something wrong? Are you okay?' I sit forward.

There's a moment's silence. 'Can you come down to Rosie's gallery?'

'Now?'

'Immediately.'

'Of course. But why? What's happened?'

'Please just come now. As quickly as you can.'

She hangs up before I can respond and I hold my mobile in mid-air, in front of my face, frowning.

Jon walks back into the lounge, now wearing his lecturer's clothes. He sees my expression. 'Something wrong?'

'I don't know. That was Priscilla on the phone. She wants me to go down to Rosie's gallery immediately.'

'Why?'

'She wouldn't say. Do you think there's a problem with the private view?'

'I can't think why they would need you for that.' Jon shrugs. 'It's probably nothing, just Rosie getting her knickers in a twist over some minor issue.'

'Are you sure?'

He smiles. 'I've no idea. Look, I'll come with you, on my way to work. It's time I left anyway.'

It's only a ten-minute walk to Rosie's gallery from our house and when we reach it, the entrance door is wide open. That's unusual for late morning. We walk in apprehensively, as if we're trespassing uninvited into someone's front room. It's eerily quiet.

'Hello?' I call out. 'Rosie? Priscilla?'

I hear running footsteps and Rosie appears from another room. Her face is tear-stained and she looks terrible. She scampers up to me and throws her arms around my neck.

'Oh, Caroline, I'm so sorry. I'm so sorry.'

I gently touch her back and turn my head towards Jon. He frowns. I ease the gallery owner away from me. 'Rosie? What's happened?'

Rosie wipes the back of her hand under her nose. 'It… it's your painting.'

'My painting? What about it?'

'It… Oh, God. I can't believe it.' She grabs my wrist. 'You better come and see.'

She tugs me urgently through the atrium and towards the back of the gallery. Jon follows closely behind. We walk through a door that leads to her office and the storeroom at the rear of the building, and as we reach the room where she keeps the art that is not on display, I see Priscilla, standing in the middle of the floor facing away from me, staring down at a canvas. She hears us come in and turns to face us. She isn't crying but her face is ashen, her mascara smudged from where she must have been rubbing her eyes. She shakes her head and takes a step sideways.

And I stop in my tracks as I see what she was looking at.

The canvas on the floor. My canvas, my artwork.

I sink to my knees. Oh my God.

My commission for Priscilla, the work into which I have invested so much time, creativity and mental effort, of which I am so proud and expect so much from its future, now has four long paint streaks running from corner to corner sprayed right across it. Graffiti from a deep red aerosol spray-can discharged onto my art as if it's a broken wall in a disused railway tunnel.

It's ruined.

My head lolls forwards and I feel dizzy. I reach out to stop myself from collapsing onto the floor. But I don't cry; for some reason, no tears come. But I feel nauseous, as if I'm going to retch any second.

There's no sound in the room, other than the occasional sob from Rosie. I feel a hand gently touch my shoulder. I know it's Jon. I reach up and lay my fingers on his. I look back at my art and find the sickness is replaced by anger. I squeeze Jon's hand and haul myself to my feet.

'What…' I clear my throat. 'What the fuck happened?'

Priscilla has her hands clasped tightly together, her thumbs aggressively massaging each other.

'We found it this morning, like this. When we got here…' She looks at Rosie.

Rosie takes a step forward and stops. 'The back door was broken. The padlock…'

'Someone broke in?'

'They must have. Last night. After we left it here.'

'But… why? Why would someone do this? Why?' My voice is rising.

Priscilla folds one arm across her chest and knocks her chin with a knuckle. 'We don't know. Unless… well, there is the one possibility.'

'Which is?'

'The jewellery company, Esposito, it has received… threats in the past. For its supposed acceptance of, ah, what I think you call blood diamonds.'

'Blood diamonds?'

'Yes, they are——'

'I know what they are,' I snap. 'What have they got to do with my artwork?'

Priscilla takes a deep breath. 'There are activist groups who have threatened the company before, said they would do something to bring them down. But they have been... all mouth until now. No action. We had no reason to believe they would attack us in such a way as this. It makes no sense.'

'And yet here we are. Here it is,' I blurt out.

'Yes. It seems it is.'

The two women fall silent. I walk across the final few feet to where my canvas is propped up on the floor and kneel in front of it. I reach out tentatively towards the paint-sprayed lines as if I expect them to electrocute me. It is dry. So yes, this must have been done last night. My shoulders slump again.

I hear a mumbled conversation behind me, Jon's voice mingling with Priscilla's and the gallery owner.

'Of course,' Jon says. 'Yes, I'll look after her.'

He comes across and sits down beside me, wraps his arms around my shoulders and hugs me into him. I sink into his chest. I'm not sure how long we stay like that, but when I finally look up, we're alone. Jon gently pulls me to my feet. I stare again at the broken back door and start to move towards it, but he touches my elbow.

'Don't disturb anything,' he says quietly. 'Rosie says the police are coming later and they might find some sort of evidence if we're lucky.'

I snatch my hand back, clasp my fists to my stomach. Nod urgently, decisively. Jon places his palm on my back and calmly leads me back into the main gallery. Priscilla and Rosie are standing by the front entrance, not speaking. They both hug me before we leave.

'We still want you to create something for the company,' Priscilla says. 'Something new. When you are ready. We will support you, believe me.'

'And if we learn anything more about what happened, we'll let you know immediately,' Rosie says.

I nod glumly. Jon and I walk slowly home.

When we reach our house, Jon encourages me to lie down on the sofa while he makes tea. 'Unless you want something stronger?' he asks.

I shake my head. Not yet.

'I'll be back in a minute, I just have to let work know I won't be coming in today.'

He leaves me alone and I lie back and stare at our ceiling.

My mind is blank.

Sometime later – ten minutes? half an hour? – Jon reappears with a pot of tea and I sit up. We exchange a few words about his work and then we fall silent again.

'What time is it?' I ask after a while.

Jon looks at his watch. 'Close to one. Are you hungry?'

'No.'

'Are you sure? It must be nearly seven hours of actual time since we had breakfast if you include the period when we were at the Amy Winehouse gig.'

'Maybe a little bit.' I shake my head. 'I can't believe we were there only a few hours ago. It seems so much longer.'

'I know what you mean. But I… wait, hang on a minute.' Jon sits upright. 'I've had an idea. The time machine. Maybe we could use it, to go back to last night I mean. To Rosie's studio. Get inside before the perpetrators and find out who did it. Wait for them!'

I think for a second. 'Really? We could do that?'

'Of course. It's a time machine!'

'Wow. I mean, okay. Do you really think…'

Jon stands up and starts pacing around. 'We could do it. There wouldn't be any problem getting there. But..' He stops and sucks air in through his teeth. 'The problem is, how would we explain our being there? How could we have got in, broken in without any evidence of doing so? And why would we be there? Shit, I hadn't thought of that.'

'Oh, I see what you mean.'

'That might be pushing it. But, oh, what the hell, we'll think of something. I mean, we could be uncovered as time travellers anytime. Maybe this is the right occasion for us to risk it. What do you think?'

I sit back on the sofa and clasp my face. I stare at my husband's excited but clearly worried face. I can't believe what he's saying: that he would risk all that we have done, everything that he has created just so we can potentially trap the people who destroyed my art. What an amazing man he is. How much I love him.

I smile weakly. 'Oh, darling. That is such a lovely thought. Thank you! But we can't risk it, can we? Not even for my painting.'

'We can.'

'No, it's not right. You know it's not. As you've always said, if anyone does find out what you've invented, who knows what could happen next. Something far worse than a stupid piece of art being damaged.'

'It's not stupid.'

'You're right, it's not. But in the great scheme of things, it isn't on the same level as your invention. I can create more art, a better painting. And anyway.' I sigh. 'We might be seen by the perpetrators, as you call them, before they actually do anything. They could wait for us to leave or just come back another time and do it then. I don't think it would help.'

Jon looks as if he wants to argue further but I stand up and wrap my arms around his neck, bury my head in his shoulder. He hesitates and then hugs me back. I hold him until my arms ache and then I kiss him on the lips.

'You should go to work, darling.'

'What? No, I need to be here with you. Make sure you're okay.'

'I'm fine! Really.' I stand back and throw my arms out. 'Look!'

'Caz…'

'Okay, I'm not fine, and I don't suppose I will be for some time. But I'm not going to feel any better moping around this room all day. I need to do something. Do another painting, go out, whatever it is.'

'Are you sure?'

'Your students need you! How are they going to complete their projects if you're not there? That was what you said to that girl, Elise, yesterday, right?'

For a second, Jon looks surprised. Then he furrows his brow and gives me a wry smile. I grin back.

'Go already.'

Jon kisses me softly and a few minutes later, he calls out to say goodbye and closes the front door behind him.

I slump back into the sofa. Okay, I lied. I don't want to go out or do any painting. I'm still heartbroken. I want to phone Bee, but if I do I'll just break down again and feel twice as bad. I will call her but not just yet.

I curl up on the cushions, close my eyes and damn the jewellery company for investing in blood diamonds and curse the day the activists were born.

14

I rouse myself when I hear our grandfather clock strike five. Jon will be home soon and I don't want him to find me here, still lying on the sofa. I urge myself upstairs, jump in the shower and decide to cook a proper dinner. That's genuinely a good thing to take my mind off everything.

When Jon comes in, I'm still in the kitchen. He comes up behind me and kisses me on the back of the neck. 'Is dinner ready?' he asks.

'Ten minutes.'

'Excellent. I've just got to do something downstairs in the lab.' He rushes off.

When he comes back upstairs, I bring our food into the dining room and we switch our mobiles to silent. Jon enquires how I feel, then updates me on the classes he held today. I eat morsels of food while he talks.

'I mean, they're amazing students, but damn, they drive me crazy sometimes.'

'Uh-huh.'

'You wouldn't believe what excuses they come up with if they haven't done something I've asked.'

I rest my chin on my palm and push my food around the plate with a fork.

Jon puts down his cutlery. 'Oh, Caz, I'm sorry. Here I am waffling on about my work and you're still feeling like shit.'

'I'm fine.'

'Yeah, I know you said that, but you're forgetting how well I know you.'

He slides his fingers across the table towards mine. I nudge his back with my fingertips.

'Listen, I have an idea. I was going to discuss this later but what the hell.' He licks his lips. 'Look, I may not be able to use the time machine to help find the people who destroyed your artwork, but I can use it for what I invented it for.'

'I know.'

'I've been thinking about this all day. How I can make it up to you for what happened.'

'There's nothing for you to say sorry for, darling.'

Jon picks up his fork again, twiddles it around between his fingers. 'Well, anyway. I know that we normally go for days, even weeks without going to a gig sometimes, but I've had an idea. I think we should go see someone else now. Tonight.'

I look up. 'Tonight? Already?'

'It will help take your mind off what happened, I promise.'

'I don't know. So much has happened today and as you said earlier, it's been an even longer day in terms of our actual time. I'm quite tired.'

'You won't be when you hear my plan.'

He's like a man who's just about to give someone a puppy. I half smile, shake my head. 'Go on.'

Jon sits back in his chair. 'It came to me while I was

teaching this afternoon. I was thinking about who we've always said we must go see but never have. Which lead me to one obvious answer: Bruce.'

'Springsteen?'

A flicker of excitement pulses through me. Jon is right, we have always wanted to see a Bruce Springsteen concert, but for some reason we've never done it.

My husband grins. 'A trip to 1978. What do you reckon? Shall we go? We've got plenty of dollars left from our other trips around that era. And the good thing about the greenback is that it barely changed for years in its design. We can use notes from the sixties or even the eighties and it should fool most people.'

'Why '78?'

'He plays three nights in August 1978 in Madison Square Garden, part of his Darkness tour, so we should be able to get a couple of seats. And it'll be a lovely time of year to visit New York.'

Jon is right, he does know me, understands just how to press my buttons. *Darkness on the Edge of Town* is my number one favourite Springsteen record. There's a reason that it's listed in *Rolling Stone* magazine's top two hundred albums of all time – although it should be higher. I think quickly about the songs he might play from that album: 'Badlands', 'Adam Raised a Cain', 'Racing in the Street', as well as the title track; and all his classics from his prior records, 'Born to Run' and 'The E Street Shuffle'. We'll miss *The River* and *Born in the USA*, which he won't have written yet, but so what? The Boss is renowned for playing three-hour concerts, so we're bound to hear everything from before that time.

'Can we get tickets?' I ask.

'We'll take our chances and buy from a tout. No doubt

we'll have to pay over the odds, but I don't care. And it shouldn't be that bad.'

'But have you got another time-pen ready? We only went to see Amy Winehouse this morning.'

'That's what I was doing downstairs. Printing one double quick.'

I stare across the table at my amazing husband. He looks so keen, his eyes are bright; we could be going on one of our first gigs he is so excited. I fidget with my earrings, come to a conclusion.

What the hell. Why not? Maybe he's right, maybe this is the best way to help me forget about all I've been through today.

I grin. 'Why not?'

Jon laughs. 'Cool. I'll have everything ready in an hour.' He bounds off while I go upstairs to change into my seventies' outfit and grab the vintage handbag that I took to our Hendrix trip. I come back down and go back into the dining room to pour myself a small glass of wine to give me a kick. Jon's mobile is lying on the table by the wine bottle where he left it, and when I nudge it to one side, the screen lights up in lock mode. The first few words of a message are visible on it:

Can we talk abt 2morrow? Can't wait til…

I down my wine and take the phone downstairs where my husband is already in the basement, dressed in his own seventies' gear and fedora hat. He's tinkering with the computer.

'Jon, have you got something important happening at work tomorrow?'

'Hmm?'

'You've just got a text. Sorry, I didn't mean to look but I think it might be important.'

'What?...' Jon takes his phone from me, skims his fingers across the screen and rolls his eyes. 'No, that's okay. It can wait till later. Thanks for pointing it out.' He puts the mobile on a shelf.

I tap my fingers on the countertop. 'Where are we going to arrive in New York?'

'We can land in Washington Square Park again, where we arrived for Hendrix. It's a half-hour walk to the stadium, but we can soak up the atmosphere of seventies Manhattan. Pretty neat, eh,' he finishes in a bad American accent.

I grimace but even that doesn't concern him. He's hyperactive this evening. He laughs, punches a button on the keyboard, jumps – literally jumps – onto the metal plate in the centre of the floor and holds out his hand. I join him and take his hand. We watch the countdown, disappear from our London house, land in the New York park and after a few seconds, I orient myself to where I am. Historically, it's twelve years after our Hendrix visit but the park has barely changed: still the same thrum of musicians, jugglers, hippies, weed sellers, pill pushers and Frisbee throwers – they're just wearing different fashions now.

As we leave the park, I can't help but think sadly how Jon has continually thwarted my wish for a trip to see Edward Hopper when he had his studio here. Maybe I will ask him again after this trip.

We stroll up 8th Avenue, and as we meander by the cafes and bars, delis and fast-food outlets, walk beneath the tall buildings, hear the blare of nearby sirens, my mood lifts and I begin to enjoy myself. All tiredness is forgotten and I feel alive. We pass billboards advertising Radio City, *The Wiz*, Coca-Cola. A big old yellow metal bus steams past. The eclectic New Yorkers walk, cycle and roller-skate by us, dressed in wide lapels, funky skirts. The yellow cabs, the Greenwich Village brownstones, the subway stations. So familiar, but forty-two years before my real-time.

We reach Madison Square Garden an hour before the concert is due to start. I wipe the sweat from my brow because although it is late afternoon, August in Manhattan is hot and humid. Jon begins to haggle with the touts. Being New York touts, they don't take kindly to hard bargaining but Jon doesn't care; we're only here once so he can piss them off for all it matters. He'll just keep going until he finds one that says yes to our price. Which he does.

As we enter the huge indoor stadium, I catch my breath. I'm not normally a fan of large concert halls, but The Garden could change my mind.

It's some sight: there are multiple tiers of seating reaching up to the high roof that pans above us – I have to crane my neck to see the top row – allowing twenty thousand people an unobstructed view of the vast floor in the centre of the arena, which is so large it can be reconfigured as a basketball court or ice-hockey rink when those sports are played here. Tonight there are metal chairs lined up row after row in front of the massive stage built at one end. I'd love to be on the floor level but our view from one of the lower tiers is still incredible, worth every twentieth-century cent Jon paid.

The atmosphere is already jumping with anticipation.

'Everyone looks so young,' I say to my husband.

'Bruce is only twenty-nine himself at this time,' Jon reminds me. 'This was a period when his popularity was starting to grow. One of the reasons he played one hundred and twelve concerts this year.'

'He didn't!'

'That's nothing. He played over two hundred a few years before this.'

Surely not! How can anyone have the energy to do that? Before I can question that, the houselights dim, the crowd hoot and a spotlight picks out Vini 'Mad Dog' Lopez as he strikes the first beats of 'Summertime Blues' on his drums. I'm about to find out first hand where Springsteen's vitality comes from. Bruce walks on wearing his ubiquitous jeans and unbuttoned shirt, sleeves rolled up to his biceps, and leans into the microphone. He greets us and starts to sing.

Oh God, I am so lucky. I've seen some incredible concerts since Jon invented the time machine. Small clubs, large festivals, underground gigs where only we knew how good the artist is at the start of the evening, and now I am witnessing one of America's foremost rock stars from the last thirty years.

The concert is like no other I have ever witnessed. An initial set, then an intermission, a second set and encores. He doesn't just play the songs as they are on the record, he changes and enhances and plays longer versions: a piano and guitar prelude for 'Prove It All Night', an extended piano and harmonica intro to 'Promised Land' – one of Springsteen's political songs, in which he emphasises the distance between the American promise and American reality. We all sing along. He plays songs from *Darkness*, he plays 'Rosalita', 'Sherry Darling', 'Paradise by the C'. He is forever running across the stage to stand by Clarence Clemons, 'The Big Man' dressed in a bright red suit, as Clarence's saxophone soars through the darkness. It's so sad to think that Clemons dies in 2011, aged just sixty-nine.

During 'Thunder Road', Springsteen jumps onto the piano, then runs into the audience, the veins bulging on his neck. At one point, he is on top of the speakers. At the end of so many songs, he leaps vertically into the air, pointing the guitar towards the skies as if trying to thrust it through the clouds. What drives him? What force carries him to such heights? No wonder he needs a break halfway through. He plays three songs for an encore, including 'Born to Run'.

When we leave, I am exhausted. I'm perspiring; I feel as if I was on stage myself. Even outside the arena, the crowd are singing, still calling out 'Bruuuuce', exchanging high-fives as if they've just attended a football match.

Jon and I walk up 7th Avenue a short distance ('got to be a bit careful,' Jon points out, 'it's only another seven or eight blocks to Times Square and that is not somewhere you want to be late at night in the seventies') and go for a drink at a bar blaring out music, with the TVs on the walls showing baseball games, clips of Jimmy Carter and original broadcasts of *Starsky & Hutch*. We laugh a lot, exchange terrible high-fives, we have another drink.

'I cannot believe what I just saw,' I repeat time after time.

'I told you it would be worth the trip,' Jon says. 'Did you know that Springsteen even did a two-hour soundcheck before the concert?'

'No way!'

While Jon goes to the men's room, I sit back in my chair, staring out at a city I should never be in at this time. My ears are ringing from the volume of the concert and I know that will stay with me even when I go to bed tonight. In 2021 Crouch End, England! But I don't care. These last few days and weeks have been terrible: losing Bolan, our argument over my miscarriage, our subsequent weeks of frostiness towards each other, all culminating, of course, in this morning's discovery of the attack on my artwork. But I have to admit, Jon was right. I do feel better. This trip is making me feel as if we are turning a corner. Priscilla still wants me to paint something for her, Jon is really coming through for me now, showing how much he loves me, wants to help us. Life is looking up again. I smile as I watch a couple sashay down the street, one in waist-high jeans with the broadest flares, the other wearing tight white shorts. Both wear outrageously garish glasses.

Jon returns and knocks back the rest of his beer. 'Come on, let's find a place where we can head home.'

'Aren't we going back to Washington Square?'

'We could risk it, but you saw the drug dealers hanging out even during the day. I'd rather avoid that if we can, and we don't need to go all the way back there. We can find somewhere nearby, okay?'

I nod, happy to be led.

We start to walk and Jon points up the street. 'Look, there's the Empire State Building. We went there years ago in real-time, remember? When was it – 2005? A year later?'

'I do remember. We went up just as it was closing. Right to the top. Playing Meg Ryan and Tom Hanks.'

'And if I recall correctly, when we came down we were amazed at how quiet the streets were around there. In fact, I think we were quite nervous.'

'Hmm, yes.'

I shiver at the memory and Jon wraps his arm around my shoulder. I press my body into him.

'We can use that to our advantage now,' he says. 'Let's see if we can find a quiet spot to leap home.'

We cut along West 34th and as we progress, the crowds do thin out. By the time New York's most famous skyscraper looms above us, there are far fewer people around. But it is nerve-racking; quiet streets in Manhattan at night in 1978 are not the safest place to be and I can hear police sirens not so far away. I thrust my arm more firmly into the crook of Jon's elbow.

We look around. Jon points to a sign that says 'Welcome

to Greeley Square Park'. 'There. I bet we can find some shadows there where we can leave without being noticed.'

We walk over to the edge of the park. It's not so much a park as a small triangular, pedestrianised zone of concrete with a few benches and a closed hot-dog stand. A minimal acknowledgement to grass and a few trees so it can be called a park. I spot several shady characters but there are plenty of dark corners. We make our way towards one.

A tramp with a long beard looks in our direction and cackles, but he turns away and stares up at the night sky.

'It's so bizarre,' Jon says. 'This district is known as Kore-atown in 2021. I bet this park will have been made over with trendy cafes and flowers in our time.'

'Well, it's not now, so be quick,' I urge my him. 'I don't like it here.'

He nods, flicks his head around to see if anyone is obvi-ously staring at us, and decides it's okay to leave. He pulls out the time-pen from his pocket, spins the top and holds his thumb over the button. He holds my hand.

'Ready?' he says. 'Say goodbye.'

I watch his thumb move downwards but just before it reaches the button, as I'm bracing myself for temporary giddiness, I feel his fingers slip away from mine. I grasp at thin air. Sparks fly from the time-pen.

And he disappears.

Without me.

I am still here. In New York City, late night, August 1978.

The dust that was the time-pen remains on the sidewalk for a few seconds, then a gust of wind blows it away into the darkness.

I'm alone.

15

I stand with my arm outstretched, clasping at thin air. My fingers flutter like jellyfish tentacles. My mouth is open. I think I cried out.

What has just happened?

My hand drops to my side and I stare into the dark, holding my breath, expecting Jon to reappear with a flash. He doesn't. Instead, I become aware that this park is not as deserted as we thought. The tramp is delving through a trash can, a couple is having an arms-flailing argument and a young woman wearing a Smiths T-shirt is watching me from across the street. She has a sleeve of tattoos and multiple earrings. Checking there's no traffic, she starts walking in my direction. I back away. A gust of wind rips across the square and despite the warmth of the night, I shiver. The woman keeps walking, fists clenched, long strides. I don't like the look of this. I spin around on the spot – straight into a man's chest. I crane my neck upwards. A long-haired giant is looming over me. He opens his mouth in a semi-toothless grin. He could be Jaws from the James

Bond films, and I find myself thinking, were they even released in 1978? His breath stinks.

'Hey, babe, wanna party?'

I yelp and push myself away. He makes a grab for my bag but I swing it out of his grasp just in time. I hear more footsteps behind me, turn, see the young woman now jogging towards me and I don't hesitate – I start running myself. Fast. Back towards 7th Avenue, the direction of Madison Square Garden, where I know the streets will be busier. I turn left and right, stop because I am lost, take deep breaths, double back on myself and see a sign for Penn Station. I know that's the neighbourhood I'm aiming for. And yes, there are more people around now, but it still feels edgy and I don't fit in. This isn't good. I know I have to stop and take stock of what I'm doing. Ahead, there is a brightly lit cafe-cum-coffee shop and I make a beeline for it. I slam the door open, step in and take deep breaths. It's half full of post-bar couples and late-night loners sipping coffee and eating bagels. A waitress shouts an order. Everyone is smoking. I slide myself into a booth with a Formica table and try to bring my breathing under control. A few people glance in my direction.

A Mickey Mouse clock on the wall says it's nearly one a.m.

A waitress appears, holding a glass coffee pot. She pours me a mug without even asking me. 'What can I get ya?'

I look over my shoulder and the waitress follows my eyeline before turning back. 'You need a minute?'

I nod, gratefully, and she sucks in her teeth and stalks off to another table. I wrap my hands around the mug and close my eyes.

What the hell just happened? One minute we were standing in that place – Greeley Square Park – and Jon had a hold of my hand. We were saying goodbye to New York.

The next moment, he lost his grip of my fingers and was gone. Holy shit. And then there was Jaws and that young woman – there was definitely something not right about her. Maybe Jon noticed her, too, before he left. Perhaps he was also shocked by her appearance and that's why he let go of my hand. That must be it.

So what am I doing sitting here in a cafe? I should go back to Greeley Square immediately, so I am there when Jon comes back to get me. He won't find me here. But that would mean going back to those crazies and I don't like the idea of that.

I need to think.

I take a sip of the coffee and almost spit it out. It's weak and tasteless; I'd forgotten how bad some American coffee can be considering the natives consider they live in the land of Joe. At least it's hot.

The waitress materialises beside me again like a silent assassin. 'You decided what you want?'

'Um, nothing else, thanks.'

'You sure?' I nod. 'Okay. You let me know if you change your mind.'

I nod again, gripping the coffee mug as if my life depends on it. As she walks away, I remind myself to relax, let my hands slide away from the ceramic and sit back in the booth.

I replay over and again in my mind the same scene of my last moments with Jon, but nothing changes. Our hands… his fingers… the time-pen exploding with its puff of smoke.

The time-pen. Oh God. Jon will have to build another one before he can come back to get me. That usually takes him days, although he created one in super-quick time earlier this evening after our Amy Winehouse gig. So he could be back, when? In a few hours?

I'm being stupid. It doesn't matter how long it takes him to assemble a new pen in 2021, he can come back to my time in 1978 whenever he's done that and it will be as if no time has passed for me. He could even be waiting for me back in the park now. This minute. I'm just about to stand up but I stop myself – that isn't going to happen. The wormholes. Jon can't come back to this precise time here and now, because he can't open two wormholes in the same place at the same time. Which means... shit, what does that mean? How long does he have to leave after a wormhole closes for it to be safe? Twenty-four hours? Seventy-two? Longer? I'm sure he told me once but I can't remember for the life of me.

Jon must be worried sick about me.

The reality hits me: I am trapped here in 1978 Manhattan until a new window opens. My chin drops, my eyes close, I feel my shoulders begin to heave and the first tear runs down my cheek.

I'm not sure how long I sit like this, but I suddenly feel a painful yank on my shoulder and I open my eyes to find a man with a Frank Zappa moustache tugging at my handbag. I gasp, cry out, but my bag is being wrenched away from me. I strain against him. The waitress reappears and gives Zappa a clout over the head. The man releases my bag and turns tail.

'Get outta here!' she calls after him. A few people around me cheer.

The waitress slides into the booth opposite me. She looks tired and her face has more lines than I can count; one for every year of her life, I bet. Her name badge reads JUDY, printed on one of those retro Dymo tape machines. Except, of course, it's not old-fashioned where I am now. She inhales deeply on a cigarette and offers it to me. I decline.

She blows out a trail of smoke towards the yellow-stained ceiling.

'You know how long I've been working here, honey? Thirty-four years. I seen every weird aspect of human life in that time. The old and the young, lovers and loners, low-life scumbags. And I've witnessed my fair share of sad women. So tell me, hon, what's the problem?'

The words fly out of my mouth in an instant: 'My husband's left me here on my own.'

'You don't say.'

'He didn't mean to.'

'Right.' She takes another drag on her cigarette. 'What happened?'

'One minute we were standing there, hand in hand. The next we weren't.'

'Ain't that always the way.'

'He'd gone. Disappeared.' I stare over her shoulder.

Judy frowns. 'Disappeared? Were you tripping?'

'You... could say that.' I look down, spin my mug around on the table.

'When was this?'

'A couple of hours ago.'

'What a shithead.'

I jerk my head up. 'What? No, you don't understand.'

'I understand alright. I seen this movie a million times.'

'He's coming back. He just needs to... sort out a few things.'

'That's what we all think at first, sister.'

'No, you really don't understand. I mean, I can't explain it properly. It's... complicated.'

'Of course it is.' Judy stubs out her cigarette. 'My shift ends at four. I got no problem with you sittin' here till then. After that, you may need to buy something else.'

'Thank you.'

She slides out of the booth and stands up. 'You British, hon?'

'Yes.'

'Whaddya doin' here?'

'Holi— Vacation.'

'Huh. Some vacation.'

She acknowledges another customer.

I sigh. Some vacation indeed. Some trip. Judy has topped up my coffee mug and I sip at it again, slowly. I feel slightly calmer. I must think more clearly.

So. It looks like I might have to survive here for a day or two before Jon can come back. I can do that. Find a hotel, have a bath – I need one with all the cigarette smoke in here – buy a new dress... Oh, wait. Shit. Money. I need money. Cash. Do I have any on me...? I automatically cuddle my handbag tightly into my stomach, glance around furtively, but no one is paying me any attention. I open the clasp and peer inside, slide my fingers in. I find tissues, a hairband, nail file, a tube of hand lotion, and tucked away in the corner I feel the raggedness of American dollar bills. Oh, yes, I remember – this is the same bag I brought with me on our Jimi Hendrix trip, nearly three years ago, when Jon used his traveller's cheque to buy a tie and he gave me half the change. I've never spent any of it, so I must have close to forty dollars. Thank Christ. I blow out my cheeks. That must be enough for me to survive on in 1978 for the few days I need to be here.

There's a greasy laminated menu on my table and I gingerly swivel it around. A coffee costs thirty cents, fried chicken two dollars. Okay, so I can afford to eat. But a hotel, in Manhattan, that's not going to be cheap. Even in the seventies. Do I have enough cash? Plus, I don't have a credit card or passport – Jon is insistent that we never carry such things on our trips – so how will I find a place that will let me stay without them? I scratch at the menu with my finger-nails. There must be some hotels who don't insist on ID, although I expect they'll be at the other end of the scale to The Hilton.

I turn everything around in my head. And repeat. Repeat…

As the hours go by, the cafe begins to empty out. Mickey's hands tell me it's nearing four a.m. I reckon a genuine clock like that would be worth ten times its original price in 2021.

My waitress comes up to me again. 'I gotta go now, honey. You gonna be okay?'

I nod. 'Judy, can you help me with something? I need somewhere to stay for a few days until my husband comes back. Somewhere… not too expensive.'

'You ain't got a hotel?'

'No…'

She looks down at me, sadly. I know what she's thinking and I don't blame her.

'Give me a minute, hon.'

She returns to the counter at the back of the cafe, rummages underneath and comes back to my booth. She places a grubby business card on the table. There's a large red K at the top left and an address below it.

'You know the Y?'

'Er…'

'The YWCA. Jeez, honey, you Brits! Well, this place is the same concept, run by Kathy, but she's less, ah, fussy about the sort of people who stay with her. No religious bullshit either. It's women-only, so you'll be fine there. Plenty others in your boat.' She places a hand on my shoulder. 'You take care of yourself, honey. The first few weeks are the worst, but it'll get better, I promise.'

The first few weeks?

Then she says, 'And Kathy don't mind coloureds, either, so you should get a room.'

My jaw drops. I watch Judy leave but I'm not paying attention to her. I'm in shock over what she's just said: Kathy don't mind coloureds. So matter of fact. With everything else I've been thinking about for the past few hours, it never occurred to me that I have an additional problem. But I do. In 1978 America, I am a 'coloured person'. With seventies racism. I can well remember the bigotry I experienced when I was growing up - I had hoped we had left some of that behind. But it seems I'm about to be thrust back into it all over again.

I stay in the cafe for another two hours. I finally feel hungry so I select pancakes from the menu and a stack the size of the Empire State Building arrives at my table. I won't starve while I'm here. At six a.m., I pay with a five-dollar bill and ask the white-haired man at the counter to give my tip to Judy; he says he'll do so.

'Can you tell me how to get to East 24th Street?'

'You walkin'?'

He gives me directions, says it'll take me thirty minutes.

I exit back onto the street. The humidity is already beginning to build and the temperature must be in the low twenties. I don't know what that is in Fahrenheit. I tuck my arms in, clutch my bag to my side and walk briskly down 7th Avenue.

Down at my feet, the ubiquitous New York steam launches out of the tarmac, office blocks tower above and early morning commuters rush past, ignoring me. Trucks rumble by and horns blare. The only good thing about being out at this time of the morning is that all the crazies from last night appear to be tucked up on a park bench somewhere. At least Manhattan's grid system means that all I have to do is find West 24th Street, then just follow it left until it becomes East 24th. But the cafe proprietor was right, it takes me over half an hour to get to Kathy's.

As I walk down East 24th, the facades of the buildings get grimier, the sidewalk has more litter. Even this early, it has an edge. I know when I've reached my destination because there's a two-foot-high red K bolted to the wall above a doorway. The paint on it is peeling off. I steel myself and walk in.

No one is at the reception desk. There's a stand-alone water cooler in the corner with a few cracked, plastic cups propped on top, a couch that has seen better days and a poster on the wall promoting the Staten Island ferry, its bottom corners peeling up. There's a musty smell. A ceiling fan rotates slowly, providing an illusion of coolness. This isn't the sort of accommodation I'm used to.

I press a bell by the reception counter. A middle-aged, worn-down woman appears behind the desk – Kathy? – and flicks her head at me.

I smile. 'Hi. Can I get a room, please?'

'Single?'

'Please.'

'That'll be thirty bucks for the week.'

'Oh, but I only need it for one or two nights.'

The receptionist shrugs. 'Same price. We only rent by the week.'

Shit. Thirty dollars would almost clear me out. I might have just enough left to buy food and drink, but it would be touch and go.

'Do you have anything cheaper?'

'If you don't mind sharing a room, you can have a bed in a triple for fourteen bucks.'

'Is that en suite?'

The receptionist curls up her lip. 'Funny woman. You British?'

'Yes.'

'Don't get many of you stayin' with us.' She flips open a broad, lined notepad on her desk. 'Sign here. Payment in advance.'

I sign the register, fumble in my bag for a twenty-dollar bill. Kathy – it must be her – gives me change.

'Room four oh two. Elevator's out but I guess you ain't got no luggage. Turn right when you come out on the fourth floor. There's another like you in your room so you should get along fine.'

'Another British woman?' I'm amazed.

'No! Another coloured woman. Hey, we're gonna have some laughs with you, ain't we.' She hands me a green key and a towel. I accept it as if she's handed me a small kitten. 'There's a locker in your room, use the one that matches the colour on your key. I advise you to keep all your valuables there.' She looks me up and down. 'If you have any.'

'Thank you.'

'Have a nice stay.'

I walk up the four flights of stairs, accompanied by the same musty smell from the reception, perspiring when I reach the top, turn right as instructed and walk along the corridor until I reach room 402. Opposite is a door with 'Bathroom' stencilled on. I guess my question downstairs was rather dumb.

I unlock the door to my room and walk in.

The room is stark, white painted walls, linoleum floor with a tatty rug in the centre as if it's covering something the owner wants to hide. It's just big enough to accommodate three single beds, one under the window and one along each side wall. Another feeble ceiling fan. There's a lone wardrobe, a bedside table by each bed and a small fridge hums in the corner. The only unoccupied mattress is the one under the window, so I tiptoe across to that, trying not to wake the occupants of the other two beds, who appear to be fast asleep. On one of the walls is a poster informing me how wonderful the Metropolitan Museum of Art is. I stand by my bed and crack open the curtains. The window is wide open and I can see another soulless building opposite, cars parked all along the street below. I let the curtain fall back. It feels more like a hospital ward than a hotel but at least the room is clean and the musty aroma is less prevalent here.

I take off my shoes, slide them under my bed and lie down. My cot creaks. I stare up at the ceiling. I begin to think about Jon and Bee and Bruce Springsteen and I want to plan what I will do today and work out again when I think Jon will be able to come back for me. I think of my sister and how the magic of time travel means that at least I don't have to worry about Veronica because when Jon does come back, we will return to the same time he left; I won't miss any of my visits to her.

As I lie there, my eyelids start to close. I am exhausted. I climb under the sheets, face the wall and clutch my handbag to my chest. I fall asleep in seconds.

16

I'm woken by the sound of clumping feet. It takes me a moment to recall where I am, but when I turn over, I focus on two women getting dressed, putting their shoes on, and it all floods back.

A young black woman, I'm guessing mid-twenties, with compact braids, tight-fitting top and a short skirt is sitting on one of the beds, forcing her feet into knee-high boots. Her tattoos and earrings remind me of the girl I saw last night in Greely Square Park. She grunts when she sees me watching her.

'Hey, new girl. What's up?' I prop myself up on my elbows. 'Oh, not such a girl.'

'Uh,' I manage.

'Articulate, too.' The woman leans forward on her haunches. 'You got a name, new girl?'

I clear my throat. 'Caroline.'

'Sweet.' The woman grins. The other inhabitant of the room, half Asian, I think, looks over and laughs. The two of them exchange a high-five.

'See ya,' the half-Asian woman says and skips out of the door.

'That's Ling,' the black woman says, 'and I'm Nancy. And yeah, I know, strange name for a black chick, huh. My parents named me after Nancy Wilson the jazz singer. I've just about forgiven 'em now.'

Nancy slides off the bed, squats in front of me. I remember when I could hold that pose without straining; not any more. She fixes my eyes. 'There's only one rule here, sweet Caroline. Keep your hands off my things, dig? Follow that and we'll get along fine.'

'Um.'

'Cool.' She straightens up. 'Later.'

And she's gone. It's silent for a matter of seconds before I hear a screech of tyres and a horn blares outside. I notice Ling has a small, square alarm clock on her bedside table – actually a bedside locker, I see now – that says eleven o'clock. I've only had about four hours' sleep; no wonder I feel so groggy. And it's so hot. I fall back on my pillow and do some calculations.

It must be almost twelve hours since Jon disappeared last night – is that enough time to have passed for him to be able to open another wormhole and return for me? I know we had a discussion on one of our trips about how long we should leave before it would be safe – in Liverpool, I think, when we went to see The Beatles. What did he say? I strain to remember: three or four days should be fine, but one or two days was risky. I think that's right. In which case, it's unlikely he'll come back for me today, but you never know. If ever there was a time to risk such an endeavour, it would be now; when I'm trapped here without him. In which case, I'd better get back to Greeley Square and wait there, just in case. But first, I need a shower.

I grab the towel Kathy gave me and circumspectly ease

182

open the bedroom door. No one's in the corridor so I slip quickly across to the room marked bathroom. I pee, take a lukewarm shower and put the same clothes back on – no choice there. I shouldn't need to worry about smelly garments for long. Back in my room, I see that Nancy has an antiperspirant spray on her table. Surely she won't mind me having a quick shot of that. I shake the can and spray under my arms, place it carefully back on Nancy's locker in the position I hope she left it.

When I step out of Kathy's, the humidity and heat smack me across the face once again. I spend another few dollars on breakfast in another cancer-inducing cafe – God, I hadn't realised how good it is having smoke-free eating places in 2021 – and start walking back towards 6th Avenue and Greeley Square Park, where Jon disappeared.

I've often thought of Manhattan like a film set when I've visited before, but this is stranger. Because now I'm walking through a TV set straight out of *Starsky & Hutch* or *Taxi*; I half expect to see Judd Hirsch drive up beside me. But rather than watching through the comfort of a twenty-first-century box set, I'm walking down real streets having to keep an eye out in case someone draws a knife or pulls a revolver. It's more like a real-life video game, a potentially deadly one.

It's early afternoon by the time I reach the square/park. In the light of day, I can see it's on the corner of two streets and Broadway, and cars drive by on all three sides of the small triangular area. I find a free bench and... wait. The park is different in the daytime: there are still the loners and tramps, but there are plenty more people from multiple different cultures, families, too, the odd business person and a man selling hot dogs; the onions smell so good.

But the number of people and the non-stop traffic presents a problem: there's no way Jon could appear suddenly in the middle of this park without causing wide-spread amazement, more likely high consternation. Would he know that? Of course he would. With any luck, he'll try to land somewhere else, maybe back in Washington Square Park, and make his way up the island. But that, in turn, makes me think of something else.

'Where should I wait? I thought I should come here, but maybe I should go to Washington Square. I mean, what if he does go to that park and expects me to be there, too? If he can't find me inside a few hours, he'd have to go back and then he couldn't return again for another, I don't know, one or two days again. More. Shit. What should I do? Where should I wait? What would Jon expect me to do?'

An old man with a ragged coat and long beard is sitting at the other end of my bench – the tramp I saw last night. He growls at me. 'What the hell sort of question is that? You want me to tell you what?'

'What? No, I... What?'

Holy crap. Did I just say all that out loud? What was I thinking?

My neighbour stares at me for a few more seconds and then cackles and slaps his thigh. 'Good one, man. Sister. Good one!'

I sit stock still. But he doesn't say anything else. And no one else comes up to me, even looks at me. In a city where too many people have mental health issues and go around talking to themselves, another mad woman sitting on a bench nattering to herself isn't so abnormal. All the same, I better watch myself.

My self-examination does help in one way. Because the last point I asked myself has given me the answer to my original question: I have to wait where I am. As we both agreed at the Knebworth Festival when Bolan ran off and Jon chased after him, Jon knew he had to come back to find me where he had left me. He said that himself. So this is where I must wait. I think.

What will Jon be doing now? Whenever his 'now' is; it's an ethereal concept. I hope he is building a time-pen, but I remember that text he received just before we left for the Springsteen concert. That might mean he has a work commitment. What was it the text said? *Can we talk abt 2morrow? Can't wait.* Something like that. Not that it matters. He can go to whatever appointment that was and still print another time-pen when he gets home and it won't make any difference to my time here.

I remain in and around Greeley Square Park for the rest of the afternoon and into early evening, but there's no sign of my husband. It's hot but there is some shade in the square. Several times I reach automatically for my mobile phone before remembering I don't have it and it wouldn't make any difference if I did. But I do find a copy of yesterday's *New York Times*, August 21st 1978. It tells me President Carter is on a family vacation rafting down the Salmon River, a man in Massachusetts has kept a Frisbee aloft for 15.2 seconds, and there's a review of Stephen King's soon-to-be-published novel, *The Stand*. Zaina would find the Frisbee story hilarious. I wonder what she's doing now? I do a few exercises; again, no one blinks as I pace and stretch. I listen to conversations and hear discussions on everything from a meeting between US vice president Walter Mondale and Russia's leader, Leonid Brezhnev, through to the New York Yankees (a baseball team, I think) and what John Travolta is like in his latest film, *Grease*.

I finally cave in and buy a hot dog. It keeps me going till the evening. I stay in the park as long as I dare, even after it turns dark, as I half suspect Jon is more likely to arrive under cover of the night. Not only am I getting tired, but the atmosphere in the park changes significantly. Gone are the tourists, the worker reading a newspaper in their break and the hot-dog seller. The evening brings the druggies, the pushers, men who just stare at me and don't look away. I'm too scared to sit here any longer. I walk back to Kathy's. Today was more hope than belief for me, anyway; tomorrow onwards is when I really feel Jon is more likely to come back.

My room-mates are still out when I get back so I retire to bed and fall asleep.

17

I'm woken the following morning by someone slamming something on the foot of my bed. I open my eyes to see Nancy glaring down at me.

'Hey, new girl, what did I tell you yesterday?'

'Um…'

'Keep your fucking hands off my shit. That was the only thing I said. What part of that did you not understand?' She waves her antiperspirant at me. How the heck did she know I even used it?

'I'm sorry. It was so hot, I had to go out.'

'Ain't my problem. Buy your own. Don't use mine.' She thuds it back down on top of her cupboard. She could of course shut it away in her locker but that's clearly not her way. 'Do it again and I'll make sure Kathy moves you on.'

She slams the door as she leaves. Ling isn't in the room so I'm left alone. What jobs do these girls have that mean they come home late at night and leave late morning? Never mind. With any luck I won't see either of them again when Jon comes back for me today.

I get up, shower, leave Kathy's, walk towards Greeley

Square Park again. My dress is beginning to reek and my underwear is sticking to me. The first thing I'll do when I get home is have a long bath.

I get back to the park, sit down on the bench again. The tramp who I accidentally talked to yesterday is staring up into the sky; he sees me, does a jig on the spot and cackles. I give him a wry smile. This would still not be a place I would choose to hang out, but I can handle it. The sun beats down. I watch tourists buy hot dogs, an ambulance blares past, an Asian family – Korean? – play for a while on the small patch of grass, the temperature continues to rise...

The next moment, my neck snaps up uncomfortably. I must have dozed off for an instant. Shit, that won't do. The one thing I've learned is that if I drop my guard for a second then someone will try to steal my handbag. I clutch my bag closer to my body, twist the band around my wrist. I glance around more nervously, see the tramp, a few tourists taking photos and a young woman standing on the north side of the square outside a tall, elegant building. She's wearing a short dress, has a hairstyle that doesn't seem to suit her and a sleeve of tattoos and... Oh my, she's the same girl I saw the night Jon disappeared. I found her disconcerting then and I do so now. She sees me watching her and is clearly deliberating something, pulling uncertainly at various of her earrings. She starts to walk in my direction. I have two choices: confront her or run. I choose to run. She scares me and I've no desire to get into an argument, or worse – I can't imagine the consequences if I was to get hurt or, God forbid, get involved in a skirmish that got the police involved. I'd be royally screwed: no passport, no ID, little money – God knows what would happen.

I turn my back on her and run down Broadway, nipping between tourists, dodge around a parked car, into a department store, pause, walk smartly out again. I spin around but

I can't see the girl. I keep walking south, turning left and right until I find myself on 5th Avenue, surrounded by tourists and workers. I breathe in and stand with my back against a shop window. A businesswoman walks past me, wrinkles her nose.

I clasp my hands together. 'What am I going to do? I have to go back to Greeley Square but I'm too nervous to go back in case that girl is there. Which is stupid. Why am I worried? I should have confronted her, told her to piss off. I can't keep running away if Jon's going to meet me there. Stand up and fight your corner, Caroline.'

'You tell him, girl.' A black woman with a pushchair punches her fist in my direction – approvingly, not aggressively.

I've done it again – started talking to myself. I half laugh and push my hair back. So, what to do? I think of returning to Greeley Square, but instead, I walk down 5th to Washington Square Park, where Jon and I arrived. There's still a chance he could turn up there.

I reach the square and find a vacant bench near the end of the park where we landed for the Springsteen concert. I sit back and stretch out my legs. It's so warm; I wish I had a hat or sunglasses. But I'm watching every cent I spend for now. I watch the families play in the fountain, the buskers entertain the tourists and marvel again at the Frisbee players and roller-skaters. For a few minutes, I let myself sink into a seventies vibe while I admire my surroundings. There is so much going on that when I look back at the trees where Jon and I arrived, I understand immediately what a smart landing place that was. It would be extremely unfortunate if anyone happened to look at the specific tree that we appeared behind just as we did so, and even if they did, I reckon there's a good chance they would simply think we had just been hiding there. In theory, therefore, it should still be simple for Jon to arrive here again. Now. So why isn't he? I know that it's only the second day since he left and he, therefore, has to consider the risk of clashing wormholes, but surely this is the time to accept such risks and come and get me.

As the afternoon gets hotter, my skin gets clammier and my throat gets dryer. My willpower diminishes and I buy a vanilla scoop from an ice cream bicycle cart. It's delicious. The way the kids point at the man on the bike, it must be a vintage conveyance even now in 1978.

But there's no sign of Jon.

A couple with a screaming child walk past my bench, arguing, flinging their arms out in exasperation at each other's remarks. I start thinking about the last few months of my life and how tough it's been for Jon and me: my painting being vandalised, Bolan leaping out of my arms and running away. And Jon's disappointment and subsequent attitude to my decision that I didn't want to use the time machine to reverse history to prevent my miscarriage. That episode and the loss of our cat hit him hard. There were days, or even longer, when I felt that my husband truly resented me, even hated me.

I sit upright. A sickening thought thrusts itself into my mind. He did hate me, I know that. He even said he'd never forgiven me over my refusal to prevent my miscarriage. But, could he hate me so much, could he resent everything he feels I've done to him to the extent that... that he wouldn't come back and rescue me? Just abandon me here forever? Surely not. He couldn't do that, he wouldn't. Would he?

As I consider this and watch the couple with the braying child disappear into Manhattan, it hits me for the first time that if ever there was a man who would do such a thing, then Jon is that man. As Bee once said to me, you know better than any of us how he can blow hot and cold. I do know. I know exactly how he can be.

And now I think about that, it fucking terrifies me.

I pull my legs onto the bench and hug my knees. 'This isn't helping,' I chastise myself. 'Do not think like this, Caroline. Even if Jon does hate me, he will not abandon me here in another time. Even he wouldn't be that vindictive. It's simply the fact that I have only been here two days and he needs another few hours before he can return. I know that. I know that.'

I rock back and forwards on my bench. A man in a trilby hat carrying a briefcase walks up as if to sit down on the other end of my seat, takes one look at me and hurries away. I eventually stop rocking, close my eyes and turn my head towards the sun, willing it to burn away all these thoughts.

It's only hunger and the need to pee that finally drives me out of the park.

I head back to Kathy's, ordering myself to remain calm, driving my concerns out of my mind. Whatever happens, I have to survive here for at least another night. And tomorrow, I might find I'm a complete fool and Jon will turn up. That is more likely, isn't it? I wipe my brow. In fact, now I think about it, I probably have mild sunstroke from sitting outdoors all day and that's what is causing all these spurious thoughts. My God, of course – I feel better already. I push my shoulders back and stride along the sidewalk.

On my way back to the hostel, I find a department store and dip into my funds to buy new underwear, the cheapest dress I can find and a new bottle of antiperspirant for Nancy. I'll have to check when I'm back in my room how much money I have left, but I must still have a few dollars.

I reach my accommodation late afternoon and go upstairs to my room. When I open the door, I see that

Nancy is lying on her bed, wearing a cropped black top and short skirt. She doesn't move when I walk in. A small transistor radio sitting on her bedside cabinet is playing a tinny version of 'Roxanne' by The Police, fading in and out as the FM reception comes and goes.

I sit down on my mattress. 'I always wanted to see Sting live.'

Nancy looks over at me. 'Aren't you a bit old to go to gigs?'

'I... don't think so.'

'Anyway, Sting is just the singer. You mean The Police.'

'Ah, yeah. I forgot that.'

I rummage in my plastic bag from the department store and pull out the antiperspirant. I place it beside Nancy's radio. She glances across.

'I'm sorry I used your spray. You were right, you did tell me not to. I shouldn't have done it.'

Nancy sits up on her bed, back pressed to the wall, picks up the deodorant and turns it upside down. Then she tosses it back to me. I fumble as I try to catch it and Nancy grins.

'Keep it. You smell like you need it more than me.'

'Ah, thanks?' I smile back. She's right, of course.

My room-mate turns down the radio. 'So what's your story, Sweet Caroline? You ain't like most of the girls staying here. And do I detect a British accent?'

'I'm from London.'

'Cool. I'd love to go to England one day. What are you doing here? You're not staying in this dump while you're on vacation?'

'No, I, ah…' I sigh. I might as well tell her the truth, or an element of it. 'I came to New York with my husband, but he's… disappeared. I'm waiting for him to come back for me.'

'Ah, shit. That sucks. Men are such dorks. You really think he's coming back?'

'Of course.'

'And you want him to? You'll go back to him?'

'I… it's not like that. It's… more complicated.' I hear myself repeating what I told Judy, the waitress. I know it sounds a crap answer, but I am right. I am.

Nancy snorts. 'You know how long I been here? One and a half years. You know why? Eighteen months ago, I came from Ohio to New York with my boyfriend. We were gonna get jobs, make some money in the Big Apple. A new life. Two days after we arrived, he ran off with a white chick from New Jersey. Prick.'

'I'm sorry.'

'Three years we'd been together. He stole all my cash and took our gun.'

'You had a gun?'

'Hell, yeah. You gotta be careful in Gotham, new girl. Hey, no need to freak out about that.'

'We don't have guns in England. At least, not with the same liberal ownership that you have here.'

'Well, I ain't got one now. I couldn't anyway, Kathy would kick us out if she discovered we were packin' heat.'

She lies down again, puts her hands under her head. 'Fuck him and his honky. I'm doing fine now.'

'Good for you.'

'Wasn't how I imagined celebrating my twenty-fourth birthday, but hey.'

'So you've got a job?'

'I work in a bar in the village. Cool place. Good music. Joe Cocker came in once.'

'I've seen him live.'

'Damn, you are a dark horse, ain't you, new girl.' She turns the radio back up. 'Can I give you some advice?'

'Sure.'

'Take a freakin' shower and use that spray. You do not smell good.'

I laugh. When I come back into the room, dressed in my new clothes, Nancy is pulling on her boots.

'You got a shift?' I ask.

'Uh-huh.' Nancy stands up and runs her fingers through my hair. 'Ain't you got no shampoo? No? Look, you can borrow mine.' She flicks her head at her cabinet. 'Ling and I don't lock 'em; we trust each other. She works all night, too, so you won't see her so much.'

'Thanks.' I look at Nancy's braids. 'How do you keep your hair looking so beautiful? Isn't it expensive?'

Nancy grins. 'I got a sweet deal with a guy I know. No, not like that. I help him, you know, get some gear and he does my hair for me. I can introduce you, if you like.'

'I'll remember that,' I say. But inside I'm praying I can go to my hairdresser in Muswell Hill very, very soon.

'No problem. We gotta stick together, right? No one else is gonna look out for us.'

'Sure.' I see a paperback of Toni Morrison, *The Bluest Eye*, lying on Nancy's bed. 'Could I borrow your book if you don't mind? I've got a lot of time on my hands right now...'

Nancy nods, leaves for work. I wash my original dress and underwear, take the book and go out to find some cheap food.

I immerse myself in Nancy's novel and forget everything else.

18

I wake on my third day alone in New York City with my thoughts from yesterday rolling around my head. I skip breakfast and head up to Greeley Square Park. I still believe that this is where Jon will look for me. I sit on the same bench. The tramp I saw before is rooting around the bins of the park, but at least the young woman with the tattoos hasn't reappeared. But neither is there any sign of my husband.

I mull over everything I considered yesterday. Okay, I have to consider this rationally: even if Jon doesn't want to be with me anymore, would he really abandon me in another time and place? Is he that callous? I pick at my fingernails. I feel dejected and apprehensive. I guess I'm going to find out soon enough.

I sit and contemplate the tall building on the north side of the square. I heard someone say it was a welfare hotel for homeless families. Must be one heck of a lot of homeless in the city if that's the case. I bet these people wouldn't believe that would still be the case forty years from now. So much will change but plenty will stay the same.

Take that payphone in the corner of the park. Not an old-fashioned telephone booth, but a simple, open-air plastic box with a phone attached to it. Come to think of it, I haven't seen many of the older phone booths – Clark Kent would have serious problems getting changed in 1978 New York! But even the number of payphones will diminish in the years ahead. It's one of the strangest things to accept with my shift from the twenty-first century, not being able to easily phone someone on my mobile or send a text. In any other scenario where I was 'lost abroad', I'd just send a message to Jon or Bee and they'd get in touch instantly. Jon was forever checking his mobile when we were at home, receiving messages and calls from work at all hours of the day; that last text he got, for example, before we left for the Springsteen concert.

That text... I didn't think about it at the time. But now I'm wondering... I had automatically assumed it was a work message but what if I'm wrong and it wasn't from someone at work? What if it was from someone else, about something else? *Can we talk about 2morrow? Can't wait...*

My mind spins.

My God!

Is that possible? Could Jon have been arranging to meet someone else? Another… woman?

I clutch at my chest, swallow, grab the arm of my bench. I close my eyes and think. Maybe I'm jumping to conclusions again. It's a big step to go from someone is texting him about work to something… less innocent. That's ridiculous. On the other hand, *Can't wait...* Why would someone from his office be saying they can't wait? Unless it was a critical issue they needed to discuss, in which case surely Jon would have said that and called them back as soon as I handed him the phone in our basement. But if that does mean he's – go on, say it, I tell myself – having an affair, then who is it? Who would the damn hussy be?

I grit my teeth. It could of course be anyone. Why would I have to know her? In fact, it's more likely I wouldn't know her. It could be someone on our street, someone he met in a pub, or, I bet, someone he met at work. That's where most affairs happen, isn't it? A colleague, another lecturer, even a student…

I grab my head. An image drops into my mind. That day I went to his office before our dinner with Priscilla and Rosie, those three students sitting in his tutorial. The redhead, I can't recall her name, and the young, pretty blond girl, Elise. Elise. That name, he's mentioned her more than once or twice in the last few months, now I think about it. She was the one who gazed more intently at me, and when I walked into his office, she was the woman who pushed her necklace under her shirt collar…

The necklace.

I close my eyes. I don't want to do this but I must do. I have to know.

I replay that scene in my mind: I walk in, see the three students, Jon looks surprised, I look at Elise, see a flash of silver hanging around her neck and she hides it away. A flash of silver… I wind back my memory and freeze-frame it. And then I see it. What I missed when I was actually there. The flash of silver wasn't just her necklace, it was a pendant, a silver feather dangling from the end of it. A silver feather that Jon had bought only weeks earlier in Camden when we went back in time to the Stereophonics gig, and that I had presumed was a gift to surprise me. Well, it has surprised me. Just not in the way I had expected.

'He bought it for her,' I say aloud. He bought the necklace for Elise.

And just like that, it all falls into place.

The text he received, the necklace, and as I think back over recent months, the times he mentioned her name, that phone call he took in our kitchen when he told me his colleague had been assigned to jury service and he had to cover for him at a conference in Manchester. What's the betting that there was no conference, that he was organising a few days away with that slut instead? The little bitch.

Add all that to my realisation yesterday that he does hate me and there is only one conclusion: he is not coming back. I am fucked.

I push myself off the bench, stagger a few steps before I feel sick and have to lean forward, rest my hands on my knees. I'm sure there are people all around me but all I can hear is air rushing into my ears as if I have two conch shells strapped to the side of my head. I straighten up and lurch away from my seat, towards one of the roads that surround the park, the noise of the cars, the blare of their horns. I stand looking blankly across the lanes of traffic. See the hotel for the homeless on the other side of the square. I walk heedlessly towards it, tyres screeching, drivers screaming obscenities at me. I ignore them all. I gaze up, count the floors: sixteen. How many rooms are inside it? For some reason, I want to know.

I turn around and look back at the park. Is this where I will have to spend the rest of my life? Will I end up like that tramp?

I wipe my forehead. Damn, it's hot, and damn it but I'm sweaty. And damn Jon, damn him to hell.

Out of the corner of my eye, I sense a fast movement, someone running in my direction. I turn and see a man wearing sandals and a string vest sprinting down the street towards me. Within seconds, I can see the stubble on his unshaven chin, smell the sweat from his armpits. Before I know what's happening, before I can do anything, he barges his shoulder into my face, sending me flying onto my back, snatches up my bag and races off with it. I lie on the sidewalk and watch my life's belongings disappear up Broadway. No one runs after him, no one even shouts, and only two or three people even look down at me.

Slowly, I push myself up into a sitting position and gingerly stand up. I groan and reach for my lower back; I must have landed on my coccyx. It's agony. My elbow is bleeding, my thigh is already bruising and the skin on the palms of my hands is grazed and cut. I straighten up, ignore the pain in my spine and glare at passers-by, defying anyone to come near me. I needn't worry, no one is going to.

I close my eyes for a few moments, forcing the pain to go away. When I open them again, a child is standing in front of me; she can't be more than seven or eight. She holds out her hands and presents me with my bag. My jaw drops.

'I saw him run that way,' she says, pointing up the street where my attacker fled. 'He dropped the bag, so I fetched it for you.'

'Thank you. That's very kind of you.'

She smiles, skips away. I open my bag but with no belief that I will find anything of value in it. I'm right; my tissues and hand lotion are inside, Nancy's book, thank Christ, and so are a few coins, but nothing else. All the rest of my money, gone. All that for what, twenty bucks?

I cringe, roll my shoulders and begin to hobble back to my hostel. The only good thing about the pain is that it stops me from thinking further about Jon. Well, for some of the time.

When I push open the door to my room, Nancy is getting dressed for her evening shift. I collapse on my bed.

'Holy shit, new girl, what happened to you?'

'Mugged,' I lisp. My lip has ballooned up where my assailant's shoulder hit me in the mouth.

'Damn, stay there.'

Nancy disappears out of the door and returns with a bowl of water. She dips a cloth in it. 'Lie back. Let's sort you out.'

She wipes down my arm and leg, dabs my lip – I wince but I won't cry out – and forces me to roll onto my front. She gently prods my back; that does make me hiss.

'Hmm, nice bruises developing. But I think you'll live. What happened?'

I turn onto my side and tell her. She swears loudly. 'So you've no money left?'

'Just the coins in my bag.'

'Can you get some wired from home?'

'That could be... problematic.'

'Why?'

'I just can't.'

'Shit, Caroline, there's things you ain't telling me. I know that.'

'You wouldn't believe me if I did,' I say hoarsely.

'Well, you better hope that husband of yours comes back soon.'

'I don't think he is coming back.'

'Ah, that's just the shock talking, Caroline. He'll come find you.'

I shake my head. I'm pretty sure now that he won't.

Nancy says she has to go to work. I reassure her I'm fine and she slides out of the room. But she leaves me with a packet of aspirin, commandments on how often to take them and a bottle of water. I swallow two immediately.

They may help my physical pain, but I can't hold back my emotions. My shoulders heave, my eyes twitch and I bury my face in my hands and burst into tears. I hate myself for it, but I can't help it. I cry and cry and then I throw my head back and howl. A long, primal scream. My chest heaves further but my tears dry up. I lie staring at the ceiling. I'm sure someone must have heard my wail, but if they did, no one has come rushing in to check on me. Maybe this is normal for the inhabitants of Kathy's.

I cast my mind back to the meal we had in our house just before we left for the Springsteen concert. Jon was being so nice to me. So appeasing and complimentary. But all the while, he was buttering me up, preparing me for my final trip – to abandon me in the past. Damn him. No, fuck him. Fuck him to hell. Who needs a divorce if you can simply consign your wife to another era?

'But why didn't he just drug me, place me on the launch pad and send me spinning off to some time in history?'

The answer to that is obvious too: his fail-safe. He had, of course, programmed the time machine to always check we had the time-pen on us when we went on a trip, to ensure we weren't trapped in another time by accident. So he had to come with me. Of course, once we had arrived, he could have simply left me here in 1978 at any point, but even then, his vindictiveness and selfishness clearly kicked in and he went through with the whole Springsteen charade, the bar afterwards, our romantic stroll to the Empire State Building.

'Bastard.'

I close my eyes again. Tight, until I can see lights dancing on the inside of my eyelids. If all this is true, if I have worked out what he has done, then I am one hundred per cent truly and utterly screwed. I am stuck in 1978 forever, with no ID, no passport, in another continent with no one I know, now with no money, and with no chance whatsoever of returning to my time in 2021. I will never again see my house, my studio, my sister, Bee, my other friends. Anyone I know.

I stare at the wall opposite me for a long, long time.

Only when I can stand the pain in my back no longer do I take two more of Nancy's pills. It isn't long before I fall asleep, and thankfully, I'm dead to the world. They must be strong painkillers. I register Ling coming in at some hour of the night but I barely stir.

19

The next thing I know, light is streaming in through the window. Both my room-mates are asleep in their beds. As soon as I move, I cringe; I feel like a horse has kicked me. I want to get up to pee but I can tell that moving is going to hurt like billy-o. Eventually, my bladder wins and I slither onto the floor, ease myself to my feet and creep to the bath-room, doubled over like an old lady. I shuffle back to my room, collapse on the bed and prescribe myself two more aspirin. Sleep comes soon.

When I wake again, Nancy is sitting up on her bed, reading another novel. At first, I assume she hasn't gone to work yet, but the light outside indicates it can't be that early. I turn my head and see Ling's clock says three o'clock. I must have been sleeping for the best part of twenty-four hours.

Nancy notices I've woken up. 'Hey, how you feeling, sweet Caroline?'

I swivel my back. 'Not so bad.'

'That'll be those pills. I told you to only take one, remember?'

'Ah...'

'Ye-ah. You've had how many?'

'Ah... six?'

'Fool that you are. At least you're still alive.'

I mumble apologies. Nancy grins. 'Next time, baby, listen to me. Here.' She picks up what looks like a Chinese takeaway box from her bedside table and brings it over to me. 'You must be starving. Eat this when you're ready.'

'What is it?'

'Chinese take-out. What the fuck's it look like?'

I laugh and wince as my back spasms, but it's not so bad now.

'I really gotta go to work. Steve'll kill me if I'm late. You gonna be okay?'

'Sure. Thanks.'

'Get that food inside you. We can't have you looking emaciated when that dickless husband of yours turns up.'

I don't bother repeating that is unlikely to happen. I smile, nod slowly and carefully. Nancy leaves, not before removing all her pills except for a single one, which she allows me to keep for later. I try to sit up in bed, but my back is still painful. I take a pillow, put it on the floor and then sit on that with my spine hard up against the wall. That feels much better and I hesitantly take a mouthful of Nancy's Chinese. It's good, despite being cold. I wolf down the rest.

I rest my head against the wall and listen to the noises from the street below. My back actually feels much better; still sore, but I can twist it now with only minimal twinges. I examine my elbow; it still looks grazed, but it's fine.

The only pain is in my mind as I repeat to myself all that I was thinking about yesterday evening. I wonder again whether I'm right. I think so. But – and I'm not sure whether this is consoling or immensely depressing – there is still the possibility that I am wrong and Jon is coming back for me. But as this is day four after his departure, I will know by midnight. Because I am absolutely positive that, unless he's dead or he's lost his memory, neither of which I believe for a second, that four days is more than enough time to elapse for him to be sure it would be safe to return. That was the top end of his scale.

So, he has nine hours to prove to me I'm wrong.

I push myself into a standing position and accidentally brush something off the top of my bedside cabinet. I bend down. It's a five-dollar bill and a note from Nancy that says she is lending it to me until I get back on my feet again. I'm gobsmacked; I bet that must be close to twenty bucks in a 2021 comparison, and that can't be cash she can easily throw around. I swear to myself I will pay her back somehow. Although right now, I have no idea how.

I spend the rest of the day in Greeley Square Park. If there is any possibility that Jon will turn up, that will be where he comes. And rather than feeling scared about going back to where I was mugged, where I saw that young woman with the tattoo sleeve, I find I am quite nonchalant about it. If life has got anything else to throw at me, bring it on! I don't give a toss anymore. Someone can stab me for all I care. They won't get any money from me. What am I going to do now anyway? Live at Kathy's for the rest of my life?

I sit in the park, another hot and humid August afternoon, and watch the world go by. My back feels fine. I'm worried for a while that I can't see my long-bearded tramp, but he soon appears. The hot-dog seller is still here. One or two other faces I recognise. I sit and enjoy overhearing conversations again: politics, music, relationships. And, of course, the Yankees – they are having a tumultuous season by the sound of things. I wish I knew what happened to them this year, then I could reassure the fans that it would all be okay. Although no doubt Jon would chastise me for breaking the rule of the butterfly effect if I did that.

This does make me think of something: why is Jon apparently unworried about his precious butterfly effect by leaving me here? I'm considering this when my tramp sits down beside me on my bench. I smile at him; he doesn't worry me anymore. I don't even notice his smell; unless that means my aroma is just blending in with his.

'Back again?' he asks.

'You don't know the half of it,' I say.

He cackles. 'Tell me.'

I think for a moment. Hell, why not? Maybe there are some people you can talk to about time travel without it being an issue. After all, I told Veronica about our trips. Surely this man is another such case.

'I have a sister, you know,' I say to him. 'She has Huntington's disease. It's still not curable, even in 2021. That's when I'm from. And as it looks like I'm stuck here, the saddest thing, the most vindictive thing that my husband is doing through this plan of his, is to ensure that I will never see Veronica again. But she will remember me. She'll be okay because Zoe will take care of her until she dies, but it breaks my heart to think that she'll believe I don't care about her anymore. That's terrible, isn't it?'

The tramp frowns, mimes confusion.

I shake my head. 'I'm sorry, I'm not making much sense, am I? Let me start again. My husband left me here four days ago when you first saw me.' The tramp spits on the ground. 'Yeah, my thoughts exactly. But that's only part of the story. Because what he actually did was return to our time in 2021 without me. What do you think about that?'

The tramp tugs at his long beard.

I carry on. 'That is seriously fucked up, isn't it? Because

I've been thinking: wouldn't he be concerned that by sending me back in time and leaving me here, I could do or say anything? Why would he risk that?' The tramp shrugs. 'Mind you, I'm not sure what I could say that would disrupt history. I don't know my American politics very well, except for the presidents and post-2000, like most people. You know, Nine-eleven, Obama, Trump. But even the year 2000 is twenty-two years away. If I'm still here then, I'll be... good God, sixty-four. I can't even contemplate that. Jon knows I'm not going to kill anyone, or I don't know, invent the internet before that should happen. The best I could hope for would be to follow Andrew's advice and invest in a small unknown company called Apple whenever Steve Jobs forms that. If I had any money.'

The tramp nods seriously.

'But now I know he hates me. He despises me because of everything he thinks I've done to him. Because he clearly wants to be with a woman twenty years younger than me. But he doesn't want to divorce me, he could never kill me, so abandoning me, banishing me to a time quite literally before I was born, is the perfect tactic for him.

'Actually, that's an interesting point. I will be born in England in two months' time. How freaky is that? If I could board an aeroplane, I could go and witness my own birth!'

We both laugh.

'No, when it comes to Jon's butterfly effect, my guess is that he thinks "the timeline" will fix itself, in the way he claimed it would if we had gone back to 2010 to help me have a baby. Although, I wonder... What if we had done that? What would have happened then? Would I still be here? Would Jon still have had an affair?

'Or am I wrong? Now I'm here, before my own birth, will I disappear from Jon's timeline? Will my friends forget I even exist? Surely not; I'm still alive and I lived my first forty-two years with them. Well, twenty-five years since I met Bee and everyone at Bristol. I'm just in another time zone at this moment, the same as when Jon and I went on our trips. I don't think Bee was forgetting me when we were doing that.'

I turn to look into the tramp's eyes. 'It's enough to make you go mad, isn't it?'

The man beside me rubs his chin. 'You don't sound any madder to me than most people.'

We contemplate that in silence. And as the daylight dwindles and the night comes on, as the tourists disappear and the night crawlers come out, as the wail of the sirens increases, we sit side by side on our bench while the world goes on around us. No one stabs me. No one even threatens us.

The crowds have all but dispersed from Broadway. But I have no idea whether it's ten p.m. or one in the morning. I turn to my companion. 'Do you know what time it is?'

The tramp holds up a finger and thrusts his hand deep into his coat pocket. He retrieves an exquisite gold watch on a chain, like something you see in the movies. He hands it to me and I turn it over in awe. I hold it to my ear and hear it ticking methodically. It says eleven forty-five; fifteen minutes left for Jon to make me eat humble pie. We sit together and watch the hands on the timepiece move around. It's mesmeric and beautiful. When it reaches midnight, I stretch and hand back the watch to the old man. He grins and returns it to the depths of his pocket.

I stand up and walk away.

20

I walk back to Kathy's and go to bed but I'm awake most of the night. Nancy and Ling come in some time in the small hours. I pretend to be asleep. I don't want to talk to them now. I do need to talk to Nancy in the morning, but it can wait until then.

The girls rise around ten and I stretch and join them. I thank Nancy for the five dollars and she waves it away.

'I know you'll pay me back, new girl.'

'I will, I promise.'

'Cool.'

'But to do that, I do need to earn some money.'

Nancy pauses while buttoning up a shirt. 'Do I detect a new ploy, sweet Caroline?'

I sit down on my bed. 'I don't think Jon's coming back for me.'

Nancy and Ling exchange a glance. 'I gotta shoot,' Ling says. 'See ya both later.' She slips out of our bedroom. Nancy sits down beside me.

'I'm sorry, Caroline.'

'You were right. Men are shits.'

'Some men.'

'Yeah, I know.'

'What changed your mind?'

'I just know. He had four days to show up. He hasn't. And I'm pretty sure that's that. He's left me here to fend for myself.'

'And you really don't know anyone in England who can send you money?'

'Believe me, if I did, I would do that in a flash.'

'You could go to your embassy. They might lend you some or repatriate you.'

'I've thought about that,' I lie. 'I will do, but it's going to take time to organise. In the meantime, I need cash now. My rent's coming up and I have this debtor I owe a wad of greenbacks and I don't want to get on the wrong side of her again.'

Nancy punches me in the arm. 'She'll understand. As long as you drop that goddamn awful attempt at our slang.'

'Thanks.' I turn to face my room-mate, my new friend. 'I think I only have two choices.' I hold up my left hand and wiggle my fourth finger. 'I could pawn this, but I'm not ready to do that yet. That's my last resort. Which means I've got to get a job. Without a visa or ID. So, I was wondering, do you think there might be any vacancies in your bar?'

Nancy narrows her eyes, doesn't answer immediately. 'There's something you ain't telling me, sweet Caroline.'

'There is. But I can't. I'm sorry. Maybe one day, but not now.'

'Hmm, I don't know. Don't take this the wrong way, but all the waitresses are... closer to my age than yours.'

'Please, Nancy. I don't know what else to do. All I'm asking is that you introduce me to your bar owner. I'll do the rest.'

Nancy blows out her cheeks. 'We can ask. Steve is partial

to a little melanin so you have a shot. Don't expect him to pay you minimum wage, not if you're gonna get paid under the table.'

'Thank you.'

'And don't expect the barflies to go easy on you. Most are fine, but some wanna just call me out as a nigger.'

I try not to look as shocked as I feel. I fail miserably.

Nancy shrugs. 'I've met racist shits all my life. You know how that feels.'

I don't. Not like she does. I lean over and hug her. It hurts like hell to remember that the last time I embraced a woman half my age was when I hugged Melanie that evening at Bee's.

I put on the dress I arrived in and we walk across Manhattan to Greenwich Village. 'It saves me a few bucks to walk there,' Nancy explains. 'But after a late shift, I usually catch a bus home, or every now and then Steve throws down for a cab. I guess if you do get a job, we can share a taxi home together! Hey, I like that.'

'Did you waitress back in Ohio?'

'Once or twice. I left school with no qualifications so I worked wherever I could. Bars, shops, office receptions. I even had a few gigs in sideshows and carnivals for a summer or two, travelling around the state. You know, "Come and see the freaks: the strongest man, the smallest woman..." But I never held a job for long. Not that I cared. I was more concerned about getting my next score, finding a jam session.'

'The circus. Wow, sounds... exciting.'

'Hmm. Not all of Ohio is the picture-perfect, beautiful tourist photos you see of Columbus. I'm from Dayton. The crime rate there is double the national average, you know that? These last few years, manufacturing jobs have been disappearing in their thousands and NCR have been laying off guys like there's no tomorrow. That's another reason why my shithead boyfriend and I came here. At least there are some jobs. What about you? I assume you've got experience of working in bars in England?'

'Of course,' I say and drop my eyes.

You know when you're in Greenwich Village no matter what era you live in. The shop names may change, the cars and lapels grow larger or smaller with the fashion, and the streets are certainly cleaner in 2021, but you still see the same brownstone buildings, those familiar iconic metal fire escapes running up the sides of the structures, cast-iron stair bannisters on the stone steps and the coolest bars. We walk along West 9th Street and I recognise where I am. Washington Square Park is two blocks away – could Jon still be waiting for me there? No, I scold myself. He won't be. He's not coming back. Nancy leads me past The Stonewall Inn, up and across a few streets and we stop on a corner outside a bar: Steve's Tavern. The door is wide open and I can hear rock music pounding from inside. A chalkboard on the outside wall lists bands that are playing here in the coming days; no names I recognise.

'It ain't too busy this time of day,' Nancy says. 'Come on, let's find Steve.'

We walk in and I have to remind myself I'm not on a TV set. There are small, square wooden tables packed in tight, names scratched into the tabletops from years of drinkers' carvings, rickety chairs alongside them. Paper menus promote burgers, fries, chilli dogs, club sandwiches. The bare brick walls are covered with photos, mostly black and white shots of musicians, but there's the odd sportsman and a couple of a man holding an enormous fish. There's barely space for any more frames, although a Stars and Stripes is draped at the back of the room, right above a huge clock straight out of an old American movie. Like you see on a station concourse. A few barstools stand in front of the long mahogany bar, beer taps lined up along it, and shelves and shelves of bottles of spirit behind, all colours of the rainbow. I can't see the speakers where the music is coming from but it's loud.

Nancy grabs my wrist. 'Steve'll be in the back room.'

We walk through the main bar into a second room, furnished very similarly to the bar except for a low stage at the far end. The music from the main bar is muffled. Standing on the podium is a musician playing an acoustic guitar in front of a microphone. He's being watched by a man sitting on a chair with his feet propped up on a table. He interrupts the singer.

'Yeah, thanks, dude. We'll let you know, okay.'

'Come on, Steve,' the guitarist says miserably, 'give me a break.'

Steve swats away the man's plea, turns around and sees Nancy and me.

'Hey, Nancy, about time. Wanda's just skipped out on me so I need you to do a double shift, okay?'

'Yeah, okay,' Nancy says heavily.

'Great, now leave the customers alone and get to work.'

'This ain't a customer, Steve, she's my mellow. She's looking for work.'

Steve grins. 'Dream on, Nancy. Come on, let's go.'

Nancy flicks her head at me. I approach Steve. He's dressed in a half-unbuttoned lumberjack shirt and jeans, hair down to his shoulders, a cheeky smile, but he could be my age.

'Hi, I'm Caroline. I really am looking for a job. It'd be great to work here.'

'Hey, a Brit. Love your accent. Nancy, get this fox a drink. First one's on the house, babe.'

'Thank you. But I don't want a drink. I do want a job.'

'You're joshin' me.' Steve laughs, looks me up and down. 'You look good for your age, I'll give you that, but my customers expect someone a little younger, you dig?'

'Oh, right, you mean like Wanda. The girl who's just run out on you.'

'So?'

'Well, I guess you've got to ask yourself, do you want a young bimbo who's gonna skip off with the first man who flatters her, and may or may not turn up.' I turn to Nancy. 'Sorry, Nancy, no offence.' Nancy holds her hands up in mock horror. 'Or do you want a hard-working reliable woman who knows the ropes and digs the scene? Someone who won't cause you any problems.' I see Nancy out of the corner of my eye grinning like the Cheshire Cat.

Steve's smile has gone. 'Are you serious?'

Now the guitarist has left, I can hear the music wafting through from the main bar. I put my hand to my ear. 'This is Zeppelin, right?'

'Yes.'

'Shall I tell you about the time I met Robert Plant and he offered to take me for a ride in his limousine?'

Steve purses his lips. I wonder if my last lie was too much. The bar owner waves a hand at my room-mate. 'Okay, Nancy, off you go.' He beckons me closer. 'I'm presuming you haven't got a visa.'

'Have all your staff?'

'Touché. Well, I guess my customers will love your accent. Tell you what, I'll give you a trial. Starting tomorrow.'

'I thought you said Wanda hadn't turned up.'

'Jeez, you're a spunky chick. Alright, get behind the bar, ask Nancy to show you the ropes.'

'Thanks, Steve. You won't regret it.'

'I know.'

I push my hair behind my ear. 'Um, there is one more thing. I don't suppose I could get an advance on my wage?'

'Don't push it, babe.'

'I know, I'm sorry. It's just, my husband's run off, I'm here alone. I need to pay this week's rent and I'm down to my last nickel…'

Steve lifts his chin. 'Okay, I know how hard it can be to get back on your feet when you're going through rough times. Look, I'll pay you today's wages tonight, and then you get paid weekly in arrears, yeah?'

I dash off to find Nancy before he can change his mind. At least I'll be able to pay Kathy for another week's rent. But that's where my good news ends.

The next ten hours are a baptism of fire.

I waited tables at a small cafe in Bristol when I was a student, but that's my only similar experience. And it shows. I get orders wrong, I forget orders, I give out the wrong change, I don't clean down the tables when customers leave. I've never heard of half the drinks and once or twice I can't even understand what the patrons have asked for. Nancy does her best, chivvying me along, covering for me when I screw up, placating the angrier customers with a wink or an extra shot. I try to ignore the constant cigarette smoke, but I'm not used to it and it stings my eyes. Steve stands behind the bar, alternating between shaking his head and looking amused. The customers themselves, the regulars I guess from the way they talk to the bar staff, don't know what to make of me. As Steve predicted, some appear taken by my English accent, but others ask Steve bluntly and in front of my face why he's taken on a middle-aged coon.

By midnight, the place is heaving. I've been on my feet most of the night, but I've spent years standing up for hours at a time painting so that doesn't bother me. But it's so hot in the bar, and the aircon unit at the back of the room shouldn't be allowed to call itself that. Although I've tied my hair up, I feel sweaty under my arms, on my nape, even down the backs of my knees. A huge man in a lumberjack shirt calls me over to his table, and as I weave towards him carrying a full tray of drinks, another guy sticks his leg out and I trip right over it. The drinks go flying and customers are standing up and shouting or laughing, depending on how drunk they are.

Steve appears by my side. 'Take a break, Caroline. Come back in five.'

I nod, stand behind the bar and curse myself. Why did I think I could cope with this? Surely there have to be easier ways to make a living? More appropriate ways for a forty-something-year-old. I curse Jon silently for the tenth time today and simultaneously wish I could cry on his shoulder.

I wipe my skin and look back at where Steve and Nancy are cooling down the customers. I wonder if Steve will even let me keep the job after this. The bar owner whispers in Nancy's ear then heads off to another part of the bar. Nancy fetches more drinks and gives me a brief fist punch. I try to smile back. I watch her glide between the tables as if they don't exist, carrying a tray laden with bottles one-handed. She places them on a table and bends over to pick up the empties. Which is when one of the men at the table smacks her on the rear. Hey, he can't do that! Nancy, however, just grimaces, rolls her shoulders and carries on loading the tray. I have to remind myself that this is 1978 and that sort of thing is pretty much acceptable. But just as Nancy is about to stand up, the same guy grabs the front of her shirt and tries to pull her onto his lap. Nancy has both hands on her tray and she can't do anything to protect herself. This is too much for me to take.

I stride across to the table and, standing behind Nancy's aggressor, yank the man's hair. Being the seventies, there's plenty of hair for me to grab. He yowls and whirls around, but at least he lets go of Nancy's shirt. Seeing me, he shoves back his chair and stands up. 'Why you little—' he starts and pulls back his arm. I brace myself for the punch but at that moment, Steve slides in-between us, grabs the customer by his lapels and drags him out of the bar. Around us, other customers cheer and I feel hands slapping me on the back and arms held aloft to offer me high-fives. I vaguely slap my wrist at one or two like a floppy fishtail.

Steve appears by my side. 'Come with me, Caroline.'

He guides me behind the bar and into a small room with a desk and filing cabinets; his office, I presume. It's quiet in here. I'm breathing heavily and my hair has fallen down over my shoulders again. My brand new boss perches on the edge of the desk.

'What were you doing in there?' he asks softly.

I wipe my hand down my cheek, across my mouth. 'I'm sorry, Steve. I saw that man grab Nancy. I couldn't let him get away with that.'

'So I saw.'

'I know I shouldn't have got involved. It wasn't the right thing to do. But from where I'm from, we don't allow that sort of thing. I had to try to help her.'

'I know.'

'So.' I take a deep breath. 'Let's get this over with.' I hold my arms out. 'Say what you want before you fire me and I'll get out of your hair.'

Steve folds his arms. 'Are you freakin' kidding me? Why would I fire you?'

'What? But I, I mean…'

The bar owner grins. 'Okay, I admit it. Right up until that point, I was going to fire you. But if there's one thing I value most in an employee, it's loyalty and support to other staff. And that's what you showed there. The jerk had it coming. You did the right thing and I applaud you for it.'

'Oh. Thank you?'

Steve shakes his head. 'I do need you to improve your waitressing skills. I'll get Nancy to give you some one-to-one tomorrow. But we can show you how to do that. I can't show you how to stand up for your colleagues. Thank you.'

He walks around behind his desk, unlocks a drawer and removes a roll of dollar bills. He peels some off and hands me the cash. 'Let's call it a night. I'll see you tomorrow.'

'Thank you! I won't let you down again.'

He nods. I leave his office and stand behind the bar. Nancy sees me and mouths 'wait there'. She skids over and throws her arms around my neck. I hug her back gently. Several of the customers sitting at the bar bang their palms on the counter and whoop in the way that only Americans know how.

I wait for an hour until Nancy finishes her shift, chatting with the regulars, and then we share a cab back to Kathy's. In our room, Nancy presses her finger to her lips and pulls out a bottle of Listerine from her bedside table. She uncaps it and takes a swig, holds the bottle out to me.

'Oh. No,' I say politely. 'It's not my thing. I mean…'

Nancy swivels the bottle with her wrist. 'It isn't actually mouthwash, you dumb Brit. But Kathy doesn't let us have alcohol in our rooms, comprendé?'

'Ah…' I take the bottle from her, sniff it and swallow a mouthful of, I'm not sure, whisky or brandy or something strong. I cough violently and Nancy peels with laughter. We're still giggling half an hour later when Ling comes in. Nancy tells her what I did this evening. Ling is impressed and tells me I did good. Then, she and Nancy start a story about how Ling once chased a cyclist down the street after he nearly ran over one of her friends.

I sit and listen and laugh along. If I was to close my eyes and swap their accents, I could be back in my halls in Bristol twenty-five years ago, pissing myself at something that Bee or Teri had done the previous night in the student union bar.

I have to blink back the tears when I think about how I'll never see either of my friends again.

21

The next eight weeks are some of the most tiring, surreal but occasionally fun times of my life. I get better at wait-ressing thanks to Nancy's patience, and as I promised Steve, I am hardworking and reliable. My accent does gain me tips and I discover that there are plenty of customers who prefer the 'more mature woman', as Steve says. It makes Nancy howl with laughter when the men flirt with me.

I am right that many of the other staff at Steve's Tavern are like me; immigrants with no visa or green card, probably being exploited terribly by the bar owner, but hey, he's given us all jobs. He pays promptly.

Slowly, my life becomes, well, my life. Everything is so different when you're working in a foreign city and not a time-travelling tourist. We adapt as humans, even to living in a different era, apparently. I have to learn the layout of the city, find cheap places to eat when I'm not working at Steve's, go to the launderette. I don't miss my car, email, taking the Tube; I do kind of miss my mobile phone. And my studio and my friends, of course. Sometimes, music I hear reminds me of a trip Jon and I went on, and for a moment, I don't hate his guts. That doesn't last for long when I remember I'll never again see Bee.

All my money is going on rent, food, day-to-day necessities, more than one set of clothes, and, one time only, a haircut at a cool stylist. It only takes Nancy two days to suggest that I need to visit her hair salon. We go down to the Lower East Side one afternoon and she introduces me to Jeff, a hip black guy who happily gives Nancy a styling session in exchange for a few grams of weed. I don't ask her how she gets that. I have nothing to barter with so I pay for my haircut, thankfully at a reduced rate.

'Who cuts your hair?' Jeff asks me as I sit in his chair.

'I… it was done in England.'

'That's the style there?'

'It was when I left.'

'So whadda you want? Braids like your girl here? Afro? You could carry off a Jayne Kennedy look.'

'Who?'

Jeff and Nancy exchange a look of horror.

'The first African-American woman to be crowned Miss Ohio. Where've you been, sister?'

'England!'

'So?'

I had been thinking about this. 'I want something completely different.'

'Okay…'

'Do you know Liza Minnelli?'

And so, much to Jeff's chagrin, I come out with short hair; far easier to manage and a homage to Teri. When I look in the mirror, I barely recognise myself. I doubt anyone from 2021 would. What would Bee say! It makes me yearn even more for my friends from England. And Veronica. I miss them all terribly. What do they think has happened to me? What has Jon told them about my sudden disappearance? I'll never know.

On one more occasion only do I walk back up to Greeley Square Park just in case there's any message for me, something scratched into a tree or written on a bench. There isn't. I'm not surprised.

But most of the time, I work at Steve's Tavern, sleep on my days off or visit New York tourist spots I've never seen before: the Statue of Liberty, Grand Central Terminal, Carnegie Hall. Nancy and Ling find it most strange that I want to visit the World Trade Center.

I do forget myself once or twice. Steve has good connections in the underground music scene and some of the bands that play in his backroom are fantastic. I haven't recognised any of the artists yet (although Steve is forever boasting that Debbie Harry sang here before she was famous), but when I overhear Steve talking about Cafe Wha? I mention that I saw Jimi Hendrix there.

'That was twelve years ago!' Steve says. 'When he played as Jimmy James and the Blue Flames. What made you go to Cafe Wha?'

'Ah… my husband,' I say honestly.

'You came all the way over here just to go to a gig?'

'Nooo. He came here on business, and I came, too. He'd heard about Manny Roth and he wanted to visit his club. It was just serendipity we happened to be at the hootenanny when Hendrix was playing.'

'You went to *that* gig?'

It earns me great kudos with my boss.

We're both sad when news of Keith Moon's accidental overdose is announced in September. Steve reminisces about seeing The Who live on their *Quadrophenia* tour in the early seventies. I keep my mouth shut about Woodstock.

I also come close to saying all sorts of things when news

breaks that a millionaire called Donald Trump is renovating the derelict Commodore Hotel in midtown. I have to bite my tongue for days. Fortunately, most news is new news to me, too – even international reports about what James Callaghan's government is doing in Britain, so I steer clear of any temporal indiscretions concerning that.

On October first 1978 I celebrate my forty-third birthday and my birth day; because October first 1978 is the day I was born – am being born – in London, England. It freaks me out to think about it that way – what a screwed up concept. As it's a Sunday and Steve's Tavern is quiet, our boss lets me have a mini-party in the evening. Officially I'm working, but there's only him, Nancy and a dozen or so regulars in the tavern. I drink far too much and go from happy to morose in no time.

Nancy joins me at a table where I am staring into my glass. 'Why the long face, sweet Caroline? It's your birthday. Let your hair down!' She runs her fingers across my very short hair. 'One or two strands anyway.'

'Thanks, Nancy.' I raise my glass to her.

'Are you still thinking about him?' she asks.

'Jon? I can't help it. He's up here.' I tap my temple. Along with my friends and my sister, I say in my head.

'I still don't get why you don't want to go back to your crib. Even if he is there.'

'I know. Maybe I'll tell you one day.'

'When you're ready.'

'When I'm ready.'

'Did you like your present?'

I twist a thin silver bracelet around my wrist. 'I love it, Nancy. I hope it wasn't expensive.'

'With what Steve pays us?' We laugh. 'Hey, it might mean I can't get a new tattoo this month, but that's cool.'

'Jon gave me a Steve Harley CD for my birthday last year. It took a lot for him to buy that, to not buy the vinyl version, but it meant I could listen to it in my studio.'

'He gave you a what?'

'A C—' My tongue sticks to the roof of my mouth. Shit! What am I saying? The first commercial CD wasn't released until the early eighties. Damn, this living in the past is so difficult. Especially when you're drunk. I think fast – what would Jon say?

'It's… an inside joke. We… I got drunk one time and kept slurring my words. You know, Stevey… see dee.' I flap my hands in front of my face. 'Not funny, I know. But it meant something to us.'

Nancy drums her fingers on the table. 'You're weird sometimes, new girl.'

I shrug. 'I can't deny that.'

Steve drops into a chair opposite us, bringing Des with him, one of our regulars – a beautiful black man. 'Did I hear you call my name?' our boss inquires.

Nancy stands up. 'It was a private conversation. There is more than one Steve in the world, you know.'

'Only one that matters,' Steve says with a wink.

'Ego the size of this bar, wouldn't you say?' Des says.

I clink my glass against his a bit too forcefully and liquid slops out of both our drinks.

Steve grins. 'I'll get you another, Caroline. On the house, don't worry – it is your birthday.'

He tells Nancy to get me whatever I want and returns to schmooze his regulars. Des and I are left on our own. He smiles broadly. Damn, he's good looking.

I don't go back to Kathy's when my shift/party finishes. Des lives in Chelsea, just north of the village, and he invites me back to 'see the views of the Hudson River'. It's as good a line as any. I wonder if I should do what my body is yearning to do – I am still married, formally, and it's less than three months since Jon left me. But fuck it, that's the point – he left me. I go back with Des.

I don't see Nancy until late the following evening, when she arrives back to Kathy's from her shift. I am already lying in bed, reading. Ling is still working. Nancy bounds in, jumps into my bed with me and tells me to 'spill the beans or else'. I feel like a twenty-year-old again! My room-mate listens, squeals and jabs me in the ribs. She digs out her mouthwash bottle and lights up a spliff, taking care to smoke out of the window so Kathy doesn't notice. ('Although she's not that stupid,' she says, 'she tolerates us okay.') We lie in bed together and listen to the car horns and late-night party-goers on the street four floors below.

'How come you're so comfortable talking to me?' I ask Nancy. 'When I was your age, I would never have gone drinking with a woman, um…'

'Twenty years older than you?'

'I'm not that – yes, well, nearly.'

Nancy inhales. 'In case you hadn't noticed, I ain't like the other girls. Ha! Corny line, eh. But it's true. When I was in high school back in Dayton, the other chicks didn't dig me. I found it hard to make friends – it's one of the reasons I split – so most of the women I knew then were those who hung around with my mother. I enjoyed listening to their tall tales and their lewdness. You… no, you don't remind me of them, you're even easier to be with.'

I give her a hug. That's the nicest thing anyone has said to me in months (other than Des, but he had ulterior motives).

'What about your father?'

'He trucked out when I was at preschool. We don't know where he is now.'

'So why did you decide to come to New York?'

'I told you once before, right? I came with my cheese weasel of a boyfriend to make some money.'

'And that was all?'

Nancy shifts her body. 'I dunno. I guess at one point I thought I might be the next Shirley Chisholm.'

'Who?'

'You been hiding under a stone, new girl?'

'I'm from England, remember.'

'Ah, yeah. Well, she was the first-ever female candidate to run for president, back in seventy-two. I thought I could follow in her footsteps in some small way.' She takes a drag on her spliff, offers it to me. I wave it away. She blows smoke out of the window. 'Turns out racism and disempowerment of women in New York ain't somethin' that is just in *All in the Family* – bigotry is alive and kickin' in real life.'

I know a bit about *All in the Family*. It was a controversial US sitcom in the seventies, some say groundbreaking, that tried to address all sorts of social issues, from racism and antisemitism to the Vietnam War. The main character, Archie Bunker, would have got on well with our Alf Garnett.

'There are some decent black sitcoms aren't there?' I say. 'What about *The Cosby Show*?'

'The what? You mean *Fat Albert and the Cosby Kids*?'

'Er, yes…' Damn, maybe *The Cosby Show* hasn't started by 1978. I still need to watch my mouth.

Nancy shakes her head. 'Yeah, well, I don't know whether I dig how that portrays blacks either, but I guess it's better…'

'So what happened? Have you given up on emulating Shirley Chisholm?'

'No. But it ain't that easy.'

'So what do you want now?'

She shoots me an indignant look. 'Damn, Caroline, you sound like my school counsellor.'

I stroke her arm. 'Come on, Nancy, you know what I mean.'

'Shit, I don't know. Earn enough to send some cash home to my mom, that'd do for now. I guess ultimately I wanna be in control of my own destiny. I ain't got no qualifications so I don't wanna be reliant on lookin' to someone else to give me a gig. And yes, I'd like to meet someone again.' She pauses, twists her head away from me. 'Someone I can trust, who wants to look after me.'

'You must have a dozen men you could choose from.'

'Yeah, right. You seen the type of dude I meet in Steve's. That the kind you wanna shack up with?' She turns to face me again. 'Anyway, I could ask you the same question.'

'I'm married.'

'He ain't comin' back, sweet Caroline.'

'I know that.'

Nancy sits up, cross-legged and looks down at me. 'So come on, enough of your evasion. Tell me the truth, new girl. What's your real story?'

I stare up at the ceiling. 'The truth? Okay. I'm a time-traveller from the year 2021.'

Nancy giggles. 'Solid! I can almost believe that. So tell me about your future family, other than that shithead husband of yours.'

'Well, my sister, Veronica, she has Huntington's. It's a shitty disease. She's going to die from it soon.'

'Way to cheer me up.'

'That's how it is. But if you want cheery, then there's my friend, Bee. I met her at Bristol University on my first day and we've been best buddies since.'

227

'Best friends, Caroline. I've told you before, you can't do American.'

'Okay. So she's married to Andrew, he's a bit of a know-it-all, but we all go back to our freshers year, so we have shared history.'

'And they can't wire you money?'

'Don't, Nancy.'

'Okay.' She sighs, takes a toke. 'It must have been so different back then.'

'Yes, well, not that different, I mean it was only...' Shite. When would it have been? I can't say it was 1996 when I met Bee. Or '97, when I was introduced to Jon. If I'm not careful, I'm going to blunder into more transgressions of time as I did with the Cosbys and last night when I mentioned CDs. I do some quick calculations in my head. 'Well, yes, it was the mid-fifties so we didn't have fancy things like VCRs and seatbelts.'

'Was it just like *Happy Days*?'

'Oh my God! Yes, it was just like *Happy Days*. I was Joanie and Jon was The Fonz.' I clip Nancy playfully across the head. 'Trust me, growing up in England in my time was nothing like Milwaukee in the fifties.'

We lapse back into a comfortable silence. Jon was as cool as The Fonz to me then. The bastard. Why didn't he stay cool and just tell me he wanted a divorce? I stroke Nancy's hair, and I can't help but think, is this what it would have been like to have had a daughter? I've never had a girlfriend Nancy's age, and with Bee's kids I was always Auntie Caroline, who played with them, spoiled them and listened to their woes about their parents, but I never had conversations as I find I'm having with Nancy. It's quite seducing. I close my eyes. The strains of Paul Simon's 'America' filters through our open window from a building across the street. I steady my hand.

A flicker of an idea enters my mind.

'Nancy,' I murmur. 'You know what happened when you came to New York with your boyfriend?'

'You mean when the scumbag skipped out on me?'

'Yes, that. If you... I mean...' I need to choose my words carefully. I try again. 'If you could warn your younger self what was going to happen when you came to New York, that your boyfriend was going to run off with another girl, would you do that?'

'Mmm, what?'

Nancy is falling asleep, but I want to ask this. 'Would you warn yourself? If you could go back in time and do so.'

'What are you talking about?'

'And if you would, then would you avoid coming to New York?'

Nancy doesn't answer. Her breathing is slower now, the alcohol and weed working their way through her. Just as I think she's fallen asleep, she mutters, 'Sure I'd still come. But if I went back in time before that, I'd go and kick his sorry ass so that he never came near me in the first place.'

I stifle a laugh. Of course, that is exactly what she would do. Me, I don't have that luxury. It's what I was sort of going to do that night before Jon had so smoothly suggested we go see Bruce, but that would have been the end of our relationship, it wouldn't have stopped it happening. And even if I could do that, if I had Jon's time machine here, now, at my disposal, I still wouldn't go back to 1997 and tell myself not to fall for Jon. That is what I did, that is what my life became. I don't want to change that.

But I might still go back in time and tell me not to go to New York with my husband. And I'm starting to have the first inkling of an idea for how I could do that.

22

I'm worried about Nancy. It's now the middle of October and the more time I spend with her, the more I enjoy her company. She's like no other friend I've ever had, and from what she says, it's the same for her. There may be twenty years' age difference between us (and another forty years she doesn't know about in terms of our real timelines), but that doesn't seem to matter. Living in the same room, working at the same place means we've learned a lot about each other's habits and nuances.

Which is why I've noticed a change in her demeanour for the last few days. This afternoon, she even asked Steve if she could go home halfway through her shift because she was feeling unwell. Very unusual – she's not taken as much as an hour off in the time I've known her. I walk back to Kathy's from my stint at the bar hoping that she's feeling better. As I put my key in the lock, someone inside our room coughs. I walk in and Nancy is sitting on her bed, her back propped against the wall. She wipes the back of her hand across her nose, glances up at me. Her eyes are red and puffy.

'Nancy? Are you okay?' Nancy shakes her head. I sit on the edge of her bed, near her feet. 'Is there anything I can do?'

She looks down at her waist and rubs her thumbs together aggressively. 'No,' she whispers.

'What's wrong?'

She shakes her head. 'Can't say.'

'Why not? What is it?' A tear rolls down her cheek. I've not seen this steadfast young woman cry before. I lay my fingertips on her ankle. 'Are you sure? No one's hurt you, have they?'

'No.' Nancy sniffs. 'No one's done anything to me. I've done this to myself.'

'What?'

Nancy scratches the back of one hand, opens her mouth, closes it again. Then she takes a huge gulp of air and says, 'Oh, Caroline, the rabbit died!'

'The what?' I'm flummoxed.

'I'm pregnant, you fool!'

'Oh! Oh. Nancy!' I scoot up the bed and clasp her hands. 'Oh, that's amazing. That's wonderful news.'

'Wonderful?' Nancy pulls her hands away from my grasp, stares me in the eyes at close quarters.

'Yes, of course.'

'Why is it wonderful?'

'Because you're going to have a baby. Aren't you happy?'

'Do I freakin' look happy?'

'Oh, I mean… Oh, when I heard, I thought you were... they were…'

'Tears of happiness?'

'Yes…'

Nancy snorts a stifled laugh. 'I thought you were getting to know me, Caroline.'

I let this sink in. 'So, you mean you don't want it?'

231

'Of course not. How can I look after a baby?'

'You'd manage.'

'As a bartender? Living here? Listen to what you're suggesting.'

'You're a strong, independent woman, Nancy. You'll make a great mother.'

'Caroline, I don't want to have a baby. Don't make me feel guilty for saying that.'

I sit back. That's the last thing I want to do. I realise I'm pushing my wishes and personal history onto my friend when I should be supporting her. I soften my voice.

'So you're planning to have an abortion.'

'That's why I'm cryin'.'

'Because you don't want one?' I'm so confused.

'Because I can't afford one.'

Ah. That makes sense. 'Do you have health insurance?'

'What do you think? I earn just over three bucks an hour.'

Stupid question, Caroline. I look at my friend. She shouldn't be doing this on her own. This might be indelicate, but... 'Do you... do you know who the father is?'

'It doesn't matter.'

'Of course it does. He's responsible, he should help.'

'Maybe where you're from.'

'Nancy...'

Nancy takes a deep breath. 'You're gonna think I'm real bad.'

'No, I'm not.'

'I... I'm not sure who it is. It could be one of two guys I know. Maybe even a third.'

That does surprise me, although I check myself immediately. Why would Nancy want a steady boyfriend right now? She went through a bad time with her previous man so I can understand why she'd be happily carefree since then.

I have an idea. 'If you know who it might be, we could force them both to have a DNA test.'

'A what?'

Oh, God. Maybe that isn't invented yet. I shake my head. 'Just something I read in a British magazine, an idea for the future, I think.'

'That's not much use to me now, is it, new girl.'

She's right. And I remember now, I think we're still ten years or so away from DNA testing being possible. I recall a story of how the British police first used DNA to catch the murderer of a schoolgirl in the late eighties when I was ten or so. It made quite an impact on my friends and me at the time.

Nancy looks miserable. I try again. 'Look, I don't know anything about your health system here. You're telling me you have to pay for an abortion in the States?'

'Where they let you. And yes, at least here in New York you are allowed.'

'Well, how much does it cost?'

'Give or take, about a hundred and fifty bucks.'

I do some calculations in my head. I've become adept at doing that from all the times Jon and I had to work out our buying power when going back in history. That would mean such an operation would cost around, wait, that's close to a thousand dollars in 2021 terms. My God. For a woman like Nancy who's living day to day on a shitty wage plus tips, in a shared bedroom in a hostel, that sort of money is so far out of her league. I can't believe it's so expensive. Every woman should be able to have an abortion if she wants to. I hadn't realised how lucky we are in Britain in 2021 that we can get such procedures funded by the NHS.

I tap my fingers together. 'What about your mother? Can she help?'

'She struggles to keep her head above water as it is. She's

still paying the mortgage, has her loans. Anyway, she'd tell me that having an abortion ain't the Christian thing to do.'

'But you don't believe that?'

'You askin' if I believe in God? Why the fuck would I believe in God? I mean, if there is one, then he – and it would have to be a he, an old, white dude, that's for sure – clearly doesn't give a shit about his coloured creations. There's more chance of Nixon making a comeback as president than there is of finding God exists. And even you must know that has precisely zero chance of happening.' She pauses. 'Don't get me wrong, I still love my mom, but she's the last person who would want to pay for me to have an abortion.'

That's a pretty clear message. I moot another option. 'Well, we can ask Steve. Surely he'll lend you the money.'

'A hundred and fifty bucks? Are you kidding? How long would that take me to pay back?'

'We can ask him.'

'No.'

'Why not?'

'I can't tell him, he mustn't know.'

'Wait… he's not one of the possible, um…'

'Steve?' Nancy's eyes widen. 'Are you tripping? He's old enough to be my father. No, he'd just fire me, Caroline.'

'Okay.'

We lapse into silence.

'I don't know what to do, new girl.'

'We'll think of something, Nancy, I promise.'

Nancy grips my hand. 'Please think quickly. I ain't too sure how long I can carry on like this.'

For the next twenty-four hours, there are only two things on my mind. The first is my new idea, which I had the day after my birthday when I was telling Nancy about my life in England. It's the one thing giving me hope that I might have a chance to break out of this timeline I am trapped in; the only thing I can think of that could help me achieve that.

Ironically, it revolves around a trip that Jon and I went on.

I vividly remember Jon suggesting the concert because I was so excited: how about we go and see Simon and Garfunkel in Central Park, September 1981, he said. I jumped at the suggestion.

It was a fantastic event: a free benefit concert on the Great Lawn in New York's most famous estate, in front of more than half a million people. They kicked off with 'Mrs Robinson' and 'Homeward Bound' and went on to sing 'America', 'The Boxer', so many others. A greatest hits album played live. When Paul Simon announced that their plans for pyrotechnics had been disallowed, and had followed that up with 'Let's have our own fireworks!', the crowd had lit up the sky with cigarette lighters, as if hundreds of thousands of fireflies were flitting through the air. Jon and I had wandered around the streets of Manhattan for hours afterwards, partly because it took us that long to find a quiet spot to leap home, but also because, as with so many other great concerts we had witnessed over the years, we couldn't simply travel straight back to a North London basement – we were too high. Too elated. So incredulous, as far as I was concerned, that we were even doing this, and going back to our own time immediately seemed like anathema.

Would that I could return home so easily now.

Those events are going to unfold in just under three years from now. That still feels an age away, but it's the closest intersection I have between my current timeline and my 2021 self. And it's my only idea. If I can find

2021 Caroline in Central Park on the day of the concert, wait until she is alone for a few minutes – Jon went off several times to buy drinks and use the loo – then I can talk to her, warn her, tell her what a bastard of a husband Jon truly is. Persuade her that she shouldn't go to the Bruce Springsteen concert. I know I can talk to her because Jon proved we can communicate with our younger selves when he stupidly did that at the Stereophonics gig. Ironically, I have to thank him now for doing that.

That should mean that if I do speak to her and she doesn't go to see Springsteen, then I won't be here! I will remain in England in 2021. Although I realise that if I don't come here then I can't warn myself I shouldn't come... and so on and so forth – the ultimate time paradox. But as Jon said, the timeline will sort itself out. I trust. And as much as I'll miss my moments with Nancy, I have to attempt it.

Of course, the question is, why would 2021 me believe it when I approach her, claiming to be a future version of herself? With different hair, new clothes, a great deal slimmer, if I'm honest. Would I believe that? Would I accept the possibility? I think so – I hope so; after all, she is already a time-traveller. And I can tell her things that only she/I know. Surely she would be open to my account. But even if she does believe me, the next question is, how would she use that knowledge?

It's a risk, it's paradoxical, it might not change a thing. But it's the only plan I have.

I also think a lot about Nancy. She wants an abortion and I want to help her so much. I can do that even if I do make it back to my real-time. She helped me during the biggest crisis of my life, and I don't know what I'd be doing now or where I'd be if I hadn't met her. So I owe her. And I think I've thought of a way to help. It's not a sensible idea, but I can't think of any other solution. But to pull this off, I need Ling's help.

The following morning, I wait until Nancy goes to work and then I grab Ling.

'Ling, I need to find someone and I wonder if you can help me?'

Ling stops lacing her boots. 'What makes you think I can help?'

'It's not a specific person, more of a... type of person.'

She sits down on her bed. 'Go on.'

'The thing is, I need to borrow some money. And if you hadn't guessed, I can't go to a bank or the usual sources.' Ling raises an eyebrow but doesn't ask for details; she's not stupid. 'I need to find a private... moneylender, and I wondered if you might know where I could find one.'

'A moneylender?' There's heavy intonation in her voice. 'Are you sure?'

'Yes.' I don't say loan shark, but I might just as well. She knows what I mean.

She grimaces. 'You know you'll get charged extortionate interest.'

'I guessed.'

'And if you don't pay it back, they'll come after you.'

'I know.'

Ling leans forward on her knees. 'How much do you need?'

'One hundred and fifty dollars.' It sounds so little in the context of my 2021 life. I could lay my hands on a thousand dollars quite easily if I was living in my Crouch End house, but here in 1978 New York, with no ID and no income, it might as well be a million dollars.

'And why do you think I can help?'

Because you've evaded all my questions to date about what you do for a job but from what I understand from Nancy you work in a shady line of business. I don't answer. I simply say, 'Can you?'

Ling crosses her legs. 'Are you sure about this? You haven't got any other options?'

'Trust me, if I did, I would use them.'

She studies my face. 'Give me a few hours. I'll let you know tomorrow morning.'

I breathe out. 'Thank you. Oh, and Ling, please don't tell Nancy.'

She nods. She understands. I don't think she knows that Nancy is pregnant but she understands about keeping one's confidence.

She leaves for work and I fall back on my bed. I hope I'm not getting myself in too deep. My reasoning is simple. I will pay back the loan shark as quickly as I can but the irony of my situation is that even if I can't, then I can do a runner and it would be nigh on impossible for the moneylender to find me. After all, I don't have an identity, I'm not real in 1978 by any economic or political understanding, so I could disappear into the backwaters of this huge country and be pretty sure I could survive working in bars and farms. And I'd only need to sustain that for three years anyway, because if my plan to go to the Simon and Garfunkel concert in September 1981 works and my younger self doesn't go on our Springsteen trip, then this timeline will automatically end and I won't be here. That's as innovative a way as any of evading a loan shark, if you ask me!

A few days later, Nancy and I walk back to Kathy's together at the end of a lunchtime shift. I desperately want to update her on what I've done but I haven't had a chance yet, and I need to do so in the privacy of our room, not in a tavern or on the Manhattan streets.

She's been working hard to maintain a happy disposition at Steve's, but as we head home, her shoulders drop and I know she's increasingly distressed. When we reach our room, she immediately collapses on her bed, looking miserable. She stares at the ceiling.

'I don't know how long I can carry on doing this, Caroline. Steve's already watching me suspiciously when I'm working. If he finds out I'm pregnant, that's me outta there.' She turns away from me. 'I might have to go home to Dayton.'

I bend down to unlock my bedside cabinet and pull out a padded envelope. Turn it around in my hands.

I've had this twenty-four hours, since Ling arranged my meet with the loan shark. (I might as well call him what he is.) I met him in a bar in Brooklyn and I've rarely been so on edge. Ling's message was to look for a man with a red rose lapel pin and matching earring, but when I saw him, he wasn't what I expected: smartly dressed, neat hair and well-groomed moustache, classic seventies large spectacles.

'You Caroline?' he asked as I sat down opposite him.

I nodded nervously. 'And you are?'

'You can call me Mr Smith.' He sipped his drink calmly. 'You understand the payment details?'

'I think so.'

'Then here's the lowdown. You got eight weeks to pay me back. Including interest. Catch my drift?'

'Eight weeks? Is that all?'

He leaned backwards. 'You got a problem with that?'

'I... thought I'd have longer.'

'Normally it'd be four weeks, but I said I'd do Ling a favour.'

'Oh.'

He taps his fingers on the table. 'Tell you what, I'll add on a few days for Christmas. That'll make your deadline the end of the year.' He bares his teeth. It's not what most people would think of as a smile. 'Take it or leave it, it's your call.'

I did some maths in my head. I calculated I can just about meet the payments, but it's going to be tight. But what option do I have? There's no loan shark website for me to shop around for the best rates, so if I want to help Nancy, this is all I can do. I'll just have to work as hard as I can and if it doesn't work out then it's back to plan B – get out of dodge.

Now, sitting on Nancy's bed, I place my hand on my friend's back. 'Nancy, please turn around.'

Nancy sighs and rolls so she's facing me. I hold out the envelope. Nancy's eyes narrow and then widen as she realises what I'm offering her. She sits up.

'What are you doing, new girl?'

'What's it look like? I'm giving you the money for your operation.'

'But… what? You can't. How have you got the cash? That's not possible.'

I swat away her questions. 'It's fine, just take it.'

'I can't, Caroline. Don't be so dumb.'

'Take it,' I say, pushing the envelope into her hands. She takes my offering, then half pushes it back to me, but I force it towards her and this time she clutches it tightly.

'Caroline. I… don't know what to say.'

'Thank you is fine.'

'But why? How?'

'Because I wouldn't be sitting here today if you hadn't been here when I needed you. And because where I come from, we believe that having an abortion is your fundamental right as a woman. As for how.' I shrug. 'Contacts.'

'You don't have any contacts.'

'Maybe I do.'

Nancy turns the envelope around in her hand. 'You could fly back to England with this.'

The thought had occurred to me. Except, I can't: no passport, no British ID, and it wouldn't help anyway – I'd still be stuck in 1978 with no hope of regaining my old life, I would just be in England instead of here. Meeting myself at the Simon and Garfunkel gig in Central Park is still my best escape plan.

'Nancy, you've been the best thing that's happened to me in months. Years. I want to help you. Now take it, organise the abortion and make sure you can still cover for all my mistakes at work.'

Nancy's eyes are teary again, but whereas she was upset last time I saw her cry, now I can see her relief and elation. She throws her arms around my neck and hugs me more tightly than I've ever been hugged.

Steve's not stupid, so when Nancy and I both ask if we can have a day off at the same time he allows us to do so, but as I'm leaving he pulls me to one side.

'Take care of her, Caroline. She's been through a lot this last year or so.' He slips a five-dollar bill into my hand. 'In case you need to get a cab or something.'

I support my friend as much I can when we get to the clinic. She's the one having the abortion, but I can hold her hand before and after. It's impossible for me to be here without my mind turning back, or is that forward, to 2010 and everything that Jon and I went through after my accident. It doesn't matter how much I despise my husband now, that episode was something I wouldn't wish on my worst enemy. How different would my life have been if that hadn't happened? I guess I wouldn't be here now. How would it have changed if I'd agreed to Jon's plan to go back in time and prevent the incident? Ditto, I expect. But I can't think like this, not if I'm to remain strong and help Nancy, and not unless I want to put myself through all that mental torture again. While Nancy has the operation, I allow myself a few tears in the clinic's small, walled garden and then I go back indoors, wait for my friend to reappear.

When she does, I use Steve's cash to ensure we get back to Kathy's as safely and quickly as we can. I help her upstairs and she lies down readily on her bed. I stroke her forehead.

She smiles. 'Thank you, Caroline. For everything. I won't forget this.'

'I'm glad I can help.'

'I'll pay you back.'

'You don't have to.'

'Well, when I'm married to a rich dude, I'll steal his car and you can have that.'

'I look forward to it.'

Nancy holds up a palm and I perform my usual poor attempt at a high-five. She laughs, then coughs.

'How are you feeling?' I ask her.

'Rough. Tired.'

I stroke her hair. Nancy closes her eyes. I crane my neck and look out of the window, roll my head around and stare up at the poster on our wall promoting the Metropolitan Museum of Art.

'Have I told you I used to paint a bit back in England? A would-be artist.'

'You're full of surprises, new girl.'

'Yes, well, it didn't work out.'

'Why not?'

'Oh, the last piece I did should have got me on the map, but it got damaged, vandalised before it could be displayed.'

'Shit.'

'Yeah. It was a bad time'

'What happened?'

'I was due to have a private view. Nothing swish, a small gallery near our house. Jon and I went to a gig, er, just before the event, and when we came back someone from the gallery phoned me...'

I stop talking. Something has just occurred to me. Nancy slurs 'go on' but I think she's falling asleep. I don't reply. Instead, I close my eyes and think back to those twelve hours. I replay the gig in my memory: waiting for Amy Winehouse to come on stage, Jon buying drinks, Jon puts his arm around me – what am I trying to spot? – I notice what I thought was blood on his finger... My mind switches to my ruined painting, the red spray-paint... It seemed to me at the time a strange way for anti-Esposito activists to behave. I mean, why would Italian protesters go to all that bother over a tiny private view in North London? But Priscilla and Rosie had been so sure. But what if it wasn't? What if... what if the red on Jon's finger wasn't blood, but red paint? I wind back a few more hours in my mind to the night before that, when Jon had been downstairs and I had been in bed, and then it had gone quiet and I thought he was in the basement... the rain outside, his wet T-shirt...

And I see what happened so clearly.

'The fucking bastard,' I whisper.

And with this realisation, the last of my feelings for my husband disappear. If I do ever see him again, he'd better pray that I don't have one of Steve's kitchen knives with me.

23

Late October, I'm in the middle of an afternoon shift at the bar when Steve calls me into his office. He's aggressively chewing a pencil behind his desk.

'I've got some bad news, Caroline.'

I sit down opposite him. 'Okay…'

'A guy who owns a bar in Soho came to see me last night. We go back a few years together and know each other well. He has an inside contact in ICE.'

'Ice?'

'Immigration and Customs Enforcement.'

'Oh.' My stomach turns.

'Yeah. He says they're gonna be doing some random raids on Manhattan bars and restaurants in the next few weeks, looking for illegal aliens.'

'Shit.'

Steve leans forward. 'I'm sorry, Caroline. I like you, you're a terrific worker, the customers love you. But I can't afford to risk my licence.'

'Can't I just take some time off and come back when they've gone?'

'I can't risk it. They might come any time, and they could return just to make sure we weren't hiding anyone.'

'But after that?'

He sits back. 'It's not just you, Caroline. You know I've got a number of staff... in your position. If I can't employ you for several months, then I'll need other people to cover your shifts. Sure, if it's all quietened down in six months or so then I'd be happy to look at other options with you. Maybe you can get a work visa during that period?'

I wish. But that isn't going to happen. My shoulders slump and I pull at my fingers, one hand after the other, pinch them tightly. I twist my wedding ring around. I nod once and stand up.

'If there's anything I can do...' Steve says.

I walk out of his office. Nancy is waiting by the bar. She holds out her arms and gives me a hug.

'Steve told me his problem,' she says in my ear.

I touch her shoulders with my fingertips but I can't bring myself to hug her.

'Caroline.'

I hear Steve's voice behind me and I crane my neck. He beckons me to him; Nancy follows me.

He taps his fingers together. 'Listen, there's someone else I know, a guy who owns a... business in Brooklyn. By the harbour.'

Nancy catches her breath.

'Go on,' I say.

'He's always on the lookout for help. You're a smart cookie, I'm sure he could do with someone like you. I could give him a call?'

'Steve, no.' Nancy steps forward.

'Sure,' I say. 'That sounds good.'

'No,' Nancy repeats.

I look at my friend. 'What's your problem, Nancy?'

She turns to him, avoiding my gaze. 'Steve, you can't send her to Paolo.'

'Paolo?' I ask.

'It's not your choice,' Steve says to Nancy.

Her face darkens further. 'You know what he'd do to her. How he'd use her. That ain't right.'

'Hey,' I interject, waving my hands. 'I am here, you know. You can talk to me direct.'

Steve sucks in his breath. 'Paolo has a legit business, Caroline, that's what I'm suggesting I ask him about. Although that doesn't stop him employing whoever he likes, visa or no visa. But he also… deals. You understand?'

I grit my teeth. 'I do.'

'He's not just any old dealer,' Nancy says.

Steve glares at her. 'Nancy, you can't have it both ways. You do business with the man already. You can't choose if and when you don't like the fella.'

Nancy crosses her arms. 'That's exactly what I can do. I know the risks I'm takin'. Caroline doesn't.'

'For God's sake, Nancy,' I say. 'I'm standing right here. And it's my choice to decide what risks I take or not. And if Steve says he can get me an intro to… Paolo? Then that's good enough for me.'

'Listen, new girl—'

I throw my arms out. 'What choice do I have? Let's be blunt. I don't have a visa, I can't go home—'

'I keep telling you to go to the British embassy.'

'I need a job, Nancy. You don't understand.'

'Only because you won't tell me.'

Steve holds up his hand. 'Let me phone him, Caroline. He might not even need anyone right now. Give me a call later and I'll let you know what he says.'

Nancy shakes her head, but I squeeze her fingers and tell her I'll be fine.

I walk back to Kathy's, lie down on my bed and stare up at the ceiling. There are marks on the plaster I know better now than my bedroom in Crouch End. I fold my hands under my head.

What the hell am I doing? Is this really my life now? Borrowing money from a loan shark? Being sacked as a waitress from a common New York bar because I don't have a visa? Being put forward for a job with... well, I don't know who yet, but a man who at best appears to be slimy and by the sound of it is more of a drug baron than a businessman. And yet, what choice do I have? As I said yet again to Nancy today, I can't go to the embassy, I can't go home. Jon has properly screwed me over. If ever I see him again, I will make his life hell.

I do have my plan to visit myself at the Simon and Garfunkel concert, but I still need to stay in America for nearly three more years before that happens. And if I'm going to manage that, I need money; I need a job. And I have to pay Smith his loan back plus his exorbitant interest. If Steve doesn't come through and help me find a new position somewhere, then I might even need to resort to plan B to evade the loan shark and hit the road. That's the last thing I want to do, but if it ends up that way...

Later that evening, I find a phone booth and call Steve at the bar. He tells me he's fixed me up with an interview (although he laughs when he uses that word) with Paolo the following day. He gives me an address in downtown Brooklyn and tells me to be 'savvy'.

Savvy! Ha! If I was even half as shrewd, I wouldn't be here now. But I am.

I prepare for my meeting with the mafia.

. . .

One week later, I have a new job in Paolo's 'office' in Brooklyn. I'm still lodging at Kathy's, even though to get to my new employment means taking the subway, changing lines halfway, and in winter I bet it'll be an icy walk at both ends of the journey. I hate the commute and I already hate my job. It's everything that working at Steve's wasn't: boring, tense, cold (Paolo doesn't like paying electricity bills) and the other people who work here are so rude and arrogant that I desperately try to ignore them, or too skittish to want to make conversation with me. The poorly lit room I work in – I can't call it an office – is a chilly unwelcoming space with creaking furniture standing on dusty floorboards, on the fifth floor of a dilapidated warehouse almost under the shadow of the Brooklyn Bridge. A window looks out over the East River and my one pleasure is watching the diverse crafts that ply up and down the waters.

But it pays me a wage. Albeit a shit one. And Paolo does not appear to be as noxious as Nancy was making out. Yes, he has consumed far too much rich food in the fifty-plus years of his life, but he dresses smartly, speaks politely and sports a boxer's gold tooth.

'Steve tells me I can trust you, is that right?' he asked me at my interview. 'The previous incumbent of this role, I couldn't rely on her at all.'

I forced my gaze away from his mouth. 'Of course. You can depend on me.'

'And you're good with numbers?'

'I hope so.'

'You know what two and two makes?'

'Four?' I offered.

He sipped a coffee. 'Normally, yes, you'd be right. But if I say it adds up to three, would you believe me?'

I nodded nervously. He gave me the job.

Consequently, I've ended up as an assistant accountant

for him, doing the books. I'm no financial officer, but I have years of experience managing my own accounts, and the sort of income/expenditure that our Brooklyn company does is very simple: x widgets are bought, 3x widgets are sold. The ledgers I manage are the ones that would be presented to the IRS should the revenue service ever come knocking. Not that they do, apparently.

I still worry about how I'm going to pay back Smith in time.

24

Both Nancy and Ling were uneasy about me taking the role with Paolo, but after four or five weeks of me coming home bored and tired but untroubled, they've begun to calm down and rarely lecture me anymore. Nancy even relaxed enough to accept my invitation to go to see George Thorogood and the Destroyers at My Father's Place, an iconic Long Island concert hall that Jon used to talk about but we never visited together. It made me feel good, on the one hand, that I was giving my husband the virtual finger from three thousand miles and twenty-two years away; and simultaneously terribly sad.

Winter is a rotten season in New York, with temperatures plummeting to freezing. In late November it snows, two inches, and although it's washed away inside twelve hours the elements remain wet and vile. I buy a man's overcoat in a thrift shop and thrust a woollen hat over my short hair. At least Kathy's is warm, so I spend more evenings alone in my room, reading.

When I'm not reading, I'm thinking of my plan for the Simon and Garfunkel gig, my old life in 2021 and, of course, how long it will take me to pay back my loan shark. Maybe I'll be able to negotiate with Smith; after all, he's in this business for the money – surely he'd rather receive his full repayment over a longer period than not get it at all.

Nancy went home to her family in Virginia for Thanksgiving. She said she wanted to invite me but added, 'I can't bear the thought of introducing you to my dysfunctional brood. Plus, my shitting ex-boyfriend might be in town and I can't predict what I'll do if I meet him.'

I didn't mind. I'm slowly coming to accept that this is what my life will be for the next two and three-quarter years until the concert in Central Park. If I'm lucky, I might get my old job back at Steve's, but I'm not hopeful. I still go and drink at Steve's Tavern when I have a day off, and I mooted the idea of returning to work for him recently, but he avoided answering me directly. Nancy confirmed they had been raided by ICE soon after I was fired: 'Two of the staff who had told Steve they had work permits turned out to be illegal immigrants from somewhere in Central America. So I think he's a bit jumpy right now at employing anyone who isn't fully legit.'

One evening in early December, I'm sitting on my bed, reading, when there's a knock on my door. This is most unusual; no one ever visits us. Once or twice, Ling or Nancy have forgotten their key, but they tend to bang on the door and holler through it. I pull the door open and a black woman I vaguely recognise as one of Kathy's tenants is standing outside. She scratches her arm.

'You Caroline? Kathy says there's someone to see you downstairs.'

'For me? Are you sure?'

She shrugs. 'Just passing on what Kathy said.'

I grab my key and walk downstairs slowly. I can't think of anyone I know in New York who would visit me here. I stop halfway down a flight of stairs as a thought enters my head: it couldn't be Jon, could it? Surely it can't be him. But if so, how on earth has he found me? I descend the rest of the way slowly, step by step, my heart beginning to pump harder in my chest.

It isn't Jon. As I walk into the reception area I wonder if my (ex?) husband would have been preferable. Because standing by the broken water cooler is a man I recognise instantly: Smith, my loan shark. He smiles unpleasantly when he sees me.

'Caroline. Good to see you again. Shall we take a walk?'

I wrap my arms tightly around my body. 'It's not eight weeks yet.'

The man holds out his arm. 'Just a quick walk. We won't be going far.'

'I haven't got my coat.'

He ignores me and spirals his outstretched wrist several times to indicate I should leave the hostel. I rub my forearms and walk ahead of him as requested. We exit Kathy's onto the street. The cold bites into me immediately. It's well below freezing. I'm only wearing a sweater and jeans and although the man presses a warm, gloved hand firmly on my back, my teeth are chattering within seconds.

He leads me twenty yards up the street and stops. There's no one else around. He lights up a cigarette and offers me one. I decline, continue to hug myself.

'You sure?' he asks. I nod quickly. He blows a ring of smoke. 'This is just a courtesy visit,' he says. 'Just to check how you're doin' and to give you a polite reminder that your debt is due at the end of the year.'

'I know. I'll have your money.'

'I know you will. I just wanted to assure you, just in case you weren't sure, that we know where you live.'

My stomach flip-flops. My ears feel as if they may drop

off from the cold. I've never been in this situation before, but I recognise a threat when I hear one. I nod again.

'And also to let you know one more thing.' He pulls on his cigarette. 'I know you're not going to do this, but please don't think about skippin' out on us, 'cos you know we'd track you down.'

'I... what?'

'And if you did do something as foolish as that, then we'd still need back our... investment in you. So in the meantime, your friend would find that she'd be in hock instead. You dig?'

Now my stomach does cartwheels and I feel physically sick. 'You mean Ling?'

'No.'

Nancy. Oh my God.

'But, hey, as I said, this is just a polite reminder about our agreement. I'm sure it won't come to that, will it.'

It's not a question. He stubs his cigarette under his shoe. Grinds it purposefully, slowly into the sidewalk. Looks up at me. 'You better get back inside. A woman stands out here too long in this weather, she'll get frostbite.'

Pulling up his collar, he walks away. I actually wait five seconds, watching him disappear up the street before I realise I can't feel my ears anymore. I think I might vomit. I run back into Kathy's, straight upstairs and jump into my bed.

I pull my blankets around me and lie quaking on the mattress with my knees tucked up tight. I can't tell if I am shivering from the cold or pure fear. Maybe both. Up to now, I told myself that I knew what I was doing, and if I got myself into this sort of shit then that was my problem. I must have been kidding myself – pretending that I'd never have to pay it back or simply take my own time to do so. Suddenly that's no longer the case. Now, it's all very, very real and my oh-so-clever plan of disappearing into the hinterlands of America rather than pay back my loan has gone up in smoke. Because if I do that, Smith and his cronies will come after Nancy. And she doesn't have two cents to give them. I don't want to contemplate what they might do to her.

Which leaves me with one option: somehow, in the next three and a half weeks, I have to get hold of three hundred dollars. The price you pay for borrowing from a loan shark.

How the hell am I going to raise that?

I've never done anything illegal in my life. I've not even had a parking ticket. Even when I was arrested at the Stop the War protest rally in London, that was a mistake by the police and they let us go. So the fact that I am now contemplating how I can commit a crime scares me to the depths of my soul. But I can't think of any other solution to my problem. If I don't have Smith's money by the time my debt is due, I may end up in the East River I've been admiring from Paolo's window.

Needs must.

On the second Thursday in December, I'm finishing up my work for the day in Brooklyn in our cold 'office'. There's only been a handful of us here today, I don't know where everyone else is, but once they've all gone, I walk down a corridor towards Paolo's personal office. I pause outside his door, take a deep breath and knock. A grunt comes from inside and I hope that's an indication I can enter. I open the door.

Paolo is sitting behind a huge desk on a leather chair, blinds covering the only window in the room, and there's a sorry-looking potted plant in the corner. He curls a lip, beckons me in with his finger and leans back in his seat. I sit down in a wooden chair opposite him.

'Car'line, what can I do for ya? I trust everything's swell with you?' He puts his feet up on the desk.

'I want to enquire about the possibility of… more work.'

'More work? I don't pay you enough?'

'No, you pay me well, Paolo, thank you. But…' I swallow. 'You see, I need some extra cash. Quite urgently. And, well, since I've been working here I couldn't help but notice you sometimes send people out. To do… deliveries.'

Paolo raises an eyebrow, swings his legs down off his desk and leans forward onto it. 'And why would you think I need more help with that part of my business?'

I lick my lips and recite my prepared speech. 'I'm guessing that you need someone who's reliable, you know I'm that, who can keep their mouth shut – that's fine by me. And I'm sure you have plenty of those sort of people, but I would think you also need people who are… unassuming, inconspicuous. Low profile,' I add. Paolo's face changes and a glimmer of a smile appears on one side of his face.

'I got plenty of those. Why do I need you, too?'

'I've never seen a woman leave on any deliveries. Surely I could be the most different, plain delivery person you have.'

Paolo leans back in his chair again. His eyes bore into me. He shakes his head. 'I dunno. Car'line, I usually work with people I've known longer. It's a matter of trust.'

'Did Steve tell you why he employed me?'

Paolo gives me a gold-toothed grin. I focus on his eyes. 'You mean how you beat up some guy for leering at one of his waitresses? Yeah, I liked that.'

I don't correct the exaggeration. 'Look, Paolo. Why not give me a small tester? I can learn the ropes and you can make sure I do a good job. If I don't, I won't bug you again.'

'Well—'

'Please, Paolo.'

My boss sucks in through his teeth. 'Okay, Car'line, you got yourself a deal. Come back here tomorrow evening and we'll send you out.'

I leave the building with my knees trembling.

The next day, the same time, I am sitting opposite Paolo again in his office.

'All you gotta do is take a bus to this address—' he scribbles on a piece of paper '—and drop off the package. The host there'll give you an envelope in return – don't open it. Just bring it back here. Capiche?'

Capiche? Is Al Capone going to walk in any minute?

I nod.

He slides open a drawer in his desk. 'This is for you.' He pulls out a wad – there's no other word for it – of cash and peels off several twenty-dollar bills. He pushes them across the desk towards me. I glance down – there must be eighty dollars there. That's nearly a week's wages and will carve a good notch into what I owe Smith. This is exactly what I was hoping for.

All for what, just dropping off a package of, well, I'm not going to think about that. And surely it'll be safe, otherwise he wouldn't be doing this sort of thing so frequently. If his deliverers continually got hurt or attacked, what sort of business would he be running?

I wipe a sweaty palm along my thigh. 'Okay, Paolo. I can do that.'

'Wonderful!' He sits back in his chair and smiles. 'Go downstairs. Kelvin will give you the package.'

He returns to his papers; I'm dismissed. I find Kelvin, a huge, bald black man who often follows Paolo around. He looks surprised at my entrance but gives me further instructions and points me towards a Walmart bag on the floor. I pick it up – it's heavy; must weigh at least as much as two bags of sugar. I walk out of the building as casually as possible and find the bus stop I was told to go to. I stand and wait, suddenly petrified. It's a dark and gloomy evening. The traffic's crazy, the noise of vehicles and commuters incessant. The buildings looming above seem to be sinisterly whispering to me. The only thing that stops me dropping the bag and running away is knowing what Smith will do to me if I don't get his money. Assuming Paolo doesn't get to me first.

I concentrate on a billboard promoting the release of *Superman*, starring Christopher Reeve. I remember seeing that on TV. Several times.

The bus comes, already busy. I climb on and squeeze my way to the back. I feel as if everyone is staring at me, knows what I am carrying. I'm sweating, but that's just as likely to be the heat of the bus and all the bodies pressing into me. I hoick up the bag so it's clutched to my chest and count the bus stops. I was told to get off at the fifteenth stop. I disembark, take out the piece of paper that Paolo gave me, orient myself with the street signs and begin to walk in what I hope is the right direction.

This is not a friendly looking neighbourhood. The shops that are open are closing for the evening, but many are permanently boarded up. Piles of trash line the sidewalks. Groups of young, mostly black men sit on the stoop outside the brownstone buildings, leering, pushing each other jovially, laughing. Older folk shuffle down the streets carrying their shopping bags, eyes cast firmly downwards. I grip my Walmart bag even tighter, pull my coat around me. Kelvin gave me one more directive before I left: 'If anyone comes up to you, you tell 'em you're doin' a delivery for

Paolo. They'll know not to mess with you.' I pray I don't have to do that.

I count the house numbers as I walk down the street until I reach my destination. It's a terraced house, curtains drawn, the relatively new trend of rap music pumping out from inside. Overflowing trash cans in the front yard. Two men in black coats stand at the foot of the steps leading up to the entrance. They look me up and down, surprised, I'm sure, to see a woman approaching them. But maybe the colour of my skin helps me for the first time since I got here.

I clear my throat. 'I've got a, um, delivery. From Paolo?'

One of the men raises his eyebrows. He flicks his head at the front door. I walk up, press the doorbell and wait. A woman with a vest top, flared blue jeans and a huge afro opens the door, does a double take at seeing me and motions for me to come into the hallway. I hand her the Walmart bag. She peers inside.

'Wait here, sugar.'

I wait. It's hot, and the music is so loud it's pulsating through my bones. Two minutes later, she's back with a padded envelope. I push it deep inside my handbag. She smiles wryly and opens the front door for me. I walk back down the street, the chill in the air that I hadn't noticed earlier now nipping at my cheeks. My heart is thumping as loudly as the rap music. As I sit on the bus heading back towards the Brooklyn Bridge, I find I'm more nervous than I was on my outward journey. What if someone mugs me now? I don't think mentioning Paolo's name will save me at this point. I grasp my handbag so tightly, my knuckles turn white. I wonder how much money is in the envelope? I've no idea what the going rate is for a kilo or two of marijuana but it must be hundreds. Thousands?

A thought enters my mind. I dismiss it but it won't go away. I let it out: what if... what if I ran off with all this cash? However much it is, it could keep me going for some if not all the time I need before my planned visit to the Simon and Garfunkel concert in September '81. I could skip the state, cross the country, disappear. Only return nearer the day itself. Surely that wouldn't be difficult. Would it? I mean, how could Paolo find me in a landmass the size of the United States? Hell, I might even be able to buy passage out of the country and come back in three years. That's a great idea.

I look down at my handbag. My fingers flutter on the clasp. I lick my lips.

Then I wrap my hands around the bag and sit back. What the hell am I thinking? If I've learned anything from gangster films and TV cop shows, not to mention Smith's threat, it's that the gangster always pursues those who slip off with their loot. It's a matter of honour. It doesn't matter if the escapee is a middle-aged, mixed-race woman from Crouch End, she would still have her fingers cut off, or her ears, or whatever drug lords do to those who cross them. I must be stupid even thinking about this. And this is real, not a low-budget seventies TV show. Anyway, Paolo has paid me my eighty dollars – that's a fair amount extra. I value my fingers, ears and my life much more.

I head back to Paolo's office, climb the stairs and find him still behind his desk. He acknowledges me as I walk in and points to a chair. I sit. It's after seven now and the rest of the building is silent. I remove the envelope from my bag and hold it out for my boss. He taps his desk and I place the money on it. I'm still breathing heavily but I think I'm managing to mask my fear. Paolo doesn't even open the package, just sits back in his chair and grins at me.

'You did good, Car'line. Enjoy your bonus.'

I leave my workplace, half jog to the subway, remain paranoid all the way back to Kathy's that someone will mug me. It's not until I am safe inside my room that I begin to feel normal again.

At least I made it and I got my cash. It scared the crap out of me, but I'm safe. I'm already dreading having to do it again.

25

The following week, Paolo asks me to take a package to the heart of Queens. Gives me a hundred dollars for delivering it. He even lets me take a cab there, although he tells me I must be dropped off at least three blocks away from the street I'm visiting. I complete the task with my heart rate a tiny bit slower than the previous time. But I'm on my way to saving enough to pay back Smith. If I do one more job for Paolo, I might even be able to buy some decent new clothes. And a Christmas present for Nancy – I'd really like to do that.

I need a few extra dollars for myself this Christmas as it appears that this season of celebration will be the most miserable I have ever experienced. Nancy goes home to Dayton again, still sad that she can't take me with her, and even Ling slips off before noon on Christmas Eve, saying she won't be back for several days. It's a Sunday, so I stay in my room until mid-afternoon and then I think, fuck it, I want a drink. And I want companionship. I'll go to Steve's bar; maybe Des will be there!

I walk across Manhattan to Steve's tavern. I've seen a

hundred films and TV shows about Christmas in New York: clean white snow, presents under Christmas trees, chestnuts and carols – I don't see any of that on my way to Steve's. The tavern itself has a few decorations hanging from the ceiling and it's busy, loud music blaring out, but Steve spots me as soon as I enter. He hugs me and sits me down at the bar with some of the regulars; sadly, no Des. But Wanda, originally from California, with a booming laugh, toasts me and we do shots.

'Is this your first New York Christmas?' she asks.

'It is.'

'We should drink to that!' I smile sadly; feel tears prick the corners of my eyes. 'Ah, baby, are you okay?' Wanda says.

I sniff. 'Yes, I'm just, you know, thinking about where I was this time last year.'

'Where was that?'

'London. England.'

'London!' She slaps the bar. 'God damn, that must be a wonderful place to spend Christmas. Not as wonderful as this shithole, of course.'

'Yeah, you're right. But it's the people, you know.'

'I do.'

'I miss my friends, my sister. I even miss my bastard of a husband a tiny bit. Well, not him personally, but having someone like him.'

Wanda raises her glass. 'Hallelujah to that. Did you not think about going home?'

'I... can't. Not yet.'

'Still too painful?'

'Something like that.'

We do more shots. I don't know if it's because my tolerance level for alcohol has increased because of working and drinking here, but whatever the reason, even several shots don't make me feel drunk. Just sad. Very sad. Wanda wanders off to chat with a guy she fancies and I order a beer for myself. I never used to drink beer! That was more Jon when he went out. I wonder what he's drinking now? Is he toasting Elise in our fucking lounge? Snuggling up on our sofa? I wonder what he told her when I didn't come back? And would he have shown her the time machine? No, he wouldn't have dared. She almost certainly wouldn't guess what he'd done to me, but he'd know there was still a risk. He's not that stupid. Or brave. And what about Bee, Teri, Zaina? Veronica – is my sister even alive? My head flops forwards and I rub my eyes, refuse to cry.

'Caroline!' I hear someone call my name and I raise my head. Steve is waving the tavern phone in the air. It's one of those classic American telephones, with a cable the length of Broadway. 'Call for you,' he shouts.

'Me?' I point to my chest. Who the hell is calling me? Who knows I'm here?

'Yeah,' Steve yells. 'Come on, take it.'

I slide off my barstool, pick up the receiver and slip behind the bar. I shove a finger in one ear. 'Hello?'

'Car'line, it's Paolo.'

'Paolo. Hello.'

'How ya doing? Merry Christmas 'n' all that.'

'Ah, thanks.' My heart is beating fast. 'How did you know I'd be here?'

'Just a hunch. Listen. I gotta favour to ask.' He pauses. 'I been let down. I really, really need someone to do a delivery. It's a big job. Very important client.'

This could be it. My chance to get the last tranche of money I need to pay off my debt. But I need to play it cool – don't sound desperate.

'I don't know, Paolo. It's Christmas and I, well, you know…'

263

'I know.' My boss's voice softens. 'You got family you're seeing, right? I should have thought of that.'

He stops talking. I wind the telephone cord around my finger. 'Well, no, not exactly.'

'Oh, well, in that case. Come on, Car'line, I need someone badly. And this delivery carries a big bonus, I promise.'

'It does? I... how much?'

'Two hundred and fifty.'

Two hundred and fifty dollars? I forget about playing it cool. That would be equivalent to a thousand dollars in 2021 currency. Even more in terms of buying power in 1978. Heck, if I do this, I can pay off Smith and I might even be able to take a short vacation. Do some travelling, see the country. If I'm stuck here for another three years, I should try to make the most of it. I run my hand through my short hair.

'O-kay.'

'Wonderful. Jump in a cab and get over here pronto. Kelvin will give you the details.'

I tell Steve I have to leave, go to work. He looks at me apprehensively. 'Be careful, Caroline. You have any problems, give me a call.'

I laugh off his concerns, hail a taxi and head to Paolo's office. It's after eight when I arrive, starting to rain. There are fewer people around than normal; no one is working in downtown Brooklyn on a Sunday when it's Christmas Eve. It's dismal and kind of eerie. I find Kelvin and he hands me a smaller package than normal, slightly heavier than a can of soup.

'Be careful with this one, Caroline,' Kelvin says in his deep voice. 'Paolo tell you it's a valuable client? Cool. Take a cab there, and back, dig?'

'Sure.'

A taxi. That's great. Much safer and far warmer. I might even make it back to Steve's for a final drink this evening!

The address is towards the southern end of Brooklyn, but to get there we head west around the Belt Parkway, skimming the edge of the bay. The highway is quiet and I can see Christmas lights across the water on Staten Island. Happy families, laughter, Christmas trees. We always had a wonderful Christmas tree in our hallway in Crouch End. I try not to think about what my friends are doing in London.

We turn inland and as before, I ask the driver to let me out a few blocks from where I'm heading and walk the rest of the way. He tells me he can wait for half an hour if I pay him in advance.

I focus on what I have to do. The streets are quieter than normal. The large American cars still trundle along but the sidewalks don't have so many people hanging out. It's a more upmarket neighbourhood than my first two drop-offs; more trees. Even so, not all the streetlights are working. I walk through pools of darkness with the hairs on the back of my neck standing up.

I reach my address: it's a detached clapboard house, a neatly kept garden, no music blaring out from inside. Across the street are two large, black cars – what we'd call SUVs in 2021. A richer client, I assume. I guess I may not be carrying marijuana this time, but it's too late for any concerns about that. I knock on the front door. A woman who doesn't look so different from me opens it, peers over my shoulder suspiciously and ushers me in. As usual, I'm told to wait. There's a chair in the tastefully decorated hallway and I sit down. I hear something outside, footsteps, I think. Maybe people coming to a Christmas Eve party here, hence their order to Paolo. I stretch my neck backwards and close my eyes.

An almighty thump on the other side of the front door

makes the doorframe rattle. I turn my head. What the—? Then another.

The front door bursts open.

Men in black jackets, combat trousers, helmets and, oh my God, carrying rifles flood in. Three, six, ten of them. More behind. They're shouting, yelling, pointing a gun at me. I instinctively hold my hands up.

'On the floor!' one of them screams in my face. 'On your fucking stomach! Hands behind your head!'

I obey as quickly as I can, pain shooting through my kneecaps as I drop flat. More feet pound past me and there are shouts of panic from inside the house as similar commands are unleashed from the uniformed men. I turn my head to the side and feel someone yank my hands behind my back. I cry out in pain. They're kneeling on my legs. Something cold and metallic is slipped over my hands. I hear a click and I yelp as the metal pinches my wrists.

'What are you—' I start, but my head is immediately slammed to the floor. I'm dazed. I taste blood, from my tongue or cheek, I'm not sure. As my eyes refocus, I see the woman who answered the door being led away in front of me, handcuffed, one eye shut, dragging her heels. She's followed by two men similarly bound up. Someone hauls me to my feet and I'm pushed into the chair I was sitting in a few moments ago.

'You have the right to remain silent…' he commences. One man is left to guard me and others charge upstairs. I see on the back of their flak jackets the letters DEA.

I close my eyes again. But this time tears are pouring out of them. I know what's happening. It doesn't take a genius to work it out. It's a raid. A drug bust. And I've been caught right in the middle of it. Delivering God knows what.

I am in deep shit.

This is my nightmare scenario. Arrested with no ID, no

story that can explain who I am, what I am doing here. What the hell is going to happen to me?

It's not long before I am marched out of the house, still handcuffed. The street outside is teeming with blue flashing lights: cars, vans, SUVs. Where were they hiding when I arrived? I am bundled into the back of a van, told to sit on a bench. It's incredibly painful with my hands cuffed behind my back. The woman who greeted me at the house is seated opposite me; she glares and spits at my feet. An officer beside her clips her ear. She doesn't flinch. We speed off. When we stop, the van doors are flung open and I'm half dragged into a brick building with the Stars and Stripes hanging outside. I'm separated from the other woman, I have my mugshots and fingerprints taken, my jewellery removed. ('Where's your ID?' they ask. 'I've lost my passport,' I tell them). I'm led down a flight of stairs and along a concrete corridor with a series of heavy iron gates ahead of me: police cells. Women hoot and holler from inside the cubicles as we walk past. I am told to stop outside one, my handcuffs are removed and I am pushed behind bars. The door slams shut.

In the cell is a single bench and one other woman: black, young, tattoos all the way up both arms and across her throat. She gives me a single glance and then ignores me. I sit as far away from her as possible, stare straight ahead, out of the cell doors. A police officer ambles down the corridor, swinging his baton.

Memories flood back to me of my arrest with the Stop the War coalition in 2003, but that wasn't anywhere near as frightening or serious as this, and at least I had Jon with me then.

If Jon was here now, I'd wrench that truncheon out of the cop's hands and crack my husband over the head until he stopped moving.

. . .

The following twelve hours are a blur. I only know the time because I walk past the same clock on the wall both times I am taken to the interview rooms. We go through the same conversations, just in different orders.

'Name?'

'Caroline Tangent.'

'Date of birth?'

'October first…'

'What year?' I don't answer. What do I say? 'What year?' the white officer repeats more harshly.

'I'm forty-three,' I reply.

'Jesus.' My interviewer shows his frustration. He counts on his fingers. 'So you were born in 1935, right?' I shrug. He shakes his head.

'Nationality?'

'British.'

'A limey drug trafficker, whaddya know.' He grins at his colleague. 'What are you doing here? You on vacation?'

'Sort of.'

'Damn, some holiday.' He tries a terrible English accent. 'So where are you staying?'

'Kathy's. On East 24th street.'

'You're shittin' me. This gets even better! You coloured folk sure go budget.'

I glare at him, but he just grins. 'And you told our guys earlier that you've lost your passport?'

'Yes…'

'That's convenient.' He looks me straight in the eye. 'Who were you delivering the cocaine for?'

So that's what it was. I avoid his gaze. He taps his fingers on the table between us.

'We have your fingerprints on the package, honey. And

photographs of you walking up to the house. There's no point denying it.'

Fuck. I am screwed.

'I don't know. The house you found me at. Number seven one—'

'No. I mean who sent you? You clearly ain't a dealer yourself.'

I suspected this was coming and I've been thinking about my strategy while I've been in my cell. Yes, Paolo gave me a job in his accounts team but I don't owe him anything. He used me just as Nancy predicted. On the other hand, I know what the mafia do to snitches, wherever I end up after this. I've decided how I'm going to respond.

'I don't know.'

'You don't know? So what happened? You just met a man on the street who asked you to deliver five hundred grams of powder and you said yes?'

I shrug again. Try to look disinterested. But I know I'm shit at doing that. They'll break me eventually.

'You know who I think you're working for?' the officer says during my second interview. 'Paolo Romano. Big-time Brooklyn crook. You know him, do ya?'

For a split second, my eyes widen. I blink immediately, look up at the ceiling. But it's too late, the officer saw my reaction and he sneers.

'He's a nasty piece of work, ain't he. Sending you on a trip like this. Doin' his dirty work for him.'

I sip the water I've been given. Say nothing.

The officer sits back in his chair. 'Look, honey, you don't owe that creep nothin'. You tell us what he's been doing, give us the information we want, we'll cut you a deal. You might get less than ten years. But otherwise, phhh...'

Ten years! That does shock me. I wasn't expecting that. I thought they'd see me as a low-level delivery girl and rap me over the wrists. Or even, knowing I was British, simply assign me for deportation back to the UK. Seems I was wrong. They're going to lock me up here in the States. For a long time. Holy shit.

The officer sees he's made an impression on me. 'You're a unique case, limey. You say you're British, you claim to have lost your passport but we have no record of you entering the country. We don't know who you are or what you're covering up, but we know what you've done.' He stands up. 'Tell you what. You go back to your cell and have a think about it. We'll talk later.'

They offered me a phone call earlier, asked if I wanted my attorney to be present. What attorney? I didn't even bother considering that at the time. Now I think I need to. I phone Steve. It's six o'clock in the morning by this time but he wakes up quickly when I tell him what's happened. He tells me to sit tight and he'll make some calls. Two hours later, I'm hoisted back out of my cell and returned to the interview room. Sitting at the table on her own is a black woman in a suit. She's about my age, slim, untidy hair. She offers her hand.

'I'm Aliyah, from NY Human Rights. We offer pro bono legal services.'

'Did Steve call you?'

'The guy from the tavern?'

'That's him.' I sit beside her. 'Thank you.'

'Let's see if we can help you. The police tell me you're British but you've lost your passport. Are you telling the truth?'

'I am British and Caroline Tangent is my real name. I entered the US here in New York back in August. I... can't tell you more, you wouldn't believe me.'

'I don't know how much I can help if you don't tell me more.'

'I can't. Really…'

Aliyah regards me sadly. 'Caroline, no matter what you've done, you deserve a fair hearing. I can help ensure you get that, but only if you cooperate. Do you understand?'

I bite my nails. 'That officer told me I could get ten years or more. Is that true?'

'Maybe. Yes. You were caught trafficking five hundred grams of cocaine. You can get anywhere between five and forty years for doing that.'

'Forty years!'

'Don't worry, it's unlikely you'll get such a sentence. It's your first offence, or so you claim, although we can't corroborate that without formal ID.'

'But I'm British. I thought they would just deport me.'

'That's an option for them. But drug offences are high on the city's agenda. Doesn't matter where you're from if they want to make an example of you. And you're a coloured woman.'

'Oh, Christ.'

I drop my elbows to the table and bury my face in my hands. And the tears start to flow. I've held them back until now, but hearing all this is too much. Aliyah gently rubs my shoulder.

'Caroline, I can help you. But you have to trust me. You have to tell me the truth.'

I nod, rocking my body on my elbows. Aliyah tells me that she will come with me when they take me before the judge today to apply for bail.

It's late morning when I'm taken to the courthouse. My accusation is read out, along with my refusal to provide formal information on my identity. The judge refuses bail on the grounds that I might abscond, and I'm ordered to a detention centre to await trial. Aliyah protests but he won't change his mind. I don't blame him. He's probably right. I would run away if they released me now, even in the unlikely circumstance that I could raise the money required for bail.

'What's a detention centre?' I ask Aliyah.

She doesn't answer directly, tells me she will come and see me there as soon as possible.

I'm taken from the court to a waiting police vehicle and driven away. We leave Manhattan and head north along an interstate. After around an hour, we turn off the main highway onto a tree-lined minor road that on any other occasion I would find scenic and relaxing. But when we pull up outside a high fenced-off area, barbed wire running all along the top, two people standing guard with rifles, and I see a few hundred yards beyond an enormous grey building with hundreds of narrow windows, I understand where I am heading.

Detention centre is simply another word for prison.

What can I say about Taconic Correctional Facility? It houses over five hundred prisoners and is a godawful place where we are locked in our room most of the day, three women to a cell. I'm sharing with a black woman and an Asian woman; the irony is not lost on me that that's the same composition as Kathy's. I wear a prison-issued grey dress that barely comes down to my knees and a cardigan. It's absolutely freezing. The only positive information I have is that Taconic's sister establishment, the Bedford Hills Correctional Facility for Women is even more brutal. What if I end up there?

Aliyah visits me in the new year, pleads with me again to tell her more information about myself, but I repeat my line that I can't. I've thought about it, but what can I possibly do? I can't give her my real date of birth, I can't confirm my supposed year of birth that the police calculated. She's visited Kathy's and Kathy has, of course, confirmed that I never showed her any ID and I didn't leave any documents in my room. She doesn't mention finding a large stack of cash in my locker and I'm guessing that Kathy has helped herself to that.

'You aren't going to tell me anything more, are you?' she says at the end of our meeting.

'I can't, Aliyah. I know I'm not helping myself but that's the situation.'

Aliyah taps her pen on the table. 'You should know that it's extremely unlikely they're going to deport you.'

'Okay.'

I'm torn by this news. I'm terrified, of course, of spending time in jail here in America, but I've been considering the alternative of being sent home to Britain, to 1979 as it would be now, and that fills me with dread. Not only would I also struggle there with the authorities in terms of my identification, but how would I live where another version of me is growing up? What would that do to both of us and to the 'time continuum' or whatever I should call it? I'd have to go and live as far away from London as possible, avoid everyone I knew, and without a national insurance number I'd be confined to working in the 'grey economy'. I suppose that might be possible in the seventies but it would get increasingly difficult the more the world turned to technology. That would be compounded by the fact that in 2003, after my arrest in London, my fingerprints would be on record with the police and if they ever caught the 'new me' after that time and fingerprinted me again, all hell would break loose.

There's part of me that thinks it would be a worse nightmare than doing time here.

Aliyah says, 'So I have a recommendation. It's my job to

tell you that your best case is to plead guilty now. Instead of a trial.'

'No trial?'

'It's common practice. Eighty, ninety per cent of federal criminal cases are resolved by a guilty plea.'

'Why?'

'So you get a more lenient sentence.'

'But I did nothing wrong.'

'Caroline, you were found carrying and selling a large amount of cocaine. Unless you have some secret information, you are guilty of drug trafficking.'

'I was doing a favour,' I say weakly.

'I hear that every day of the year,' Aliyah answers.

I pick at my nails. 'How does it work? Pleading guilty.'

'Most cases involve a plea agreement. You plead guilty and therefore forgo a trial in exchange for the prosecutor recommending a more lenient sentence. I've talked to the cops. They know you're a pawn for whoever was paying you, they believe it's your first offence even if we can't prove it and they don't even think you're a menace to society. But they won't drop the charges on a drug case like this. And your refusal to cooperate with giving them more information about yourself isn't helping.'

'So what would it mean? If I did plead guilty.'

'As a sentence?' I nod, my heart thumping. Aliyah locks her fingers, taps her thumbs together. 'You might only get five years.'

'Only?'

'That's the minimum sentence for your conviction. Although you could still apply for parole at some point. Ultimately, the judge has to approve any agreement we make with the DEA.'

I'm returned to my cell, where I tell my cellmates what

274

I've learned. They tell me I'd be 'fucking stupid' not to jump at such a deal.

So I do.

I plead guilty.

In January 1979, I'm given a five-year sentence for drug trafficking.

I'm a forty-three-year-old mixed-race British artist from another time who should be at home in her North London house and I'm going to spend the next five years of my life in an American prison.

How on earth am I going to get through this?

26

It's June 1982. My parole hearing is next week. I can only hope it is granted. I used to dream of the outside world, now I'm happy if I don't have nightmares of my life inside.

I am a different woman to the one who entered Taconic Correctional Facility three and a half years ago: less substantial physically, yet paradoxically, fitter and more toned; mentally stronger; colder, more bitter. I don't like much of myself.

My initial weeks inside were spent silently raging about Jon. What I would say to him, what I would like to do to him, how I would kill him. I had to suppress those feelings or I would have sent myself mad.

The first eighteen months were the toughest and I received several beatings from inmates, which the guards didn't rush to break up. I was initially worried that Smith might have snitches inside the prison and it wouldn't be long before I'd have my throat slit. When that didn't happen, I worried that my loan shark would go after Nancy instead. So, when my friend came to see me only a few weeks into my sentence, I was convinced that Smith had caught up with her.

'There's a guy you need to know about, Nancy,' I said uneasily. We were sitting opposite each other at a visitor's table amongst a room of convicts, many of whom had done far worse crimes than me, but I still lowered my voice. 'I have this debt with him and he… told me he'd go after you if I didn't pay up.'

'Smith? Yeah, I know all about that,' Nancy replied.

'What? How?'

'Ling told me once she heard you'd been arrested. But don't worry, Steve sorted it.'

'Steve?' I rocked back in my chair. 'You don't mean he paid Smith?'

'No, but—'

'Wait. How did Steve know I had borrowed the money?'

Nancy gave me a withering look. '*I* knew you'd borrowed it, Caroline. I just didn't know who from until Ling told me about Smith. Once I did know, I put two and two together and I went to talk to Steve.'

'Why?'

'I figured he might be able to help somehow. He wasn't surprised, just sad - told me he'd already guessed something was up at Christmas when Paolo called you at the bar.'

'He had?' My eyes opened wider.

'He's a smart guy. Anyways, he called Paolo and persuaded him to intervene. And Paolo, because you didn't squeal on him, contacted Smith and cut him a deal. Even so, I wouldn't go see either of them when you get out.'

'My God. How ironic is that?'

I was so far out of my depth. Thank God Nancy and Steve had my back.

Once I realised I was at least safe from outside influences, I tried to settle into a daily rhythm, mostly by ignoring people unless I couldn't avoid a conflict. When I was confronted, I tried to play innocent or act dumb as much as I could. After my first few months, I gained a reputation as a weird Brit, which I was more than happy to cultivate. As I grew more resilient, I realised I could use that supposed eccentric character to my advantage, and in the summer of 1980, I started to spread a rumour I was a secret clairvoyant.

'What can you see in your crystal ball, Tangent?' one of the prison bullies said. 'Me beating you to a pulp?'

Her flunkies hooted.

'I can foretell deaths,' I said.

'Your own?'

'Someone is going to be shot in New York City this December,' I replied, ignoring her.

'That's news?'

'December the eighth. One of the Beatles will be killed.'

'Are you crazy, Tangent? Which one?'

'I'll tell you nearer the time,' I answered.

The other inmates sneered but they did steer away from me for a while. As it got closer to December, they started mocking me that my prophecy was coming soon, whispering what they would do to me when I was uncovered as a fake.

It was a mixed day for me when I was proven right. When Mark David Chapman's assassination of John Lennon was announced, I was immediately shunned by the vast majority of the prison population. That didn't bother me, I was glad of it. But I was so sad the shooting did happen. If ever there was an event in history that should never have occurred, that never added anything to our world and surely could only have brought a positive outcome if I could have corrected it, then this was it. I wonder what I would have done if I had been free to visit The Dakota that evening.

I have also learned skills I never thought I would: dress-making (for others, not me), keeping my head down but standing up for myself when I have to, the art of making friends with people who I would shun if I was living a normal life and how to overcome hours and hours of sheer boredom by keeping my mind as active as possible. I've been taught by other inmates how to pick a lock, acquire a fake ID, pickpocket and even poison someone with naturally occurring plant extracts. One of those four might well be the most useful ability of all.

That said, for all the fear and anguish, the confusion and frustration, the initial beatings and subsequent skirmishes I endured, there was one thing that drained me more than everything else: the knowledge that I wouldn't be able to visit my younger self at the Simon and Garfunkel concert in September 1981. I held out hope for the first two years, believing I might still get early parole and make the concert, but the authorities didn't even acknowledge my applications.

I began to consider alternatives for what I should do when I got out. I even contemplated if I *should* go back to England, somehow wait seventeen or eighteen years and tell my younger self not to go off with Jon that day – to leave him instead. But then what would happen to me 'now' if I do that? Maybe I would disappear and this timeline would never have happened? That has to be a good thing, right? But, when I scrutinised this plan more seriously, I remembered all the challenges and potential jeopardies of living in the UK for all that time without a valid ID and knowing I could bump into someone from my earlier life. Could I really hack eighteen years like that, on my own?

Instead, I came up with one more idea, but I think now that it might have been a terrible decision to pursue it.

After two years, Nancy was still coming to visit me every few months. I couldn't believe her support and I looked forward to her next visit the instant she left each time. In May 1981, I decided to ask for her help.

As usual, she sat down with such an anguished look that I spent the first few minutes telling her she had nothing to feel bad about.

'I've told you this a million times, Nancy – it was my fault, it was down to me.'

'You wouldn't have had to do it if I hadn't got myself pregnant.'

'It was my decision. I wanted to help you. You warned me about Paolo and I didn't listen. But I can't say I didn't know what I was doing. Of course I did. I was just naive. I never thought I'd actually get caught.'

'It still hurts me, new girl.'

'Don't let it.'

We chatted more. Then I lowered my voice.

'I do have one favour to ask. One... incredibly large favour.'

'Anything,' Nancy said eagerly.

'I need you to listen, not to judge me, keep an open mind.'

'Of course.'

'Do you remember that night after I, um, had that fling with Des?'

Nancy grinned. 'You bet. Hey, you want me to ask him to come see you? Bring some special photographs?'

'No. Although that would be nice. No. Listen. You asked me then to tell you the truth about myself.'

'I remember.'

'And I told you that I was a time-traveller from the year 2021. Well... that is the truth. Seriously. My husband, Jon, who I told you about, invented a time machine. But subsequently, he grew to hate me so much that he abandoned me here with no way of returning to

280

my time. And there's only one way I can think of to get back to 2021.'

I glanced at Nancy. She looked horrified. But I ploughed on.

'In September this year, my younger self and my husband will go to the Simon and Garfunkel benefit concert in Central Park. It's the only occasion when my current timeline and my previous life will cross over in America. I was intending to go tell my younger self what a shit Jon really is and to persuade her to never come here with him in 1978. But now I can't. Obviously.

'So, that's what I have to ask you to do. I need you to go to that concert, find me as I was then and tell her I've sent you. I can tell you exactly where we stood at the event, I know when Jon left to buy beers, and that's when you can give her the information. Do you understand?'

Nancy didn't say anything. She sat there, staring at me, looking sadder than when she had walked into the prison. I bent my head even lower to the table. 'I can tell you what to say to persuade her. But I need you to do this. You're my only hope.'

I looked expectantly into the eyes of my friend and ex-room-mate. But where I had wanted to see excitement and alacrity, or at the very least amusement, I saw disbelief. And tears.

'Oh, Caroline,' Nancy whispered.

I sat upright. 'You don't believe me?'

Nancy bit her lip and rubbed her palm down her cheek. I craned my neck left and right, trying to catch her eye, but she wouldn't look directly at me.

'Nancy?'

She stood up. 'Goodbye, Caroline. Thank you again for everything you did for me. I won't forget you, I promise.'

'Nancy, wait!' I stood up. 'Nancy! It's the truth! Please

listen to me. You have to do this. Nancy!'

'Tangent!' One of the guards yelled. 'Sit down!'

I didn't. I stood and watched my closest friend in America walk away.

She never visited me again.

All the hatred I had for Jon, all the anger and seething I felt for him, doubled in that moment.

I held out one final glimmer of hope until the morning of September 20th 1981, the day after the Simon and Garfunkel concert. Maybe Nancy would come through for me, perhaps she would visit the park out of curiosity and spot me – say something after all. But when I woke that day and I was still in Taconic, I knew Nancy hadn't gone.

Which means it's now too late. Nancy was my last roll of the dice. Even if I get parole, there's nothing I can do to change what's happened.

I am now stuck permanently in this timeline, this twenti-eth-century American hell into which Jon has exiled me.

I am stranded here forever.

* * *

The good news is that my parole has been granted and the process is underway. The bad news is that my release from prison means the Americans now want to deport me. But they can't. I'm learning a lot about American law, red tape and, of course, time paradoxes.

'We have a problem,' my parole officer explains to me. 'You're something of a unique case. We don't want you here, we need to deport you, and yet, although you say you're British, the Brits are refusing to acknowledge you.'

'Why is that a problem?'

'Because US law states that the receiving country of a person being deported must agree to accept them and issue travel documents. And Her Majesty's government,' he says this heavily, 'won't issue any documents because they say you don't exist. So what the hell do we do?'

Considering how difficult I know it would be for me to live in Britain in the eighties, I'm relieved by this news.

This goes on for weeks, months. It's now early 1983. I can't believe I am still in prison. I've been granted parole, but they won't let me go.

I've requested a special hearing and this morning, after breakfast, I'm transported in a prison van to another secure building outside Taconic, in the northern suburbs of Manhattan as far as I can tell, to meet someone who I'm told might be able to help me. I hope to God he can.

It's overcast and drizzling horribly when we arrive, which reflects my emotions. I'm led into an unnamed building, a single-level prefab, and placed alone in a plain room with no windows, no pictures, a single fluorescent strip light. The only furniture is a plastic table and two matching chairs. I sit down in one. At least they uncuff me. A few minutes later, a white man with a beer belly walks in. He's wearing a creased suit, a huge Rolex watch and a hairstyle that reminds me of a young Brad Pitt – except it doesn't suit him because he must be in his forties. He drops a manila file on the table and slumps into the other chair like a bored teenager, leg slung over one of the arms. This is the man who's going to help me? Shit. I remain stony-faced; I've learned to do that in prison no matter how someone acts.

'Caroline Tangent,' the man says. I flick my fingers up for an instant. He curls a lip. 'My name's Mason. Playing the hard woman, are you? Bit much for someone your age. Jesus.' He looks tired, rubs his palms up and down his face fast, several times.

'So what are we gonna do with you, Tangent, huh?' I shrug. Mason grimaces. 'You've been granted parole, we're ready to deport you, but we're stuck in a fucked-up dead-lock. Christ.'

He likes his biblical references, clearly. He taps a pen on the table and looks up at all four corners of the room. I subtly follow his gaze.

'The good thing about this room,' he says, 'why I asked for it today, is because there's no cameras, no two-way mirror or any of that shit, and we can talk man to, well, old woman.'

Still I don't rise to his bait. His shoulders lift and fall in an enormous sigh. He taps the file in front of him.

'You're just a pain in the ass, you know that? All this paperwork and time and those goddamn limeys refusing to take you 'cos they say they can't process you. You got amnesia or something? Jesus H. But you know what? Today is your lucky day. Because I may be the man who can fix this conundrum.'

Mason leans forward conspiratorially and, despite myself, I do the same. If he's serious, I need to listen, and I don't need him to think I'm being awkward. Time to be a nice person. I smile encouragingly.

He cocks his head. 'Say, you want a coffee? I want a coffee, I know that. There's a kitchen down the corridor where I could make one. I might go do that, and while I do, maybe I'll leave this door open. It'll take me at least five minutes or so to make a joe, and you know what might happen during that time? No? I think you might not be here when I return. Because if you were to walk out this door, turn right and keep going around the next corner, you'd find a fire door that leads directly to the outside. No one guards that. And from there, well, I bet you could sprint away in no time at all. You could be lost somewhere in this country for years, decades, and we'd never find you. Whadda ya reckon?'

I reckon my eyes are the size of saucers. Everything I've learned inside about keeping a poker face and playing it straight has just gone straight out the window. Is this man serious? Is he... letting me go? Or is it a trick? Am I being tested while I am still formally awaiting parole? I need to be careful. I'm not losing my pardon because of some sleazy official.

'I guess I could,' I say cautiously. 'But why would I do that when I'm going to be released on parole anyway?'

'Because you goddamn well won't be let out if we can't sort out this shit box. Holy mother of...' He catches himself and pushes his hands through his hair.

'Look. It often happens that illegal aliens drop out of the process. We don't care about you, Caroline Tangent, you're just one person who was caught at the wrong place at the wrong time. I know you were Paolo Romano's stooge.' He throws his arms out. 'Hell, I'd welcome you to our country compared to all the spics and Latinos we have trying to get in. I ain't got no beef with you coloureds. We have far bigger fish to fry with all them Mexicans and the like. But.'

He runs his tongue across his teeth. Opens the file in front of him. I watch as he does so. Sellotaped to the inside cover is a compact, plastic Ziploc bag, and inside – I gasp – are my mother's opal earrings. I had them taken from me when I was arrested over four years ago and I haven't seen them since. I raise my hand to my mouth, I can't help it. Emotions and memories flood into my mind.

Mason bares his teeth. 'The thing is, if all that is to happen, well, I need it to be worth my while. Know what I mean? I'll still have to fill out a shitload of forms and get them lost in the bureaucracy of this shitty government I work for. So I'm thinking, well, my wife would love a new pair of earrings. You know?' He pauses. 'What do you think?'

I hover my fingers over the Ziploc bag. 'May I?' I ask.

Mason rocks back in his chair. 'Knock yourself out.'

I pull open the bag and tip the earrings into my palm. Manoeuvre them between my fingertips. The opal has never been bright but now it even seems dimmer than it was. I think about how much I love them. What they mean to me. But if I don't say yes, I may never get released until (if) the British government do accept me, and even if/when they do, I will face all the issues and dangers I worked out before of having to live in England at the same time as my other self and with no British ID either. At least this way, I can take my chances in the New World.

I slide the earrings across the table. 'I don't think they're worth very much.'

Mason frowns. 'How long have you owned them?'

'Twenty years. Bit more. My mother gave them to me.'

'Don't tell me, they were her mother's, too, yes? Sweet story. Well, would it surprise you to know I had them valued already and they're definitely worth a few bucks? Enough to make me and my wife happy. But – I understand if they're so valuable to you regardless of price. I guess it depends just how much you value your freedom, right?'

He grins lasciviously. 'Tell you what, let me sweeten the deal for you.' He flicks the file over and inside the back cover is another Ziploc bag. And inside that, my wedding ring and a twenty-dollar bill. 'You can take that with you. That must mean more to you, yes?'

'You sure you don't want to swap?' I ask.

'Oh-ho! Like that, is it? Sorry, no dice, sweetheart. These are the bargaining chips right here. You want in, say yay. You don't, well, I can't force your hand. But I don't know where we're gonna go from here.'

I stare at the file. Think of where I am. Reflect again on Jon and what he did. Remember my mother. I close my eyes. If I believed in fate, I would say that this is why she gave these earrings to me. Unfortunately, I don't. But I do believe I know what's best now. It breaks my heart, but at this moment, I need to be the steely, cold woman I created inside Taconic. I'm sorry, Mum.

I pick up my wedding ring and slip it onto my fourth finger. On my right hand. Mason grins. I look him in the eyes.

'Go get your coffee.'

He acknowledges with a wag of his chin, sweeps up the earrings and file and gently eases open the door. He turns left and I hear his footsteps disappear down the corridor. I wait for fifteen seconds in case anyone immediately enters. No one does. I stand up, take a deep breath and poke my head out of the doorway. All clear. It's mousey quiet. If this is a trap, I'll find out soon enough. I pad as quietly as I can in the opposite direction, turn the corner as instructed and see the fire door. I push the horizontal bar down. It clanks and I wait for an alarm to sound. Nothing happens. I step outside.

It's a cold, dreary March morning, but at least it's stopped raining. We're in an industrial estate of some sort: anonymous ochre buildings, a few trucks parked up, a road rising to my left with a small copse at the top. It's time to stop pussyfooting around. I leave the fire door open and sprint away. Thirty seconds later, I'm in amongst the trees, catching my breath. More importantly, I'm out of prison. I may be formally on the run, but somehow I think my man will keep his word and I don't expect to be chased down. He might be a sleazebag and a corrupt official, but he's no reason to lie.

'I hope your wife likes her new earrings,' I mutter to myself and start walking.

27

Imagine watching a movie with a friend where they've never seen the film before but you have. And how hard it is for you not to say, 'Oh, this is a really good bit coming up,' or 'That isn't going to last'. That's what it's like for me for much of the next ten years. I've seen it all before and now I'm seeing it all over again. The swell of optimism after the fall of the Berlin Wall in 1989, the Gulf War in the early nineties, the tragedy and impact on America from the 1993 World Trade Center bombing. And of course iconic events such as Live Aid in 1985, Nelson Mandela walking out of prison in 1990. I also witnessed for the second time the emergence of iconic bands such as Guns n' Roses, The Smiths, the Gallagher brothers; many other acts I'd forgotten had hits during these years.

I learned to act surprised, fake happiness, keep my mouth shut and my opinions to myself. I cried at night when I thought of those who would die, but I believed in Jon's butterfly effect – I wasn't going to change history.

I wouldn't have re-experienced any of this if it hadn't been for Steve helping me out the first few nights of my new-found freedom. Once he'd overcome his surprise at seeing me walk into his bar in a prison uniform, my teeth chattering from the cold, he let me crash on a couch in the small room above his tavern. When I asked after Nancy, Steve shook his head sadly.

'She doesn't work here anymore, Caroline. But she was worried about you, I know that.'

'She was so good to me. Came to see me every few months when I was first inside. Then she stopped coming.' I bit my fingernails; there was a tiny part of me that was worried whether Nancy might have mentioned my confession to Steve. 'I wish I knew why. Did she say anything?'

'She was concerned about... your mental health.'

'Did she say anything more?'

'Nothing specific.'

I exhaled an invisible, huge sigh of relief. Even when she had every right to tell someone else what I had said, Nancy had kept it to herself. I was so upset I'd lost her as a friend.

I didn't want to burden Steve, so I immediately made use of what I'd learned inside and, pawning my wedding ring (I was glad to be rid of it), bought myself a fake ID, taking the opportunity to 'change' my name to Caroline Turner. It was a surprisingly simple process in 1983 to get a counterfeit ID, but I knew that the more the government computerised their records over the coming years, the higher the chance I'd get caught. I'd worry about that later. In the meantime, I'd stay off-grid whenever I could.

That one accomplishment meant I could truly move on and, as Mason had indicated, get lost in America. That was my plan. Go upstate, find a small community, get a job. Start a new life.

Which I did. In Manchester, a small town in southern Vermont, on the edge of the Green Mountain National Forest. I found a job as a waitress in The Equinox Cafe, rented a neglected but warm enough cabin on the outskirts of town (a cash deal, I was careful to ensure) and tried to forget all about Taconic Correctional Facility, New York, Paolo, time machines and England.

That said, for the first year or so, I was constantly looking over my shoulder to see whether anyone who walked into the cafe was an ICE/immigration officer, but progressively, I started to relax. In 1984, I did up my cabin to the background of Bruce Springsteen's new album, *Born to Run*, and listening to the news that the space shuttle *Discovery* had made its maiden voyage. While Mikhail Gorbachev became the leader of the Soviet Union in 1985, I also started to make new friends, felt my emotional wounds closing up. I even converted an old tool shed outside my cabin into a studio and started painting again. Not my musically inspired art from my younger days; my new artwork reflected my more recent experiences: betrayal, loneliness, anxiety, but also recovery and reconstruction. It not only helped my mental state, it enabled me to pursue my creativity in directions I never would have dreamt of investigating before.

And in 1988, when Damien Hirst launched himself at what I knew to be the famous Freeze show in London's Surrey Docks, I sold my first painting in America. I made a hundred dollars. I was proud and delighted. Gradually, I started to sell more.

Although I was pleased to make friends in Manchester, I was wary of getting too close to anyone. I knew I still harboured resentment deep within me, lacked the ability to trust, and although I allowed myself occasional flings, loving another man again was not something I saw in my future. Then I met Roger.

One of the things I did enjoy about my new life was that I could go for a drink by myself, as a single woman, without the stigma attached to such an activity that we have in England. Without the constant concern that I was going to be hit on. Hence, in the spring of 1989, I was sitting on my own at the end of a bar in a local Manchester inn when the tumultuous events of Tiananmen Square started to unfold on the inn's TV. I watched in disbelief and turned away from the screen, shook my head sadly. As I did so, I saw a man at the other end of the bar counter shaking his head in unison, his palm rubbing his short, white beard. We caught each other's eye.

'Can't believe what I'm watching,' the man said.

'I know, it's awful. And yet at least it is being beamed across the world.'

'Beamed?' The man smiled gently, the creases around his eyes softening his face.

'Oh, too *Star Trek*?'

'Now there's a show I haven't thought about for years.'

I caught my breath. At least it wasn't completely out of time.

'I'm more of a *Six Million Dollar Man* fan myself,' he continued and moved his arms in a slow-motion, Steve Austin running movement while still perched on his barstool. I laughed. 'Well, actually, a six hundred-dollar man since my divorce, but I feel much better for it.'

The bar was playing old easy-listening tunes as background music. I flicked my head at one of the speakers. 'At least the theme tune is more exciting than this stuff.'

'What's wrong with Karen Carpenter?'

The man sounded hurt. I opened my mouth and then raised my fingers to my lips in embarrassment.

He smiled. 'I'm Roger.'

'Caroline. And I should warn you, I prefer my Rolling Stones to Celine Dion.'

'Who?'

'You'll find out. She's Canadian.'

'Oh, well, in that case.'

We spent the rest of the evening discussing music and politics and putting the world to rights. Roger was fifty-six, a couple of years older than me, divorced, and the sweetest man I had encountered in the US. By the time we said goodnight, I felt I had made a good friend but nothing more.

For a while, we remained just good friends. He took me to see Tony Bennett, I made him go to The Smashing Pumpkins. I learned he had been a radical architect in his youth, but now he was content designing eco-homes and greener factories, splitting his time between New England and California. I found myself opening up about some of my previous life, carefully, but not hiding the fact that I, too, had been married in England and even how I had dabbled in a bit of painting. Roger never pushed me for details, just accepted whatever I told him at face value. When we became lovers it seemed so natural. Even then, we kept our own accommodation because we still valued our independence as well as our companionship.

I only rarely thought about my old life.

But it was tough sometimes. If I was having a bad day and a mother walked into the cafe with a pram, I would occasionally wonder whether I should have accepted Jon's offer to have gone back to 2010; prevented my car accident – kept our baby. Wouldn't that have been better than this? A fifty-something-year-old waitress in a nowhere town in New England? Then I would see in my mind's eye the text from Elise or the vandalised painting in Rosie's studio, and I'd kick all such thoughts into touch. Most of the time.

As the new decade started, I was still very aware that my fake ID could be uncovered at any time. I wanted to be in a position where I could live fully off the grid with no government interaction. But to do that, I needed money, a lot of money. My opportunity came in June 1992.

I was working a shift at the Equinox and serving a group of holidaying English men who were talking excitedly about an upcoming football tournament called the European Championships.

'I can't believe Denmark has been allowed to play,' one of them said. 'They've only got in because Yugoslavia was disqualified.'

'Yeah, but they've got no chance,' one of his mates replied. 'The bookies have got them as rank outsiders. We'll thrash them!'

The whole table laughed.

As I listened, I suddenly realised what they were talking about and I was transported back to the night of our Paul Weller gig in London, back in June '92. The evening when Jon and I got so outrageously drunk with those Danes. And as the English boys boasted further about how they would wipe the floor with all the other teams, a plan slowly hatched itself in my head. They were wrong, I knew what was going to happen: Denmark was going to win. Surely I could use that to my advantage. Which meant one thing: I had to bet on the outcome. It was an absolute one hundred per cent dead cert.

The problem, I discovered, was that betting on sports was illegal in most of America in the nineties. I couldn't believe that when I heard; I remember bookmakers being on the high streets of England even when I was a child in the 1980s. But not in the US of A. In America, betting and gambling were only legal in certain states. One such place, I learned, was Las Vegas, which ran 'sportsbooks'. I'd never been to Vegas so I asked for a few days of leave, withdrew all my savings from the proceeds of my paintings and flew to sin city. Where I proceeded to try to bet on Denmark winning the Euros. That wasn't as easy as I had hoped because most of the sportsbooks only ran odds on American sports. I finally found three places I could place a bet, and I decided to split my stake across all three, rather than cause suspicion with one large bet at a single bookmaker. The odds on Denmark winning the Euros were, on average, twenty to one. I had three thousand dollars to invest. I felt quite light-headed at what that meant.

I arrived in Las Vegas during the first week of the tournament, so I placed my bets and then spent ten days travelling around the region, visiting Zion National Park, Bryce Canyon and, of course, the Grand Canyon. A breathtaking journey. I returned to Vegas with my heart thumping. I knew I couldn't lose but for some reason, I wasn't convinced the sportsbooks would pay out. Would they be suspicious? The first one I went back to was incredulous when I turned up.

'Lady, that is some win.'

'Thank you,' I replied cautiously.

'What made you risk a thousand bucks on… Denmark?'

'Just a hunch, I guess.'

'You kiddin'. Some hunch. Where is that, anyway?'

'Denmark? It's part of Scandinavia.'

'But they're still allowed to play in a European tournament? Huh, well, I guess you Brits know your soccer.'

I walked out with my winning cheque and my heart thumping.

It was the same story at the other two bookmakers, which meant I returned to Vermont in a state of euphoria with sixty thousand dollars in my bank account. Think twice that for the equivalent in 2021.

I waited a week before telling Roger about my windfall. I explained my mother had died and left me her inheritance. Roger couldn't believe the sum I announced I had.

'You never told me she was so well off,' he said.

'She wasn't, in terms of savings. But British house prices have been going up and up for years.'

As I always ensured, I never lied to Roger, but I used my words carefully to insinuate and imply.

'And sadly it's just for you.' He folded his hands around mine.

I had told Roger about Veronica and I knew by now, in my original timeline, she must have died.

I nodded wistfully. 'But it does mean I can move on now. Or rather, we can move on. If you want to.'

'What do you mean?' Roger asked.

'I've been thinking. As much as I enjoy living here, I don't want to be a waitress forever. I'd love to buy a small area of land, build a modest house, continue my artwork full-time. I was hoping you might… help me.'

'To design your house?'

'No, you silly man. To come and live with me! Please. Let's move in together.'

So we did.

In 1992, we bought Veedon Fleece.

28

It's seven years now since we bought our smallholding. It wasn't called Veedon Fleece then; I think it was something mundane like Green Mountain Farm. Roger didn't mind what we called it. But he knew it was important to me, still is, and he's so laid back he went with the flow. Apart from which, it was mostly my money that paid for the farmland, so he happily accepted my eccentric name.

It's tucked away in the rolling hills of the Vermont/New Hampshire border. That can be an overused depiction of a landscape but that is exactly what this part of the States is like. To reach our homestead, you leave the interstate and highways far behind, head down route 38, go through a few small towns and after a few dinks left and right, you come to the foot of our 'driveway' – a winding, hundred-yard track that leads up to our few acres. We have a comfortable house on the hillside, designed by Roger, obligatory dogs and chickens, and my studio, which is set back and away from the other buildings with a view over the valley. It brings me inspiration every day. We hold an open-house policy where anyone can visit my studio anytime to buy my art.

That's where I am now. It's late afternoon on a beautiful Vermont summer's day, the sun casting long shadows across the land. I'm standing at the entrance of my studio, holding a paintbrush, observing a white compact Nissan crawling up our rough track. It's a classic rental car being inched slowly forward by a typical vacationer who isn't familiar with driving. I hope he or she has good insurance. The car stutters to a stop, straddling two of our guest spots, and the driver gets out. It's a young woman with a pretty floral dress and a shoulder bag, that's all I can see from this distance. I hope she's a potential customer; I could do with selling a painting or two this week.

She holds her hand over her brow to shade her eyes from the afternoon sun, appears to see my studio and starts to walk up the path towards me. It's a bit of a steep climb. I put down my brushes and wait. When she's about ten or twelve yards away, she sees me and waves. I raise my hand to acknowledge her – and my arm freezes in mid-air.

Unless I'm mistaken, I recognise this girl. A sleeve of tattoos, a collection of dangling earrings, slightly longer hair than when I last saw her, but other than that she's hardly changed, barely looks a day older. And as I last set eyes on her nearly twenty years ago, that shouldn't be possible.

She walks up to within a few feet of me and then, I presume, sees the look of shock on my face and stops. She bites her lip.

'You,' I say. 'It is you, isn't it?'

The woman casts her eyes down demurely. 'I guess that depends on who you think I am.'

'The girl from New York. When I first arrived, waiting in…' I search my memory. 'Greeley Square Park.'

'Mmm.'

'But that's… that's not possible. It can't be.'

'I can explain, Caroline. If you'll let me.'

297

'What? How do you know my name?'

She has an English accent, very home counties. She smiles and her eyes shine, and I recognise those eyes. Not because I've seen them before, but there's something else that is familiar. My hand flies to my mouth.

'Oh, no. You can't be. You can't have.'

'Caroline—'

'No. No! I cannot believe that. I can't.'

The woman holds her arms out as if she's offering herself. I stand still, shaking my head. Wondering if there is any other explanation. But I know there isn't. I glance down the hill. The solar panels on our farmhouse roof are shining brightly in the afternoon sunlight. Roger is probably ensconced in the kitchen, making dinner or baking. Or maybe just reading on the veranda. This girl and I, we have plenty of time to sort this out.

I calm myself down. Flick back my hair – now long again, a hint of silver – and take a deep breath. 'Would you like some ice tea? I've become quite fond of it over the years. I know we don't drink it much in England, but it's very refreshing, I promise.'

'Thank you.' The girl takes a step forward and I turn and head into my studio. It's something of an upgrade on the shed at the end of my garden in Crouch End. My current construction is large, with a high vaulted ceiling and floor-to-ceiling windows, more like a modern, open barn. It has a mezzanine level and internal 'walls' that are only half the height of the building, which Roger and I installed so I can display my artwork on them. I even have a compact kitchen at the rear and two small couches.

The girl walks in and gazes around my studio with a look of delight. Goes right up to one of my pieces and peers closely at it then brings her palms together in front of her chin. That makes me happy.

'You obviously know who I am,' I say, pouring the ice tea, 'but I don't know your name.'

'Suzi.' She takes the glass from me and holds my eyeline. 'Suzi Tangent.'

Obviously.

I nod. Our largest dog is snoozing on one of the couches. I indicate Suzi should take the other. 'And... how old are you?'

'Twenty-six.'

'How old were you when I saw you in New York?'

She hesitates. 'Twenty-six.'

'And how long ago was that for you?'

'About three months. You've given me the run-around since. It's taken me that long to track you down again.'

'But here you are.' I sit down on the opposite couch, beside my dog.

'It was a lot of detective work, trust me. A lot.' She gives me a half-smile. 'Well, and some slightly dodgy hacking.'

'Hmm. You know, you have your father's eyes. I can see that now.'

'I wish you'd noticed when you saw me in Manhattan.'

'How could I? It was dark the first time and I was terrified. Jon had just fucked off and you scared the crap out of me.'

My dog raises its head for a moment. I stroke her ears and she curls up again.

'I'm sorry,' Suzi says.

I wave away her apology. 'It wasn't your fault. I'd just been dumped alone in another time in a frightening city, and the next thing I know, this strange girl is staring at me. I thought you were going to mug me. And the next day, well, I didn't know what you were doing following me, so I ran off quickly. I didn't have time to study the genetics of your eyes.'

'I get it. You gave me the slip so easily.'

'I'd been walking up and down those streets for a couple of days by then. I knew them well.'

'So I realised. Too late.'

I sip my drink. 'You say you're twenty-six.'

'That's right.'

'So… what year are you from?'

Suzi crosses her legs. She has a slim physique and a punky hairstyle which wouldn't look out of place from the early 2000s, but apart from Jon's eyes, I can't see much else of him in her. I presume her mother's genes were stronger. She smiles.

'2050.'

'Woah.' I chuckle. 'That's freaky. That would make Jon… er, seventy-five?'

'Yep. An old seventy-five.'

'So now he's twelve years older than me. That's weird.'

'I know what you mean. I'm finding it hard seeing you now in 1999 as a sixty-something-year-old woman. You were forty-two when I saw you last, right? That's only three months ago for me! And the only photos I've seen of you are when you were in your twenties, I think.'

'Jon still has photographs of me?'

'A few. I had to, well… I'll come to that.'

I shift in my seat. Enough of the pleasantries. We've been dancing around the question I have to ask. But it's time now.

'So, Suzi, why have you come? I presume your father sent you for some reason?'

'What?'

'Has he got all melancholy and regretful in his old age? Does he want to apologise? If so, he can stuff it.'

'No, that's not it.'

'Well, why else are you here?' A thought slips into my mind. 'He's not trying to... tie up loose ends, is he?'

'What do you mean by that?'

'You know. Maybe he's sent you to stop me permanently from ever going back to England. In case I do something. Because if that's the case, then I can tell you—'

'No!' Suzi smacks her thigh with her fist, spilling ice tea over her leg. She rubs the liquid angrily and smears it on her dress. 'He doesn't even know I'm here.'

'What?' Now it's my turn to be surprised again. 'Then... why are you here?'

'If you give me a second, I'll tell you.'

I hold out my hands. She has her father's temper, that's for sure.

Jon's daughter takes a deep breath and composes herself. 'I'm here to rescue you, Caroline.'

'Rescue me?'

'Yes. I'm here to offer you the chance to get your life back.'

'Wait, what are you saying?'

Suzi leans forward and hovers her fingers above my knee. 'Caroline, I want to help you. I want to make things right. I want to give you the chance to go back to that night in North London in 2021 when my father stranded you here in the past and stop that from ever happening.' She sits back and smiles broadly. 'I'm here to help you change back time.'

In my wildest dreams, I never thought this day would come. After the disappointment of not being able to meet myself at the Simon and Garfunkel concert in Central Park eighteen years ago, I gave up hope of ever leaving this timeline. And then I went from resigned to accepting to truly embracing my new life. So to be suddenly given the opportunity to change everything, reverse everything, go back to how I was, I can't take it all in. My mind is whirring; I could even go back to 2021, stop John from leaving me here, and instead, tell him I've decided to accept his proposal to prevent my car accident in 2010 and have our baby.

I could change my life twice over in a matter of minutes.

I ask Suzi if she would mind going for a walk around our estate and come back later. I'll have an answer for her then. She's happy to oblige.

I need something stronger than ice tea, so I find a demi-bottle of white wine that I have tucked away at the back of my studio fridge and sit in my Adirondack chair outside the doorway of my workroom and survey our land below. I see Roger a few hundred yards away; he is pointing at the figure of Suzi who is wandering along the very border of our farm, past our wind turbines. He opens his arms in a large, inquisitive shrug. I give him a thumbs-up sign to let him know it's okay. He reciprocates and goes back into the farmhouse.

When Suzi has done two laps of Veedon Fleece and said hello to one of the dogs, she climbs back up to where I'm sitting. She sits on the ground at my feet, cross-legged.

'I haven't asked you,' I say, 'but I presume you have a time-pen, such as we used to get home?'

'Time-pen? Oh.' Suzi pulls something out of her bag and holds it up. It looks similar to the pens we used, a little larger, more plastic, more sci-fi. 'You mean this? I've made a few improvements.'

'Such as?'

'Well, as I understand it, Dad had to build a new device every time you went on a trip because the returner exploded when he used it.'

'The returner? Is that what you call it?'

'It's as good a name as any, isn't it? Anyway, my device

stays intact so you don't need to create a new one all the time. I just charge it up when I return home. Plus, I have a second one that I keep fully charged in case I want to go on another trip immediately.'

'Very smart. Anyway, assuming that means you can return to the same moment you left, I guess you don't have anything to rush back to. In which case...' I pause. Sigh. 'The thing is, I need more time to make such a far-reaching decision. So, would you like to stay for dinner? Spend the night here if you like.'

Suzi's face lights up. 'I'd love that. Thank you.'

We descend towards the house.

'We'll tell Roger you're the daughter of one of my friends from England, and I told her to look me up if she ever came over. And you've come instead.'

'It's almost true.'

'Just be very careful what you say. It's taken me a long time to train myself so that I know I'll never again slip up and say something that Roger might find suspicious.'

'You mean mention something from the wrong time?'

'Exactly.'

'Okay. Just kick me if I do say anything inappropriate.'

'I'll kick you out.'

Suzi grins. 'Is Roger your husband?'

'Partner. Neither of us feels the need to get married again. We're perfectly happy just being here together.'

'He knows nothing about your background?'

'He knows I grew up in England and about Jon. He even knows about my time in... New York. I haven't lied about anything. I just haven't told him the whole truth.'

We reach the side door to our farmhouse. I put my hand on Suzi's forearm.

'One more question for now. Your mother. Would I be right in thinking she is Elise?'

303

Suzi nods. I curl up my lip. Suzi lowers her voice. 'If it makes you feel any better, I hate her, too. Now that dad's old and feeble and they're divorced, well, she's twenty years younger than him and she spends most of her time with rich playboys.'

'Divorced?'

'Some years ago.'

'Hmm, that's the second time you've said Jon is elderly. He's only seventy-five. Surely he can't be that frail. He must have years ahead of him.'

'That's another part of my story,' Suzi says quietly. 'Shall we save that for later? Tomorrow, maybe?'

I smile and let her take my arm as we walk indoors.

I introduce Roger and Suzi. Suzi is charming, another trait she's learned from her father, and Roger is entranced by her. Suzi, in turn, listens intently to Roger's account of growing up in America during and after the Second World War and laughs herself sick when he tells her his story of chasing a pig and a chicken around his friend's house when their parents were away. I sit with my arm around my partner's neck and reflect how lucky I am to have such a wonderful man who I am (could that be 'was'?) planning to grow old with. I love his tranquillity, his empathy for my needs, his cooking, of course, and I even love his chunkiness and white, scraggly beard; facial hair was never my thing when I was younger, but I can't imagine Roger without it.

Suzi manages to go almost the whole evening without making a faux pas. Until her third glass of wine when she accidentally infers that her father and I were close once. Roger raises an eyebrow and Suzi's hand flies to her mouth.

I swirl the wine around in my own glass. 'I did kiss Suzi's father once,' I say coyly. 'It was a long, long time ago.

Nothing came of it in the end. But we stayed in touch until I left England.'

'You still surprise me, even now,' Roger teases me.

I do a little upper-body dance movement while sitting in my chair.

Suzi puts her glass down. 'I think I'd better go to bed.'

'Of course. I'll show you where you're sleeping,' I say and lead her upstairs.

'I'm so sorry,' Suzi whispers once we are in the guest bedroom.

I grin. 'Don't worry. I said a lot worse when I was living in New York. And if that's the worst of your blunders, we'll be fine.'

We've both had a few glasses of wine and for some reason, we both go for a hug and break away slightly embarrassed.

'I'm only my father's daughter by blood,' Suzi says seriously. 'It doesn't mean I'm the same as him otherwise. You need to know that.'

I leave her in the eaves of our house and go back downstairs to the man I love.

29

'I'm going into town for supplies and taking Suzi with me,' I say to Roger the next morning. 'I'm going to show her around and then we might go for coffee or a spot of lunch.'

'A spot of lunch?' Roger echoes. He pokes me gently in the stomach. 'A few hours with a fellow Brit and you're talking all elegant.'

I tickle him back.

'I love your farm,' Suzi says as we walk towards my pick-up. 'You're fully off-grid?'

'We even have our own water supply now.'

'Amazing.'

I drive her towards our local town, Burley.

'Is that a rental car you arrived in?' I ask.

'Of course.'

'I'm surprised you need to drive in 2050. Isn't it all driverless cars in your time?'

'Ninety-five per cent. Once I realised I would have to rent one coming here, I had to learn on a retro computer simulator in my bedroom. I think I did okay.'

'Hmm. Just drive carefully. But why didn't you simply land at the bottom of our drive and walk up?'

'I didn't know exactly where you lived. I discovered you'd bought a farm in this area called Veedon Fleece, but I couldn't pinpoint it.'

'Ah. So how on earth did you get a driving licence?'

'I researched what they looked like and, er, printed one at home,' Suzi says.

I laugh loudly. 'Oh my, you are your father's daughter.'

'What do you mean?'

'Didn't Jon ever tell you about how we gathered banknotes for the periods we visited?'

'No. I always wondered that. No one uses cash in 2050, and it's been one of my biggest problems since I've been trying to track you down. I can land anytime, anywhere, but I can never stay for long because I don't have any money I could spend on food or hotels. How did you do it?'

I tell her how we forged a traveller's cheque. When she doesn't answer, I glance across at the passenger seat. She is staring open-mouthed through the windshield. I start laughing all over again.

We buy supplies in the market and I take her to my favourite cafe. The weather is gorgeous again so we sit outside in their back garden and share a pizza and salad.

'They still have pizzas in 2050?' I ask.

'You know, in some ways, 2050 is not that different to 2021. Yes, we have driverless cars, the oil has all run out, and the computing power is off the scale compared to what you had. But we still have pizza, TV, the internet, right-wing idiots, and the rich-poor divide is even worse, if anything.'

'That's depressing.'

'I know.' Suzi puts down her cutlery. 'So have you decided what you want to do?'

'You're very direct, aren't you?'

'I've waited so long to meet you, Caroline. Now that I have, I can't help but ask. It's so important to me.'

'I still have some questions I'd like to ask you first.'

'Shoot.'

'Let's start with the obvious one.'

'Why am I doing this?'

'Yep.'

Suzi runs a finger around the edge of her empty plate. 'When I was a little girl, neither of my parents spent much time with me. Dad was too morose, so self-centred. I don't remember him ever playing with me. And Mum, I think after the first few years of being with my father she realised what a bore he was. As I said last night, she's twenty years younger than him. By the time I was eight or nine, she was already meeting other men in the evening while dad stayed home and got drunk on whisky.'

'Which is why she left him?'

'Not immediately. They tried to patch it up for a few years, but they both soon returned to their old ways. She moved out when I was twelve. Dad hit the bottle even harder and he's not stopped since. He never did anything for me, barely loved me. Then one day, I found out exactly what sort of man he was.'

She hesitates, blinks quickly. I wait for her to continue when she's ready. After a few seconds of silence, she takes a deep breath.

'It was a rare occasion when he was actually going out for the evening. He insisted on employing a babysitter for me even though I was thirteen. Not that I really minded, because Isobel, the girl who came over, was pretty cool. I enjoyed being with her for a few hours. Her sister was in my year at school. Anyway, it must have been about seven o'clock and I wandered into our lounge, looking for a book I'd been reading, and that's when I saw Dad with his hands all over Isobel, while she was desperately trying to push him away. He didn't notice me immediately and kept pawing at her. Just as his hand went to loosen his belt, Isobel called out my name and Dad jerked around. He stopped touching her but he didn't look embarrassed or worried, he just sneered. Hoicked up his trousers and stalked past me. Isobel smiled and told me everything was okay, but she cried later that evening when she thought I couldn't hear her. She was only seventeen.' Suzi pauses. 'I never saw her again. After that, I lived with Mum for a short time, but she packed me off to boarding school as soon as she could. I couldn't stand it. I hate them both.'

I grit my teeth. My ex-husband has become a monster. I wonder if there were other Elises or Isobels I never knew about when we were married.

I make myself focus on Suzi again and ask, 'But you're still living at home now?'

'One thing that hasn't changed is housing prices and the cost of renting. When I finished my degree I had to move back in with one of them. I chose Dad. He was the best of two shit options. Trust me, I would love to get out, but I can't yet.'

'Wait, you're not... he's not still in our house in Crouch End, is he?'

'No. I think he sold that a couple of years after he abandoned you. I grew up in their new house in Enfield.'

'None of that explains how you know about me, or what Jon did to me.'

'I always knew about you. Even when I was young, my parents would fight over you. Mum would say that he loved you more, and Dad would say that she was pathetic and nothing compared to you.'

I can't hide the shock on my face. I never expected to hear that. A tiny part of me – hell, no – a significant part of me fills up with schadenfreude at Jon's anger and sadness. Fuck him, I say to myself, he deserved every minute of shit he had after he left me in Manhattan.

'Then, one night,' Suzi continues, barely registering my astonishment, 'I must have been fifteen or so when I was back home for the summer, Dad got drunker than I had ever seen him. He clambered up into the attic, started rummaging around and then I heard him go back to the lounge. I crept downstairs and peeped in. He was sitting in his chair, flicking through old photographs. And he was sobbing, not just a few tears, proper deep heaving. Bawling. As much as I disliked him, I couldn't do nothing, so I went to his chair and knelt down beside him. And he started talking. Told me everything he had done. To you.'

'You mean, about the time machine?' I say hoarsely.

'And your trips and how much fun you had. He told me he tried to force you to go back in time to have a baby and how much he still wished you'd said yes, and about your cat – Bolan? – and how he sabotaged your most important artwork. I couldn't believe what I was hearing.'

'Did you believe him? Didn't you just think it was the ramblings of a drunkard?'

'At first, yes. But the more he talked and the detail he went into, he couldn't have made that up. He doesn't exactly have a great imagination. He showed me the photo of the two of you at the Jimi Hendrix gig, and John Lennon's autograph and note to you on the Cavern Club headed paper. I guess it sort of made sense. And then he told me how he had tricked you into going to see Bruce Springsteen in 1978 and left you there. I was gobsmacked. I mean, I hated him already, but this took my anger to a whole new level.' She fiddles with one of her earrings. 'And there was what happened next.'

'Did he say something the next morning? Ask you not to tell anyone?'

'You're kidding. The following day, he couldn't even remember he had been talking to me.'

'So what did happen next to persuade you he was telling the truth? And how on earth did you learn how to invent a time machine? Unless everyone can do it in 2050?'

Suzi laughs lightly. 'No, of course not. It took a long time, I can tell you that for nothing. First off, when he got drunk next time, I went up to the attic and had a look around. I found John Lennon's note again, a set of these old-fashioned computer screens and a tiny thumb-sized device in an envelope. It had a small silver plug at the end.'

'His USB stick!'

'Yeah, but I didn't know it was called that at the time. I took it round to a friend of mine, a guy called Remi. He's a technology genius and he loves retro stuff. He recognised it as a... USB thing and managed to hook it up to his comput- ers. He got all Dad's files off it in a matter of days – 2021 encryption is a piece of cake for Remi to crack. He gave them all to me and I started to read them. That's when I discovered they were his notes about the time machine and I started to believe a bit more.'

I sit back in my chair. For a moment, I am transported back to my first ever conversation with Jon about the time machine, in our lounge in Crouch End, and his paranoia over anyone finding printed notes about it. Hence his use of the memory stick. How weird - that was in 2018; here in 1999, USB drives don't yet exist; and in 2050 it appears they've been all but forgotten.

Suzi is still talking. 'But what convinced me was when I had your note from Lennon and McCartney authenticated. I scanned it into my computer, sent it off to a graphologist who specialised in music memorabilia, and his report came back saying there was a ninety-eight point five per cent likelihood that it was genuinely written by John Lennon. But that was impossible, right, for my father to have met The Beatles, because Dad was only five when Lennon was shot. Which meant he had to have been telling the truth. That's when I swore to myself that I would try to find you, help you.'

She sips her water. 'Mind you, that was easier said than done. I had to teach myself physics, mathematics, algorithms, you name it. I chose a degree in quantum mechanics so I could understand it all better. And I learned all about wormholes and Albert Einstein – he was a bloody genius, wasn't he – and then I had to adapt all that into new technology that I could use in the 2040s. Took me years. I gave up several times, but then I would remember what he had done to you and I couldn't imagine what you would be doing now and how awful it must be for you, and I would start again.'

Suzi grimaces, scans the cafe garden. A look of absolute pleasure crosses her face. 'You wouldn't believe how I felt the first time I got it to work.'

'I think I would,' I say.

'Oh, yeah, maybe!'

We laugh.

'But, are you telling me you did all this in your bedroom? Jon had an enormous great machine in the basement of our house.'

'Like I said earlier, the power in my cheapo computer in my bedroom is equivalent to one of the supercomputers of 2021. Hook that up to a virtual server on the internet and I can harness almost unlimited capacity. I don't need any metal launch pad or whatever my father created.'

'There must be some of your father's genius in there,' I say, pointing to Suzi's head.

'You keep saying that. Seriously, I'd rather go around an entire Logan Jacksdotter exhibition than be compared to him.'

'Who's that?'

'Jacksdotter? He's a famous artist in my time. Christ knows why, he's terrible. Creates the most godawful art.'

'I'm glad there's something of Jon in you.'

'Yes, well. I guess as long as I can use it for good then that's okay, I can accept that.'

'You are doing. You're incredible.'

'Thanks, Caroline,' Suzi replies. 'That means a lot.'

I think about what Jon's daughter has told me, her self-lessness and drive. I believe her account, why wouldn't I, but there's something that doesn't sit quite right with me. I lean back into my chair and catch her eye. 'Suzi, is there anything you're not telling me?'

'Like what?'

'Well, I realise how much you hate your father, and it's admirable that you want to help me, but you'd never met me and I'm not even related to you really.'

'That means I shouldn't rescue you?'

'Of course not. I'm so happy you're here. But, well, you said you didn't have any money. How could you afford to build a time machine? Even using your 2050 technology, surely that would require specialist equipment?'

Suzi looks down, nudging her glass away from her. 'She said you were smart, I should have known you'd see through me.'

'Who?'

'I didn't know if I should tell you this. I hoped I might not have to. But you deserve to know.'

'What? What should I know?'

She taps her fingernails on the table. 'I told you already I knew about you when I was young, yes? I mean, Mum knew of you and Dad occasionally talked about you, so why wouldn't I. And then there was Uncle Andrew and Auntie Bee.'

'Ohhh.'

Two other groups in the cafe garden turn around. I wave my hands in embarrassment at them and smile. They turn away again.

'Sorry,' Suzi says, 'I should have warned you I was going to say that.'

'Don't worry. Carry on,' I say urgently.

'One of my earliest memories is going round to their house with Dad, I can't remember if Mum was there. Anyway, they were lovely and I always enjoyed it when we visited them or they came to see us. So, a few years later, I must have been about eight or nine, Andrew and Bee had come to our house for dinner. I guess it must have been about twelve years after Dad had dumped you. I knew they were all drinking because I could hear the noise from the dining room downstairs. I crept onto the landing to listen.'

'What were they saying?'

'Bee kept repeating the same thing: "I still don't believe you, Jon, tell me the truth." Then Dad would shout back that he was telling the truth, and Andrew would try to intervene. Then I heard Bee scream, and I mean scream, "I don't care what you say. I know that Caroline would never just walk out on you and not tell me. She's my best friend. I know you did something to her, I know you did." There were more tears, more arguing, but I'd got the gist of it.'

'Oh my God.'

Poor Bee! What an exceptional friend she was. Is. Still speaking out for me so many years after I'd disappeared. I sniff; it's all I can do to hold back my own tears.

'I mean,' Suzi continues, 'obviously, I thought that Bee was saying that Dad had killed you or something. I couldn't believe he'd do that, but I understood where Bee was coming from. Something didn't make sense. So a little while later, when I was staying over with her and Uncle Andrew one night, I asked her point-blank about you and what had happened. She cried for a while but she opened up to me: back in 2021, Jon had turned up at their house in a terrible state saying that you had been having an affair and now you had left him, run away. She didn't believe him then and she still didn't, she said. It astounded me. Something like that makes a big impression on you when you're eight.'

She takes a deep breath. 'So. Back to when I was fifteen. Once I'd started reading Dad's notes from his USB stick and got John Lennon's note authenticated, and I realised that his story about leaving you in the past was almost certainly true, I thought again about what Auntie Bee had said when I was young. So... I went to see her. And I told her. Everything. What my father had said, the Hendrix photo, John Lennon's note, what I was reading from Dad's USB stick.'

'And?' I whisper.

'She asked me a hundred questions about how that could be possible. I tried to answer but I knew it sounded a wild story. In the end, she told me to go home while she thought about it. But the next morning she called and said she believed me. Said she had been thinking about some of the things you and Jon had insinuated when you were younger, at your dinner parties. And now it all made perfect sense. She even recalled that when they were driving home from one of your parties, Uncle Andrew had told her that he'd been into your basement and seen a machine that Dad had claimed was a Faraday cage, but now she realised might even have been the time machine.'

'I remember that night. I was so angry with Jon for letting Andrew down there.'

'She also reiterated that she'd known that Dad had done

something, that you would never have left without saying goodbye, and she knew you would have tried to contact her again if you could. She admitted that she thought my father might have killed you, but she'd always clung on to the belief that he hadn't.'

'Oh, Bee.' I miss you so much.

'So, when I told her I had thought about whether I could build a time machine myself, she urged me to do it. Said she would do anything to help, including paying for all my equipment.'

'That sounds like Bee.' I smile.

'We agreed we should keep it a secret. We wouldn't tell Uncle Andrew and we definitely wouldn't let Dad know that we'd found out what he'd done.'

'Sensible.'

'We thought so!'

My brain is working double time as I process what Suzi is telling me. 'So… does that mean… wait, are you saying that Bee knows I'm here? I'm alive? If so, why didn't she come with you, or instead of you? You could have sent her to New York!'

Suzi leans forward. My hands are resting on the table and Suzi gently places her fingers over mine. 'That was the plan, Caroline. But it's taken me so long to build it and, oh, I don't know how to tell you this.'

She swallows. I try to. But my mouth is so dry, I can barely part my lips.

'Go on,' I croak.

'Bee was diagnosed ten years ago with cancer.'

'Oh God.'

'They kept it at bay for a few years but it was so aggressive, they tried a new experimental drug on her. She would have died very soon otherwise. We thought it was working, but it turned out that the side effects impact the brain.'

316

'How?'

'The easiest way to describe it is that it leaves the patient as if they've got dementia. She still has a reasonable long-term memory but everything else is muddled up.'

'But it stops the cancer?'

'No.'

'And now?'

Suzi's face drops. 'She's still alive, but she's not been given long. She's in a specialist care unit. I still visit, she still remembers me. They look after her very well…'

I nod, shake my head, put my head in my hands, start rocking in my chair. It's all too much. I push my seat back and as Suzi stands up, I motion her to wait and I walk out of the cafe garden and down the street. Tears are streaming down my cheeks. People stare at me as I pass them but I don't care. I find a bench outside a grocer and I sit down. I bawl my eyes out.

My best friend I ever had is dying from a horrible disease and there's nothing I can do. Just like Veronica's Huntington's, a time machine can't stop that from happening.

I go over in my mind what Suzi has just told me. I've always wondered what Jon told our friends. I'd guessed it must have been something along the lines of what Suzi said, but to hear that confirmed… All the pain that I felt twenty years ago begins to rush back into me. I knew Bee would be upset when I didn't come back, but I never thought she would carry the anguish with her for nearly thirty years. What a terrible thing to have to endure. Then another decade waiting for Jon's daughter to build her a fabled time machine. And then just as she was given hope that she might find me, the cancer arrived.

What a fucking bastard my husband was. Still is. What an absolute shithead. He doesn't deserve to live.

I sit on the bench for another twenty minutes, then walk slowly back to the cafe. Poor Suzi is still sitting at our table. At least she's ordered herself another drink. Relief floods her face when she sees me.

'I couldn't come and find you,' she says, distressed. 'I don't have any money to pay the bill!'

Much to my surprise, I laugh. I give her a hug.

'What was that for?' she asks.

'For helping me make up my mind,' I say.

We walk back to my car. I sit in the driver's seat but I don't turn on the ignition. There's something else I have to know.

I clear my throat. 'Can I ask you one more question?'

'Of course.'

I look down at my lap. 'Did you know about my sister? Your Auntie Veronica?'

'Yes,' Suzi says quietly.

'And do you…do you know what happened to her?'

She doesn't answer immediately. Then she says, 'Dad told me she died before I was born. I'm sorry.'

I wave my hand and brush the corner of my eye. 'Don't be. It's okay.'

'Caroline…'

I clutch my mouth and start to cry, silently. Since the day I realised I couldn't get to the Concert in Central Park, I've had to accept that Veronica would die without me in my original timeline and I thought I'd reconciled that, but being told explicitly that did happen brings it all back to me. One of the worst consequences of Jon's vile act of abandonment was to leave my sister thinking I couldn't be bothered to visit her anymore, and I couldn't bear the thought that she would believe that for a long time. At least I now know.

We drive back to Veedon Fleece in silence, and once

we're home, I squeeze Suzi's hand and tell her she's taken a huge weight off my mind. She looks relieved.

We climb the slope and sit outside my studio overlooking the valley. It's such a beautiful spot. One of the dogs lies with us; she snaps at a passing butterfly and looks proud of herself when it flutters off. Suzi giggles.

'Ah, butterflies,' I say. 'Did your father write in his notes about the butterfly effect?'

'All the time. He was clearly anxious about it.'

'And then we discovered it can have a positive effect, too, with The Beatles note on their album cover.'

'So it doesn't worry you? Being here now for so long?'

'You mean in terms of impacting negatively on history?' Suzi nods. 'What can I do? I have to live, I'm not going to retreat into a hermit's cave for the rest of my life.' I stroke the dog. 'But yes, I think about it. I wonder if Roger should have been with someone else, what that might mean. I'm rather glad to hear that there's no apocalypse in 2050, so I can't have done anything too bad.'

'What about... well, it's 1999 now, yes? In two years, Nine-eleven will happen. That's still discussed in my time as a pivotal moment in American history. How do you feel about that?'

I sit back in my Adirondack chair and survey my view across the hills. 'I've thought about it. But even if I wanted to warn someone, even if I could persuade the FBI or the CIA that I wasn't a madwoman, what would that really do?' I clasp my hands together. 'You know, we discussed this very thing once at a dinner party in London. And as Andrew or Jon pointed out, I can't remember who, even if someone was to stop Nine-eleven from occurring, what would happen instead? Could it be worse? Does the war on terror, as shocking as that was, prevent an even more diabolical thing from happening?' I shake my head. 'I'm not going to knowingly change anything in my new timeline. I decided that years ago.

'Which does bring us back to your reason for being here. Because in theory, if I come back with you and warn myself in 2021 not to come, then I would bring everything back into its expected equilibrium, yes?'

Suzi looks away. 'That's right,' she says quietly.

'I need to know one more thing. You keep saying you had to track me down. How did you do that? And why such a long gap between Greeley Square Park and now?'

'Because you're so good at covering your footsteps.'

'I have good reasons.'

'I understand. Well, our first idea, Bee's and mine, was to intercept you as soon as you were abandoned on your own in New York. I mentioned Dad told me you had gone to see Bruce Springsteen in New York in 1978, right? He said that he had left you in a tiny park near the Empire State Building after the concert. Looking at maps of the time, Greeley Square was the only place it could be. It was easy to find out Springsteen played three nights in August. I was lucky I found you on the first night.'

'So, wait. When I saw you, did you go back to 2050 and then return the following night?'

'Of course.'

'But I thought, I mean, Jon said that creating two wormholes so close together was so risky that they might clash or something, and we could disintegrate into nothing!'

'He was right – using the algorithms and technology he had in 2021. I've improved the exactitude of the time machine so that I can return to the same place just twelve hours later and I know I won't disrupt the previous wormhole.'

'Wow, you're a genius.' Suzi shrugs. 'So after I ran away

from you the second time, why didn't you try to contact me again?'

'In Manhattan? Firstly, I could see how scared you were when you saw me and I didn't know how to approach you to overcome that. And after you did escape the second time, I couldn't find you again for months. Your months, I mean. I didn't even know where you were staying in New York.'

I tell her about Kathy's and meeting Nancy and getting a job at Steve's.

'Nancy sounds a wonderful friend,' Suzie says. 'So why did you end up in prison?'

I jolt forward, spilling my drink. 'How the hell do you know that? I haven't told you.'

'Sorry.' Suzi grins, embarrassed. 'After I lost you, I had to start thinking differently. I trawled all sorts of government databases searching for your name, but I couldn't find you. Well, when I say I searched, I mean my friend, Remi, helped me again. A 1978 database doesn't have any security he can't hack with his 2050 software.'

'You told him about the time machine?' I'm aghast.

'No, no, don't worry. I asked him to load his hacking software on my handheld computer, so I could do it without needing to involve him, and then I travelled back to 1978 and ran my checks there.'

'How? There was no Internet then. No Wi-Fi.'

'That didn't matter. I just transported myself straight into a government building at night, connected my computer directly and worked there. Much easier.'

I chuckle. 'You're quite the undercover agent.'

'But it wasn't until I scanned the Department of Justice that I found your name. It was quite a shock, I can tell you.'

'Not as much as it was for me.'

'What crime did you do?'

I tell her, finishing with my fortunate escape. Suzi accepts it without judgement.

'Nancy was lucky to have you as a friend. And that also explains why I lost you after that,' she says thoughtfully. 'I knew you had been accepted for parole, but then you just dropped off the map. I was going to approach you again the day you left prison, but there was never a date recorded for your final release.'

I check that Roger hasn't sneaked up on us, although I know he would never do that. Even so, I lower my voice. 'That's when I acquired my new identity as Caroline Turner.'

'Ohhh. I get it. That all makes sense now.'

'That's good to hear. What does?'

'I thought you had just changed your name for your artwork. But of course, you needed a new identity, I should have thought of that.'

'Okay. So explain this, then: I was never on any database as Caroline Tangent except the DOJ, then I got a new ID, changed my name and yet here you are. How did you find me?'

'It took me months of scanning historic records.'

'By visiting the eighties again?'

'No, I did all that in 2050. You see, I finally began trying to think like you. I mean, if I was you, what would I have done to make a living given your horrendous circumstances? I asked Bee what she thought and she reminded me that you had been an artist when you were married to Dad, so she guessed that would be the thing you would return to, to make money.'

'Bee is so smart.'

'She said you were really talented and you could have been far more famous if it hadn't been for one of your paintings being vandalised. I couldn't bring myself to tell her that Dad had done that.'

For the first time in close to fifteen years, I think about what Jon did to my artwork that night at Rosie's gallery. I close my eyes for a moment but remain calm; this isn't the time to drag up my pain from that episode.

Suzi continues. 'Anyway, I began to research your artwork. The sort of paintings you did, that famous piece you painted for Bugatti. When I found your Hendrix piece, which a collector bought, I laughed so hard.'

'Not because it was bad, I hope.'

'No, I loved it. But Dad had shown me that photo of the Hendrix gig, so I realised what you'd done. That was beautiful, Caroline.'

I smile. 'Thank you.'

She looks over her shoulder, through the open door of my studio. 'But your new work, what you have here, it's so much more... dynamic. Provocative.'

'I've moved on.'

'I can tell. After that, I did the only thing I could do. Started searching websites and American archives for signs of your existence. Hoping you were mentioned as an artist in an exhibition, a gallery, an interview, whatever. That was a labour of love, I can tell you, even using my automated search software.'

'How did you do that?'

'Methodically! I started searching websites and old journal archives for artists in that period, moving outwards geographically from New York. I did search for your real name, but as you know, that never turned up, so I widened it to terms like "artist", "British", your possible ages, other stuff I guessed could help. I even requested some archives from specific art magazines that aren't published anymore. It took me *months.*' We both laugh. 'Which is when I came across an interview you did about four weeks ago in the summer '99 edition of a magazine called *East Coast Encounters.*'

I frown. 'I didn't even know that interview had been published yet.'

'It has in my time, if you see what I mean. Actually, I didn't know for certain that it was you, initially, but my search terms gave me a high probability rating. When I read the interview, I saw the name Caroline Turner and a photo of someone who I thought could be you, and you were mentioned in the article as the right age as you are now, so I took it to Bee. Even with her condition, she was pretty positive the photograph was you, and when I read out that the artist was living on a farmstead called Veedon Fleece she almost broke down because she remembered that was your favourite Van Morrison album. I think if it hadn't been for her cancer, she would have insisted on coming today.

'I just prayed we were right and it was you. You can't believe how relieved I was when you confirmed it with your shock of recognising me. I guess my trips to New York were worth it after all!'

I look at the young woman sitting beside me. I marvel at her. What she has done solely for Bee and me in the last ten years of her life is nothing short of miraculous. The kindest, most unselfish acts of altruism that any person could display. There was no need for her to do any of this, no benefit for herself, she did it because Bee had asked her to and she thought it was the right thing to do. Unbelievable. What will she think when I tell her my decision?

'Let's go for a walk,' I suggest.

We start to ramble slowly across my land. I show her the planting we've done, all Roger's improvements that mean we can live off-grid and point to local landmarks on the horizon. As we stand and look towards Burley, I take her hand.

'Suzi, I need to tell you that you are such an amazing woman. Intelligent, charming, selfless.' She looks embarrassed. 'And after all you've done to find me, I feel as if I'm letting you and Bee down when I say this, but I have to say it: I don't want to go back to that night in 2021 when Jon abandoned me. Not anymore. I've no need to warn my younger self what's going to happen. In fact, I don't want to. This is my life now. This is who I am. I want to keep that.'

Suzi bites her lip. I continue.

'It's the same thing I felt when Jon tried to persuade me to go back to 2010 to stop my miscarriage so we could have a baby. By 2021, I knew I didn't want to do that, I'd come to terms with it, I had my new life. You shouldn't change who you are and your experiences. It's about accepting it and learning from it. Even if you can alter your history with an incredible invention called a time machine, that's wrong. It's cheating yourself. Lying about history and who you are. And going back wouldn't change who Jon is. Or was. He was still a man who had or wanted to have an affair. Why would I want to go back to that?'

Suzi nods. She doesn't seem disappointed. I hope she's not pretending.

'But also,' I add, 'I don't want to go back because I have a wonderful new partner here, a man I love. And I'm painting, selling my artwork, I live in a beautiful place. I don't want to walk away from this, forget all this.'

'I understand, Caroline.'

I let go of Suzi's hand and clench my fist. 'However, I still hate Jon for what he did to me. And my friends. And now you. I thought I'd buried all his vile, selfish deeds deep inside a dark closet of my soul, never to be excavated, but these last two days with you have made me realise that isn't the case. Just because I won't go back and change things doesn't mean I don't want to see the bastard suffer. I want retribution. Who would miss him?' I turn my head to face my fellow time-traveller. 'So, maybe I can suggest an alternative plan.'

I tell Suzi my idea.

30

The next morning, Suzi and I leave my house just before seven. I tell Roger it's our guest's last day on her vacation, so I'm going to take her out all day, go on a long sightseeing adventure.

'I'll be back late tonight,' I say.

My plan means we take Suzi's car. Unfortunately, my visitor from the future is still not au fait with real cars and as we jerk down our track towards the main road, I grip my grab handle tightly and hope we live long enough to implement the rest of my scheme.

Suzi is oblivious to my nerves. 'I can see why people enjoyed driving,' she says, turning onto the thankfully empty road without looking.

We head towards Burley, where we'll leave Suzi's car. We won't need it again, but someone from the rental company should find it eventually. The road is quiet at this time of the morning and as I watch the countryside rush by, I think about what I'm going to do and say when I arrive in 2050. The problem with time-travel is that every time I think about how I fit in, another question pops into my head.

Now I have another conundrum I want to pose to Jon's daughter.

'Tell me,' I say. 'When you were trying to track me down, why didn't you come back to a much earlier time? Before 2021, when Jon and I were living in Crouch End. It would have been much easier to find me and you could have come to my house any day when Jon wasn't there and told me everything.'

Suzi grips the wheel, stares straight ahead through the windshield. 'You wouldn't have believed me if I'd come then. What I was saying, the concept of who I was. Would you have wanted to accept at that time what I would be telling you about your husband?'

'I suppose not.'

'Which is why I had to wait until after he deserted you.'

'And why it could have worked if we had gone back to the night before we left for the Springsteen concert and I could tell myself about Elise and Jon's attack on Priscilla's commission. Because I would be far more likely to believe myself by that time. And, of course, it would have been me telling me, not you.'

Suzi nods.

I massage my eyebrows briefly. 'God, I haven't had to think like this for so long, it gets so confusing.' I ponder this more carefully. 'You know, if you and I had gone back to 2021 and I had persuaded myself not to leave, then, in theory, this timeline, the one I'm living in now, would cease to exist, right?'

'That's the idea.'

'But, also, Jon and I might have patched things up, he could have broken off his affair with Elise and we could have stayed together.'

She nods again, blinks several times and bites her bottom lip.

'In which case… my god. In which case, Jon wouldn't have gone off with Elise and you wouldn't have been born.'

'Yes,' Suzi whispers.

'So, when you came here, in your words, to rescue me, you were quite literally risking your life. You were jeopardising your entire existence.'

'It was a risk.'

'And you did that just so you could help me. That's extraordinary. You're extraordinary.'

Suzi shrugs. 'It was a risk I had to take. I told you, I had to do the right thing. For Bee and you.'

I can't take my eyes off this incredible young woman.

I blow out my cheeks. 'Mind you, with what we both know about Jon, he might still have left me and you might still have been born. Or I might have persuaded Jon to adopt a baby after all, and we might have found you that way.'

'Sounds unlikely.'

'True.' I look ahead. 'But if you were my daughter, I'd be very proud of you.'

Suzi smiles, sniffs, wipes her hand under her nose.

We drive on in silence, enter Burley, find a place to park the Nissan. We get out.

'One more thing,' I say to Suzi.

'You're always saying that.'

'I know. I can't help it. There is always one more thing!' I hesitate. 'If I had said yes to going back to 2021, and I hadn't worked out what I said in the car, would you have told me what would happen to you?'

'No. I'd come to terms with that.' She swings the keyring around her forefinger. 'Mind you, I'm glad you didn't decide to do it – I don't want to cease to exist in a puff of smoke!'

I hug her tightly.

It's so early, there's barely anyone in town. Still, we walk behind a tree that hides us from the street. Suzi pulls out her version of the time-pen.

'Ready?' she asks.

'Not really. But I don't know if I ever will be. I stopped believing this day would come years ago.'

We hold hands and Suzi presses the button.

Moments later, I feel a sensation I haven't experienced for over twenty years: temporary dizziness, a need to blink to adjust to new light and the awareness of a different texture under my feet. I look down. I'm standing on carpet. In a bedroom. A room painted in pale green, single bed pushed up against the wall, a standard looking bedside light on a low-level chest of drawers. The curtains are drawn over the window, although a crack between them shows it's dark outside. Above the bed is my first clue that we're not in 1999 anymore or even the early twenty-first century: instead of pictures, there's what looks like a thin computer screen hanging on the wall with a changing 3D scene of seascapes. The only nod to bygone times is a classic black-and-white pop poster taped to the back of the bedroom door: a young Morrissey and Johnny Maar of The Smiths stare out at us, superimposed above faded text at the foot of the poster: 'The Smiths Debut Album February 20th 1984'.

But all of that is incidental compared to what dominates the room. Along one side of the room are two wooden desks pushed together, and standing on them are more computer screens, mounds of electronic gadgetry and three micro versions of what I recognise as the lightning rods that Jon created in our basement; but these are no bigger than a large ballpoint pen. Stuck to the wall above the desks are sheets and sheets of paper, many of the edges curling up, with mathematical algorithms and equations, diagrams, drawings, lots of scribbling out. I can guess what they must be.

'Welcome to 2050,' Suzi says.

I raise my eyebrows. 'Wouldn't it bother you if your father saw all this?'

'He's not been in here for ten years, and I've got a fingerprint lock on my door. But even if he did come in, he wouldn't know what I was doing.'

'Hmm.'

'But just in case, I don't leave my most important things on display.'

She slides open a drawer and presses a button on what looks like a remote control. The picture-screen on the wall flashes and new images appear. Copies of my paintings. Some from my time in America, but one or two from my life before I left England. I cover my mouth, watch the pictures change.

'This is what kept me going,' Suzi says. 'This is what reminded me what was important.'

Before I can get emotional, a clock on the wall strikes an old-fashioned chime and I roll my neck. 'Come on. Let's get our plan started.'

Suzi sits in front of one of the computer screens on her desk and taps briefly at her keyboard. She reaches into a box and pulls out another 'returner', her spare one I assume. She hands it to me. 'Give me a minute while I get the other stuff.'

She disappears out of her room and I gently spin the device around between my fingers. I go over my plan once more, make sure I haven't missed anything. If I get it wrong, I'll be in deep shit and I've no desire to see the inside of any more prisons. I'm ticking points off on my fingers as Suzi returns.

She holds out her arms. 'Here you go. They're a bit musty, I don't think he's worn them for years.'

I take her offering: one of Jon's old coats and his fedora

hat. I can smell my ex-husband on the overcoat and it rockets me back twenty years and simultaneously repels me. I slip on the coat, turn up the collar and push my hair inside it so it's hidden from view. I hold up the hat in front of my face and turn it slowly around. 'I used to think Jon looked so cool in this. I guess he did, really.'

'It didn't mean he wasn't a bastard underneath it. He still is.'

'I know.'

I circumspectly place the hat on my head. It's too big for me, but when I tug it down, it nestles conveniently on my hair.

Suzi points at her returner. 'As soon as you collect what you want, you can press the button to come back. Remember, you need to time it perfectly so the cameras don't see you clearly.'

'No problem.' I tuck it into one of Jon's coat pockets. 'So you can really land me within a few feet of where it's hanging?'

'Absolutely. We've got the floor plans. This is what I've been doing for ages – I've perfected this. And it will be the middle of the night so there'll be no one around.' She grimaces. 'All the same, I'd feel a lot happier if I came with you and controlled the returner, while you just take it.'

'No, I'm not risking that. If anything does go wrong, you have your whole life ahead of you. This bit is down to me.'

'I hate him as much as you.'

'And here and now you are as much a part of this as I am. I couldn't do this without you.'

'Okay, okay.' Suzi sucks air in through her teeth. She touches one of her computer screens. 'Ready, then?'

I nod. She presses a button on her keyboard.

A moment later, I feel the carpet under my feet disappear and I am standing on a hard wooden floor. My knees waver for an instant. I find my stability and catch my breath. Suzi could not have positioned me any better.

The room I'm in is vast, with high ceilings, dimly lit, and on the far side I can see the night sky through an uncovered window. It's deathly quiet. The entire space is unfurnished except for some low benches dotted around for visitors to admire the works of art. Hanging on all the walls are other pictures I would happily spend hours perusing. But not tonight. Tonight is about military precision.

I tug Jon's hat further over my brow and, keeping my head down, take two paces forward. Suspended at eye level on the panel in front of me is my target. I've seen it in a hundred books but never before in reality: it's twenty-two inches high by twenty-five inches wide and even in this light, its genius takes my breath away. But I don't allow myself even a second to admire it, I'll have plenty of time for that in a minute. I reach out and ever so carefully ease it off its fixtures with my right hand. With my left, I pull Suzi's returner out of my pocket, holding it close to my chest. I stand up straight, still facing the wall and hold my breath. Sure enough, within a few seconds, the bright bulbs in the room are activated and an ear-piercing siren shatters the silence. I wait for a flash of light to illuminate me and press the button on my returner.

I'm back in Suzi's bedroom.

I wobble and Suzi quickly leans over to take the painting from me. I hold out my hands to balance myself and sit down on her bed.

'Okay?' Suzi asks.

I nod. 'Just as we planned.' I plant my palms either side of me on the mattress and puff out my cheeks. 'My God, that was so easy. Too easy. Jon was absolutely right all those years ago when he said that in anyone else's hands this could be a doomsday machine. Just think what a master criminal could do!'

'Yes, well, don't go getting any ideas. This is a one-off. For a specific purpose.'

'Of course.' I wrench off Jon's coat and hat and discard them on the bed. 'First things first. Let's check we've created a new timeline.'

Suzi sits down at her computer. I stand behind her, biting my nails. My partner-in-crime searches the internet, scrolls through a few pages and selects a hyperlink. 'Here it is. Just as we predicted.'

I lean over and read what she's pointing at. It's an article from the *New York Times*, dated January fourth 2035. Fifteen years before my current time with Suzi. The headline reads: 'Mystery of the Century as $10m Artwork is Stolen'. We both laugh and manage a decent high-five. Then we read the rest of the news item.

In what experts are calling the crime of the century, Edward Hopper's famous painting, Office at Night, *valued at over ten million dollars, was stolen last night from the Walker Art Center in Minneapolis. Police are baffled as to how the thieves entered without any signs of a break-in or indication of how they escaped. Somehow they evaded the museum's high-tech security and all but one CCTV camera. The only clue is a single photograph of the back of a man dressed in a long coat and hat. We understand the search begins today, with the mayor of Minneapolis stating, 'We will not stop until we find the thieves and they are locked up forever.'*

I straighten up. 'I hope they've stopped looking by now. Fifteen years is a long time to be searching in vain.'

We burst out laughing. I clap my hand over my mouth. 'Shit, what if Jon hears us?'

Suzi scoffs. 'He won't hear a thing. He'll be too drunk to even notice our footsteps. I once dropped a pile of books outside his lounge door and when I poked my head in to apologise, he didn't know what I was talking about.'

'Fine. So, can you print me out a copy of that article, and then, please can you check if there has been any wild butterfly effect because of what we've done. I know you won't find every little thing, but I don't want to make anything wickedly awful.'

While Suzi is doing that, I take Edward Hopper's masterpiece and prop it up on her bed, against the wall. I stand back. *Office at Night*. It is so compelling I cannot remove my eyes from it. Now I can see the oil painting with all its brush strokes and nuances, it is so much more vivid than I ever imagined. The man at the desk, the woman beside him – is there a secret relationship? What is in the drawer she's leaning into? Where does the window over-look? Never did I think I would be able to examine this incredible piece of art in such detail and so privately.

I am so immersed in my study that I don't register Suzi's voice.

'Hey, Caroline! Did you hear me?'

'Sorry, what?' I tear my gaze away from the painting. Suzi is looking amused, her finger tapping the screen in front of her. She grins.

'I was saying, I've discovered something.'

'Oh?' I give her my full attention. 'What? Has something bad happened? Don't tell me we have to take it back.'

'No, everything's fine, as far as I can tell. Except for one thing.'

'Which is?'

'Remember I told you about that famous artist, Logan Jacksdotter?'

'The man whose work you hate?'

'Yes, him. Well, he always said that seeing *Office at Night* was one of the key influences on him when he began to paint. Now it appears that he never became an artist after all! There's barely a mention of him anywhere online. I can only presume that he never got to see the painting because we stole it! How fantastic is that!'

'Are you sure?'

'Absolutely. That's what I call a wonderful outcome of the butterfly effect!'

'Hmm. And, of course, you didn't know how he had admired that painting before you proposed we steal that particular piece?'

'Hey, you suggested swiping an Edward Hopper. We could have taken any one of his works.'

I shake my head, but I'm not angry. Suzi deserves a small victory for herself, considering everything she's doing for me. I fold the printout she hands me of the *New York Times* article and put it in my pocket.

'Shall I send the email now?' Suzi asks.

'Do it. And I'll wrap up this valuable painting so you can hide it with Jon's hat. Then you can show me where your father is. I've got a lot to say to him.'

Once we complete our tasks, Suzi opens her bedroom door. We exit onto a landing that could be from any post-1990 era and she leads me downstairs. There are more picture-screens on the hallway wall, some showing family photos of Jon, Elise and Suzi, and one with a rather mundane image of the night sky that flickers but doesn't change. In 2050, technology still has its glitches, it seems. Suzi points at a closed door opposite and mouths 'good luck'.

I straighten my back and run my hands down my dress. I've taken care to wear something that shows me off at my best – I want Jon to know I'm in my prime and feeling good about myself. I cautiously push open the door and step inside.

The room has low lighting but I can see the furniture: sofa, armchairs, sideboard and a fake computerised fire-place with, for some reason, a real companion set stationed beside it. I'm standing beside a tall bookcase housing faded paperbacks. I spy two loudspeakers on the wall opposite and I automatically scan the room for a record deck; I can't see one. Seems those days have come and gone.

But I can see an old man sitting in one of the armchairs. And I'm shocked. Suzi said that Jon has been drinking for many years, but if I didn't know he was only seventy-five, I would have placed him ten years older. He's skinnier than I've ever seen him, with pronounced veins on his hands, scraggly white hair clinging to his scalp, and his face – oh my – I have to look beyond the folds of skin and sunken eyes to see the man I used to know. He's there, but only just. He's holding a near-empty whisky glass, and there's a half-full bottle of liquor on a low side table beside him. His shirt is partly unbuttoned and there is a damp patch under his collar.

It's only when I step forward into the room that he looks up. Incredibly, his face doesn't change. In fact, rather than look scared or shocked, he half smiles.

'Ah, it's you,' he croaks. His voice is as weak as the rest of him appears to be. 'Come to visit me once more?'

I'm taken aback. This is not what I expected. How can he be so blasé? I take another step towards him.

He raises his glass as if he's toasting me. 'Haven't seen you for weeks. I thought I must be getting over you again.

337

Appears not.' He pats the bottle beside him. 'Trust my old friend JD to sort that out.'

I cock my head. 'Do you know who I am?'

Jon cackles. 'Caz. Caz, Caz, Caz.'

'Then… you think I'm not real?'

'As real as I want you to be.'

'I'm in your imagination?'

'Hee, this is a good one. You haven't talked to me for a while.' He sips from his glass. 'I must be having strong memories tonight. You look so good.'

I'm dumbfounded. I can't believe this is happening. How can I achieve what I've come to do if he doesn't know I'm real? I place my hand on my hip, glare at him. He smiles back happily, swirls the ice around in his glass. I watch the ice cubes come to a stop; I know what I must do.

I take two strides towards my ex-husband, snatch the glass out of his hand and knock back the remaining contents. I gasp as the liquid burns my throat, but I stand up straight and thrust the empty tumbler back into his hand.

His jaw drops and he holds the glass up before his face, turns it upside down and jerks backwards, as if he can't believe nothing is pouring out. His hand shoots out sideways and he drops the glass onto the table beside him before slamming his palm into his chest, clutching at his shirt collar, scrunching it up. He looks up at me, eyes widening. Now I see the fear on his face.

I cross my arms. 'Oh yes, Jon, it genuinely is me. The real Caroline. The woman you left in New York over twenty years ago. No, thirty years for you. Hey, how about that? I have ten years on you now.'

'Caz?'

'Yep.'

'Caz? Is it truly you? Not a dream?'

I'm standing close to him. He reaches out, caresses my

338

dress, flinches as if he's been scalded, then inches his fingers towards me again and brushes the back of my forearm. I shiver. I can't help it. His touch makes my skin crawl.

'But… but…' I wait for him to finish. 'How?'

I ignore his question. Instead, I push my hair back, reach down for his glass and refill it. Now the whisky has warmed me, it feels good. I'd like another shot. I begin to saunter around the room, running my finger along the sideboard, admiring the cornices decorating the ceiling.

'Nice room, darling,' I say. 'Comfortable for your old age.' I face him again from across the lounge. 'Not like the prison cell I spent four years in.'

'The what?'

'Oh, but why would you care about that? Why would you give two hoots about my incarceration, or the months before that when I was sharing a room in a rundown hostel.'

'Caz, I don't understand.'

'Of course you don't!' I yell. 'You know nothing about what happened to me. Nothing. You didn't give a fuck for me then and you don't now. You're a lousy, godforsaken piece of shit, Jon, and I hate you. Hate you!'

'Caz…'

'Four days I waited for you in that fucking park. Four whole days. And nights sometimes. I even got mugged while I was waiting. But I was sure you were coming back for me. Positive. I mean, why wouldn't you? Your fingers had just slipped from my grasp, right? It was all a terrible mistake. All I had to do was wait a few days for you to build a new time-pen, ensure your precious wormholes wouldn't conflict with each other, and then you'd return. Yes?' I stamp my foot. 'No! Fucking no.'

'Oh, Caz.'

He sounds so contrite. Just as he used to do so often when we were married, I remind myself. I scowl and push back my shoulders. I march over to the armchair opposite him and sit down abruptly. But I don't spill a drop of whisky. I hover the glass by my lips. Sip it casually.

Jon leans forward. 'Lights up,' he says, and the room becomes brighter.

I squeeze my eyes shut for an instant and blink them open, adjusting to the illumination. Voice technology appears to have advanced.

Now I can see my ex-husband more clearly, he looks even worse than I thought. Decrepit is the best word I can find. Or cadaverous. I tap my fingers on the arm of my chair.

'So what have you got to say, husband? Eh? Husband. Because, actually, you know what? I don't think I've ever had my marriage annulled. I think I'm still owed half of whatever you have.'

Jon looks momentarily panicked.

I flap my hand in front of my face. 'Oh, for Chrissakes, don't worry, you old curmudgeon, I'm not here to take your money. There was a time when I would have snatched it out of your bony old fingers, but I don't need it anymore.'

He licks his lips. I say again, 'You left me there, you bastard. How could you?'

Another look of guilt crosses his face. 'It wasn't like that, Caz. Honestly.'

'What do you mean? Of course it was.'

Jon shakes his head, wildly. 'No, it was a terrible, terrible mistake. One I've had to live with ever since. As you said, every day for thirty years.'

'What are you talking about?'

'Listen, I did let go of your hand, I admit that. But I didn't mean to. My fingers did slip.'

'Right. And that's why you never came back.'

'No. That was the worst part. I couldn't.'

'What do you mean you couldn't? All you had to do was wait a few days for your goddamn wormholes to be far enough apart, and then you could return.'

'No. The time machine, Caz. It never worked for me again. Something had gone wrong. No matter what I did, I couldn't fix it.'

'Never? You could never fix it?'

'I tried, Caz. You have to believe me. I tried.'

I scratch my wrist. Is this possible? Is that what actually happened? Have I got it wrong all these years?

'But you left me there,' I say.

'I never meant to.' He holds his arms out. 'Remember Knebworth? What I said?'

'I...'

'I said I would never leave you and I meant it. Even after Bolan, I told you I'd never do that. I told you.'

I can't believe what I'm hearing. Could Jon really have tried to come back to get me but not been able to, and I've been blaming him all this time, calling him every name under the sun? I look back at him. Look away again. I think about what we went through together. Our lives at uni, our marriage, all the trips we did. I know he was having an affair, but as I thought on those first nights in New York, surely he'd come back to me despite that. Maybe... maybe I was right at the time. My God. I turn back to this old man sitting opposite me.

'I didn't know. How long did you try to fix it?'

'Years, Caz.'

'Years? When did you stop trying?'

'I... don't remember exactly. It was a long time.'

'What was wrong? Why wouldn't it work?'

'I never found out. It was as if... time didn't want me to do this anymore.'

'Time didn't what?'

341

I lean forward. Stare my ex-husband in the eyes.

And I see it.

Just for a moment, just the tiniest of emotions: a flicker in his eyes as he glances down at his feet before looking back at me. I see his deceit.

'You lying bastard.'

'What?'

'That's not true. None of it.'

'It is, Caz, it is. I promise.'

'Promise? *Promise?*' I slap my palm hard onto the arm of my chair. Jon twitches. 'You expect me to believe your *word*? After everything you did? Everything you ever said?'

'I... It is... Honestly...'

I hold my finger up, pause, then turn it into a clenched fist. 'You knew I would find out about that slut you were running around with.'

He blinks rapidly. 'What? Who?'

'Elise, you fake. That hussy you ended up marrying. You were already having an affair when we went to New York, remember? You couldn't even tell me to my face that you didn't want me, that you hated me. And now you think I'll believe your story? Forgive you?'

'It is true, Caz. The time machine is broken. No one can ever travel that way again.'

I open my arms, wide. 'Then how do you explain how I'm here?'

'I... assumed you had just been waiting.'

'Since *1978*?'

'Well, yes. Haven't you? Just been biding your time?'

'Are you insane? I was forty-two when you abandoned me in 1978. If I had lived non-stop since then, that would make me... over one hundred and ten years old. Do I look that old?'

Jon's eyes open wide. I see understanding cross his face.

Then dismay. His arms slump to his side. He looks dejected. Humiliated. Fucking good. I was right. I am right. Fuck. Him.

I take another drink. 'Shall I tell you my story? What happened to me? That's why I'm here.'

'I…'

'Good. Then let's start. Settle back, darling. We're going for another little ride through time.'

And I tell him. In every gruesome detail. Of my first days in Manhattan on my own, of Kathy's, my desperation, drug running for Paolo, my arrest and my time in Taconic Correctional Facility. I give him the full, unedited version of that. I tell him how much I grieved for Veronica, how much I missed Bee and Teri and Zaina. How much I hated him, loathed him, wished I could batter him over the head with that police officer's truncheon. But then I sit back and change my tone. I tell him how I started painting again, met Roger, bought Veedon Fleece.

'I managed to forget all about you,' I say. 'And then, guess what? I met Suzi. I learned what actually happened after you came back from New York. What you said after you abandoned me, what you told our friends, what you didn't tell that slut of a second wife of yours. But the best thing, and I mean this, darling, I really do, the best thing I discovered is that you're now a wretched, drunken, tormented old man who has wasted half his life because he couldn't face telling his first wife that he was a lecherous, lying shit. And who has consequently spent the last fifteen years inside a bottle, miserable and alone. Even his own daughter despises him. And guess what? I'm so happy about that. So happy. Because it's what you deserve, you bastard. Every last goddamn second of it.'

I pour the rest of the whisky down my throat, stand up and walk over to the decorative fireplace. I pick up the real

343

poker and slap it several times in my palm. I glance over at Jon. He's pushed himself back into his chair, his eyes darting around as if searching for something. I wonder if he has a panic button, or he might have a voice-activated alarm to call the police. I doubt it, Suzi would have told me; but, Christ, that would take the biscuit, wouldn't it? I come back to my original time and get picked up by the cops, where they could ID me in two seconds!

Let's get this over with.

I walk back to stand in front of Jon. I can't believe that I ever loved this quivering wreck of a man. He took the best time of my life and made it hell. He deserves what's coming to him. I know that.

It would be so easy. The perfect murder. Hit him over the head, walk out and return to another continent. Fifty years prior to now in 1999. Sure, the police might find my fingerprints on the murder weapon, but what would they do when they find they belong to the deceased's ex-wife who apparently disappeared thirty years ago and was declared dead? Launch a manhunt for me? I'd like to see them try.

I stand over Jon and raise the poker. He cowers, raises his bony arms to his head and closes his eyes.

I pause.

I drop the poker onto the floor. It thuds on the carpet and bounces away from the armchair. Jon opens his eyes and lowers his hands. He is still shaking. I bend down, rest my palms on the arms of his chair and lean into his face. I think I might vomit, but I swallow, hold it back.

'I'm not going to kill you, Jon. Not now, anyway. I want you to live. I want you to carry on feeling despair every day, knowing what you did to me, your friends, your new family. Knowing how happy I am now with my new life.' I stand up. 'Besides, there's a far more important reason I want you alive.'

Jon is still pressed back into his chair. He looks so pathetic. He frowns, shakes his head nervously. Good. Time to tell him what's coming. I smooth my hands through my hair.

'You see, I've been catching up on what's been happening over the last thirty years. There's been some fascinating developments, hasn't there? Especially in the art world. And I've been delving into the whereabouts of Edward Hopper's work. Remember I always wanted to go back and meet him? But you always refused. Never even countenanced it. So I never did get to meet him. But I have managed the next best thing.' I fix his gaze. 'It appears there was a famous art heist of his painting, *Office at Night*, fifteen years ago. It was worth over ten million dollars and thieves stole it in the dead of night. An unsolved crime. The mystery of the century, they called it. Oh, you didn't know that? Ah, well, that's because it only happened half an hour ago in real-time. But wait, look. Here's an article from the *New York Times* from January fourth, 2035. Would you like to read it?'

I hold out the printout. Jon reaches out warily. I snatch back the paper.

'Why don't I go through it for you? Just in case you miss any of its relevance.'

I start to read. As I do, Jon's face changes from fear to perplexity to deep confusion, and when I finish, I can see he is trying to work out what this means. I cross my arms and wait for a moment, but I can't resist sliding the ace out from up my sleeve.

'So, darling husband, guess where the painting is now?'

I crane my neck slowly backwards and look up very deliberately, as if I'm peering through the ceiling. Jon mirrors my movement. After a moment, I roll my eyes downward so I can see his face again. Now there is clear understanding on it. Now he is worried. His eyeballs bulge as he puts his hands on the arms of his chair and tries to lever himself up. I place a single fingertip on his chest and push him back down into his seat.

'You won't find it. Don't even bother looking. The only people who will know where to search are the police, who right about... now, should have received an anonymous email tipping them off as to its whereabouts. I'd say they'll be here in less than twelve hours.'

'Caz, please.'

'Oh, no. You don't get to plead this time. This time it is the end of the line for you. You will spend the rest of your sorry life in prison. Banged up, where you deserve to be. Whether or not it's for the crime you committed. Still, at least your daughter will have a lovely house to live in.'

'Caz...'

'Unless, of course, you decide to take another way out before the police arrive. I guess there are multiple options for that.'

Jon lifts one of his hands and with great effort, makes a fist. But he can't hold it. His arm slumps again onto his lap.

I drop the printout of the article at his feet, turn and walk out of the room.

I close the door quietly behind me, lean against it and take deep breaths. I close my eyes. When I open them again, Suzi is waiting for me. She's fiddling with an electronic mobile device of some sort.

'You okay?' she asks. I nod. 'Did you tell him what we've done?'

'He'll work it out. The only question is whether he waits for the police, or...'

'He hasn't got the guts to do that. He'll be here when the cops arrive.'

'Which means I'd better not be.'

She gives me a hug. When she releases me, I let my body relax like a rag doll, feeling all the tension seep out of me. A coy smile appears on Suzi's face.

'Hey, I've just been doing some research on the NFL.'

'American football?'

'Correct. Did you know that in January 2000, the St Louis Rams won the Superbowl twenty-three to sixteen, but at the start of that season, no one gave them a chance? Must have been some good odds on that, I reckon.'

I grin. 'I'll bear that in mind.'

She pockets her mobile tech. 'So are you ready for your penultimate trip?'

I take another deep breath and nod.

Suzi programs her time machine carefully. We've selected a specific time: 2041, after Suzi told Bee what Jon had done, but before Bee's cancer had reached its zenith. A late-autumn day, which Suzi remembered because she had visited Bee at her home in the afternoon, and Andrew wasn't due back until the following day because of a work trip.

'I was updating her on my progress,' Suzi says. 'Or lack of it at the time.'

It's also exactly twenty years for Bee and me, in our own timelines, since we last saw each other. And we'll both be near-enough the same age.

We land in a park near Bee's house under the cover of dusk. I came to this park so many times over the years with Bee and her children – it's so remarkable to be returning now. We walk down the street towards Bee's house. The houses haven't changed, but there are far fewer cars parked outside them and I notice a complete lack of telephone poles. I'm just about to cross the road, but Suzi holds me back.

'Wait a minute.'

'What is it?'

Suzi points to a young woman a little way off.

'It's you!' I say under my breath. 'Leaving Bee's.'

'Age seventeen. I look so young.' She grins. 'I've never done this before. It's weird.'

'Remind me to tell you about our trip to see our younger selves at a Stereophonics gig. That was weird!'

We let younger Suzi disappear into the distance and then walk up to Bee's house. It's so familiar. We've agreed that Suzi will go in alone while I wait outside for Jon's daughter to prepare Bee for what's going to happen. Suzi rings the doorbell. I crouch down behind a car, but I can still hear their conversation.

'Oh,' Bee says. 'Hello again. Have you forgotten something?'

I have to clamp my hand over my mouth to stop myself crying out when I hear her voice. I can already feel tears spring into my eyes.

'Sort of,' Suzi replies.

'Wait a minute.' Bee's voice changes. 'You weren't wearing those clothes just now. And you look different. What's happening?'

'Let's go in. I'll explain.'

The door shuts, I stand up. I wipe my eyes, take a huge gulp of air and try to prepare myself. Despite the cool evening, I am sweating. My hands are shaking as if I'm about to do an exam. I don't know what I'm going to say.

It's at least ten minutes before Bee's front door opens and Suzi is silhouetted in the entrance. She beckons me in. She closes the door quietly and I stand in the hallway of a house that I know so well but which I never dreamt I

348

would ever see again. New floor, different wallpaper, same feeling.

'She's in the lounge,' Suzi says softly.

'How is she?'

'Completely freaked out. Uncontrollable. She could barely accept I was from the future, but when I told her you were here too she almost collapsed. I don't know if she really believes me. I was going to give her longer to pull herself together but I don't think any amount of time will do that! You just need to go in.'

I hug Suzi. She wishes me luck. I wipe my hands down my sides and open Bee's lounge door. I walk in.

Bee is pacing on the far side of the room, brushing her fingers across the closed lid of their piano. When she hears me open the door, she stops and looks across. Her hands fly to her mouth and she gasps.

I'd recognise her anywhere. She looks so beautiful. An older but reverent version of the woman I last saw. Her hair is cropped short but she's kept her figure, and the blue dress she's wearing could have been tailor-made for her. And her eyes, although full of tears, are exactly as I remember.

We stand like statues for a few seconds before I take a step forward and we fly into each other's arms. We hug and cry and say that we love each other and how much we've missed each other. 'I can't believe it's you,' is repeated over and over. Then Bee collapses on the carpet and wails and I crouch down and pull her into my embrace. I gently rock my best friend until her tears dry up.

'The fucking bastard!' Bee finally says.

'Yes,' I reply. 'But I've dealt with him.' Bee's eyes open. 'No, not like that, don't worry. He deserves what's coming to him.' I pat the cushions on her sofa. 'Come on, I'll tell you all about it.'

For the second time today, I tell someone in my future

the story of the past twenty years of my life. Bee doesn't interrupt once, but her expression changes every thirty seconds. At some point, Suzi enters carrying a tray with a teapot and cups and we all hug again. Bee retrieves an old photograph album with pictures from our university days and the years soon after that. We howl with laughter. Suzi leaves us alone again.

'Aren't you violating every part of Jon's edict on the butterfly effect by being here?' Bee asks.

'Probably. But I don't care. And I trust you.'

'I can't tell Andrew, can I?'

'You can't tell anyone. Not even your version of Suzi. But you can give her plenty of encouragement.'

'I'll do that. Not that I need to – she's so eager.'

'She's amazing.'

'Thank goodness!'

We sit quietly.

'I'm so glad you came now,' Bee says.

'Good!'

'No, I mean the timing. You see–' Bee clasps my hands '–I have to tell you something, Caroline.'

'Okay.' I know what's coming.

'This is so difficult. You see, I… I have cancer.'

'I know.'

'You do? How? Oh… of course. Oh, that's so strange.'

'I'm just about used to it by now.'

'Oh, well.' She smiles. 'I'm on these new drugs. If it wasn't for them, I'd probably be dead already. But at least that means you can visit me lots more in the coming years!'

I bite my lip, look down. Blink rapidly.

Bee's shoulders fall. 'Oh, it's like that, is it?'

I nod.

'Ah, well. Maybe it's best I know. I can make the most of the time I do have.'

'There is one thing we could do together,' I say. 'Now.'

'Of course. What is it?'

'Can you get hold of one of those driverless cars? Oh, and do you have a torch?'

Bee orders one of the electronic vehicles to her house. I give her the destination and she programs it in.

It's a two-hour trip to the Suffolk coast, even at night-time with the traffic moving smoothly and no possibility of traffic jams. We continue to talk about everything we've missed in the last twenty years: her children's birthdays, her granddaughter, who is now a young woman herself, even their visits to Jon's. I tell her more about Roger and Veedon Fleece and how Nancy helped me so much.

When we arrive, we get out of the car and meander through Veronica's village in the dark. It hasn't changed much since the last time I was here and it warms my heart to think that some parts of our future remain untouched. We wend our way to the village church. I flick on the flash-light and we enter the graveyard holding hands. It should be a spooky place to be at night, but I feel serene. It takes us ten minutes to find my sister's headstone. It's a simple monu-ment, the engraving informing me she died in January 2022. I cry, but I'm relieved she didn't live much past my final visit. I kneel down and stroke the stone. Bee caresses my hair.

We return to the car and head back to Bee's house. It's nearly midnight when we walk in. Suzi is still here, flicking through Bee's photos, looking amused and bemused. Bee and I sit down and carry on talking. We're still going at six a.m., but it's going to be time for me to leave soon. Now comes the hardest part of all.

I hold my best friend's hands. 'I think I have to say goodbye.'

Bee nods. 'We can't do this anymore, can we?'

'No. Your cancer will deteriorate soon and I don't want to remember you like that.'

'Me neither.'

'I wish I could be here to support you.'

'I wish I could meet Roger and see your new studio!'

We spend another half an hour exchanging last-minute desires and words of advice. I'm sure it will take months for both of us to get over this, but I know there will be nothing left unsaid. How many other friends get that sort of chance?

When I finally, finally force myself out of the lounge, Suzi takes my hand and moments later we are back in her bedroom in 2050. The same minute we left.

'I can't go home yet,' I say.

Suzi points outside. 'The garden's pleasant at night. Dad keeps a gardener to look after it.'

We wait until we hear Jon clump upstairs to his bedroom. Suzi checks that he's passed out and I walk downstairs to sit outdoors, stare up at the few stars I can see and try not to wonder what Bee is thinking now back in 2041.

I'm not sure how long I stay there, but eventually, I feel too cold and I go back upstairs to Suzi's bedroom. I sit down on her bed while she programs her time machine.

She touches her computer screen. 'We left about seven a.m., right? Better make it so we arrive, say, thirteen hours after that, just to be safe.'

She holds out her hand and seconds later, we are standing at the foot of our drive leading up to Veedon Fleece. It's a balmy summer Vermont evening.

'Should be about eight o'clock,' Suzi says.

We hug.

'You know where I am now,' I say. 'And you're welcome to visit again anytime.'

'Is that anytime or any time?' Suzi asks.

I smile. 'Just ensure you're an appropriate age for whenever you come.'

She nods, flicks her time-pen and she's gone.

I walk up our track to the farmhouse. I find Roger sitting on the couch, listening to NPR on the radio. He turns it off. 'Hey, I didn't hear a car drive up.'

I sit down beside him, kiss his lips. 'Suzi dropped me off at the end of the drive. She was in a rush for her flight.'

'Nice kid.'

'The best.'

Roger turns on the radio again. We listen for a while.

I stroke my partner's arm. 'Darling, I've got a bit of a hunch. What do you reckon on the chances for the St Louis Rams this season?'

THE END

CAROLINE AND JON'S GIG LIST

(amongst others!)

October 1935 – Edith Piaf – Le Gerny's, Paris
December 1962 – The Beatles – The Cavern Club,
Liverpool
August 1966 – Jimi Hendrix – Café Wha?, New York City
April 1968 – Janis Joplin – San Francisco
August 1969 – Woodstock – Bethel, NY State
September 1971 – Led Zeppelin – Osaka, Japan
July 1973 – David Bowie – Hammersmith Odeon, London
August 1974 – Knebworth Festival – England
August 1978 – Bruce Springsteen – Madison Square
Garden, New York City
February 1981 – Pink Floyd, The Wall original tour –
Dortmund, Germany
September 1981 – Simon and Garfunkel – Central Park,
New York City
March 1985 – Robin Trower – The Marquee, London
June 1992 - Paul Weller – Subterania, London

November 1998 – Stereophonics – The Forum, London
July 2003 – Amy Winehouse – The Cobden Club, London
June 2015 – Glastonbury Festival, England

IF YOU ENJOYED THIS BOOK...

Wonderful - that's great! I'm very happy.

Book reviews can help independent authors enormously. If you feel you would like to write one (for this or any novel!), please do consider leaving a review on Amazon, Goodreads or any other similar website. Thank you!

And if you would like to hear more about my writing, you can sign-up to my newsletter on my website at www. ivanwainewright.com. If you do so, you will also receive a free bonus chapter from *The Other Times of Caroline Tangent* which tells of a trip that Caroline and Jon took to see James Brown in Boston in April 1968, the day after Martin Luther King Jr was assassinated...

Many thanks,
    Ivan
    March 2021

(There does remain one unanswered question: what happened to the people who *should* have got into the gigs which Caroline and Jon went to instead? I wonder...)

ACKNOWLEDGMENTS

Firstly, my thanks to everyone who read my early drafts and gave me encouragement; in particular, my brother, Max, and Sarah Clarke and Ruth Buller, all of whom gave me feedback and very helpful criticism.

Enormous thanks to both my editors: Carrie O'Grady, who helped me restructure and enhance all sorts of elements in the story which I wouldn't have thought of; and Lucy York, whose detailed editing and suggestions vastly improved the final version. I highly recommend both.

To Sophie Burdess, my cover designer, for all the times I asked her to change just one more thing...

To all the musicians I have ever seen live (in real-time or potentially with a future time machine...), thank you for all your inspiration; I wish I were half as talented as all of you.

I've tried to ensure that all the details about the gigs and concerts which Caroline and Jon went to are accurate - any mistakes are mine, so if you do see one, you are welcome to let me know.

And as before: I would still like to thank my A-level examiners, because if they hadn't given me the crap marks which they did bestow on me, and which meant I had to subsequently change my whole plans for the following years, then my life would never have turned out the way it has. And I'm eternally grateful for that. So thank you – whoever you were.

ABOUT THE AUTHOR

Ivan Wainewright lives in Kent with his partner, Sarah, and their slightly neurotic rescue dog, Remi. Before moving to Kent, he lived in North London, Leeds and Singapore.

When not writing, he can be found watching (and occasionally playing) football, running, listening to music from Chumbawamba to Led Zeppelin, arguing over politics and trying to cook. He has been an independent IT consultant for many years, working solely with charities and not-for-profit organisations.

The Other Times of Caroline Tangent is his second novel, and he is currently working on his next book.

facebook.com/ivanwainewrightauthor

twitter.com/ivanwainewright

instagram.com/ivanwainewright_author